THE VIRIDIAN BOOK
OF OCCULT FICTION

EDITED BY

BRENDAN CONNELL

THIS IS A SNUGGLY BOOK

ISBN: 978-1-64525-141-5

THE VIRIDIAN BOOK
OF OCCULT FICTION

Brendan Connell was born in Santa Fe, New Mexico, in 1970. His works of fiction include *The Architect* (PS Publishing, 2012), *Lives of Notorious Cooks* (Chômu Press, 2012), *Miss Homicide Plays the Flute* (Eibonvale Press, 2013), *Cannibals of West Papua* (Zagava, 2015), *Against the Grain Again: The Further Adventures of Des Esseintes* (Tartarus Press, 2021), and *Spells* (Snuggly Books, 2023). As editor he has worked on various projects, including *The World in Violet: An Anthology of English Decadent Poetry* (Snuggly Boos, 2022), and *The Neo-Decadent Cookbook* (Eibonvale Press, 2020), which was co-edited by Justin Isis. As translator his efforts include *Alcina and Other Stories* (Snuggly Books, 2019), by Guido Gozzano, which was co-translated by his wife Anna.

CONTENTS

INTRODUCTION

THE current volume is the fifth in the series of books of occult fiction of many colors. The first, *The Zinzolin Book of Occult Fiction*, dealt with the occult revival of the British Isles from 1888-1911; the second, *The Vermilion Book of Occult Fiction*, dealt with the French occult revival of the nineteenth century and the early part of the twentieth century; the third, *The Zaffre Book of Occult Fiction*, dealt with the occult revival of the British Isles from 1908-1937; the fourth, *The Alabaster Book of Occult Fiction*, again dealt with the French occult revival of the nineteenth century and the early part of the twentieth century. The present volume, *The Viridian Book of Occult Fiction*, switches its focus from Europe, to the United States of America, covering the American occult revival from 1824-1917.

Occultism, though having much of its origins in Europe, manifested itself somewhat differently in the United States—a country, after all, in its own dubious mythology, founded by those wishing to escape religious persecution in England. The country, abiding under the constitutionally protected "freedom of religion," escaped many of the prejudices that occurred in France and England—and the vastness of the land, with a burgeoning press and a reasonably efficient postal service, allowed for the dissemination of new ideas between the large cities of the East Coast to those of the remote West, and the countless intermediate places.

Biography and fiction are never far apart, and this was certainly the case with the various occultists, spiritualists, mediums and mystics who appeared in the cities and frontiers of America.

Robert Matthews (1788-c. 1841) emerged in upstate New York, calling himself the Prophet Matthias, an incarnation of God. Joseph Smith (1805-1844) was visited by an angel, received the golden plates, and started Mormonism. Andrew Jackson Davis (1826-1910), the son of a shoemaker, had clairvoyant revelations and began mesmerizing people and, while in states of trance, dictated *The Principles of Nature, Her Divine Revelations, and a Voice to Mankind* (1847), a highly influential book which helped earn him the moniker of the John the Baptist of Modern Spiritualism.

Edgar Allan Poe (1809-1849), always fascinated with mes-merists and other odd cases, became quite interested in Davis, as he mentioned him more than once in his writings and, after attending one of his lectures, wrote the short story "The Facts in the Case of M. Valdemar" (1845). Poe, himself, as varied as his influences were, was certainly one of the most influential of all writers on fiction, occult and otherwise, and one of his early and most immediate influences was on a young writer by the name of George Lippard (1822-1854).

Poe had met Lippard in 1843 in Philadelphia, where both were in the newspaper business. Lippard had been a reporter for the *Spirit of the Times* and right around the time of making Poe's acquaintance became assistant editor on a paper called *The Citizen Soldier* where he began serializing a novel titled *The Ladye Annabel, or The Doom of the Poisoner*, from which Lippard's piece in the present volume is derived. When the novel came out in book form in 1844, he gave a copy to Poe who offered it some words of praise, though implying that the author might consider reigning in his freneticism. According to the famous occult author R. Swinburne Clymer (1877-1966), Lippard was a Rosicrucian; it is impossible to know if the subject of Rosicrucianism had come up in their conversations while they were sitting in Poe's home on Seventh Street, but it is worth noting that Poe did write "The Fall of the House of Usher" (1839), a story which seems to hint at Rosicrucianism, while living in Philadelphia and it is not a far-reach of the imagination to think that the subject had come up with his young protegee.

Though another writer in the current volume, F. C. Ewer (1826-1883), seems to have been inspired by Poe as well, his "The Eventful Nights of August 20th and 21st" bearing some similarities to "The Facts in the Case of M. Valdemar," he, Ewer, denied having ever read the story. A curiosity of Ewer's piece is that, upon publication, while some might have viewed it as an imitation of Poe, others saw it in a very different light, it being immediately reprinted in at least two Spiritualist newspapers, *The Sacred Circle* and *The Christian Spiritualist*,—the former of the two certainly believing it was a work of non-fiction, for its editor claimed to have had spiritual interviews with the principal character, the fictitious writer John F. Lane!

In this manner Ewer's story was later seen as a hoax he committed on the Spiritualists, but it is doubtful if that was his original intention—and though much fun has been poked at Spiritualism, it is from that movement that the American Occult Revival sprang.

Andrew Jackson Davis has been mentioned as one of the early influencers in the rapidly moving phenomena of Spiritualism, but he was certainly not the only one.

P. T. Barnum, in 1841, bought Scudder's American Museum in New York City, on the corner of Broadway and Ann Street, which already had a somewhat strange reputation, showing, instead of paintings or sculptures, curiosities such as a magic lantern, a two-headed lamb, a giant snake, etc., and changed it into Barnum's American Museum, and, instead of de-emphasizing this aspect of museum's reputation, amplified it even more, bringing in a dwarf who he named Jumpin' Tom Thumb, a mermaid from Fiji, and other oddities.

As part of this "upgrade," he hired, in 1844, a fortune teller by the name of Mrs. B——, whose working name was Madame Rockwell, and who was a specialist in the occult art of lithomancy, or divination through the use of stones.

The Fox Sisters have widely been credited with giving the first public demonstrations of mediumistic faculties, their first public performance being in November of 1849. Madame Rockwell, however, had, for a number of years before this been offering her services for the price of 25 cents.

Barnum had previously been a newspaperman, and, knowing the power of print, released, in 1849, a book titled *The Prophetess, Being the Life, Natural and Supernatural, of Mrs. B——, Otherwise known as Madame Rockwell.* This volume, purporting to be a true biography of the mystic, tells the story of how the woman underwent initiation from an Indian medicine man and developed her supernatural abilities. Certainly one of the early works of occult fiction to be published in the United States, the book is structured in a way that would become a hallmark of the genre, the blending of fact and fantasy and the author either using themselves as the central character, or some thinly veiled version of themselves.

"Lara" (1861), the story in the present volume by Paschal Beverly Randolph (1825-1875), falls firmly into this latter category and Randolph's fictional works were mostly tied, in one fashion or another, to his real biography, which itself is as interesting as any novel.

Randolph was born in New York City, the son of a white father and a black mother, and spent his early youth in the

Five Points, not far from the American Museum, which he was certainly aware of, writing in his novel *The Wonderful Story of Ravalette* (1863):

> The great multitude had gathered about him as city sight-seers gather round the last new novelty in the museum—a child with two heads, a dog with two tails, or the Japanese mermaid— duly compounded of codfish and monkey . . .

It is highly likely that he was aware of Madame Rockwell and though it is impossible to say if he read her book or not, the fictionalized writings he composed of his own life bear some resemblance.

Though he would later reject Spiritualism, in the early part of his career Randolph was an important member of Spiritualist circles and worked as a medium—his fame becoming great enough that, in 1855, he was selected to journey to England, for the World's Fair, in order to spread the messages from America, and in 1857 and 1861, made two more trips to Europe and the Near East. During these voyages he met "reputed Rosicrucians" such as Edward Bulwer-Lytton and Hargrave Jennings. In France he became involved with mesmerists and, in Egypt and Jerusalem, received magical instructions and studied ancient manuscripts.

Randolph had been attempting to found a Rosicrucian lodge in the United States called the Third Temple of the Rosy Cross since 1855. These efforts went through various manifestations, including the Supreme Grand Corner Stone Lodge and the Triplicate Order of Rosicrucia, Pythianae and Eulis; and then, in 1874, he founded the Brotherhood of Eulis, which seems to have been the basis of the Fraternitas Rosae Crucis. Through all this, naturally, Randolph had accumulated a certain number of disciples.

In *Seership!; The Magic Mirror* (1875) he wrote:

> Mystery never opens her dark doors to the impatient seeker, has been the result of all my experience, and that of every true Rosicrucian that ever lived, from Thoth-Mor, King of Egypt and high priest thousands of years before the both of the present materialistic phase of civilization, down to Freeman B. Dowd, the selected grand master of the magnificent order. From Tao-Tu in his palaces, three miles square, on the banks of ancient Nile, to Dowd in Davenport, Iowa, in the shores of mightier Mississippi, each and both, and all the links between, will tell the same story, and recount the same experience, that mystery refuses knowledge to the impatient soul!

The Freeman B. Dowd (18??-1910) to whom he refers was one of his most adamant followers, who, as is implied by the above quote, became the Grand Master of the Imperial Order of Rosicrucia.

As Randolph had used fiction as a vehicle for his own biography, so did Dowd, in 1895 publishing the remarkable novel *The Double Man*, from which his contribution in the present volume is taken.

It should be said regarding Randolph that, until recently, the chief source of information on his biography, aside from what he wrote himself, was the writings of the previously mentioned R. Swinburne Clymer, who became head of the Fraternitas Rosae Crucis in 1905, and put a good deal of effort into the organization's hagiology, often at the expense of accuracy. He said that Lippard and Randolph were friends and seems to imply that it was due to Lippard that Randolph became a Rosicrucian. He further ties Randolph to numerous other figures, including W. P. Phelon, the founder of the Hermetic Brotherhood of Luxor, Atlantis and Elephante, who he says Randolph, in 1871, "introduced to his Egyptian associate, the *Orthman Asward el Kindee*, then attaché of the khedive of Egypt."

If we are to believe documents left by the Brotherhood itself, the organization was founded in Chicago in 1874, one year before the Theosophical Society was founded in New York by H. P. Blavatsky (1831-1891) and Henry S. Olcott (1832-1907).[1]

In Blavatsky's *Isis Unveiled* (1877), she mentions that her teachings had been derived from the Brotherhood of Luxor. What precise connection that Brotherhood had to Phelon's is unknown, and both Phelon's and Blavatsky's were certainly tied in various ways to the similarly named Hermetic Brotherhood of Luxor, which, though ostensibly founded in 1884, was claimed to have been established as early as 1870.

The relationship between the H. B. of L. and the Theosophical Society is a complicated one, not only because the two organizations were in rivalry, but also because a large part of the members of the H. B. of L. were also members, at one point or another, of the Theosophical Society. Phelon, for example, was a member of both, and his piece in the present volume, "My Ancient Cat Theosophuz," shows his own peculiar take on these various teachings.

The H. B. of L. was supposedly founded by a Polish Jew by the name of Max Théon (1848-1927) and his wife Alma (1843-1908), who had in the early 1880s been going by the sobriquet of Una, the High Priestess of Pan.

Théon's students were Peter Davidson (1842-1929), a Scottish violin maker, and Thomas H. Burgoyne (1855-

---

1 A privately circulated group of lessons for initiates bearing the date 1918 says the Hermetic Brotherhood of A. L. and E. was founded in 1875, but an 1891 example of Phelon's stationery indicates a founding date of 1884, the same year Clymer gives for the organization's foundation.

189?) a grocer from Leeds who had spent time in jail for advertising fraud. Together in 1885 they published *The Occult Magazine*, writing columns under the pseudonyms of "Zanoni" (Davidson) and "Mejnour" (Burgoyne). In 1886 they decided to immigrate to the United States in order to set up a utopian community under the tenants of the H. B. of L., and travelled from England to Georgia, but once there, went their separate ways.

Davidson remained in Georgia where he promoted the H. B. of L., published materials, and stayed in contact with Europe, and it is said that it was he who initiated Phelon into the H. B. of L., and some association is all but certain, as he quotes him in his *Book of Light* (1891).

Burgoyne went west and propagated the H. B. of L., giving lessons, preparing his magnum opus, *The Light of Egypt* (1889), and gathering in students. Two of these were Henry Wagner, a homeopathic doctor, and his wife Belle M. Wagner, of Denver, Colorado, who, in order to aid Burgoyne in his efforts, offered $100,000, at least part of which was used to form the Astro-Philosophic Publishing Company, which published various works, including Borgoyne's *The Language of the Stars* (1892) and *Celestial Dynamics* (1896), and also reprinted his *The Light of Egypt*. Henry Wagner had, furthermore, printed, in 1886 or 1887, "The Mysteries of Eros," a work which was distributed to the advanced members of the H. B. of L and which was almost completely derived from Randolph's "The Mysteries of Eulis."

Burgoyne passed away sometime around 1894-1896, but his publishing career was not yet over, for, in 1900, a second volume of *The Light of Egypt* appeared, this time dictated by the author to Belle M. Wagner, whom he had chosen as his spiritual successor and as the Scribe of the H. B. of L.—the work being dictated from "the subjective plane of life through the law of mental transfer."

This process might not have been entirely new to Mrs. Wagner, however, since the year before, in 1899, she had published the piece which is in the present volume, "Within the Temple of Isis," in which hints are given in the publisher's preface[1] that the novel had been transmitted to her from "spirit realms" and she, in her introduction, requests the reader to accept the work "not as fiction, but as divine truth as to the laws herein revealed."[2]

Aside from the Rosicrucian order that Randolph ostensibly founded, the Fraternitas Rosae Crucis, two other major Rosicrucian orders appeared in the United States, the Rosicrucian Fellowship, which was founded in 1909, and the Ancient and Mystical Order Rosæ Crucis, which was founded around 1915. Since the subject of this latter organization goes beyond the scope of this book, I will confine myself to a few words about the former.

The Rosicrucian Fellowship was founded by Carl Louis von Grasshoff (1865-1919), a Danish immigrant who went by the sobriquet of "Max Heindel." Though other Rosicrucians might have claimed their lineage from ancient Egyptians, Persian magi or enlightened Eleusinians, Max Heindel received his instructions from the etheric Temple of the Rose Cross that had been formed in the year 1313. Near Oceanside, California, a piece of land was purchased which he called Mount Ecclesia, and on it a temple was built. In 1913 he launched the organization's journal *Echoes from Mount Ecclesia*, the name of which was soon after changed to

---

1 Written by her husband and omitted from the text of the present volume, as is the case with the author's introduction.

2 Though "Within the Temple of Isis" was published at least three years after Burgoyne's death, he still seems to have managed to blurb it, presumably also "through the law of mental transfer," as, upon the publication of the book, he wrote, under his "Zanoni" pseudonym: "This is an Occult Novel of rare value, as it contains a vast deal of Occult lore on many subjects. Soul-Transfer and Soul-Marriage are especially dealt with in a scientific manner. Everybody should read it."

Rays from the Rose Cross—and it was in this publication that his piece in the present volume, "The Last Hours of a Spy," is taken, as well as a piece by one of his followers, Blanche Cromartie, titled "A Dream of Roses."

✳

The information in this introduction comes from numerous sources, and while the bulk of them are primary, not all of them are. In the latter category I would like to acknowledge my indebtedness to two invaluable books: *The Hermetic Brotherhood of Luxor: Initiatic and Historical Documents of an Order of Practical Occultism*, by Joscelyn Godwin, Christian Chanel and John Patrick Deveney (1995), and *Paschal Beverly Randolph: A Nineteenth-Century Black American Spiritualist, Rosicrucian, and Sex Magician*, by John Patrick Deveney (1997).

I would further like to thank Anna, my wife, for her help transcribing "My Ancient Cat Theosophuz," and to Damian Murphy, Justin Isis, and Daniel Corrick for occasional feedback.

—Brendan Connell

THE VIRIDIAN BOOK
OF OCCULT FICTION

THE ADVENTURE OF THE GERMAN STUDENT

by *Washington Irving*

IN a stormy night, in the tempestuous times of the French Revolution, a young German was returning to his lodgings, at a late hour, across the old part of Paris. The lightning gleamed, and the loud claps of thunder rattled through the lofty narrow streets—but I should first tell you something about this young German.

Gottfried Wolfgang was a young man of good family. He had studied for some time at Göttingen, but being of a visionary and enthusiastic character, he had wandered into those wild and speculative doctrines which have so often bewildered German students. His secluded life, his intense application, and the singular nature of his studies had an effect on both mind and body. His health was impaired; his imagination diseased. He had been indulging in fanciful speculations on spiritual essences, until, like Swedenborg, he had an ideal world of his own around him. He took up a notion, I do not know from what cause, that there was an evil influence hanging over him; an evil genius or spirit seeking to ensnare him and ensure his perdition. Such an idea working on his melancholy temperament produced the most gloomy effects. He became haggard and desponding. His friends discovered the mental malady preying upon him, and determined that the best cure was a change of scene; he was sent, therefore, to finish his studies amidst the splendors and gayeties of Paris.

Wolfgang arrived at Paris at the breaking out of the revolution. The popular delirium at first caught his enthusiastic mind, and he was captivated by the political and philosophical theories of the day; but the scenes of blood which followed shocked his sensitive nature, disgusted him with society and the world, and made him more than ever a recluse. He shut himself up in a solitary apartment in the Pays Latin, the quarter of students. There, in a gloomy street not far from the monastic walls of the Sorbonne, he pursued his favorite speculations. Sometimes he spent hours altogether in the great libraries of Paris, those catacombs of departed authors, rummaging among their hoards of dusty and obsolete works in quest of food for his unhealthy appetite. He was, in a manner, a literary ghoul, feeding in the charnel-house of decayed literature.

Wolfgang, though solitary and recluse, was of an ardent temperament, but for a time it operated merely upon his imagination. He was too shy and ignorant of the world to make any advances to the fair, but he was a passionate admirer of female beauty, and in his lonely chamber would often lose himself in reveries on forms and faces which he had seen, and his fancy would deck out images of loveliness far surpassing the reality.

While his mind was in this excited and sublimated state, a dream produced an extraordinary effect upon him. It was of a female face of transcendent beauty. So strong was the impression made, that he dreamt of it again and again. It haunted his thoughts by day, his slumbers by night; in fine, he became passionately enamoured of this shadow of a dream. This lasted so long that it became one of those fixed ideas which haunt the minds of melancholy men, and are at times mistaken for madness.

Such was Gottfried Wolfgang, and such his situation at the time I mentioned. He was returning home late one stormy night, through some of the old and gloomy streets of the Marais, the ancient part of Paris. The loud claps of thunder rattled among the high houses of the narrow streets. He came to the Place de Grève, the square where public executions are performed. The lightning quivered about the pinnacles of the ancient Hôtel de Ville, and shed flickering gleams over the open space in front. As Wolfgang was crossing the square, he shrank back with horror at finding himself close by the guillotine. It was the height of the reign of terror, when this dreadful instrument of death stood ever ready, and its scaffold was continually running with the blood of the virtuous and the brave. It had that very day been actively employed in the work of carnage, and there it stood in grim array, amidst a silent and sleeping city, waiting for fresh victims.

Wolfgang's heart sickened within him, and he was turning shuddering from the horrible engine, when he beheld a shadowy form, cowering as it were at the foot of the steps which led up to the scaffold. A succession of vivid flashes of lightning revealed it more distinctly. It was a female figure, dressed in black. She was seated on one of the lower steps of the scaffold, leaning forward, her face hid in her lap; and her long dishevelled tresses hanging to the ground, streaming with the rain which fell in torrents. Wolfgang paused. There was something awful in this solitary monument of woe. The female had the appearance of being above the common order. He knew the times to be full of vicissitude, and that many a fair head, which had once been pillowed on down, now wandered houseless. Perhaps this was some poor mourner whom the dreadful axe had rendered desolate, and who sat here heart-broken on the strand of existence, from which all that was dear to her had been launched into eternity.

He approached, and addressed her in the accents of sympathy. She raised her head and gazed wildly at him. What was his astonishment at beholding, by the bright glare of the lightning, the very face which had haunted him in his dreams. It was pale and disconsolate, but ravishingly beautiful.

Trembling with violent and conflicting emotions, Wolfgang again accosted her. He spoke something of her being exposed at such an hour of the night, and to the fury of such a storm, and offered to conduct her to her friends. She pointed to the guillotine with a gesture of dreadful signification.

"I have no friend on earth!" said she.

"But you have a home," said Wolfgang.

"Yes—in the grave!"

The heart of the student melted at the words.

"If a stranger dare make an offer," said he, "without danger of being misunderstood, I would offer my humble dwelling as a shelter; myself as a devoted friend. I am friendless myself in Paris, and a stranger in the land; but if my life could be of service, it is at your disposal, and should be sacrificed before harm or indignity should come to you."

There was an honest earnestness in the young man's manner that had its effect. His foreign accent, too, was in his favor; it showed him not to be a hackneyed inhabitant of Paris. Indeed, there is an eloquence in true enthusiasm that is not to be doubted. The homeless stranger confided herself implicitly to the protection of the student.

He supported her faltering steps across the Pont Neuf, and by the place where the statue of Henry the Fourth had been overthrown by the populace. The storm had abated, and the thunder rumbled at a distance. All Paris was quiet; that great volcano of human passion slumbered for a while, to gather fresh strength for the next day's eruption. The student conducted his charge through the ancient streets of the Pays Latin, and by the dusky walls of the Sorbonne, to the great dingy hotel which he inhabited. The old portress who admitted them stared with surprise at the unusual sight of the melancholy Wolfgang, with a female companion.

On entering his apartment, the student, for the first time, blushed at the scantiness and indifference of his dwelling. He had but one chamber—an old-fashioned saloon—heavily carved, and fantastically furnished with the remains of former magnificence, for it was one of those hotels in the quarter of the Luxembourg palace, which had once belonged to nobility. It was lumbered with books and papers, and all the usual apparatus of a student, and his bed stood in a recess at one end.

When lights were brought, and Wolfgang had a better opportunity of contemplating the stranger, he was more than ever intoxicated by her beauty. Her face was pale, but of a dazzling fairness, set off by a profusion of raven hair that hung clustering about it. Her eyes were large and brilliant, with a singular expression approaching almost to wildness. As far as her black dress permitted her shape to be seen, it was of perfect symmetry. Her whole appearance was highly striking, though she was dressed in the simplest style. The only thing approaching to an ornament which she wore, was a broad black band round her neck, clasped by diamonds.

The perplexity now commenced with the student how to dispose of the helpless being thus thrown upon his protection. He thought of abandoning his chamber to her, and seeking shelter for himself elsewhere. Still, he was so fascinated by her charms, there seemed to be such a spell upon his thoughts and senses, that he could not tear himself from her presence. Her manner, too, was singular and unaccountable. She spoke no more of the guillotine. Her grief had abated. The attentions of the student had first won her confidence, and then, apparently, her heart. She was evidently an enthusiast like himself, and enthusiasts soon understand each other.

In the infatuation of the moment, Wolfgang avowed his passion for her. He told her the story of his mysterious dream, and how she had possessed his heart before he had even seen her. She was strangely affected by his recital, and acknowledged to have felt an impulse towards him equally unaccountable. It was the time for wild theory and wild actions. Old prejudices and superstitions were done away; everything was under the sway of the "Goddess of Reason." Among other rubbish of the old times, the forms and ceremonies of marriage began to be considered superfluous bonds for honorable minds. Social compacts were the vogue. Wolfgang was too much of a theorist not to be tainted by the liberal doctrines of the day.

"Why should we separate?" said he; "our hearts are united; in the eye of reason and honor we are as one. What need is there of sordid forms to bind high souls together?"

The stranger listened with emotion: she had evidently received illumination at the same school.

"You have no home nor family," continued he; "let me be everything to you, or rather let us be everything to one another. If form is necessary, form shall be observed—there is my hand. I pledge myself to you forever."

"Forever?" said the stranger, solemnly.

"Forever!" repeated Wolfgang.

The stranger clasped the hand extended to her. "Then I am yours," murmured she, and sank upon his bosom.

The next morning the student left his bride sleeping, and sallied forth at an early hour to seek more spacious apartments suitable to the change in his situation. When he returned, he found the stranger lying with her head hanging over the bed, and one arm thrown over it. He spoke to her, but received no reply. He advanced to awaken her from her uneasy posture. On taking her hand, it was cold—there was no pulsation— her face was pallid and ghastly. In a word, she was a corpse.

Horrified and frantic, he alarmed the house. A scene of confusion ensued. The police were summoned. As the officer of police entered the room, he started back on beholding the corpse.

"Great heaven!" cried he, "how did this woman come here?"

"Do you know anything about her?" said Wolfgang eagerly.

"Do I?" exclaimed the officer; "she was guillotined yesterday."

He stepped forward; undid the black collar round the neck of the corpse, and the head rolled on the floor!

The student burst into a frenzy. "The fiend! the fiend has gained possession of me!" shrieked he; "I am lost forever."

They tried to soothe him, but in vain. He was possessed with the frightful belief that an evil spirit had reanimated the dead body to ensnare him. He went distracted, and died in a mad-house.

LIGEIA

by Edgar Allan Poe

And the will therein lieth, which dieth not.
Who knoweth the mysteries of the will, with
its vigor? For God is but a great will pervading all things by nature of its intentness.
Man doth not yield himself to the angels,
nor unto death utterly, save only through the
weakness of his feeble will.

—Joseph Glanvill.

I cannot, for my soul, remember how, when, or even precisely where, I first became acquainted with the lady Ligeia. Long years have since elapsed, and my memory is feeble through much suffering. Or, perhaps, I cannot *now* bring these points to mind, because, in truth, the character of my beloved, her rare learning, her singular yet placid cast of beauty, and the thrilling and enthralling eloquence of her low musical language, made their way into my heart by paces so steadily and stealthily progressive that they have been unnoticed and unknown. Yet I believe that I met her first and most frequently in some large, old, decaying city near the Rhine. Of her family—I have surely heard her speak. That it is of a remotely ancient date cannot be doubted. Ligeia! Ligeia! Buried in studies of a nature more than all else adapted to deaden impressions of the outward world, it is by that sweet word alone—by Ligeia—that I bring before mine eyes in fancy the image of her who is no more. And now, while I write, a recollection flashes upon me that I have *never known* the paternal name of her who was my friend and my betrothed, and who became the partner of my studies, and finally the wife of my bosom. Was it a playful charge on the part of my Ligeia? or was it a test of my strength of affection, that I should institute no inquiries upon this point? or was it rather a caprice of my own—a wildly romantic offering on the shrine of the most passionate devotion? I but indistinctly recall the fact itself—what wonder that I have utterly forgotten the circumstances which originated or attended it? And, indeed, if ever that spirit which is entitled *Romance*—if ever she, the wan and the misty-winged *Ashtophet* of idolatrous Egypt, presided, as they tell, over marriages ill-omened, then most surely she presided over mine.

There is one dear topic, however, on which my memory fails me not. It is the person of Ligeia. In stature she was tall, somewhat slender, and, in her latter days, even emaciated. I would in vain attempt to portray the majesty, the quiet ease, of her demeanor, or the incomprehensible lightness and elasticity of her footfall. She came and departed as a shadow. I was never made aware of her entrance into my closed study save by the dear music of her low sweet voice, as she placed her marble hand upon my shoulder. In beauty of face no maiden ever equalled her. It was the radiance of an opium-dream—an airy and spirit-lifting vision more wildly divine than the phantasies which hovered about the slumbering souls of the daughters of Delos. Yet her features were not of that regular mould which we have been falsely taught to worship in the classical labors of the heathen. "There is no exquisite beauty," says Bacon, Lord Verulam, speaking truly of all the forms and *genera* of beauty, "without some *strangeness* in the proportion." Yet, although I saw that the features of Ligeia were not of a classic regularity—although I perceived that her loveliness was indeed "exquisite," and felt that there was much of "strangeness" pervading it, yet I have tried in vain to detect the irregularity and to trace home my own perception of "the strange." I examined the contour of the lofty and pale forehead—it was faultless—how cold indeed that word when applied to a majesty so divine!—the skin rivalling the purest ivory, the commanding extent and repose, the gentle prominence of the regions above the temples; and then the raven-black, the glossy, the luxuriant and naturally-curling tresses, setting forth the full force of the Homeric epithet, "hyacinthine!" I looked at the delicate outlines of the nose—and nowhere but in the graceful medallions of the Hebrews had I beheld a similar perfection. There were the same luxurious smoothness of surface, the same scarcely perceptible tendency to the aquiline, the same harmoniously curved nostrils speaking the free spirit. I regarded the sweet mouth. Here was indeed the triumph of all things heavenly—the magnificent turn of the short upper lip—the soft, voluptuous slumber of the under—the dimples which sported, and the color which spoke—the teeth glancing back, with a brilliancy almost startling, every ray of the holy light which fell upon them in her serene and placid, yet most exultingly radiant of all smiles. I scrutinized the formation of the chin—and here, too, I found the gentleness of breadth, the softness and the majesty, the fullness and the spirituality, of the Greek—the contour which the god Apollo revealed but in a dream, to Cleomenes, the son of the Athenian. And then I peered into the large eyes of Ligeia.

For eyes we have no models in the remotely antique. It might have been, too, that in these eyes of my beloved lay the secret to which Lord Verulam alludes. They were, I must believe, far larger than the ordinary eyes of our own race. They were even fuller than the fullest of the gazelle eyes of the tribe of the valley of Nourjahad. Yet it was only at intervals—in moments of intense excitement—that this peculiarity became more than slightly noticeable in Ligeia. And at such moments was her beauty—in my heated fancy thus it appeared perhaps—the beauty of beings either above or apart from the earth—the beauty of the fabulous Houri of the Turk. The hue of the orbs was the most brilliant of black, and, far over them, hung jetty lashes of great length. The brows, slightly irregular in outline, had the same tint. The "strangeness," however, which I found in the eyes, was of a nature distinct from the formation, or the color, or the brilliancy of the features, and must, after all, be referred to the *expression*. Ah, word of no meaning! behind whose vast latitude of mere sound we intrench our ignorance of so much of the spiritual. The expression of the eyes of Ligeia! How for long hours have I pondered upon it! How have I, through the whole of a midsummer night, struggled to fathom it! What was it—that something more profound than the well of Democritus—which lay far within the pupils of my beloved? What was it? I was possessed with a passion to discover. Those eyes! those large, those shining, those divine orbs! they became to me twin stars of Leda, and I to them devoutest of astrologers.

There is no point, among the many incomprehensible anomalies of the science of mind, more thrillingly exciting than the fact—never, I believe, noticed in the schools—that, in our endeavors to recall to memory something long forgotten, we often find ourselves *upon the very verge* of remembrance, without being able, in the end, to remember. And thus how frequently, in my intense scrutiny of Ligeia's eyes, have I felt approaching the full knowledge of their expression—felt it approaching—yet not quite be mine—and so at length entirely depart! And (strange, oh strangest mystery of all!) I found, in the commonest objects of the universe, a circle of analogies to that expression. I mean to say that, subsequently to the period when Ligeia's beauty passed into my spirit, there dwelling as in a shrine, I derived, from many existences in the material world, a sentiment such as I felt always aroused within me by her large and luminous orbs. Yet not the more could I define that sentiment, or analyze, or even steadily view it. I recognized it, let me repeat, sometimes in the survey of a rapidly-growing vine—in the contemplation of a moth, a butterfly, a chrysalis, a stream of running water. I have felt it in the ocean—in the falling of a meteor. I have felt it in the glances of unusually aged people. And there are one or two stars in heaven—(one especially, a star of the sixth magnitude, double and changeable, to be found near the large star in Lyra) in a telescopic scrutiny of which I have been made aware of the feeling. I have been filled with it by certain sounds from stringed instruments, and not unfrequently by passages from books. Among innumerable other instances, I well remember something in a volume of Joseph Glanvill, which (perhaps merely from its quaintness—who shall say?) never failed to inspire me with the sentiment: "And the will therein lieth, which dieth not. Who knoweth the mysteries of the will, with its vigor? For God is but a great will pervading all things by nature of its intentness. Man doth not yield him to the angels, nor unto death utterly, save only through the weakness of his feeble will."

Length of years, and subsequent reflection, have enabled me to trace, indeed, some remote connection between this passage in the English moralist and a portion of the character of Ligeia. An *intensity* in thought, action, or speech, was possibly, in her, a result, or at least an index, of that gigantic volition which, during our long intercourse, failed to give other and more immediate evidence of its existence. Of all the women whom I have ever known, she, the outwardly calm, the ever-placid Ligeia, was the most violently a prey to the tumultuous vultures of stern passion. And of such passion I could form no estimate, save by the miraculous expansion of those eyes which at once so delighted and appalled me—by the almost magical melody, modulation, distinctness and placidity of her very low voice—and by the fierce energy (rendered doubly effective by contrast with her manner of utterance) of the wild words which she habitually uttered.

I have spoken of the learning of Ligeia: it was immense—such as I have never known in woman. In the classical tongues was she deeply proficient, and as far as my own acquaintance extended in regard to the modern dialects of Europe, I have never known her at fault. Indeed upon any theme of the most admired, because simply the most abstruse of the boasted erudition of the academy, have I ever found Ligeia at fault? How singularly—how thrillingly, this one point in the nature of my wife has forced itself, at this late period only, upon my attention! I said her knowledge was such as I have never known in woman—but where breathes the man who has traversed, and successfully, all the wide areas of moral, physical, and mathematical science? I saw not then what I now clearly perceive, that the acquisitions of Ligeia were gigantic, were astounding; yet I was sufficiently aware of her infinite supremacy to resign myself, with a child-like confidence, to her guidance through the chaotic world of metaphysical investigation at which I was most busily occupied during the earlier years of our marriage. With how vast a triumph—with how vivid a delight—with how much of all that is ethereal in hope did I *feel*, as she bent over me in studies but little sought—but less known—that delicious vista by slow degrees expanding before me, down whose long, gorgeous, and all untrodden path, I might at length pass onward to the goal of a wisdom too divinely precious not to be forbidden!

How poignant, then, must have been the grief with which, after some years, I beheld my well-grounded expectations take wings to themselves and fly away! Without Ligeia I was but as a child groping benighted. Her presence, her readings alone, rendered vividly luminous the many mysteries of the transcendentalism in which we were immersed. Wanting the radiant lustre of her eyes, letters, lambent and golden, grew duller than Saturnian lead. And now those eyes shone less and less frequently upon the pages over which I pored. Ligeia grew ill. The wild eyes blazed with a too—too glorious effulgence; the pale fingers became of the transparent waxen hue of the grave; and the blue veins upon the lofty forehead swelled and sank impetuously with the tides of the gentle emotion. I saw that she must die—and I struggled desperately in spirit with the grim Azrael. And the struggles of the passionate wife were, to my astonishment, even more energetic than my own. There had been much in her stern nature to impress me with the belief that, to her, death would have come without its terrors; but not so. Words are impotent to convey any just idea of the fierceness of resistance with which she wrestled with the Shadow. I groaned in anguish at the pitiable spectacle. I would have soothed—I would have reasoned; but, in the intensity of her wild desire for life,—for life—*but* for life—solace and reason were the uttermost folly. Yet not until the last instance, amid the most convulsive writhings of her fierce spirit, was shaken the external placidity of her demeanor. Her voice grew more gentle—grew more low—yet I would not wish to dwell upon the wild meaning of the quietly uttered words. My brain reeled as I hearkened, entranced, to a melody more than mortal—to assumptions and aspirations which mortality had never before known.

That she loved me I should not have doubted; and I might have been easily aware that, in a bosom such as hers, love would have reigned no ordinary passion. But in death only, was I fully impressed with the strength of her affection. For long hours, detaining my hand, would she pour out before me the overflowing of a heart whose more than passionate devotion amounted to idolatry. How had I deserved to be so blessed by such confessions?—how had I deserved to be so cursed with the removal of my beloved in the hour of her making them? But upon this subject I cannot bear to dilate. Let me say only, that in Ligeia's more than womanly abandonment to a love, alas! all unmerited, all unworthily bestowed, I at length recognized the principle of her longing with so wildly earnest a desire for the life which was now fleeing so rapidly away. It is this wild longing—it is this eager vehemence of desire for life—*but* for life—that I have no power to portray—no utterance capable of expressing.

At high noon of the night in which she departed, beckoning me, peremptorily, to her side, she bade me repeat certain verses composed by herself not many days before. I obeyed her. They were these:—

> Lo! 'tis a gala night
>   Within the lonesome latter years!
> An angel throng, bewinged, bedight
>   In veils, and drowned in tears,
> Sit in a theatre, to see
>   A play of hopes and fears,
> While the orchestra breathes fitfully
>   The music of the spheres.
>
> Mimes, in the form of God on high,
>   Mutter and mumble low,
> And hither and thither fly;
>   Mere puppets they, who come and go
> At bidding of vast formless things
>   That shift the scenery to and fro,
> Flapping from out their Condor wings
>   Invisible Wo!

That motley drama!—oh, be sure
    It shall not be forgot!
With its Phantom chased forever more,
    By a crowd that seize it not,
Through a circle that ever returneth in
    To the self-same spot,
And much of Madness and more of Sin
    And Horror the soul of the plot.

But see, amid the mimic rout,
    A crawling shape intrude!
A blood-red thing that writhes from out
    The scenic solitude!
It writhes!—it writhes!—with mortal pangs
    The mimes become its food,
And the seraphs sob at vermin fangs
    In human gore imbued.

Out—out are the lights—out all!
    And over each quivering form,
The curtain, a funeral pall,
    Comes down with the rush of a storm,
And the angels, all pallid and wan,
    Uprising, unveiling, affirm
That the play is the tragedy, "Man,"
    And its hero the Conqueror Worm.

"O God!" half shrieked Ligeia, leaping to her feet and extending her arms aloft with a spasmodic movement, as I made an end of these lines—"O God! O Divine Father!—shall these things be undeviatingly so?—shall this Conqueror be not once conquered? Are we not part and parcel in Thee? Who—who knoweth the mysteries of the will with its vigor?

Man doth not yield him to the angels, *nor unto death utterly*, save only through the weakness of his feeble will."

And now, as if exhausted with emotion, she suffered her white arms to fall, and returned solemnly to her bed of death. And as she breathed her last sighs, there came mingled with them a low murmur from her lips. I bent to them my ear and distinguished, again, the concluding words of the passage in Glanvill—"*Man doth not yield him to the angels, nor unto death utterly, save only through the weakness of his feeble will.*"

She died: and I, crushed into the very dust with sorrow, could no longer endure the lonely desolation of my dwelling in the dim and decaying city by the Rhine. I had no lack of what the world calls wealth. Ligeia had brought me far more, very far more than ordinarily falls to the lot of mortals. After a few months, therefore, of weary and aimless wandering, I purchased, and put in some repair, an abbey, which I shall not name, in one of the wildest and least frequented portions of fair England. The gloomy and dreary grandeur of the building, the almost savage aspect of the domain, the many melancholy and time-honored memories connected with both, had much in unison with the feelings of utter abandonment which had driven me into that remote and unsocial region of the country. Yet although the external abbey, with its verdant decay hanging about it, suffered but little alteration, I gave way, with a child-like perversity, and perchance with a faint hope of alleviating my sorrows, to a display of more than regal magnificence within. For such follies, even in childhood, I had imbibed a taste and now they came back to me as if in the dotage of grief. Alas, I feel how much even of incipient madness might have been discovered in the gorgeous and fantastic draperies, in the solemn carvings of Egypt, in the wild cornices and furniture, in the Bedlam patterns of the carpets of tufted gold! I had become a bounden slave in the trammels of opium, and my labors and my orders had taken a coloring from my dreams. But these absurdities I must not pause to detail. Let me speak only of that one chamber, ever accursed, whither in a moment of mental alienation, I led from the altar as my bride—as the successor of the unforgotten Ligeia—the fair-haired and blue-eyed Lady Rowena Trevanion, of Tremaine.

There is no individual portion of the architecture and decoration of that bridal chamber which is not now visibly before me. Where were the souls of the haughty family of the bride, when, through thirst of gold, they permitted to pass the threshold of an apartment so bedecked, a maiden and a daughter so beloved? I have said that I minutely remember the details of the chamber—yet I am sadly forgetful on topics of deep moment—and here there was no system, no keeping, in the fantastic display, to take hold upon the memory. The room lay in a high turret of the castellated abbey, was pentagonal in shape, and of capacious size. Occupying the whole southern face of the pentagon was the sole window—an immense sheet of unbroken glass from Venice—a single pane, and tinted of a leaden hue, so that the rays of either the sun or moon, passing through it, fell with a ghastly lustre on the objects within. Over the upper portion of this huge window, extended the trellice-work of an aged vine, which clambered up the massy walls of the turret. The ceiling, of gloomy-looking oak, was excessively lofty, vaulted, and elaborately fretted with the wildest and most grotesque specimens of a semi-Gothic, semi-Druidical device. From out the most central recess of this melancholy vaulting, depended, by a single chain of gold with long links, a huge censer of the same metal, Saracenic in pattern, and with many perforations so contrived that there writhed in and out of them, as if endued with a serpent vitality, a continual succession of parti-colored fires.

Some few ottomans and golden candelabra, of Eastern figure, were in various stations about—and there was the couch, too—bridal couch—of an Indian model, and low, and sculptured of solid ebony, with a pall-like canopy above. In each of the angles of the chamber stood on end a gigantic sarcophagus of black granite, from the tombs of the kings over against Luxor, with their aged lids full of immemorial sculpture. But in the draping of the apartment lay, alas! the chief phantasy of all. The lofty walls, gigantic in height—even unproportionably so—were hung from summit to foot, in vast folds, with a heavy and massive-looking tapestry—tapestry of a material which was found alike as a carpet on the floor, as a covering for the ottomans and the ebony bed, as a canopy for the bed, and as the gorgeous volutes of the curtains which partially shaded the window. The material was the richest cloth of gold. It was spotted all over, at irregular intervals, with arabesque figures, about a foot in diameter, and wrought upon the cloth in patterns of the most jetty black. But these figures partook of the true character of the arabesque only when regarded from a single point of view. By a contrivance now common, and indeed traceable to a very remote period of antiquity, they were made changeable in aspect. To one entering the room, they bore the appearance of simple monstrosities; but upon a farther advance, this appearance gradually departed; and step by step, as the visitor moved his station in the chamber, he saw himself surrounded by an endless succession of the ghastly forms which belong to the superstition of the Norman, or arise in the guilty slumbers of the monk. The phantasmagoric effect was vastly heightened by the artificial introduction of a strong continual current of wind behind the draperies—giving a hideous and uneasy animation to the whole.

In halls such as these—in a bridal chamber such as this—I passed, with the Lady of Tremaine, the unhallowed hours of the first month of our marriage—passed them with but little disquietude. That my wife dreaded the fierce moodiness of my temper—that she shunned me and loved me but little—I could not help perceiving; but it gave me rather pleasure than otherwise. I loathed her with a hatred belonging more to demon than to man. My memory flew back, (oh, with what intensity of regret!) to Ligeia, the beloved, the august, the beautiful, the entombed. I revelled in recollections of her purity, of her wisdom, of her lofty, her ethereal nature, of her passionate, her idolatrous love. Now, then, did my spirit fully and freely burn with more than all the fires of her own. In the excitement of my opium dreams (for I was habitually fettered in the shackles of the drug) I would call aloud upon her name, during the silence of the night, or among the sheltered recesses of the glens by day, as if, through the wild eagerness, the solemn passion, the consuming ardor of my longing for the departed, I could restore her to the pathway she had abandoned—ah, *could* it be forever?—upon the earth.

About the commencement of the second month of the marriage, the Lady Rowena was attacked with sudden illness, from which her recovery was slow. The fever which consumed her rendered her nights uneasy; and in her perturbed state of half-slumber, she spoke of sounds, and of motions, in and about the chamber of the turret, which I concluded had no origin save in the distemper of her fancy, or perhaps in the phantasmagoric influences of the chamber itself. She became at length convalescent—finally well. Yet but a brief period elapsed, ere a second more violent disorder again threw her upon a bed of suffering; and from this attack her frame, at all times feeble, never altogether recovered. Her illnesses were, after this epoch, of alarming character, and of more alarming recurrence, defying alike the knowledge and the great exertions of her physicians. With the increase of the chronic disease which had thus, apparently, taken too sure hold upon her constitution to be eradicated by human means, I could not fail to observe a similar increase in the nervous irritation of her temperament, and in her excitability by trivial causes of fear. She spoke again, and now more frequently and pertinaciously, of the sounds—of the slight sounds—and of the unusual motions among the tapestries, to which she had formerly alluded.

One night, near the closing in of September, she pressed this distressing subject with more than usual emphasis upon my attention. She had just awakened from an unquiet slumber, and I had been watching, with feelings half of anxiety, half of vague terror, the workings of her emaciated countenance. I sat by the side of her ebony bed, upon one of the ottomans of India. She partly arose, and spoke, in an earnest low whisper, of sounds which she *then* heard, but which I could not hear—of motions which she *then* saw, but which I could not perceive. The wind was rushing hurriedly behind the tapestries, and I wished to show her (what, let me confess it, I could not all believe) that those almost inarticulate breathings, and those very gentle variations of the figures upon the wall, were but the natural effects of that customary rushing of the wind. But a deadly pallor, overspreading her face, had proved to me that my exertions to reassure her would be fruitless. She appeared to be fainting, and no attendants were within call. I remembered where was deposited a decanter of light wine which had been ordered by her physicians, and hastened across the chamber to procure it. But, as I stepped beneath the light of the censer, two circumstances of a startling nature attracted my attention. I had felt that some palpable although invisible object had passed lightly by my person; and I saw that there lay upon the golden carpet, in the very middle of the rich lustre thrown from the censer, a shadow—a faint, indefinite shadow of angelic aspect—such as might be fancied for the shadow of a shade. But I was wild with the excitement of an immoderate dose of opium, and heeded these things but little, nor spoke of them to Rowena. Having found the wine, I recrossed the chamber, and poured out a gobletful, which

I held to the lips of the fainting lady. She had now partially recovered, however, and took the vessel herself, while I sank upon an ottoman near me, with my eyes fastened upon her person. It was then that I became distinctly aware of a gentle footfall upon the carpet, and near the couch; and in a second thereafter, as Rowena was in the act of raising the wine to her lips, I saw, or may have dreamed that I saw, fall within the goblet, as if from some invisible spring in the atmosphere of the room, three or four large drops of a brilliant and ruby colored fluid. If this I saw—not so Rowena. She swallowed the wine unhesitatingly, and I forbore to speak to her of a circumstance which must, after all, I considered, have been but the suggestion of a vivid imagination, rendered morbidly active by the terror of the lady, by the opium, and by the hour.

Yet I cannot conceal it from my own perception that, immediately subsequent to the fall of the ruby-drops, a rapid change for the worse took place in the disorder of my wife; so that, on the third subsequent night, the hands of her menials prepared her for the tomb, and on the fourth, I sat alone, with her shrouded body, in that fantastic chamber which had received her as my bride. Wild visions, opium-engendered, flitted, shadow-like, before me. I gazed with unquiet eye upon the sarcophagi in the angles of the room, upon the varying figures of the drapery, and upon the writhing of the parti-colored fires in the censer overhead. My eyes then fell, as I called to mind the circumstances of a former night, to the spot beneath the glare of the censer where I had seen the faint traces of the shadow. It was there, however, no longer; and breathing with greater freedom, I turned my glances to the pallid and rigid figure upon the bed. Then rushed upon me a thousand memories of Ligeia—and then came back upon my heart, with the turbulent violence of a flood, the whole of that unutterable woe with which I had regarded her thus enshrouded. The night waned; and still, with a bosom full of bitter thoughts of the one only and supremely beloved, I remained gazing upon the body of Rowena.

It might have been midnight, or perhaps earlier, or later, for I had taken no note of time, when a sob, low, gentle, but very distinct, startled me from my revery. I *felt* that it came from the bed of ebony—the bed of death. I listened in an agony of superstitious terror—but there was no repetition of the sound. I strained my vision to detect any motion in the corpse—but there was not the slightest perceptible. Yet I could not have been deceived. I *had* heard the noise, however faint, and my soul was awakened within me. I resolutely and perseveringly kept my attention riveted upon the body. Many minutes elapsed before any circumstance occurred tending to throw light upon the mystery. At length it became evident that a slight, a very feeble, and barely noticeable tinge of color had flushed up within the cheeks, and along the sunken small veins of the eyelids. Through a species of unutterable horror and awe, for which the language of mortality has no sufficiently energetic expression, I felt my heart cease to beat, my limbs grow rigid where I sat. Yet a sense of duty finally operated to restore my self-possession. I could no longer doubt that we had been precipitate in our preparations—that Rowena still lived. It was necessary that some immediate exertion be made; yet the turret was altogether apart from the portion of the abbey tenanted by the servants—there were none within call—I had no means of summoning them to my aid without leaving the room for many minutes—and this I could not venture to do. I therefore struggled alone in my endeavors to call back the spirit ill hovering. In a short period it was certain, however, that a relapse had taken place; the color disappeared from both eyelid and cheek, leaving a wanness even more than that of marble; the lips became doubly shrivelled and pinched up in the ghastly expression of death; a repulsive clamminess and coldness overspread rapidly the surface of the body; and all the usual rigorous illness immediately supervened. I fell back with a shudder upon the couch from which I had been so startlingly aroused, and again gave myself up to passionate waking visions of Ligeia.

An hour thus elapsed when (could it be possible?) I was a second time aware of some vague sound issuing from the region of the bed. I listened—in extremity of horror. The sound came again—it was a sigh. Rushing to the corpse, I saw—distinctly saw—a tremor upon the lips. In a minute afterward they relaxed, disclosing a bright line of the pearly teeth. Amazement now struggled in my bosom with the profound awe which had hitherto reigned there alone. I felt that my vision grew dim, that my reason wandered; and it was only by a violent effort that I at length succeeded in nerving myself to the task which duty thus once more had pointed out. There was now a partial glow upon the forehead and upon the cheek and throat; a perceptible warmth pervaded the whole frame; there was even a slight pulsation at the heart. The lady lived; and with redoubled ardor I betook myself to the task of restoration. I chafed and bathed the temples and the hands, and used every exertion which experience, and no little medical reading, could suggest. But in vain. Suddenly, the color fled, the pulsation ceased, the lips resumed the expression of the dead, and, in an instant afterward, the whole body took upon itself the icy chilliness, the livid hue, the intense rigidity, the sunken outline, and all the loathsome peculiarities of that which has been, for many days, a tenant of the tomb.

And again I sunk into visions of Ligeia—and again, (what marvel that I shudder while I write?), *again* there reached my ears a low sob from the region of the ebony bed. But why shall I minutely detail the unspeakable horrors of that night? Why shall I pause to relate how, time after time, until near the period of the gray dawn, this hideous drama of revivification was repeated; how each terrific relapse was only into a sterner and apparently more irredeemable death; how each agony wore the aspect of a struggle with some invisible foe; and how each struggle was succeeded by I know not what of wild change in the personal appearance of the corpse? Let me hurry to a conclusion.

The greater part of the fearful night had worn away, and she who had been dead, once again stirred—and now more vigorously than hitherto, although arousing from a dissolution more appalling in its utter hopelessness than any. I had long ceased to struggle or to move, and remained sitting rigidly upon the ottoman, a helpless prey to a whirl of violent emotions, of which extreme awe was perhaps the least terrible, the least consuming. The corpse, I repeat, stirred, and now more vigorously than before. The hues of life flushed up with unwonted energy into the countenance—the limbs relaxed—and, save that the eyelids were yet pressed heavily together, and that the bandages and draperies of the grave still imparted their charnel character to the figure, I might have dreamed that Rowena had indeed shaken off, utterly, the fetters of Death. But if this idea was not, even then, altogether adopted, I could at least doubt no longer, when, arising from the bed, tottering, with feeble steps, with closed eyes, and with the manner of one bewildered in a dream, the thing that was enshrouded advanced boldly and palpably into the middle of the apartment.

I trembled not—I stirred not—for a crowd of unutterable fancies connected with the air, the stature, the demeanor of the figure, rushing hurriedly through my brain, had paralyzed—had chilled me into stone. I stirred not—but gazed upon the apparition. There was a mad disorder in my thoughts—a tumult unappeasable. Could it, indeed, be the *living* Rowena who confronted me? Could it indeed be Rowena *at all*—the fair-haired, the blue-eyed Lady Rowena Trevanion of Tremaine? Why, *why* should I doubt it? The bandage lay heavily about the mouth—but then might it not be the mouth of the breathing Lady of Tremaine? And the cheeks—there were the roses as in her noon of life—yes, these might indeed be the fair cheeks of the living Lady of Tremaine. And the chin, with its dimples, as in health, might it not be hers?—but had she then grown taller since her malady? What inexpressible madness seized me with that thought? One bound, and I had reached her feet! Shrinking from my touch, she let fall from her head, unloosened, the ghastly cerements which had confined it, and there streamed forth, into the rushing atmosphere of the chamber, huge masses of long and dishevelled hair; *it was blacker than the raven wings of midnight!* And now slowly opened the eyes of the figure which stood before me. "Here then, at least," I shrieked aloud, "can I never—can I never be mistaken—these are the full, and the black, and the wild eyes—of my lost love—of the Lady—of the LADY LIGEIA."

THE DREAM OF THE DAMNED

by George Lippard

HE stood upon a lonely isle. His feet were tortured by the sensation of burning, he looked beneath in wonder, and discovered that he stood upon a rock of fire.

He looked around—he beheld an ocean of fire; as far as eye could see, nothing met his vision but the waves of crimson flame, undulating to and fro, with a gentle, yet solemn motion.

Had the waves arisen around him, in giant billows, or swept above in mountains of liquid flame, the dreamer would have rejoiced, his spirit would have joined in the tumult, his soul become the incarnation of the storm.

But that strange calmness of the waves, that quiet undulation, awed him, chilled him to the heart. He looked again over the shoreless sea, and saw with straining eyes a sight of woe—unutterable woe.

From the surface of every wave, from the waves breaking in spiral flames at his feet—afar and near, on every side—from the surface of every wave was thrust a discolored face, with burning eyes, that gleamed with a strange life, while the lips were colorless, the cheeks livid, and the brow green with decay. As the Dreamer looked, low, faint murmurs, unutterable sighs and sobs, broke on the air, and a hollow whisper, more like the echo of a thought than a sound, came to his ear—THESE ARE THE FACES OF THE DAMNED—every face you see, is the face of a *Lost-soul*—THESE ARE THE FACES OF THE DAMNED.

Aldarin turned from side to side with a horror he had never felt before. All around seemed turning to fire, fire in every shape and form, fire intangible and fire incarnate. Above, no sky with Sun of Glory gave light to that ocean of flame, with the faces of the damned, thrust from every billow. A roof of brass, vast and awful, and magnificent, arched over the waves of fire; it was heated to a burning heat, and the eye of Aldarin seemed turning to flame, as he looked upon the brazen sky.

The horizon of this fearful sky, was concealed by great clouds, rolling slowly on, and on, and on, over the waves of fire, far, far, from the isle where stood Aldarin.

And while the hollow murmur broke over the scene, and the whispering of subdued voices, and the sobs of soft voiced women, shrieking that unutterable wail, Aldarin felt the very air burn into his flesh hotter, and more torturing than the air of the simoon, he felt the rock beneath him turning molted fire, his feet were crumbling into fragments, while agony and intense pain, quivered along his veins, and the flame lapped up his blood. He burned, and yet—he burned not.

The air penetrated into his flesh, entered the pores, burning along his veins; he felt the fire at his very heart; he drank in the flame with every breath, and yet—he burned not.

No sooner did his feet crumble with the agonizing influence of the fire, than another portion of his frame, seemed renewing its life, his heart became young, and his brain flowed with healthy blood.

Again his feet renewed their flesh, and then, with a hollow voice, he shrieked, mingling in that unutterable wail of the damned, "I burn, I burn, my heart is on fire, my brain is turned to flame, and yet I am not consumed."

46

A sudden change in the shape of the islet on which he stood, attracted his attention. At first wide and extensive in form, it was now narrow and contracted. Every moment it grew smaller, and yet smaller, and the waves of fire came rolling wave after wave over its surface. Aldarin started with a new and strange horror. Terrible it was to stand on the rock of fire, his feet consuming, his brain on fire, his heart a flame; air, sky and ocean, all burning into his very soul, terrible, most terrible, but those hollow murmurs, those fearful whispers of the damned came breaking on his ear, speaking of mysteries, yet more terrible, in the Vast Beyond.

The wretched man clung to the rock. Oh! God, how fearful was the first touch of the waves of molten flame; how the liquid fire ate into his flesh and corrupted his blood, as the spiral flames cresting, each wave came hissing and curling round his limbs!

The waves rose higher and higher; the bodies of the lost, offensive with decay, the loathsome, and worm-eaten came floating around Aldarin. He raised his hands, he pushed the ghastly carcasses aside, but still they came floating on, and on, throwing their crumbling arms around his neck and fixing their livid lips upon his burning cheek, in the kiss of the damned.

They hailed him—brother—with a hollow welcome, and as innumerable voices whispered forth the sound of awful welcome, Aldarin missed his footing on the rock, he felt his form changing with decay, he raised his hands in the effort to keep on the surface of the waves, and saw his fingers with the flesh dropping from the bones; he floated on the surface of the boundless sea, he became one of the damned.

Forever and forever lost.

They were floating on and on, the boundless legion of the lost, and with them floated Aldarin.

A strange distant sound burst on the ear, he heard it grow louder and louder, now it was like the roaring of a mighty ocean, now it was like the hissing of a thousand furnaces.

Floating on the waves of fire, crowded by legion of the lost, Aldarin turned with a feeling of intense awe, and murmured the question—"What means yon sound of terror—yon murmur of fear?"

"We are floating on and on, toward the Cataract of Hell—" was the hoarse murmur of the living corse floating by his side, and a million tongues, speaking from livid lips returned the echo—"On and on toward the Cataract of Hell!"

Aldarin was carried on without the power of resistance, with no object to stay his career, on and on, every moment nearing the fearful Cataract, whose omnipresent thunder now deafened his ears, and fell upon his very brain, like the awful echo of an unrelenting Judgment.

Then came a pause of strange unconsciousness, from which Aldarin presently awoke; and opening his eyes, gazed around.

He hung on the verge of a rock, a rock of melting bitumen, that burned his hands to masses of crisped and blackened flesh as he hung. The rock flung its projecting form over a gulf, to which the cataracts of earth might compare, as the rivulet to the vast ocean.

It seemed to Aldarin as though the universe, with all the boundless fields of space, was comprised in the sweep of that awful cataract with its rocks of bitumen and red-hot ore extending for miles and miles innumerable, on either side, with the waves of fire—each wave bearing its awful burden of a damned soul—surging and foaming over the edge of the precipice, while a hissing and crackling sound, like the noise of ten thousand forests, ravaged by flame, startled the very air of hell, and mingled with the shrieks of the ******.

Aldarin looked below.

God of Heaven, what a sight! A gulf, like the space occupied by a thousand worlds—deep, vast, immense, and yet perceptible to the eye—sunk beneath him, with its surface of fiery waves, all convulsed and foaming with innumerable whirlpools, all crimsoned by bubbles of flame, each whirlpool swallowing the millions of the lost, each bubble bearing on its surface the face of a soul, damned and damned forever. Forever and forever.

And as the lost were borne on by the waves and swallowed by the whirlpools, they raised their hands and cast their burning eyes to the brazen sky, and shrieked, with low and muttering voices, the eternal death-wail of the lost.

Over the cataract, shrieking and wailing, were precipitated the millions and ten thousand millions of living-dead; each one swelling that unutterable murmur as he fell, each soul yelling with a more intense horror as it sank into night and all around, innumerable echoes bursting from the rocks or bitumen and melting ore breaking from the very air gave back the shriek, the wail and murmur of the lost. Forever and forever lost.

And over this scene, awful and vast, towered a figure of ebony darkness; his blackened brow concealed in the clouds, his extended arms grasping the infinite of the cataract, while his feet rested upon islands of bitumen far in the gulf below.

The eyes of the figure were fixed upon Aldarin, as he clung with the nervous grasp of despair, to the rock of melting bitumen, and their gaze curdled his heated blood.

Every moment he was losing his grasp, sliding and sliding from the rock, now his feet were loosened and hung dangling over the gulf.

There was no hope for him, he must fall—fall, and fall forever.

At this moment, when his burning hands clung to the rock, when his feet were dangling in the air, when his blood-shot eyes, protruding from their sockets, glared ghastily above, a new wonder attracted the gaze of Aldarin.

A stairway, built of white marble, wide, roomy, and secure, seemed to spring from the very rock to which he clung, and winding up from the cataract, encircled by white and rainbow-hued clouds, was lost in the distance, far, far above.

Aldarin beheld two figures slowly descending the stairway from the distance—the figure of a warrior and the form of a dark-eyed woman.

As they drew near and nearer, he felt a strange feeling of awe gathering round his heart.

He knew the figures, he knew them well.

Her face of beauty wore a smile, her dark eyes were brilliant as ever, brilliant as when first he wooed and won her in the wilds of Palestine. Yet there was blood upon her vestments near the heart; and *his* lip was spotted with one drop of thick red blood.

It was most fearful to see them thus calmly approach; it was most terrible to recognize every line of their features, every part of their vestments.

"This," muttered Aldarin, "this indeed, is Hell.—And yet he must call for aid, and call to the warrior and the woman. How the thought writhed like a serpent round his very heart!"

He was sliding from the rock, slowly, yet certainly sliding. Another moment and he would plunge below. There was but one hope. He might, by a desperate effort, drag his carcass along the pointed rock: by a single extension of his arm, his hand would grasp the lowest step of the stairway.

He prepared himself for the effort, his feet hung dangling below, it is true, and his body was gradually slipping, but he gathered all the strength of his living corse for that single effort.

Slowly he passed his hand along the rock of bitumen, clutching the red-hot masses of ore in the action, and with his heart all aflame, he supported his trembling carcass with the other hand, and passed the extended hand yet farther along the rock.

It wanted but a single inch, a little inch, and his hand would grasp the marble of the stairway. And, yet that inch he could not compass with the hand so nervously outstretched, all his strength had been expended in the effort, and there he hung trembling on the verge of the abyss, when had he but the additional vigor of a mere child, he might grasp the stairway—he might be saved.

Another and a desperate effort! His fingers touched the carved marble-work of the stair-way, but his strength was gone—he could not hold it in his grasp.

With an eye of horrible intensity he looked above him, ere he made the last effort. The figures stood before him on the second step of the stairway. The woman, beautiful and bright-eyed, smiled, and the stern warrior shared her smile.

"Thou, thou wilt save me Ilmerine—my wife, my love, thou wilt—drag—drag—my hand to thee, and I can reach the staircase."

She stooped, the beautiful woman, she reached forth a fair and lily hand, she grasped the blackened fingers of Aldarin.

"Thanks, beautiful Ilmerine. I have wronged thee, but— the SECRET—a little nearer—drag—drag my hand—a moment—and I will grasp the staircase—I will be saved."

She placed his fingers round a projecting ornament of the staircase, his grasp was tight and desperate.

"Ascend!" she cried in a sweet and soft-toned voice.

"Julian—oh, Julian—grasp this hand—aid me, oh Julian my brother!"

The figure of the Warrior slowly stooped and seized the other hand, and drawing it towards the staircase, wound the fingers round another piece of the carved work of the staircase.

"Ascend, Aldarin, brother of mine, ascend!" cried his deep toned and awful voice.

"Ascend, brother of mine, I would, but my strength fails—seize me, by the body, and drag me from this rock of terror—oh, seize me."

The Warrior seized Aldarin by the shoulder, and dragged him slowly along the rock, but the flesh he clenched, crumbled in his grasp. Aldarin again trembled over the verge of the abyss—the blow of a single straw, might suffice to hurl him into the world below.

"Julian my brother. Ilmerine my wife, save me—oh, save me!"

The woman, dark-haired and beautiful, stooped, she slowly unwound the fingers of Aldarin from the ornament of the staircase. And as she unwound finger after finger, she looked upon his horror-stricken face and smiled, and pointed to the red wound near her heart. He returned her smile with a ghastly grimace, he looked to the Warrior, and tightened the grasp of his other hand.

"Thou Julian, wilt save me—thou wilt not unwind my fingers, thou wilt hurl this beautiful demon aside."

"Aldarin my brother!" said the Figure in a voice of awe, as kneeling on the lowest step of the staircase, he cast the glance of his full and burning eyes upon the livid visage of Aldarin, while for a moment he wound the folds of his robe yet closer around his warrior-form.—"Aldarin, my brother, I will save thee."

He smiled—Aldarin returned his smile.

"Reach me thy hand, Julian, thy hand, or I perish."

The Warrior slowly reached forth his hand, from beneath the folds of his cloak, he held it before the face of Aldarin, and the eyes of the doomed man saw that the fingers clenched a Goblet of Gold, that shone and glimmered thro' the air, like a beacon-fire of hell.

"Oh—Fiend—the Death-bowl!"

As these words shrieked from Aldarin's livid lips, he drew back from the maddening sight, with horror, he missed his hold, he slid from the rock—he fell.

✳

A thousand fires burned before his eyes, ten thousand horrid sounds fell on his very brain, serpents loathsome and noxious crawled thro' his hair, all around, above and beneath was fire, waves of flame eating into his soul, sky of brass, burning his eyes from their sockets, all was fire and horror and death, and—still he fell.

And a hoarse hollow voice, rising above the murmurs of the damned, spoke forth the words—"*Forever and Forever*—" and all hell gave back the echo—"Ever, Ever, Ever!"

Still he fell! The whirlpool sucked him within its circles of flame, around and around he dashed, with the bodies of the living dead floating over him, with ghastly faces, upturned to his vision, with foul arms, clenching him in a loathsome embrace, around and around he dashed, joining in the low, deep murmur of the damned, and his heart gave back the murmur. This, this, is hell!

Suddenly all was dark. Aldarin heard no sound, no murmur of the lost. All was dark, all was still. He touched his brow, and was amazed to find it untortured by flame. Yet big beaded drops of sweat stood from his forehead, his frame was chilled, a feeling of unutterable Awe was upon him, he feared to stir. He had been dreaming. His dream was past, his consciousness gradually returned, he found himself reclining among the foul remnants of decay, amid the carcasses of the dead.

He drooped his head low on his bosom, his face rested on his knees, his arms were folded across his eyes, and there in that lone chamber, while the silent hours of the night wore on, with his own weird soul, communed Aldarin the Fratricide.

THE EVENTFUL NIGHTS OF AUGUST 20TH AND 21ST

by F. C. Ewer

I am about to undertake a task,—here in the silence of this room, to which I feel impelled by a combination of circumstances,—such as I believe never surrounded mortal man before. I am hurried to its accomplishment, to the unburdening of my mind, from certain strange intelligence, not only on account of an express order, which I have received, the nature and particulars of which will more fully appear below,—but because I feel that I can only relieve my mind from its insufferable weight by laying before the public the occurrences of the last two nights.

I am in a house on McAllister Street, between Hyde and Larkin. The room in which I am seated contains little furniture, save a poor bed, a large pine table, one of smaller dimensions, and a chair. The paper I write on—this is the second night I have been here—I was compelled to bring with me, together with the pen, ink, and candle. At every whisper of the breeze, as it sighs among the bushes outside, I shudder and look around me, where lies the body of a man whom I knew not until yesterday—yet to whom I feel bound by a spell such as I never experienced before. And yet I know that all is over and quiet now. The hush of silent death is in this room; and I can distinctly hear my own breathing and that of a little child—she tells me her name is Jane—who is sitting on a box at the foot of the bed, and who, although young, is just old enough to realize that she is stricken by an awful calamity, and yet knows not whether the more to be amazed or grieved. At times she will come to my side, and the tears will rise into her eyes; but at a word from me, she will check them, return to the dead body of her parent, and there gaze into the cold, still face, silently and with a mingled expression of awe and uncertainty. She, too, has been a witness of the events of the past forty-eight hours, and now that she is at last left alone, she clings to me instinctively for protection—she knows not from what, nor why. May God give me health and strength to support her, and guide her in the uncertain ways of the dark future.

She had just stolen quietly to me, put her little arms about my neck, and said:

"What are you writing, sir? Come with me. I am *very* lonesome. Come with me to father and make him talk."

I kissed her upon her fair white forehead, and said:

"Hush, child! Father will not speak to us any more tonight. You shall go with me tomorrow, and we'll take father with us."

I led her back to her seat, and turned quickly, for the tears were gushing to my eyes. But I must hasten to my recital.

I shall endeavor to state the plain facts, as they occurred, as briefly and in as simple a style as possible. For I find that it is already half-past two in the morning, and I feel quite exhausted from the excitement I have passed through. In bringing these facts before the public, I am aware that I shall subject myself to the taunts of the street, and be pointed at by the world as one of the "insane dupes of the spiritual rappers,"—and nothing but an imperative sense of duty (mistaken, it may be thought by some) urges me to submit myself to such an ordeal.

I will not (at least upon this occasion) go into the *rationale* of "spiritualism." The public are already sufficiently acquainted with the modes in which the "manifestations" are given, to understand thoroughly all I shall have to say. I will not speak of the singular facts of "odism," which have been established by Reichenbach and Liebig, with a clearness only less satisfactory than that with which the truths of electricity are proven. I will not state that no evidence of the odic fluid can be discovered in paralyzed limbs; I will not speak of the supposition, therefore, of the above-named physicists, that as mind cannot act directly on matter, and as it is impossible by an effort of mind to move a paralyzed limb, the odic fluid may be the condition necessary to lie between the mind and the arm or foot (which are matter) to account for the mysterious effect of the will in moving our bodies. The relation of these facts and suppositions is not at all necessary to a clear understanding of my story.

Night before last, (the nineteenth of August,) after I had retired and extinguished my candle, I was surprised, on laying my head upon my pillow, at discovering a pale, bluish brush of light at the other side of the room, apparently hovering over a portion of a tea-poy, on which is a Parian statuette of Venus, one or two daguerreotypes, a small pearl cross, and several other little matters of ornament. I was struck by the suddenness with which the light ceased to waver as I directed my attention to it. I started up, but immediately came to the conclusion that the strange appearance resulted from a diseased retina—(my eyes have been affected for the past six months.) I looked away, supposing, of course, that if the apparition could be traced to the cause mentioned, it would display itself wherever I gazed. This, however, I found not to be the case. And as I looked again towards the tea-poy, I thought I heard a series of faint tickings. Determined to have my curiosity satisfied, I arose and advanced towards the apparition. The tickings here grew more active. I re-lighted the candle; there was, however, no unusual appearance about the stand. But I soon found that the sounds proceeded from a small pocket-compass that was lying thereon. I opened it, and the needle was trembling and vibrating quite violently over N. Soon the north pole moved round to the south-west, and back again; and so on, three distinct times—each time pausing a moment at N., trembling violently, then sweeping round and reaching the S. W. point with a jerk. Thinking this a very singular circumstance, I hurriedly threw on some clothes, and sat down to watch it. After a pause, and while my eyes were directed intently upon the needle, it moved slowly round again, reaching the south-west point with a jerk,— repeating this three times, and then stopping. It seemed to me to act almost with *intelligence*; and I involuntarily uttered,—"What *does* this mean?" To my surprise for I was a firm disbeliever in anything like "spiritualism"—the needle, as though in answer to my ejaculation, made a rapid circuit entirely round the card, passed the north point, and resting for an instant at south-west, or rather over the fifty-first degree point, returned slowly and steadily to its place at north.

I now (half ashamed of myself) commenced a series of questions in whisper. Yet, although the needle seemed to act intelligently, I could not discover what was the nature of the information (if any) intended to be conveyed, and why, after each series of unsuccessful questions and answers, it swept with more and more vigor to south, fifty-one degrees west; and at length I reluctantly retired.

Last evening, about ten o'clock, I received a note, written in pencil, which, I was told, had been left for me by a little girl. It was brief, but exceedingly urgent in a request—nay, it was almost a command—that I should go out to the house of the writer, Mr. John F. Lane. It stated that I need fear nothing, but should start immediately upon its reception, bringing with me paper, a pen, and candles.

I learned that the little girl could not read, but by showing the superscription of the note containing only my name, had at last succeeded in finding the *locale* of my apartment on Kearny Street. But she had gone, and I could therefore learn nothing of the nature of the riddle from her.

I cannot tell how, but by some strange intuition, I associated unconsciously the note, with its singular request, its lack of any cue by which I could discover why my presence was required in a desolate and lonely part of the city at the dead hour of night, with the singular occurrence of the compass the night before. The only bond of connection between them, it is true, was the unexplained mystery that hung around both. But the human mind often finds itself at conclusions without any known steps by which it could have arrived at them, whose subsequently ascertained correctness staggers reason, and leads to the belief that there are mental processes and strange sympathies and connections in nature whose character and depths are to be sought for in the Infinite God alone. At length, however, I became convinced that some villain was working upon my curiosity, to entrap me among the sandhills and rob me; and I determined not to go, and to pay no heed to the affair at all. But I could not drive the subject from my mind, and at last I deliberately resolved, come what would, to go out to the spot designated, and solve the mystery. For precaution's sake, I relieved myself of my watch and purse, put my pistol in my pocket, and procured a lantern, before sallying forth.

At the corner of Kearny and Sacramento streets I met two of my friends—Mr. H. and Dr. L. Mr. H. asked me where I was going in that Diogenes style. In response, I related the circumstance of the note, and my determination to see the end of the affair. The two expressed their willingness to accompany me, and we proceeded together. It was then half-past eleven o'clock. We passed without molestation to the corner of

Sutter and Mason streets, and thence struck off in a diagonal direction over the sandhills toward Yerba Buena Cemetery. Contrary to our expectations, our devious walk to McAllister Street was undisturbed, save by the occasional barking of a dog. When we reached the corner of what we found on inquiry at a neighboring house to be Hyde and McAllister streets, one of my friends called my attention to a noise that sounded like a faint groan. We approached in the direction whence it came, and found ourselves nearing a small house that stands on the north side of the road, just before you come to Larkin Street. This was the house designated in the note.

I rapped at the door, and the little girl, who answered the call immediately, said:

"Father wants you to come in."

Mr. Lane, who was lying upon the bed, reached forth his hand in welcome; but was evidently surprised on seeing Mr. H. and the Doctor following me into the room. After apologizing for not having chairs enough for us, he called me to the bedside and stated that he knew I must have been surprised at receiving his note; that he was too weak to write more; that he had told Jane to see me in person, but that she, becoming alarmed at her long absence from him and at the lateness of the hour, had hastened back without obeying his instruction. He said that it was very kind of me to take so much trouble, but that he was a dying man, and had information of importance to impart to me.

"But, my dear sir," said I, "something must be done for you. Fortunately, one of my friends is a physician,"—and I called Doctor L. to the bedside.

Mr. Lane was evidently in the last stages of consumption. In fact, the Doctor told me in a whisper, that it was too late; that nothing could be done, and that his end was very near.

He overheard us and said that he knew all; that nothing remained for him but to fulfill a duty to me and to the world.

Before proceeding to the business before us, he told me briefly his previous circumstances; his early education, which was liberal; his poverty, and the fact that his little child—this patient, sweet little Jane, who, exhausted with watching, has laid her head in my lap and sunk, at last, into a slumber—would by his death be left alone in the world. He besought me, with tears in his eyes, to watch over her when he was gone, and see that she did not suffer. He did not care about her being poor. He expected she would have to work. He did not wish her to be a burden to me. But, oh! he prayed that I would guide her footsteps away from sin and its influences; that I would instill into her a love of purity, and so guard her, that she would grow to womanhood, an honor to herself and a blessing to those around her. I drew little Jane to me, kissed her, and satisfied the dying man by promising solemnly that I would do my utmost to comply with his last wish.

His mind was then apparently relieved from its only care, and he turned his attention to the business before us.

"My friend," said he, "I must premise my remarks by stating that I am a firm believer in the great doctrine of the present century; that we have at last reached that momentous period, when the spirits of the departed can, through the medium of a principle newly discovered, communicate their thoughts and wishes to mortals upon earth. I have been led to this belief by the surest of all processes—personal experience. When I am alone and find a table moving under my passive hands—moving intelligently—moving in such a manner as to give me information of events which are happening in the distant East, and which I subsequently find to have occurred exactly as stated through this mysterious agency,—nay more, when I feel a nameless sensation—half chill, half tremor—running through my whole body, apparently penetrating to the innermost recesses of my brain, and find my arm and hand moved over the paper beneath it by some influence which I cannot convince myself is not foreign,—when I find my hand writing strange, grand thoughts, such as I never conceived of before—such as at times it takes me days thoroughly to understand,—when I close my eyes and so divest myself of attention, that I know nothing, except that my hand is moving, and when I find afterwards thoughts worthy of the angels, penned, I cannot but believe we are upon the threshold of one of the most eventful changes that ever occurred upon the surface of the earth. Geology has told us of mighty epochs in the far past history of the world. Look back, my friends. Remember that whole races of the animal and vegetable kingdoms have been swept away—that whole periods of the world have moved into the still past, leaving their history legible to the mind of a subsequent period on the everlasting rocks and strata. Remember that whole continents have gone grandly down and been swallowed up in the depths of ocean; that whole oceans have swayed in volumes around the earth—from pole to pole, from the Orient to the Occident. If we stand amazed, as we contemplate the mighty changes that rest entombed in the past, ever receding from us, is it unreasonable to suppose that other changes equally momentous are approaching the world from the future? Oh! deceive yourselves not; for mankind tread toppling upon the verge of a tremendous epoch; that in which Finity can speak to Infinity,—that in which the greatest seal shall be broken, and the secrets of hereafter whispered from strange intelligences to man! I know it—I know—know."

Mr. Lane here sank back upon his pillow, exhausted.

I had stood rapt in wonder and admiration, as I listened to such sentences coming from a man apparently so humble in life. The shadow of death stretching up to meet him seemed almost to inspire him. The deliberate enunciation with which the remarks were uttered, coupled with the soul-felt earnestness with which he spoke, impressed us all; and for a moment we stood at the bedside, gazing with rapt attention at that pale face, with its spiritual expression and its closed eyes. The eyelids seemed to me so thin, as to be powerless to conceal the large jet-black eyes within, which almost appeared to be displayed *through* them.

I know not how long our silence would have lasted, had not the Doctor called my attention to the fact, that the last struggle of mind had hastened the dying man towards his dissolution; and that if he had any important information to communicate, we must be brief.

I looked again, and the large, black eyes were upon us; they seemed larger and blacker than any I had ever beheld before; and Mr. Lane continued:

"I wish this conversation recorded. At first, I regretted that you had brought your friends with you; but I am glad that you have done so, as one of them can be of service to us."

I then took the writing materials which I had brought, and after recording, as nearly as I could recollect, the remarks set down above, I delivered them to Mr. H., who moved the large table into the center of the room, and proceeded to take the notes which now lie before me, without whose assistance I should have great difficulty in preparing these remarks for the press.

Mr. Lane resumed:

"As I have told you, I am not only a believer in spiritualism, but am a medium myself. Four days ago, I was informed, by one of the spirits, that he desired me to procure some gentleman either connected with the press, or to whom the columns of some paper were open, to be with me during my last moments—that what should occur at our interview would be of importance. I knew none of the editors. I had heard, however, that you had devoted several months to the investigation of spiritualism, previously to which time you were atheistically inclined. The fact that an atheist should have looked into this matter, with any degree of assiduity, convinced me that you were a candid man, open to conviction. Was I rightly informed with regard to your previous tenets, and your investigations?"

I answered in the affirmative.

"I am surprised, then, that you have not exercised your advantages, by publishing some of the extraordinary proofs of the science. I suppose you have recovered from your atheism, and that you are somewhat of a believer in spiritualism?"

I responded that, with regard to the former, I was still quite skeptical, and inclined to a belief in materialism; and as for the latter, that my earnest investigations had only led me to the conclusion that it was an unmitigated humbug, so far as any *spiritual* agency was concerned.

Mr. Lane appeared astonished, and after a pause, asked me if I had any objection to remaining with him, and awaiting the result. I told him that I certainly had none.

At his request the small table was then drawn quite near the head of the bed. Mr. Lane, who was lying upon his back, stretched forth his thin, white hand, placed it, with the palm downwards, upon the side nearest to him, and then closed his eyes as though he were settling himself for death. I sat at the end towards the foot of the bed, and was in such a position that I could see his face distinctly. The Doctor and Jane were at the opposite side of the bed, while Mr. H. was seated at the table in the center of the room. After a pause the table tipped toward me, lifting Mr. Lane's hand. We all remained in silence, during which the dying man appeared to be putting mental questions; to which the table answered. At length, he stated that the spirit desired to transmit a written communication. Paper and a pencil were procured. The sick man's hand was moved very gently, but the paper moved with it. I then secured the sheet with my hand, and the first communication was as follows, namely:

"The time is ripe. The great truth has entered into the circle of the world silently, and powerfully,—as the 'still small voice.' There is sublimity in its silence. And thus it appeals to man. We cannot trumpet forth the truth. For voice is not to us, as hearing is to you. We appeal to you through sublimity, and silence, and an unheard, though felt power. Behold, how the great change has manifested itself in every city, and town, and hamlet in America! This is one of the great voices of your great country. She announces the glad tidings, crying: *'The gates of death are open, the ladder of Jacob is reared, and angel voices are ascending—descending from us to them—from them to us!'* We are hovering above and around and among your republic of *thought*. It was the fitting field. Had the seed dropped too early, or upon the unenlightened, it would not have fructified. Years were to roll. Years have rolled. The intellectual soil was at last prepared, and the sowers joyfully went forth. At first, the great change broke slowly upon man. It was right. There must have been doubters. But the truth is mighty and prevails. The spiritualists are numbered by hundreds of thousands. And thus as it is, that the seed has taken root sufficiently for permanence and ever-growth, spite of all calamity of skepticism and ridicule, it is right that you should advance one step further. Attend! The meaning of death is the mission of this interview. Then mayst thou indeed exclaim, 'Where is thy sting, and O grave, where is thy victory!' Attend, while the passing spirit performs his privilege and his high duty."

Mr. Lane's hand then ceased moving. The whole was calculated to render us breathless. After a pause I remarked, that the solemnity of this time would not, I freely confessed, permit me to doubt the honesty of the dying man. But I ventured to ask the spirit, if spirit it was, whether he would not give us some certain proof of the genuineness of the communication as a *spiritual message*. Mr. Lane's hand immediately traced the following:

64

"Willingly. The whole shall be in itself a test. For true it is, that one of the first elements of success in this new movement is, that you believe. *Mr. Lane shall hold a conversation with you prior to, during and after death*, in which he will give you his experience of death, and the facts and scenes, so to speak, to which he first awakes, after the heart has ceased to beat. Farewell."

I willingly dispelled doubt from my mind, and was for a time lost in thought at the solemn import of the spirit's message. The silence was only broken by the low sobbing of this dear little creature, exhausted, and pale, and scantily clad, who, thank Heaven, has forgotten her affliction for a time in sweet slumber. Her dreamy eyes have seized upon my heart. Ah! what a shadow within them lies! Will she live to womanhood? Oh! will she always love and trust me, with all my faults? Well-a-day! At length, as I gazed into the emaciated face upon the pillow before me, the lids opened the large black eyes turned upon me, and with a faint voice he said:

"I am sinking—sinking—"

His eyes then turned upon Jane with a gaze of sadness, then rolled slowly round to me again. The look was enough. I leaned toward him, and assured him with a low voice that henceforth she should be my daughter. The little thing ran round to me and fell upon my breast, sobbing violently.

"And now," said he, faintly, and with pauses between his sentences, "I am ready to die. I feel that it is good. It grows dim—dim—dim. I am losing earth—losing you all. I know that I live. It—it is a solemn passage—but what, I know not. Are you here? Touch me—touch me—that I may know that I live."

I pressed my hand gently upon his as it lay upon the table before me. It was cold.

"Are you—are you here? *Can* you not touch me?" I stooped over him and whispered into his ear that his hand was in mine.

"In mine?—in mine? There is no angel here. What was it whispered? I am in no one's keeping. I am passing—Oh!" said he, making a faint effort to rise, "Oh! that I could stay! Janie—Janie—that—that this solemn journey were but over."

Exhaustion succeeded, and for a moment he ceased breathing. I quietly re-spread his hand upon the table, and resumed my seat.

"I seem hovering—I know not where. No one is around me—no one comes to me to lift me on through this solemn gloom. I hear nothing—solitary—solitary in this fearful way. This is indeed—the valley—of the shadow of death. Where are they, my friends of the future? Is this *death*? Is this the future? *Is the spirit theory then untrue?*" at last he cried in despair.

"And am I—am I to live thus—*thus*? Oh! the fearful *hell* of an eternal existence alone!—no sight—no hearing—no God—no heaven—(as I had been told)—no light—Great God! *no darkness!* all thought! My soul is consuming—*consuming itself!*——*Can* I live thus forever?—Oh! for annihilation! for anything but this solitude! Why can I not peer through this gloom?——Horror! horror!—where are these limbs of mine?—*I feel not my body around me!* Oh! lost at length—lost to the green earth—and to my Janie—lost to the sweet harmony of companionship!——The past, *gone,*—the future, a *blank!*——Great eternity, am I a God?—am I creative?—will a world spring at my thought?——Yes, I create—but it is *thought* alone—for that is of my own essence.——I *must* be dead. If you are here and I am not yet dead—tell Janie I will *try* and seek her,—I know not how. Tell the world that in death the spirit is fearfully and forever *alone!*—Tell the world that death is terrib——"

The nervous twitching about the under jaw stopped; and from the very instant when he ceased to articulate, I was startled by finding the table slowly rising and leaning toward the bed. And as the jaw dropped and the strange shadow of death swept down like a curtain over his face, the table rose quickly and pressed firmly and steadily against the bedside, as though it were attracted towards the dead body by an immense power.

We were all now around him. The Doctor, who was on the side opposite to us, slowly laid the right hand, which he had been holding during the dying scene, upon the breast, and we remained gazing awe-struck at this strange death. I believe that, for a moment, my heart actually ceased beating. There was an oppressive pause, which must have lasted at least five minutes. During all this time the table maintained its inclined position, and we still stood speechless—almost breathless. At length we were awakened from our trance by finding the table quietly descending to the floor. It then commenced tipping on two of its legs with a gentle rocking motion. I know not why, but I shuddered at the thought of breaking the death-like silence, so I took up the pencil and wrote:

"Will you finish what you were saying?"

Imagine our terror at seeing the dead arm and hand which had been lying on the table, strike into rigidity, as though it were a piece of mechanism pulled by wires, rise slowly from the table and move toward me. When it had reached within a few inches of me, like lightning it darted forth and down upon my hand in which I was still holding the pencil. Its fingers grasped suddenly and tightly around mine. The touch was as of an icicle. A nameless thrill and terror seized me. Mr. H. fell back;—and slowly the locked hands before me moved across the paper. The dead hand was so tracing the words that *I* could read them. *They were upside down to itself.* The following was the

RESPONSE.

"No, not that death is *terrible*. The silence and the solitude were *the dying*—not *death!* Tell them that it was a fearful, silent passage to me and those before me. But that it shall be so no longer *in secula seculorum!* Silent and strange—yes. But fearful—no. It was terrible, and has been terrible from its *uncertainty.* Every spirit hath known not, when it feels that it has at length lost earth, but it was doomed to silence and solitude *forever!* The struggle to know what it is, the futile efforts to see—to hear, followed by the great, all-absorbing consciousness and conviction, that it is simply an *existence,* are fearful! But let the living listen! Hereafter, let those that die be content to pause through the change;—for the solitude lasts but a moment, when the dormant spirit gradually develops. *Then,* there was nothing around it;—*now* it knows itself and that into which it enters."

"Are you in the midst of spirits?" I asked aloud; and my voice seemed to resound unnaturally through the felt silence of the room.

RESPONSE.

"I had lost you for a time. I could see and hear nothing. I almost forgot the circumstances of my death. But then, I was not dead. Slowly a sensation of lightness came over me, and I remembered all. I knew you all. I felt calm. I saw your motions as of something apart from me very much as you look down through clear water and watch the motions of the strange monsters of the deep, whose element is different from yours,—whose actions are sometimes strange and unaccountable,with whom you have nothing in common."

Here was a pause again for about five minutes, during which the cold, dead hand relaxed from around mine. At length, I asked again:

"Are you in the midst of spirits?"

The strange, invisible wires were pulled again,—for the blue death-fingers tightened around my own, and the locked hands traced the following

RESPONSE.

"I found myself gradually taking *form*—and moving through a long, grand, misty, undulating arch-way, towards a *harmony*, as it were, of far-off music. All was indefinite. I felt the intense consciousness of my own existence—nothing more. At length, clearer and clearer I understood the new universe into which I was entering, and a part of which I formed. I was alone. I heard no voice. But as I swept through the arch, I said as it were distinctly to myself this strange word, 'FORMS.' At length it changed to 'FORMS—MOTION.' After I had swept on still farther, it changed to 'FORMS—MOTION—HARMONY.' And then after a pause, to 'FORMS—MOTION—HARMONY—THE ARCH.' Why I repeated them I know not. Soon I was, as it were, uttering 'FORMS—MOTION—HARMONY—THE ARCH—CONNECTION.' At length the word 'BEAUTY' was added; and finally I found myself repeating over and over again:

"'FORMS—MOTION—HARMONY—THE ARCH—CONNECT -ION—BEAUTY—ETERNITY—ETERNITY—ETERNITY!'

"I knew not what it could mean. I know now. I will tell you more tomorrow night. I thought, and those in the flesh think, that all they conceive of, is everything that exists, save God and the disembodied spirits. Hence they call it the universe.' I find myself now forming a part of a second universe; as I have formed unknown through all ages. All have lived and shall live forever. I know it in the dim distance. You are immortal as truly in the past, as you shall be in the future. Finity at the beginning must lead to finity at the end, and as you shall live forever, so have you lived for ever: for your life is *infinite*. I will explain tomorrow night. Your first stage was non-self-sentient. Peer not into the past. It will not advance HIS GREAT LIVING. Look to the future. You are wearied. Remember Janie—see, she sits weeping. Farewell."

"But are you in the midst of spirits?" cried I.

RESPONSE.

"Oh, wonderful—wonderful!—Oh, altogether inexplicable! As you may suppose the rose unto her leaves,—as you may suppose music unto the consciousness of man,—as you may suppose the harmonies, and ever crossing, and unheard, and dimly understood converse always going on between the elements of a landscape—the cascade and the rocks—the liquid water-ripples and the shore—the forest and the sunbeams,—so do the hosts of the new universe around me hold communion with each other. Direct, not impeded—silent, and dreamily beautiful and sublime! As different from the converse of man with man, as is color from weight. Remember Janie—see, she sits weeping. Adieu!"

"But I am not weary—*I am not weary*," cried I, quickly. "More—*more!*"

We asked and asked again for one more response—*but* one. The spirit had, however, left us. I wished to know if they experienced the passage of time in the other world. But not one word could we obtain. At the word adieu," the dead hand fell off from mine. The clock struck three, and, bewildered with the strange occurrences of the night, and intoxicated with excitement, I staggered out into the air. My friends soon joined me.

I will not say—I need not say—that for us there was no sleep that night. As I have remarked above, I staggered, bewildered, from the room into the open air, where I was followed by the Doctor and Mr. H. Not a word was uttered. In the awfulness of the occasion each seemed to respect the other's feelings. Great, silent waves of thought had rolled upon us out of profound death. And the majesty of the new universe,—from whose solemn depths a soul had just now whispered to us,—as it pressed down and around me with painful reality and grandeur, overwhelmed and stupefied me. Where was the invisible spirit, upon whom its sublimity had just burst?—the great liquid eyes, forth from which he had looked upon us, were glazed now, and set. Where was the *soul?*—could it be here, standing, silent, at my side, and gazing serenely upon me? Whence had issued those strange whispers—those fragments of knowledge?—There, in the room, were the arm and the hand—that had traced the thoughts—relaxed, and left by us in our bewilderment outstretched upon the table. But where was the *spirit*, that had stirred it—from *without!* Where was the spirit? Fled—fled into those unknown, strange regions, whither we all shall go!—Fled! Yet co-existent, co-knowing, co-working with us. I burned to learn of the NEW UNIVERSE.

While we stood in the still, dark night, thus rapt in thought, with the stars looking down from afar,—with the invisible wind sighing around us—we knew not where,—with the great city of the dead before us, where glimmered faintly in the starlight the white tombstones of the unnumbered departed,—and with the lowly, silent hall of death behind us, whence another spirit had just now lifted and sped,—as we stood thus rapt in thought, a soft hand stole into mine, and I felt upon my fingers the pressure of a gentle kiss. I looked, and it was Jane. She was kneeling at my feet—kneeling upon the damp ground, and weeping. In her desolation, sweet child, she had left the dead, to cling to the living. She had silently singled me out from the rest, with an instinct that knows no premeditation.

"Janie, my dear child," said I, "let us return to father." I lifted her into my arms, and she clasped her little hands around my neck, and laid her head upon my breast, and wept—wept bitterly. I need not say that my own tears were flowing full and fast, and dropping and mingling with hers.

We moved slowly along towards the silent room, and, as we entered, Mr. H. passed noiselessly to the mysterious bedside, and disposed the body decently.

We stood gazing upon it for a time in silence; and then, recollecting ourselves, consulted in a low voice upon our position.

For us to inform our acquaintances with what had passed, was not to be thought of. We should have had the town upon us in an hour. We had received no instructions, but the sentence, "I will tell you more tomorrow night," clearly indicated what was expected from us. At last, it was decided that Mr. H. should remain with the body during the day, (it was now nearly four o'clock in the morning,) while the Doctor and myself should return to our respective duties in the city. To prevent inquiry, it was thought best that Jane should stay with Mr. H. And we agreed to meet here tonight—or rather, last night, (for it is now nearly daylight of the 22d,) at eight o'clock, punctually. The preliminaries being arranged, the Doctor and myself took our silent way across the hills toward the city, while Mr. H. bowed farewell to us from the door, with little Janie in his arms looking tearfully after us.

Oh, the long, weary hours that dragged, leaden-footed, until night! It seemed to me that sunset would never come. Need I say that the Doctor and myself, although we separated at six in the morning, could not remain apart? The imperative call of duty summoned me at ten to my desk in the Custom-House; and when I went in, I found him there waiting for me. Our eyes met, but not one allusion was made to the occurrences of the previous night. Each felt intensely the other's knowledge. A mysterious spell bound us together. I dared not have him stay, lest remark should be excited; and yet I could not *bear* to have him leave. And so, he lingered all day. Now and then we would steal a word together. But, oh! need I say, what an effort it caused me to attend to the details of my desk, and to talk cheerfully and carelessly of the trivial events of the morning?—oh! so trivial they seemed to me, beneath the shadow of the great event that had towered about me in a night!—No, I will pass all this. Suffice it to say, evening came. And at half-past seven we were at the threshold of the darkened chamber. I entered—with Janie in my arms;—for she had watched for us from the edge of the window-curtain, and had run out to meet us, chiding me sweetly and artlessly for my long delay.

With the exception of a little more neatness in the arrangement of the simple furniture of the room, everything was as we had left it, even to the small pine table at the head of the bed.

Well, the momentous hour had arrived. The solemn arcana of hereafter were to transpire. I know not why, but we hesitated at meeting the great intelligence, and we lingered in conversation at least an hour, before we prepared to receive those communications, which we knew were in store for us. We re-read those we had already received:

"Mr. Lane shall hold a conversation with you prior to, during, and after death,—*in which he will give you his experience of death, and the facts and scenes, so to speak, to which he first awakes, after the heart shall cease to beat.*"

He had only given us a part of his experience of death, and tonight, then, he would finish the recounting of his solemn, solitary passage through the shadowy valley, and open to your view, in language, the structure and appearance of the New Universe. Where *was* this Universe? What manner of beings were the spirits? What was their form—their destiny? Did they increase in knowledge? That *must* be so, for the soul had declared it. How then was the paradox to be explained, of a spirit living on forever—forever increasing in knowledge—forever—forever—and yet never equaling the changeless God!

At length we took our seats around the table at the head of the bed, and placed our hands upon it. For fifteen minutes we remained in silent expectation, but received no manifestations of the spirit's presence. This was strange. It was, however, suggested, that Mr. Lane's hand was not upon the table; and that possibly this might be the reason of our want of success. But the body had become stiff, and the hand, when outstretched, slowly arose from the table, and returned to its place upon the breast. We then held it down; and soon found that the odic fluid (if fluid it be) was penetrating it: or, at any rate, that the arm and hand were becoming limber. Another fifteen minutes elapsed without result. The table neither tipped, nor manifested any disposition to slide, or even stir. The only indication we had received thus far was a single rap, which startled us by its loudness and brevity. Finally, in the silence of almost hopeless expectation, and as a last resort, I resumed the pencil, and, without saying anything to my friends, lifted the dead hand, placed it around my own in the position it had assumed of itself last night, and held it there to keep it from dropping off. Another anxious pause ensued, when, what was my delight at feeling the cold fore-finger pressing gently, but very perceptibly upon the back of my hand. I ejaculated with almost profane gleefulness:

"It is clutching me!"

"Hark!" said the Doctor, quickly, while both leaned forward with painful anxiety for the result.

Slowly the middle finger commenced to press down. Then the third finger. Then the little finger.—And at last, the spell of death seemed to break, for the arm violently stiffened, and the whole hand grasped mine with a suddenness that startled us, notwithstanding we were so anxiously hoping for some such result.

We breathed freely again. And I could not but contrast our feelings of placid joy with those of terror which filled us last night, when first we beheld the hand and arm rising mysteriously from the table.

But, if the reader is as anxious to learn the tenor of the communications as were we to procure them, he will wish me to come to them without more delay. In short, I must hasten to the conclusion of my task, for I have been writing since two this morning, and the dawn has already broken.

To proceed, then: My first question was, "Are you happy?"

—No response.

QUESTION, again—" Are you happy?"

After a pause:

RESPONSE.

"That is a singular interrogatory for this occasion, and one, for obvious reasons, I am not able to answer."

QUESTION.

"Why are you not able to satisfy your friends on so important a point?"

RESPONSE.

"If those who are happy could communicate the fact to their friends—*those who are unhappy* could do the same.

"But I do not see the point," said I.

RESPONSE.

"Silence is the best answer."

QUESTION.

"Perhaps if I put the question in an abstract form, the difficulty will be removed. Is there happiness and misery in your Universe?"

—No response.

After a pause, Mr. H. remarked as follows, viz: "But I am anxious to have you finish your experience of death. You told us last night that you found yourself repeating the words 'FORMS, MOTION, HARMONY, THE ARCH,' etc., and that you would tell us more tonight."

Response.

"While moving in the midst of your Universe, I had been blinded by the glare of particularities. Numberless individuals and species were around me. I saw not that which underlay and ran up through all things.

"Motion, in all its infinite varieties, is sublime. Whether I watch it flitting in the butterfly, curling gracefully in the rising smoke, or darting in the lightning—whether I contemplate it in the majestically wheeling worlds or grasp it with far-reaching conception in the slow decay of an abbey ruin—it is the same mysterious condition of nature. The boy passes into the man. It is motion. Nations rise and sink. It is motion. 'Rest' is a relative word. As the word ghost sprang from man's fear, and expresses something which never had existence, so does the word 'rest' spring from man's egotism, and expresses what never had existence. That which moves faster than man's knowledge is as much rest to man as that which moves slower, and that which moves without his knowledge is as much rest as either. The landscape appears at rest, while silently grow the trees, fabricating their slender tissues from the earths, the air and the water, with magic fingers; slowly, unseen by mortal eye, unheard by mortal ear, are the chemical and mechanical forces of nature tapping at the life-essence of the rocks and strata; shine on the stars in the heavens unseen by you—move on the worlds of the universe unfelt—flows on the eternal circle of vapor, clouds and the rain-storm. So, could you enter more minutely into nature, would you find that *all* is motion. Rest is not life. Rest is death—is non-existence. And your universe lives. It is all working—working—*God cannot rest!* Rest means that thou movest faster than some things, and slower than others. Motion is not merely a fact in your universe, here and there. It is a condition pervading your entire universe, running down to every—even the minutest part. Motion underlies and runs up through all things.

"Your universe exists by entering into forms. In its present phase it has entered as a whole into the form of revolving suns and earths, with all the forms that on and in them are. All things around you are in forms—FORMS—MOVING.

"Come now to the 'Arch.' How do the forms of your universe move? The seed drops into the ground. The plant springs up. Watch the arching of the flower. First the tender embryo upon the stem—the unshaped silky chaos. This is soon a bud. The bud swells. It bursts. The ripe flower opens to the full its fragrant form, and the sunbeams come there, and nestle in the warm beauty. The maturity is on. The key-stone is reached. But not one instant does the motion stop. Less and less grows the fragrance. Duller and duller is the blushing white—the yellow—the crimson; petal and sepal and stamen and pistil drop away; and what was a flower is nothing. And what of the plant? Certain particles have married into that form. But in the course of the months, or the years, or the centuries, the form dissolves and disappears. The *particles* are eternal. But the *form* is no more. The arching of the flower is typical of that of every form, and all the arching forms make up your universe. All forms come into being—pass, however slowly, however rapidly, up to maturity—and so—however slowly, however rapidly, down to dissolution. Where is hundred gated Thebes? The small makes up the great. This is the answer to the autumn leaf, that flits across your pathway, and to the dying girl. The great motion, which pervades your universe, is its flowering to culmination. And hearken! When it shall have reached its acme, it will descend along a bright pathway, and entering into, be lost in another grand form into which it will expand. FORMS—MOVING—in ARCHES.

"Why wonder at the fitness of things? The horse's head and neck are just long enough to enable him to reach the ground, and crop the grass which is his food. And you lift your eyes and admire the harmony, and say it was so designed.

Designing is a process of mind, requiring more or less time, and arguing imperfection. Forget thee, great man, who is thy God. God weigheth not, nor doth he consider. God resteth not, but liveth out his nature of necessity. For he cannot be anyone else, as a square cannot be a circle. Men wonder at the fitness of the horse's head and neck for the purposes for which they are used. They do not consider that were his neck and head too short to reach his food, the whole race of horses would die. Discord would defeat itself. And they are astonished, because they discover only a part of the harmony of nature. Harmony prevails everywhere from the necessity of the case. It pervades your universe. FORMS—MOVING—HARMONIOUSLY—in ARCHES.

"There is action and reaction around you. Who was he that said, 'Each grain of sand is the center of all things?' This is truth. Each form acts upon every other, and is reacted upon, in turn, by every other. Mind, even, works upon your universe. Your universe works upon mind. CONNECTED FORMS MOVING—HARMONIOUSLY—in ARCHES.

"Beauty is universal. To the mind of man a part is free. The rest is latent. This, too, is well. For mind must build, first a hut—then a house—then a temple. Mind upon earth must search out beauty—must be educated for higher works in the future. God is not discordant; so is he all beautiful. CONNECTED—and BEAUTIFUL FORMS—MOVING—HARMONIOUSLY—in ARCHES.

"Therefore is your universe not a heterogeneous mass of disjointed parts. It is a homogeneity. It is distinct and different from our universe.

"Rise now for a moment to a contemplation of Deity. To gain a conception of him, conceive of any form around you—a golden goblet. It has certain qualities—color, hardness, extension, weight—by which you know it. So has God essential qualities, which constitute him the being he is. He is an infinite being, therefore are each of his qualities infinite. Your universe is the expression of one of those qualities—mine, of another. Both are, therefore, infinite; infinite in extent,—infinite in duration, from the past and into the future. But as God, too, is an infinite being, he has not a *finite* number of qualities, as has the golden goblet; but an infinite number of qualities, each of which expresses itself in an infinite universe. The soul has within itself a germ of every universe, and it sinketh on ever from one to another. The universes are infinite in number, therefore is the soul ever-lasting; ever growing in knowledge, yet never exhausting that through which it passes. For it would require an infinity of years to exhaust the secrets of one single infinite universe, how much more, then, to exhaust those of an infinite number of universes, each of which is infinite in itself! Glorious art thou, O man, the everlasting! Glorious art thou, O man, that ever sinketh through the universes! Glorious art thou, O infinitely greater—exhaustless God!

"Thus then do I describe to you your Universe.

"Connected and Beautiful Forms Moving
Harmoniously in Arches through all
Eternity."

This extraordinary communication was followed by a long, thoughtful pause on our part. What subjects for contemplation did it not open up! the connection between universe and universe; the connection between God and his universes; the meaning of death; its necessity, as a link, between universe and universe, etc. At length, I broke the silence by the following remark, viz: "But in all this—for which we are truly grateful to you—you have not given us what we so anxiously wait for, to wit, the remainder of your experience of death. What of the arch in which you found yourself? And what species of place is the new universe, into which the soul passed at death?"

RESPONSE.

"The spirit frees itself from the cloudy arch by reasoning and testing. It finds itself *alone*. The solitude is oppressive. At first it knows not what manner of being it is. It struggles, in the solitude, to bring into existence something besides itself, that it may not be alone. But tell those that shall die, to pause patiently, until the dying has ceased. Each soul will then involuntarily test itself. At first, it supposes that all its faculties were suited to its condition and surroundings upon the earth alone. Its eyes and ears, with their corresponding mental faculties, seemed fitted alone to enable it to act in the world. Love bound it to its fellows. Sublimity and ideality enabled it to enjoy the beauty and grandeur of nature. But it knows that it has dropped nature. What use then for these mental faculties?—for benevolence, since the sick and suffering and needy are left behind; for its moral faculties, since mankind is gone; yes, even for its pious faculties, for it finds no God. Thus does it eliminate *itself* from every condition of earth. But forthwith I realized that I was *reasoning*.—I recognized the action of *selfish faculties*; for I was alone, and yearned for companionship. I remembered that I had been *observing* the long archway, with its gentle wavering, its form, its vast length, its soft, variegated opal colors. I realized that I was appreciating the surpassing beauty and the grandeur of this my passage. I noticed that I was *remembering*; and when I reached where I now am, I knew within myself an ardent desire for knowledge; I was charmed with the new scenes around me; I found new companions to love, new grandeurs to enjoy, new duties before me, new works to accomplish. I see no God. But I know that he exists. Thus did I learn myself, discovering that I still possessed all the mental faculties I had on earth."

QUESTION.

"And when you looked around you, what species of place did you find yourself in?"

RESPONSE.

"There is no 'passage' with me, as you move on earth. There is no 'place,' as you speak of 'locality' on earth. There is no 'form,' as you speak of shape on earth. The archway of death was but a condition in which I remained while testing myself, and becoming prepared to enter into my present state. Our condition here is such, that that by which each soul seems surrounded, is an out-creation from itself. When you are in a grove, the grove actually exists; and would exist were you not there. Not so here. We cannot speak of 'locality,' for there is no such thing in this life; and therein consists the difficulty of making you comprehend our condition. But that, here, which is analogous to your 'locality,' I must express by using your word. The locality, in which is each soul from time to time, does not exist outside of itself, as, for instance, does your grove, or street, or habitation; but it is an out-creation of the soul itself; and I appear to live in the midst of my out-creations;—they are all in effect as actual to me, as are your surroundings to you.".

"But this being the condition of affairs," remarked I, after a pause, "your universe must be very heterogeneous in appearance.

RESPONSE.

"Beware of materialism,—for its hand-maiden is atheism. The landscapes of earth 'appear' to the vision—and the dark blue vault of the heavens with its stars! I comprehend your difficulty, however, and will explain as best I may.

"True,—each soul lives in the midst of its out-creations; and you might suppose our universe heterogeneous in its character. But consider the various localities of earth, how they differ from each other. Where is there similarity between a room and a river flowing between its leafy banks? Bear in memory, that no two persons on earth can occupy, at the same time, the same space, and witness their surroundings from precisely the same angles, else would they be one person. So, no two souls live in the same out-creations, else would they be one soul. But, as all the different spirits—which, with their ever-varying, ingenious and beautiful out-creations, compose this universe—have, nevertheless, that something in common, which throws them together into the one class—'SOULS,'— our universe has a general effect of unity in itself, analogous to that unity which is possessed by the universe you have not yet left.

"Motion pervades this universe also. All the souls are continually varying their out-creations. Therefore is it like a vast kaleidoscope—heaving itself into new, grand forms of beauty, forever and ever!

"Thus can I dimly only tell you of that to which I awoke."

QUESTION.

"But how can your universe be infinite, when the number of spirits who have left earth is finite?"

RESPONSE.

"Look into thy heavens. Thou beholdest but a thousand of the infinite lights!"

"But *where* are you?" asked I.

RESPONSE.

"Is color above extension? Is weight above, or beneath or even among color? And yet each is different from the other, while all are qualities of the same golden goblet. Neither can I say, that we are above, or beneath, or even among your universe:—and yet each universe—yours and mine—is a part of God."

Well, we were at length satisfied with regard to the general character of the abode of the departed, and our conversation about it was long and rambling. I will not detail what we said, as no notes were taken of it, but will leave the reader to his own reflections.

At length I asked the spirit, if he could give us any information in relation to the appearance of the soul—its form, its structure.

RESPONSE.

"Mankind are wrong. The earth and their senses clog them. Every man, when he thinks of a spirit, attains to a conception of it by passing through an unnoticed, subtle series of rapid steps. He thinks of some material object—water; he passes thence to steam; thence to air, and finally, by a further etherealization, he reaches a conception of spirit. This unremembered but invariable process leads inevitably to a conception tinged with materiality. To gain an idea of spirit, think of a single thought. It has no shape—it occupies no space;—and yet it is distinct and different from every other thought. Pass thence to a spirit, which has no shape—which occupies no space, and yet is distinct and different from every other spirit. A tree is a material unit—non-self-conscious. A thought is a spiritual unit—non-self-conscious. A soul is a spiritual unit—self-conscious."

This was a new process—to me a simple and reasonable one, and I wondered that it had not struck me before.

QUESTION.

"Do the relationships of earth—the friendships, the filial loves—last beyond the grave?"

—No response.

"Have you friendships in the other world?"

RESPONSE.

"By how much the better was the spirit at death, by so much the more lovely are his out-creations as he sweeps hither-among. Thus there are grades among us, as there are among you. Thus there are similarities and dissimilarities of disposition. Free intercourse exists among the souls—free-will. Thus are there opportunities for advance and improvement, or for the reverse. Could you pass to a contemplation of the other universes—which do exist, although I see them not—then would you feel how important is improvement at every step. Awaken to a conception of a life forever! For each universe which the soul has passed through is lost to it forever with all the means of advance contained therein. And, as capacity for enjoyment widens and deepens the farther we sink along the universes, so does the disadvantage of a single unimproved universe in the past increase in awful, irremediable proportion, the farther we advance through the future. An unimproved universe is a clog forever! Beware, beware! oh! beware! Act purely,—speak purely,—but, above all, *think* purely and with dignity. For in two universes, at least, selfishness is the mainspring of the spirit's life."

QUESTION.

"But how do you converse, having left the organs of articulation upon earth?"

RESPONSE.

"As it is with you, neither can soul here pierce the depth of the soul. Each recognizes the other's out-creations, but cannot pass within them into the motives and thoughts of the soul with which he is communicating. The conversation of the pure in heart on earth is truthful; that of the vast intellect embodies great thoughts; the words of the vile are either vile or deceitful. Thus is it here. Our out-creations each arranges at will. The noble, the great, the improved, can and do naturally surround themselves with corresponding out-creations. They bear an influence among us. There are souls that originate, and souls that copy. And truth and deceit is mingled here as it is with you. You can judge of a man's motives, notwithstanding his remarks; we can judge of a soul's motives notwithstanding his out-creations. Thus, as it were, do we communicate with each other—originating and improving, or retrograding, as you do on earth. Death will necessarily make no one happy;—free no one from cares;—release no one from labors. Our condition is no happier than yours. Not only does the individual have duties to perform here,—as you suppose,—for which he should prepare himself on earth by purity and a strengthening of the mind, but races have also grand works to perform."

QUESTION.
"Must the souls advance to a definite point of perfection before they can pass from your universe to the next?"

RESPONSE.
"Why do you ask this, when it is not so with you?"
"It is generally supposed to be the fact," said I.

RESPONSE.
"No soul knoweth when it shall be summoned away— we know not whither. Our out-creations are to us here, as are your bodies on earth. When the soul is no longer able to surround itself with out-creations, it becomes unfit for duties in this universe; it cannot act among us, any more than can a corpse among you, And the soul—the 'me' when its out-creations die from around it, remains for an instant a torpid entity, and vanishes, ere we can think,—we know not whither.—*This is death with us.*"

"Do the friendships of earth continue beyond death?"

RESPONSE.

"Lift yourself to a contemplation of an *eternal existence*, and think of the fleeting friendships of earth and their uses. Is not the useless cast away?"

"It is sad to think of parting forever from a loved mother or sister," said I. "It is sad to think, that when we stand by the death-bed of a dear father, we shall see him no more."

—No response.

"I say, it is sad to feel that at death we leave our friends forever."

RESPONSE.

"The useful remaineth. God is great."

"Can you not answer us more definitely?"

RESPONSE.

"Would you have me say, that the soul of a vile son shall forever pollute the purity of a sainted mother, or that a loving sister shall forever be separated from a kind brother?"

"I would have you tell us the truth."

QUESTION.

From the Doctor. "Is the doctrine of transmigration of souls correct in whole, or even in part?" At this moment I noticed the other hand and arm of the corpse moving slightly. The odic fluid had evidently penetrated the entire body.

RESPONSE.

"Can the tree call back its leaves? We press ever onward. Death is a barrier, across which we may look back, but over which we may not pass again."

QUESTION.

"Is there communication between your universe and the one beyond you?"

—No response.

QUESTION.

"Can you tell us of the universe beyond you?"

RESPONSE.

"Did you know aught of this, until now, save that it existed?"

"It is true," said I, "but what—what of the next?"

RESPONSE.

"Knowing 'color' and 'extension' only, how could you judge what manner of quality 'weight' might be? Neither can we conceive what manner of universe the next is, for we have nothing to judge from. We only know it to be as different in its character from ours as ours is from yours, as color is from weight."

We had scarcely received the response, when I was amazed at finding the entire body strangely agitated. The odic fluid, passing through the arm, had indeed penetrated it throughout. But before I could speak, the hand dropped away from mine, and I was stupefied at seeing the corpse rise slowly to a sitting posture—evidently without any internal muscular action, but as though it were willed up from without by its disembodied soul. It was stiff and stark. The lids opened, the black eyes—they were the glazed, soulless eyes of death—stared forth into vacuity, and, to our horror, the chin dropped, the organs of articulation were moved—*the corpse spoke!*

"Great   Heavens!—I   am—I   am—*leaving   my Universe!*—my   out-creations   die   from   around   me!—I am   passing   to   the   next——Oh   where!—*where!*—I   am DYING—dy——Fare——"

And the body fell relaxed upon the bed, the right arm bounding as it struck.

When we had recovered partially from our stupefaction, we looked around us, and could scarcely believe what we had seen and heard. Could it indeed be possible, that the corpse had moved—*had uttered words?* Yes—we were all awake—all dismayed—terror-stricken; and in the ears of each of us still rang those words of awful import: "I am leaving my universe!—my out-creations die from around me! I am passing to the next!" Could our senses have deceived us? And yet, if the disembodied spirit could, through the medium of the odic fluid, move the table, or the arm and hand that once were his, why *indeed* could it not will the inhaling muscles and the organs of articulation into action? Yes, strange though it seemed, the one was no more unreasonable than the other.

We laid the body into a proper position again, re-closed its eyes, and resumed our seats.

But the spirit—the spirit—whither had it flown? It was now not even within *our* reach! A whole universe was between us!

What more is there for me to say? My task is done. I have related the strange occurrences to which I have been witness during the past forty-eight hours, as faithfully as lies in my power,—and my duty to the world is performed.

The Doctor and Mr. H. left me at two this morning, promising to return at noon. The reader knows the rest. Stealthily, hour by hour, has the night stolen away, the silence only broken by the rustling of my papers. Janie still sleeps sweetly and confidingly. One lock of hair must I clip from the marble forehead—one single memento of the departed for her who is left alone.

✳

Five days afterwards, two passed over the hills toward that silent city, beneath the shade of whose trees and among whose winding paths all eyes are closed—all hands are peacefully crossed forever. And as they left the city of the living behind them, and the din of its crowded streets died away in the distance, peace fell upon their hearts, and I knew they drew closer together, as they walked hand in hand. It was the blessed Sabbath morning. Nearer and nearer sounded the solemn, mournful roar of the great Pacific. To the elder, it seemed like the far-heard, commingled converse of the innumerable departed!

Thus they moved in silence, and entered the broad avenue, with sunny hearts. Path after path they threaded, and at last they stood before a new-made grave. Flowers were freshly planted around it, and on the headstone were graven these simple words:

"farewell—father."

And as the elder threw himself upon the grass, he knew not which was the fairer,—the younger or the flowers she tripped among.

THE LOST ROOM

by Fitz James O'Brien

IT was oppressively warm. The sun had long disappeared, but seemed to have left its vital spirit of heat behind it. The air rested; the leaves of the acacia-trees that shrouded my windows hung plumb-like on their delicate stalks. The smoke of my cigar scarce rose above my head, but hung about me in a pale blue cloud, which I had to dissipate with languid waves of my hand. My shirt was open at the throat, and my chest heaved laboriously in the effort to catch some breaths of fresher air. The noises of the city seemed to be wrapped in slumber, and the shrilling of the mosquitos was the only sound that broke the stillness.

As I lay with my feet elevated on the back of a chair, wrapped in that peculiar frame of mind in which thought assumes a species of lifeless motion, the strange fancy seized me of making a languid inventory of the principal articles of furniture in my room. It was a task well suited to the mood in which I found myself. Their forms were duskily defined in the dim twilight that floated shadowily through the chamber; it was no labour to note and particularize each, and from the place where I sat I could command a view of all my possessions without even turning my head.

There was, *imprimis*, that ghostly lithograph by Calame. It was a mere black spot on the white wall, but my inner vision scrutinized every detail of the picture. A wild, desolate, midnight heath, with a spectral oak-tree in the center of the foreground. The wind blows fiercely, and the jagged branches, clothed scantily with ill-grown leaves, are swept to the left continually by its giant force.

A formless wrack of clouds streams across the awful sky, and the rain sweeps almost parallel with the horizon. Beyond, the heath stretches off into endless blackness, in the extreme of which either fancy or art has conjured up some undefinable shapes that seem riding into space. At the base of the huge oak stands a shrouded figure. His mantle is wound by the blast in tight folds around his form, and the long cock's feather in his hat is blown upright, till it seems as if it stood on end with fear. His features are not visible, for he has grasped his cloak with both hands, and drawn it from either side across his face. The picture is seemingly objectless. It tells no tale, but there is a weird power about it that haunts one, and it was for that I bought it.

Next to the picture comes the round blot that hangs below it, which I know to be a smoking-cap. It has my coat of arms embroidered on the front, and for that reason I never wear it; though, when properly arranged on my head, with its long blue silken tassel hanging down by my cheek, I believe it becomes me well. I remember the time when it was in the course of manufacture. I remember the tiny little hands that pushed the colored silks so nimbly through the cloth that was stretched on the embroidery-frame,—the vast trouble I was put to to get a colored copy of my armorial bearings for the heraldic work which was to decorate the front of the band,—the pursings up of the little mouth, and the contractions of the young forehead, as their possessor plunged into a profound sea of cogitation touching the way in which the cloud should be represented from which the armed hand, that is my crest, issues,—the heavenly moment when the tiny hands placed it on my head, in a position that I could not bear for more than a few seconds, and I, kinglike, immediately assumed my royal prerogative after the coronation, and instantly levied a tax on my only subjects which was, however, not paid unwillingly. Ah! the cap is there, but the embroiderer has fled; for Atropos was severing the web of life above her head while she was weaving that silken shelter for mine!

How uncouthly the huge piano that occupies the corner at the left of the door looms out in the uncertain twilight! I neither play nor sing, yet I own a piano. It is a comfort to me to look at it, and to feel that the music is there, although I am not able to break the spell that binds it. It is pleasant to know that Bellini and Mozart, Cimarosa, Porpora, Glück and all such,—or at least their souls,—sleep in that unwieldy case. There lie embalmed, as it were, all operas, sonatas, oratorios, nocturnos, marches, songs and dances, that ever climbed into existence through the four bars that wall in melody. Once I was entirely repaid for the investment of my funds in that instrument which I never use, Blokeeta, the composer, came to see me. Of course his instincts urged him as irresistibly to my piano as if some magnetic power lay within it compelling him to approach. He tuned it, he played on it. All night long, until the gray and spectral dawn rose out of the depths of the midnight, he sat and played, and I lay smoking by the window listening. Wild, unearthly, and sometimes insufferably painful, were the improvisations of Blokeeta. The chords of the instrument seemed breaking with anguish. Lost souls shrieked in his dismal preludes; the half-heard utterances of spirits in pain, that groped at inconceivable distances from anything lovely or harmonious, seemed to rise dimly up out of the waves of sound that gathered under his hands. Melancholy human love wandered out on distant heaths, or beneath dank and gloomy cypresses, murmuring its unanswered sorrow, or hateful gnomes sported and sang in the stagnant swamps triumphing in unearthly tones over the knight whom they had lured to his death. Such was Blokeeta's night's entertainment; and when he at length closed the piano, and hurried away through the cold morning, he left a memory about the instrument from which I could never escape.

Those snow-shoes that hang in the space between the mirror and the door recall Canadian wanderings,—a long race through the dense forests, over the frozen snow through whose brittle crust the slender hoofs of the caribou that we were pursuing sank at every step, until the poor creature despairingly turned at bay in a small juniper coppice, and we heartlessly shot him down. And I remember how Gabriel, the *habitant*, and François, the half-breed, cut his throat, and how the hot blood rushed out in a torrent over the snowy soil; and I recall the snow *cabane* that Gabriel built, where we all three slept so warmly; and the great fire that glowed at our feet, painting all kinds of demoniac shapes on the black screen of forest that lay without; and the deer-steaks that we roasted for our breakfast; and the savage drunkenness of Gabriel in the morning, he having been privately drinking out of my brandy-flask all the night long.

That long haftless dagger that dangles over the mantelpiece makes my heart swell. I found it, when a boy, in a hoary old castle in which one of my maternal ancestors once lived. That same ancestor—who, by the way, yet lives in history—was a strange old sea-king, who dwelt on the extremest point of the southwestern coast of Ireland. He owned the whole of that fertile island called Inniskeiran, which directly faces Cape Clear, where between them the Atlantic rolls furiously, forming what the fishermen of the place call "the Sound." An awful place in winter is that same Sound. On certain days no boat can live there for a moment, and Cape Clear is frequently cut off for days from any communication with the mainland.

This old sea-king—Sir Florence O'Driscoll by name—passed a stormy life. From the summit of his castle he watched the ocean, and when any richly laden vessels bound from the South to the industrious Galway merchants, hove in sight, Sir Florence hoisted the sails of his galley, and it went hard with him if he did not tow into harbor ship and crew. In this way he lived; not a very honest mode of livelihood, certainly, according to our modern ideas, but quite reconcilable with the morals of the time. As may be supposed, Sir Florence got into trouble. Complaints were laid against him at the English court by the plundered merchants, and the Irish viking set out for London, to plead his own cause before good Queen Bess, as she was called. He had one powerful recommendation: he was a marvellously handsome man. Not Celtic by descent, but half Spanish, half Danish in blood, he had the great northern stature with the regular features, flashing eyes, and dark hair of the Iberian race. This may account for the fact that his stay at the English court was much longer than was necessary, as also for the tradition, which a local historian mentions, that the English Queen evinced a preference for the Irish chieftain, of other nature than that usually shown by monarch to subject.

Previous to his departure, Sir Florence had intrusted the care of his property to an Englishman named Hull. During the long absence of the knight, this person managed to ingratiate himself with the local authorities, and gain their favour so far that they were willing to support him in almost any scheme. After a protracted stay, Sir Florence, pardoned of all his misdeeds, returned to his home. Home no longer. Hull was in possession, and refused to yield an acre of the lands he had so nefariously acquired. It was no use appealing to the law, for its officers were in the opposite interest. It was no use appealing to the Queen, for she had another lover, and had forgotten the poor Irish knight by this time; and so the viking passed the best portion of his life in unsuccessful attempts to reclaim his vast estates, and was eventually, in his old age, obliged to content himself with his castle by the sea and the island of Inniskeiran, the only spot of which the usurper was unable to deprive him. So this old story of my kinsman's fate looms up out of the darkness that enshrouds that haftless dagger hanging on the wall.

It was somewhat after the foregoing fashion that I dreamily made the inventory of my personal property. As I turned my eyes on each object, one after the other,—or the places where they lay, for the room was now so dark that it was almost impossible to see with any distinctness,—a crowd of memories connected with each rose up before me, and, perforce, I had to indulge them. So I proceeded but slowly, and at last my cigar shortened to a hot and bitter morsel that I could barely hold between my lips, while it seemed to me that the night grew each moment more insufferably oppressive. While I was revolving some impossible means of cooling my wretched body, the cigar stump began to burn my lips. I flung it angrily through the open window, and stooped out to watch it falling. It first lighted on the leaves of the acacia, sending out a spray of red sparkles, then, rolling off, it fell plump on the dark walk in the garden, faintly illuminating for a moment the dusky trees and breathless flowers. Whether it was the contrast between the red flash of the cigar-stump and the silent darkness of the garden, or whether it was that I detected by the sudden light a faint waving of the leaves, I know not; but something suggested to me that the garden was cool. I will take a turn there, thought I, just as I am; it cannot be warmer than this room, and however still the atmosphere, there is always a feeling of liberty and spaciousness in the open air, that partially supplies one's wants. With this idea running through my head, I arose, lit another cigar, and passed out into the long, intricate corridors that led to the main staircase.

As I crossed the threshold of my room, with what a different feeling I should have passed it had I known that I was never to set foot in it again!

I lived in a very large house, in which I occupied two rooms on the second floor. The house was old-fashioned, and all the floors communicated by a huge circular staircase that wound up through the center of the building, while at every landing long, rambling corridors stretched off into mysterious nooks and corners. This palace of mine was very high, and its resources, in the way of crannies and windings, seemed to be interminable. Nothing seemed to stop anywhere. Cul-de-sacs were unknown on the premises. The corridors and passages, like mathematical lines, seemed capable of indefinite extension, and the object of the architect must have been to erect an edifice in which people might go ahead forever. The whole place was gloomy, not so much because it was large, but because an unearthly nakedness seemed to pervade the structure. The staircases, corridors, halls, and vestibules all partook of a desert-like desolation. There was nothing on the walls to break the sombre monotony of those long vistas of shade. No carvings on the wainscoting, no molded masks peering down from the simply severe cornices, no marble vases on the landings. There was an eminent dreariness and want of life—so rare in an American establishment—all over the abode. It was Hood's haunted house put in order and newly painted. The servants, too, were shadowy, and chary of their visits. Bells rang three times before the gloomy chambermaid could be induced to present herself; and the negro waiter, a ghoul-like looking creature from Congo, obeyed the summons only when one's patience was exhausted or one's want satisfied in some other way. When he did come, one felt sorry that he had not stayed away altogether, so sullen and savage did he appear. He moved along the echoless floors with a slow, noiseless shamble, until his dusky figure, advancing from the gloom, seemed like some reluctant afreet, compelled by the superior power of his master to disclose himself. When the doors of all the chambers were closed, and no light illuminated the long corridor save the red, unwholesome glare of a small oil lamp on a table at the end, where late lodgers lit their candles, one could not by any possibility conjure up a sadder or more desolate prospect.

Yet the house suited me. Of meditative and sedentary habits, I enjoyed the extreme quiet. There were but few lodgers, from which I infer that the landlord did not drive a very thriving trade; and these, probably oppressed by the sombre spirit of the place, were quiet and ghost-like in their movements. The proprietor I scarcely ever saw. My bills were deposited by unseen hands every month on my table, while I was out walking or riding, and my pecuniary response was entrusted to the attendant afreet. On the whole, when the bustling, wide-awake spirit of New York is taken into consideration, the sombre, half-vivified character of the house in which I lived was an anomaly that no one appreciated better than I who lived there.

I felt my way down the wide, dark staircase in my pursuit of zephyrs. The garden, as I entered it, did feel somewhat cooler than my own room, and I puffed my cigar along the dim, cypress-shrouded walks with a sensation of comparative relief. It was very dark. The tall-growing flowers that bordered the path were so wrapped in gloom as to present the aspect of solid pyramidal masses, all the details of leaves and blossoms being buried in an embracing darkness, while the trees had lost all form, and seemed like masses of overhanging cloud. It was a place and time to excite the imagination; for in the impenetrable cavities of endless gloom there was room for the most riotous fancies to play at will. I walked and walked, and the echoes of my footsteps on the ungravelled and mossy path suggested a double feeling. I felt alone and yet in company at the same time. The solitariness of the place made itself distinct enough in the stillness, broken alone by the hollow reverberations of my step, while those very reverberations seemed to imbue me with an undefined feeling that I was not alone. I was not, therefore, much startled when I was suddenly accosted from beneath the solid darkness of an immense cypress by a voice saying, "Will you give me a light, Sir?"

"Certainly," I replied, trying in vain to distinguish the speaker amidst the impenetrable dark.

Somebody advanced, and I held out my cigar. All I could gather definitively about the individual who thus accosted me was that he must have been of extremely small stature; for I, who am by no means an overgrown man, had to stoop considerably in handing him my cigar. The vigorous puff that he gave his own lighted up my Havana for a moment, and I fancied that I caught a glimpse of long, wild hair. The flash was, however, so momentary that I could not even say certainly whether this was an actual impression or the mere effort of imagination to embody that which the senses had failed to distinguish.

"Sir, you are out late," said this unknown to me, as he, with half-uttered thanks, handed me back my cigar, for which I had to grope in the gloom.

"Not later than usual," I replied, dryly.

"Hum! you are fond of late wanderings, then?"

"That is just as the fancy seizes me."

"Do you live here?"

"Yes."

"Queer house, isn't it?"

"I have only found it quiet."

"Hum! But you *will* find it queer, take my word for it." This was earnestly uttered; and I felt at the same time a bony finger laid on my arm, that cut it sharply like a blunted knife.

"I cannot take your word for any such assertion," I replied rudely, shaking off the bony finger with an irrepressible motion of disgust.

"No offence, no offence," muttered my unseen companion rapidly, in a strange, subdued voice, that would have been shrill had it been louder; "your being angry does not alter the matter. You will find it a queer house. Everybody finds it a queer house. Do you know who live there?"

"I never busy myself, sir, about other people's affairs," I answered sharply, for the individual's manner, combined with my utter uncertainty as to his appearance, oppressed me with an irksome longing to be rid of him.

"O, you don't? Well, I do. I know what they are—well, well, well!" and as he pronounced the three last words his voice rose with each, until, with the last, it reached a shrill shriek that echoed horribly among the lonely walks. "Do you know what they eat?" he continued.

"No, Sir,—nor care."

"O, but you will care. You must care. You shall care. I'll tell you what they are. They are enchanters. They are ghouls. They are cannibals. Did you never remark their eyes, and how they gloated on you when you passed? Did you never remark the food that they served up at your table? Did you never in the dead of night hear muffled and unearthly footsteps gliding along the corridors, and stealthy hands turning the handle of your door? Does not some magnetic influence fold itself continually around you when they pass, and send a thrill through spirit and body, and a cold shiver that no sunshine will chase away? O, you have! You have felt all these things! I know it!"

The earnest rapidity, the subdued tones, the eagerness of accent, with which all this was uttered, impressed me most uncomfortably. It really seemed as if I could recall all those weird occurrences and influences of which he spoke; and I shuddered in spite of myself in the midst of the impenetrable darkness that surrounded me.

"Hum!" said I, assuming, without knowing it, a confidential tone, "may I ask you how you know these things?"

"How I know them? Because I am their enemy; because they tremble at my whisper; because I hang upon their track with the perseverance of a bloodhound and the stealthiness of a tiger; because—because—I was of them once!"

"Wretch!" I cried excitedly, for involuntarily his eager tones had wrought me up to a high pitch of spasmodic nervousness, "then you mean to say that you——"

As I uttered this word, obeying an uncontrollable impulse, I stretched forth my hand in the direction of the speaker and made a blind clutch. The tips of my fingers seemed to touch a surface as smooth as glass, that glided suddenly from under them. A sharp, angry hiss sounded through the gloom, followed by a whirring noise, as if some projectile passed rapidly by, and the next moment I felt instinctively that I was alone.

A most disagreeable feeling instantly assailed me;—a prophetic instinct that some terrible misfortune menaced me; an eager and overpowering anxiety to get back to my own room without loss of time. I turned and ran blindly along the dark cypress alley, every dusky clump of flowers that rose blackly in the borders making my heart each moment cease to beat. The echoes of my own footsteps seemed to redouble and assume the sounds of unknown pursuers following fast upon my track. The boughs of lilac-bushes and syringas, that here and there stretched partly across the walk, seemed to have been furnished suddenly with hooked hands that sought to grasp me as I flew by, and each moment I expected to behold some awful and impassable barrier fall across my track and wall me up forever.

At length I reached the wide entrance. With a single leap I sprang up the four or five steps that formed the stoop, and dashed along the hall, up the wide, echoing stairs, and again along the dim, funereal corridors until I paused, breathless and panting, at the door of my room. Once so far, I stopped for an instant and leaned heavily against one of the panels, panting lustily after my late run. I had, however, scarcely rested my whole weight against the door, when it suddenly gave way, and I staggered in head-foremost. To my utter astonishment the room I had left in profound darkness was now a blaze of light. So intense was the illumination that, for a few seconds while the pupils of my eyes were contracting under the sudden change, I saw absolutely nothing save the dazzling glare. This fact in itself, coming on me with such utter suddenness, was sufficient to prolong my confusion, and it was not until after several minutes had elapsed that I perceived the room was not only illuminated, but occupied. And such occupants! Amazement at the scene took such possession of me that I was incapable of either moving or uttering a word. All that I could do was to lean against the wall, and stare blankly at the strange picture.

It might have been a scene out of Faublas, or Gramont's Memoirs, or happened in some palace of Minister Fouque.

Round a large table in the center of the room, where I had left a student-like litter of books and papers, were seated half a dozen persons. Three were men and three were women. The table was heaped with a prodigality of luxuries. Luscious eastern fruits were piled up in silver filigree vases, through whose meshes their glowing rinds shone in the contrasts of a thousand hues. Small silver dishes that Benvenuto might have designed, filled with succulent and aromatic meats, were distributed upon a cloth of snowy damask. Bottles of every shape, slender ones from the Rhine, stout fellows from Holland, sturdy ones from Spain, and quaint basket-woven flasks from Italy, absolutely littered the board. Drinking-glasses of every size and hue filled up the interstices, and the thirsty German flagon stood side by side with the aërial bubbles of Venetian glass that rest so lightly on their threadlike stems. An odour of luxury and sensuality floated through the apartment. The lamps that burned in every direction seemed to diffuse a subtle incense on the air, and in a large vase that stood on the floor I saw a mass of magnolias, tuberoses, and jasmines grouped together, stifling each other with their honeyed and heavy fragrance.

The inhabitants of my room seemed beings well suited to so sensual an atmosphere. The women were strangely beautiful, and all were attired in dresses of the most fantastic devices and brilliant hues. Their figures were round, supple, and elastic; their eyes dark and languishing; their lips full, ripe, and of the richest bloom. The three men wore half-masks, so that all I could distinguish were heavy jaws, pointed beards, and brawny throats that rose like massive pillars out of their doublets. All six lay reclining on Roman couches about the table, drinking down the purple wines in large draughts, and tossing back their heads and laughing wildly.

I stood, I suppose, for some three minutes, with my back against the wall staring vacantly at the bacchanal vision, before any of the revellers appeared to notice my presence. At length, without any expression to indicate whether I had been observed from the beginning or not, two of the women arose from their couches, and, approaching, took each a hand and led me to the table. I obeyed their motions mechanically. I sat on a couch, between them as they indicated. I unresistingly permitted them to wind their arms about my neck.

"You must drink," said one, pouring out a large glass of red wine, "here is Clos Vougeout of a rare vintage; and here," pushing a flask of amber-hued wine before me, "is Lachryma Christi."

"You must eat," said the other, drawing the silver dishes toward her. "Here are cutlets stewed with olives, and here are slices of a *filet* stuffed with bruised sweet chestnuts"—and as she spoke, she, without waiting for a reply, proceeded to help me.

The sight of the food recalled to me the warnings I had received in the garden. This sudden effort of memory restored to me my other faculties at the same instant. I sprang to my feet, thrusting the women from me with each hand.

"Demons!" I almost shouted. "I will have none of your accursed food. I know you. You are cannibals, you are ghouls, you are enchanters. Begone, I tell you! Leave my room in peace!"

A shout of laughter from all six was the only effect that my passionate speech produced. The men rolled on their couches, and their half-masks quivered with the convulsions of their mirth. The women shrieked, and tossed the slender wine-glasses wildly aloft, and turned to me and flung themselves on my bosom fairly sobbing with laughter.

"Yes," I continued, as soon as the noisy mirth had subsided, "yes, I say, leave my room instantly! I will have none of your unnatural orgies here!"

"His room!" shrieked the woman on my right.

"His room!" echoed she on my left.

"His room! He calls it his room!" shouted the whole party, as they rolled once more into jocular convulsions.

"How know you that it is your room?" said one of the men who sat opposite to me, at length, after the laughter had once more somewhat subsided.

"How do I know?" I replied indignantly. "How do I know my own room? How could I mistake it, pray? There's my furniture—my piano——"

"He calls that a piano," shouted my neighbours, again in convulsions as I pointed to the corner where my huge piano, sacred to the memory of Blokeeta, used to stand. "O, yes! It is his room. There—there is his piano!"

The peculiar emphasis they laid on the word "piano" caused me to scrutinize the article I was indicating more thoroughly. Up to this time, though utterly amazed at the entrance of these people into my chamber, and connecting them somewhat with the wild stories I had heard in the garden, I still had a sort of indefinite idea that the whole thing was a masquerading freak got up in my absence, and that the bacchanalian orgie I was witnessing was nothing more than a portion of some elaborate hoax of which I was to be the victim. But when my eyes turned to the corner where I had left a huge and cumbrous piano, and beheld a vast and sombre organ lifting its fluted front to the very ceiling, and convinced myself, by a hurried process of memory, that it occupied the very spot in which I had left my own instrument, the little self-possession that I had left forsook me. I gazed around me bewildered.

In like manner everything was changed. In the place of that old haftless dagger, connected with so many historic associations personal to myself, I beheld a Turkish yataghan dangling by its belt of crimson silk, while the jewels in the hilt blazed as the lamplight played upon them. In the spot where hung my cherished smoking cap, memorial of a buried love, a knightly casque was suspended on the crest of which a golden dragon stood in the act of springing. That strange lithograph of Calame was no longer a lithograph, but it seemed to me that the portion of the wall which it covered, of the exact shape and size, had been cut out, and, in place of the picture, a real scene on the same scale, and with real actors, was distinctly visible. The old oak was there, and the stormy sky was there; but I saw the branches of the oak sway with the tempest, and the clouds drive before the wind. The wanderer in his cloak was gone; but in his place I beheld a circle of wild figures, men and women, dancing with linked hands around the hole of the great tree, chanting some wild fragment of a song, to which the winds roared an unearthly chorus. The snow-shoes, too, on whose sinewy woof I had sped for many days amidst Canadian wastes, had vanished, and in their place lay a pair of strange up-curled Turkish slippers, that had, perhaps, been many a time shuffled off at the doors of mosques, beneath the steady blaze of an orient sun.

All was changed. Wherever my eyes turned they missed familiar objects, yet encountered strange representatives. Still, in all the substitutes there seemed to me a reminiscence of what they replaced. They seemed only for a time transmuted into other shapes, and there lingered around them the atmosphere of what they once had been. Thus I could have sworn the room to have been mine, yet there was nothing in it that I could rightly claim. Everything reminded me of some former possession that it was not. I looked for the acacia at the window, and lo! long silken palm-leaves swayed in through the open lattice; yet they had the same motion and the same air of my favourite tree, and seemed to murmur to me, "Though we seem to be palm-leaves, yet are we acacia-leaves; yea, those very ones on which you used to watch the butterflies alight and the rain patter while you smoked and dreamed!" So in all things; the room was, yet was not, mine; and a sickening consciousness of my utter inability to reconcile its identity with its appearance overwhelmed me, and choked my reason.

"Well, have you determined whether or not this is your room?" asked the girl on my left, proffering me a huge tumbler creaming over with champagne, and laughing wickedly as she spoke.

"It is mine," I answered, doggedly, striking the glass rudely with my hand, and dashing the aromatic wine over the white cloth. "I know that it is mine; and ye are jugglers and enchanters who want to drive me mad."

"Hush! hush!" she said, gently, not in the least angered by my rough treatment. "You are excited. Alf shall play something to soothe you."

At her signal, one of the men sat down at the organ. After a short, wild, spasmodic prelude, he began what seemed to me to be a symphony of recollections. Dark and sombre, and all through full of quivering and intense agony, it appeared to recall a dark and dismal night, on a cold reef, around which an unseen but terribly audible ocean broke with eternal fury. It seemed as if a lonely pair were on the reef, one living, the other dead; one clasping his arms around the tender neck and naked bosom of the other, striving to warm her into life, when his own vitality was being each moment sucked from him by the icy breath of the storm. Here and there a terrible wailing minor key would tremble through the chords like the shriek of sea-birds, or the warning of advancing death. While the man played I could scarce restrain myself. It seemed to be Blokeeta whom I listened to, and on whom I gazed. That wondrous night of pleasure and pain that I had once passed listening to him seemed to have been taken up again at the spot where it had broken off, and the same hand was continuing it. I stared at the man called Alf. There he sat with his cloak and doublet, and long rapier and mask of black velvet. But there was something in the air of the peaked beard, a familiar mystery in the wild mass of raven hair that fell as if wind-blown over his shoulders, which riveted my memory.

"Blokeeta! Blokeeta!" I shouted, starting up furiously from the couch on which I was lying, and bursting the fair arms that were linked around my neck as if they had been hateful chains,—"Blokeeta! my friend! speak to me, I entreat you! Tell these horrid enchanters to leave me. Say that I hate them. Say that I command them to leave my room."

The man at the organ stirred not in answer to my appeal. He ceased playing, and the dying sound of the last note he had touched faded off into a melancholy moan. The other men and the women burst once more into peals of mocking laughter.

"Why will you persist in calling this your room?" said the woman next me, with a smile meant to be kind, but to me inexpressibly loathsome. "Have we not shown you by the furniture, by the general appearance of the place, that you are mistaken, and that this cannot be your apartment? Rest content, then, with us. You are welcome here, and need no longer trouble yourself about your room."

"Rest content!" I answered madly; "live with ghosts, eat of awful meats, and see awful sights! Never! never! You have cast some enchantment over the place that has disguised it; but for all that I know it to be my room. You shall leave it!"

"Softly, softly!" said another of the sirens. "Let us settle this amicably. This poor gentleman seems obstinate and inclined to make an uproar. Now we do not want an uproar. We love the night and its quiet; and there is no night that we love so well as that on which the moon is coffined in clouds. Is it not so, my brothers?"

An awful and sinister smile gleamed on the countenances of her unearthly audience, and seemed to glide visibly from underneath their masks.

"Now," she continued, "I have a proposition to make. It would be ridiculous for us to surrender this room simply because this gentleman states that it is his; and yet I feel anxious to gratify, as far as may be fair, his wild assertion of ownership. A room, after all, is not much to us; we can get one easily enough, but still we should be loath to give this apartment up to so imperious a demand. We are willing, however, to risk its loss. That is to say,"—turning to me,—"I propose that we play for the room. If you win, we will immediately surrender it to you just as it stands; if, on the contrary, you lose, you shall bind yourself to depart and never molest us again."

Agonized at the ever-darkening mysteries that seemed to thicken around me, and despairing of being able to dissipate them by the mere exercise of my own will, I caught almost gladly at the chance thus presented to me. The idea of my loss or my gain scarce entered into my calculations. All I felt was an indefinite knowledge that I might, in the way proposed, regain in an instant, that quiet chamber and that peace of mind of which I had so strangely been deprived.

"I agree!" I cried eagerly; "I agree. Anything to rid myself of such unearthly company!"

The woman touched a small golden bell that stood near her on the table, and it had scarce ceased to tinkle when a negro dwarf entered with a silver tray on which were dice-boxes and dice. A shudder passed over me as I thought in this stunted African I could trace a resemblance to the ghoul-like black servant to whose attendance I had been accustomed.

"Now," said my neighbour, seizing one of the dice-boxes and giving me the other, "the highest wins. Shall I throw first?"

I nodded assent. She rattled the dice, and I felt an inexpressible load lifted from my heart as she threw fifteen.

"It is your turn," she said, with a mocking smile; "but before you throw, I repeat the offer I made you before. Live with us. Be one of us. We will initiate you into our mysteries and enjoyments,—enjoyments of which you can form no idea unless you experience them. Come; it is not too late yet to change your mind. Be with us!"

My reply was a fierce oath, as I rattled the dice with spasmodic nervousness and flung them on the board. They rolled over and over again, and during that brief instant I felt a suspense, the intensity of which I have never known before or since. At last they lay before me. A shout of the same horrible, maddening laughter rang in my ears. I peered in vain at the dice, but my sight was so confused that I could not distinguish the amount of the cast. This lasted for a few moments. Then my sight grew clear, and I sank back almost lifeless with despair as I saw that I had thrown but *twelve!*

"Lost! lost!" screamed my neighbour, with a wild laugh. "Lost! lost!" shouted the deep voices of the masked men.

"Leave us, coward!" they all cried; "you are not fit to be one of us. Remember your promise; leave us!"

Then it seemed as if some unseen power caught me by the shoulders and thrust me toward the door. In vain I resisted. In vain I screamed and shouted for help. In vain I implored them for pity. All the reply I had was those mocking peals of merriment, while, under the invisible influence, I staggered like a drunken man toward the door. As I reached the threshold the organ pealed out a wild triumphal strain. The power that impelled me concentrated itself into one vigorous impulse that sent me blindly staggering out into the echoing corridor, and as the door closed swiftly behind me, I caught one glimpse of the apartment I had left forever. A change passed like a shadow over it. The lamps died out, the siren women and masked men vanished, the flowers, the fruits, the bright silver and bizarre furniture faded swiftly, and I saw again, for the tenth of a second, my own old chamber restored. There was the acacia waving darkly; there was the table littered with books; there was the ghostly lithograph, the dearly beloved smoking-cap, the Canadian snow-shoes, the ancestral dagger. And there, at the piano, organ no longer, sat Blokeeta playing.

The next instant the door closed violently, and I was left standing in the corridor stunned and despairing.

As soon as I had partially recovered my comprehension I rushed madly to the door, with the dim idea of beating it in. My fingers touched a cold and solid wall. There was no door! I felt all along the corridor for many yards on both sides. There was not even a crevice to give me hope. I rushed downstairs shouting madly. No one answered. In the vestibule I met the negro; I seized him by the collar and demanded my room. The demon showed his white and awful teeth, which were filed into a saw-like shape, and extricating himself from my grasp with a sudden jerk, fled down the passage with a gibbering laugh. Nothing but echo answered to my despairing shrieks. The lonely garden resounded with my cries as I strode madly through the dark walls, and the tall funereal cypresses seemed to bury me beneath their heavy shadows. I met no one,—could find no one. I had to bear my sorrow and despair alone.

Since that awful hour I have never found my room. Everywhere I look for it, yet never see it. Shall I ever find it?

LARA
AN EXPERIENCE

by Paschal Beverly Randolph

FLESHLESS, yet living, I strode through the grand old hall of a mighty temple. I was compelled to climb the hills that bar the gates of Glory, and soon I found myself on a mighty plain, stretching out to the Infinitudes as it seemed in the short spaces wherein the vision was not obstructed by dense vapors that rose from the waters of the river of Lethe that skirted the immense prairie on which I was traveling toward my undreamed-of Destiny.

Dark, dense shadows rolled massily over the spaces—grim shadows of the dead worlds. No sound, no footfall, not even mine own, not an echo broke the awful stillness. I was alone!—alone on the tremendous wastes of an unknown, unimagined Eterne. Within my bosom there was a heart, but no pulse from it went bounding thro' my veins; no throb beat back responsive life to my feeling, listening spirit. I felt that it was changed to solid stone, all save one small point, distant as the vague ghost of a long-forgotten fancy,—and this seemed to have been the penalty inflicted on me for things done on the earth; for it appeared that I was dead, and that my soul had begun an endless pilgrimage to——What?—to Where? It seemed to be a penalty, and yet no black memory of dark-handed crime had seat within the mystic portals of my deathless soul. And I strode all alone adown the uncolumned vistas of the grand old temple, whose walls were builded of flown seconds, whose tessellated pavements were laid in sheeted hours, whose windows were wrought of the Gone Ages, and whose sublime turrets pierced the clouds, which roll over and mantle the summits of the gray mountains of Time. And so I strode through this temple alone!

With clear, keen gaze I looked forth, and my vision swept over the floors of all the dead years, yet in vain, for the objects of my longing were not there. There were trees, but all their leaves were motionless, and no caroling bird sent its heart-notes forth to wake the dim solitudes into life and music; there were stately groves within the temple, but no amphian strains of melody fell on the ear from their moveless branches, or from out their fair theatres. All was still. It was a palace of frozen tones and only the music of Silence prevailed, and I, Paschal, the Thinker, and my thoughts strange, uncouth, yet mighty—but moveless thoughts, were the only living things beneath the bending dome. Living, I had sacrificed health, wealth, fame, honors—all things, even Love itself, for THOUGHT, and by thought had risen to a throne so lofty, that mankind wondered, stood aghast, and by reason of my thought had gathered from me, and condemned me to solitude even in the busy marts of men, and in the lanes and streets of earth's crowded cities; and now, after I had quitted earth with fearless tread, assured of an endless immortality, and had entered upon the life of Thinking, still was I alone. Had my life, my thinking, been a failure? The thought was bitter—seemed true, yet was rejected by my soul in utter loathing. For a moment, the social spirit had overshadowed Reason, and caused me to forget that even though stricken with deformity, poverty, sin or disease, the Thinker is ever the only true King. I had forgotten that the name of Paschal was inscribed on the fadeless parchments of the Imperial Order of the Rosy Cross, and that to be a Rosicrucian, was to be blest with boundless knowledge. But now, as I strode along, I felt my human nature yearning for human society and affection, and in the terrible presence of its absence I—I longed for death—that deeper death which sweeps the soul from being, and crowns the intellect with the hood of limitless, eternal Night. But it was not to be; and so I laid me down in despair beneath a tree which stood out from its fellows all ragged and lightning scathed, an awful monument, telling the onlooker that God had passed that way in fierce deific wrath, once upon a time in the dead ages whose ashes now bestrewed the floors of that vast and mighty Temple of ETERNE.

It was dreadful, very dreadful to be all alone. True, the pangs of hunger, the torture of thirst, the fires of ambition, nor the flames of passion could no longer mar my peace, nor disturb my being, for I was immortal and could laugh death to scorn,—yet suffering was mine. I wept, and my cries gave back no outer sound, but they rang, in dreadful echoes through the bottomless caverns and abysmal deeps of my soul, racking it with torments, such as only lonely souls can feel, and such as are only undergone by the destined daughters of the Star-beam, the quenchless sons of Day,—the treasured children of the Empyrean.

Sleep came—a strange, deep sleep, and in it I dreamed. Me thought I still wandered gloomily beneath the vast arches of the old grand hall, until at last, after countless cycles of ripe years had been gathered back to the Holy One, I stood before a solid, massive door, which, an inscription thereabove told me, opened into the vestibule leading to the garden of the Beatitudes. This door was secured by a thousand locks, every one of which might be opened, but the opener could not pass through, unless he unfastened one gigantic master lock having ten thousand wards and bolts. A doom! again despair enshrouded my soul in this dream within what was not all another dream; for to achieve such a task without the moster key, was a task requiring the labor of a host for periods of time, defying human comprehension, so many were the locks, so vastly strong the door. Mournfully I turned away, when, as if by chance, my gaze encountered a rivetless space upon the brazen door, of a circular shape, around which was an inscription running thus: "MAN ONLY FAILS THROUGH THE FEEBLENESS OF WILL!"

Within this smooth circle was a golden triangle, in the center of which was a crystaline winged globe, surmounted with the cypher "R,"[1] while beneath this winged globe, in fiery characters, was the single word, "TRY!" The very instant I caught the magic significance of these divine inscriptions, Hope was begotten of my soul, and born of stern resolve. Despair fled to his dismal solitudes, and in the excess of my tumultuous joy, I awoke from the dream within a dream.

But what a change! During my slumber I had been transported to the summit of a high mountain, in another part of the Temple. By my side stood an aged and saintly man of most regal and majestic presence. He was clad in oriental garb, and his flowing raiment was bound to his waist by a golden band wrought in the form of a shining serpent,—the sacred emblem of Wisdom, and insignia of Power. Around his broad and lofty brow was a coronet of silver, dusted with spiculæ of finest diamonds, in the center of which was a magian character, which told me his name was Ramus the Great—the same known historically as Thothmes or Thotmor, the builder of the first Pyramid, King of Egypt, and sixty-ninth chief of the Imperial Order of the Rosy Cross.

This regal being spake kindly to me, and his soft tones fell upon the hearing of my soul like words of pardon at the Judgment Seat fall upon the repentant sinner. He pointed

---

1 Rosicrucian.

me to a vast procession of the risen dead—a spectral army, wending its way toward that part of the temple I had just quitted in such a mysterious manner. Said he: "O, Son of Time, yonder host are men and women who are seeking, as thou hast sought, the Gates of Glory, that they may pass through into the delightful garden of the Beatitudes. It is one thing to be endowed with Immortality; it is another thing to be Happy. The first is a boon granted to all the children of the earth alike; the last can only be attained by self-endeavor, on Earth and in the great Eterne alike! The way to the garden lies ever through the Hall of Silence, and each aspirant must open the door for himself and no other. Failing, as thou hast failed, each must turn back, and like thee, come hither to the Hill of Retrospection, and must search in the vales of memory for the triple key, which alone can unbar the gates of Glory! Remember! Despair not—Try!" and in an instant the glorious phantom turned from me, and with arms outstretched in more than mortal love, hied him toward the head of the moving army.

Again I stood alone, but not now in despondency and gloom, but in all the serene majesty of noble, conscious Manhood, aware of my short-comings, failures and mis-spent time, yet conscious of having meant well. . . . . In this spirit I began to search in the crypts of memory for the magic key, which I knew instinctively must consist of some three grand human deeds or virtues.

At length it seemed that I had found them—Virtues clothed in words or names, and no sooner was this thought born than I wished myself before the gate, and instantly by some magic power I found myself standing on the exact spot I had occupied during my dream within a dream. The first inscription had disappeared, as had the trine and winged globe, and in their places I read: "Speak, and tell what thou hast done toward uplifting thy fellow-men: when thou speakest the three words in which resides the magic spell and key, the door will open, and thou mayest pass!"

The writing slowly faded, and the smooth space assumed the appearance of molten gold. I spoke aloud, and to my astonishment my voice rang shrill and clear through the spaces of the grand old Hall. "I have educated myself—have developed reason, judgment, intuition—have reaped laurels in the field of letters, and surmounted difficulties without number, thus setting an example to all the world, by following which, man might elevate himself to the loftiest spheres of usefulness." While uttering this sentence of living truth, I firmly expected at its conclusion, to see the gate fly back upon its hinges. But to my horror it moved not at all, while the echoes of my voice echoed back in frightful waves, repeating my last word, "usefulness." Not being able to think of any nobler deed, I cast my eyes downward, and on raising them again, I saw across the clear space on the door, the word "Try."

Taking heart again, I said: "I have made grand efforts to redeem mankind from sloth, sin, and ignorance. I have told them of Jesus, and upheld the power and honor of the cross and the sweet religion it typifies. My aims have been to lift the veil that hides man from his own soul; and to effect this end I have endured poverty, slander, insult, disgrace; and to attain the great end I have ignored wealth, fame, honor, place, and have even been deaf to the calls of Love." I ceased. The gate moved not, but the word "Try" reappeared in greater brightness, and the vast vault echoed back with a gentle, soft, and velvet cadence the one word "Love." I tried again. "I have rebuked the high, comforted the mourner, redeemed the thief, saved the harlot, fed the orphan, and upheld the rights and dignity of Labor!" Still the door moved not; and again the echoes gave back my last word, "LABOR." "I have preached immortality, written of it, convinced thousands, been its champion; I have confirmed the wavering, beaten the skeptic, reassured the doubting, and through long and bitter years; throughout both hemispheres of the globe, from sea to sea, have I proclaimed that if a man die he shall unmistakably live again, and thus have I endeavored to banish error and superstition, and on their ruins lay the broad and deep foundations of a better faith!" As if a myriad voices chimed out my last syllable, there rang through the spacial hall the sublime word "Faith!" Instantly the bolts of the thousand locks flew back in their wards, and the ponderous gate moved forward and back, like a vast curtain when swayed by a gentle wind. Joyously I tried again, knowing that only one thing more was necessary to end my pilgrimage of loneliness, and exalt me to the blest companionship of the dear ones whom I so longed to join in their glory-walks adown the celestial glades of God's infinite gardens of Beatitude.

"I have fallen from man's esteem in pursuance of my duty. A new faith sprang up in the land, and zealots brought shame upon it. Lured by a false eloquence I yielded to the fascinations of a specious sophistry, and for a while languished beneath the bondage of glittering falsehood. At length I saw my error and theirs; I strove to correct the faults, and to sift the chaff from the rich new wheat; but the people did not or would not understand me, but insisted that I ignored both grain and tares; yet still I labored on, trying to correct my faults, and cultivate the Queen of human virtues—CHARITY!" Scarcely had this word escaped my lips, than the massive portal flew open, and a sight of supernal magnificence stood revealed before my ravished soul, whose nature I may not now reveal.

Lara—Lara, my beautiful one—the dear, dead maiden of the long agone, stood before me, just within the lines of Paradise. She loved me still—aye, the red maiden had not forgotten the lover of her early days, ere the cruel death snatched her from my arms; for the love of the Indian maiden survives the grave, and she spake, saying: "Paschal, my beloved—lone student of this weary world—I await thy entrance here. But thou mayst not enter now. Thy work is yet unfinished. Thou hast found the keys! Go give them to thy fellow men. Teach them that only USEFULNESS, LOVE, LABOR, FAITH and CHARITY, are the keys which are potent to unbar the gates of glory!"

"Beautiful Lara! I obey thee! Wait for me, love, I am coming soon," I cried, as slowly she retreated, and the gates closed again. "Not yet, not yet," I cried, as with outstretched arms I implored her to stay. But she was gone; I fell to the ground in a swoon. When I awoke again, I found the night had grown an hour older than it was when I sat down in my chair in the little chamber I occupy in this goodly city of the Golden Gate.

THE LIFE-MAGNET

by Alvey A. Adee

THERE was something about the wholesome sleepiness of Freiberg, in Saxony, that fitted well with the lazy nature of Ronald Wyde. So, having run down there to spend a day or two among the students and the mines, and taking a liking to the quaint, unmodernized town, he bodily changed his plans of autumn-travel, gave up a cherished scheme of Russian vagabondage, had his baggage sent from Dresden, and made ready to settle down and drowse away three or four months in idleness and not over-arduous study. And this move of his led to the happening of a very strange and seemingly unreal event in his life.

Ronald Wyde was then about twenty-five or six years old, rather above the medium height, with thick blue-black hair that he had an artist-trick of allowing to ripple down to his neck, dark hazel eyes that were almost too deeply recessed in their bony orbits, and a troublesome growth of beard that, close-shaven as he always was, showed in strong blue outline through the thin and rather sallow skin. His address was singularly pleasing, and his wide experience of life, taught him by years of varied travel, made him a good deal of a cosmopolitan in his views and ways, which caused him to be looked upon as a not over-safe companion for young men of his own age or under.

Having made up his mind to winter in Freiberg, his first step was to quit the little hotel, with its mouldy stone-vaulted entrance and its columned dining-room, under whose full-centered arches close beery and smoky fumes lingered persistently, and seek quieter student-lodgings in the heart of the town. His choice was mainly influenced by a thin-railed balcony, twined through and through by the shoots of a vigorous Virginia creeper, that flamed and flickered in the breezy October sunsets in strong relief against the curtains that drifted whitely out and in through the open window. So, with the steady-going and hale old Frau Spritzkrapfen he took up his quarters, fully persuading himself that he did so for the sake of the stray home-breaths that seemed to stir the scarlet vine-leaves more gently for him, and ignoring pretty Lottchen's great, earnest Saxon eyes as best he could.

A sunny morning followed his removal to Frau Spritzkrapfen's tidy home. There had been a slight rain in the early night, and the footways were yet bright and moist in patches that the slanting morning rays were slowly coaxing away. Ronald Wyde, having set his favorite books handily on the dimity-draped table, which comprised for him the process of getting to rights, and having given more than one glance of amused wonderment at the naïve blue-and-white scriptural tiles that cased his cumbrous four-story earthenware stove, and smiled lazily at poor Adam's obvious and sudden indigestion, even while the uneaten half-apple remained in his guilty hand, he stepped out on his balcony, leaned his elbows among the crimson leaves, and took in the healthful morning air in great draughts. It was a Sunday; the bells of the gray minster hard by were iterating their clanging calls to the simple townsfolk to come and be droned to in sleepy German gutturals from the carved, pillar-hung pulpit inside. Looking down, he saw thick-ankled women cluttering past in loose wooden-soled shoes, and dumpy girls with tow-braids primly dangling to their hips, convoying sturdy Dutch-built luggers of younger brothers up the easy slope that led to the church and the bells. Presently Frau Spritzkrapfen and dainty Lottchen, rosy with soap and health, slipped through the doorway beneath him out into the little church-bound throng, and, as they disappeared, left the house and street somehow unaccountably alone. Feeling this, Ronald Wyde determined on a stroll.

Something in the Sabbath stillness around him led Ronald away from the swift clang and throbbing hum of the bells and in the direction of the old cemetery. Passing through the clumsy tower-gate that lifts its grimy bulk sullenly, like a huge head-stone over the grave of a dead time of feudalism, he reached the burial-ground and entered the quiet enclosure. The usual touching reverence of the Germans for their dead was strikingly manifest around him. The humbler mounds, walled up with rough stones a foot or two above the path-way level, carried on their crests little gardens of gay and inexpensive plants; while on the tall wooden crosses at their head hung yellow wreaths, half hiding the hopeful legend, "Wiedersehen." The more pretentious slabs bore vases filled with fresh flowers; while in the grate-barred vaults, that skirt-ed the ground like the arches of a cloister, lay rusty heaps of long-since mouldered bloom, topped by newer wreaths tossed lovingly in to wilt and turn to dust in their turn, like those cast in before them in memory of that other dust asleep below.

Turning aside from the central walk that halved the cemetery, Ronald strolled along, his hands in his pockets, his eyes listlessly fixed on the orange-colored fumes and rolling smoke that welled out of tall chimneys in the hollow beyond, an idle student-tune humming on his lips, and his thoughts nowhere, and everywhere, at once. Happening to look away from the dun smoke-trail for an instant, he found something of greater interest close at hand. An old man stooped stiffly over a simple mound, busied among the flowers that hid it, and by his side crouched a young girl, perhaps fourteen years old, who peered up at Ronald with questioning, velvet-brown eyes. The old man heard the intruder's steps crunching in the damp gravel, and slowly looked up too.

"Good morning, mein Herr," said Ronald, pleasantly.

The old man remained for an instant blinking nervously, and shading his eyes from the full sunlight that fell on his face. A quiet face it was, and very old, seamed and creased by mazy wrinkles that played at aimless cross-purposes with each other, beginning and ending nowhere. His thick beard and thin, curved nose looked just a little Jewish, and seemed at variance with his pale blue eyes that were still bright in spite of age. And yet, bearded as he was, there was a lurking expression about his features that bordered upon effeminacy, and made the treble of his voice sound even more thin and womanish as he answered Wyde's greeting.

"Good morning, too, mein Herr. A stranger to our town, I see."

"Yes; but soon not to be called one, I hope. I am here for the winter."

"A cold season—a cold season; our northern winters are very chilling to an old man's blood." And slouching together into a tired stoop, he resumed his simple task of knotting a few flowers into a clumsy nosegay. Ronald stood and watched him with a vague interest. Presently, the flowers being clumped to his liking, the old man pried himself upright by getting a good purchase with his left hand in the small of his back, and so deliberately that Ronald almost fancied he heard him creak. The girl rose too, and drew her thin shawl over her shoulders.

"You Germans love longer than we," said Ronald, glancing at the flowers that trembled in the old man's bony fingers, and then downwards to the quiet grave; "a lifetime of easy-going love and a year or two of easier-forgetting are enough for us."

"Should I forget my own flesh and blood?" asked the old man, simply.

Ronald paused a moment, and, pointing downwards, said:

"Your daughter, then, I fancy?"

"Yes."

"Long dead?"

"Very long; more than fifty years."

Ronald stared, but said nothing audibly. Inwardly he whispered something about being devilish glad to make the wandering Jew's acquaintance, rattled the loose gröschen in his pocket, and turned to follow the tottering old man and firm-footed child down the walk. After a dozen paces they halted before a more ambitious tombstone, on which Ronald could make out the well-remembered name of Plattner. The child took the flowers and laid them reverently on the stone.

"It seems to me almost like arriving at the end of a pilgrimage," said Ronald, "when I stand by the grave of a man of science. Perhaps you knew him, mein Herr?"

"He was my pupil."

"Whew!" thought Ronald, "that makes my friend here a centenarian at least."

"My pupil and friend," the feeble voice went on; "and, more than that, my daughter's first lover, and only one."

"Ach so!" drawled Ronald.

"And now, on her death-day, I take these poor flowers from her to him, as I have done all these years."

Something in the pathetic earnestness of his companion touched Ronald Wyde, and he forthwith took his hands out of his pockets, and didn't try to whistle inaudibly—which was a great deal for him to do.

"I know Plattner well by his works," he said; "I once studied mineralogy for nearly a month."

"You love science, then?"

"Yes; like every thing else, for diversion."

"It was different with him," quavered the old man, pointing unsteadily to the head-stone. "Science grew to be his one passion, and many discoveries rewarded him for his devotion. He was groping on the track of a far greater achievement when he died."

"May I ask what it was?" said Ronald, now fairly interested.

"The creation and isolation of the principle of Life!"

This was too much for Ronald Wyde; down dived his restless hands into his trowsers' pockets again, and the gröschen rattled as merrily as before.

"I have made quite a study of biology, and all that sort of thing," said he; "and, although a good deal of a skeptic, and inclined to follow Huxley, I can't bring myself to conceive of life without organism. Such theorizing is, to my mind, on a par with the illogical search for the philosopher's stone and a perpetual motor."

The old man's eyes sparkled as he turned full upon Ronald.

"You dismiss the subject very airily, my young friend," he cried; "but let me tell you that I—I, whom you see here— have grappled with such problems through a weary century, and have conquered one of them."

"And that one is—"

"The one that conquered Plattner!"

"Do I understand you to claim that you have discovered the life-principle?"

"Yes."

"Will you permit an utter stranger to inquire what is its nature?"

"Certainly. It is twofold. The ultimate principle of life is carbon; the cause of its combination with water, or rather with the two gaseous elements of water, and the development of organized existence therefrom, is electricity."

Ronald Wyde shrugged his broad shoulders a little, and absently replied,

"All I can say, mein Herr, is, that you've got the bulge on me."

"I beg your pardon—"

"Excuse me; I unconsciously translated an Americanism. I mean that I don't quite understand you."

"Which means that you do not believe me. It is but natural at your age, when one doubts as if by instinct. Would you be convinced?"

"Nothing would please me better."

With the same painful effort as before, the old man straightened himself and made a piercing clairvoyant examination into and through Ronald Wyde's eyes, as if reading the brain beyond them.

"I think I can trust you," he mumbled at last. "Come with me."

Leaning on the young girl's arm, the old philosopher faltered through the cemetery and into the town, followed by Wyde, his hands again pocketed for safety. Groups of released church-goers, sermon-fed, met them, and once in a while some stout burgher would nod patronizingly to Ronald's guides, and get in response a shaky, sidelong roll of the old man's head, as if it were mounted on a weak spiral spring. Further on they intersected a knot of students, who eyed them askance and exchanged remarks in an undertone. Keeping on deeper into the foul heart of the town, they passed through swarms of idle children playing sportlessly, as poverty is apt to play, in the dank shadows of the narrow street. They seemed incited to mirth and ribaldry by the sight of Ronald's new friend, and one even ventured to hurl a clod at him; but this striking Ronald instead, and he facing promptly to the hostile quarter from whence it came, caused a sudden slinking of the crowd into unknown holes, like a horde of rats, and the street was for a time empty save for the little party that threaded it. Ronald began to think that the old man's sanity was gravely called in doubt by the townsfolk, and would readily have backed out of his adventure but for the curiosity that had now got the upper hand of him.

Presently the old man sidled into a dingy doorway, like a tired beast run to earth, and Ronald followed him, not without a wish that the architect had provided for a more efficient lighting of the sombre passage-way in which he found himself. A sharp turn to the right after a dozen groping-paces, a narrow stairway, a bump or two against unexpected saliences of rough mortared wall, two steps upward and one very surprising step downward through a cavernous doorway that took away Ronald's breath for a moment, and sent it back again with a hot, creeping wave of sudden perspiration all over him, as is the way with missteps, and two more sharp turns, brought the three into a black no-thoroughfare of a hall, whose further end was closed by a locked door. The girl here rubbed a brimstone abomination of a match into a malodorous green glow, and by its help the old man got a tortuous key into the snaky opening in the great lock, creakily shot back its bolt, swung open the door, and motioned Ronald to enter.

He found himself in a long and rather narrow room, with a high ceiling, duskily lighted by three wide windows that were thickly webbed and dusted, like ancestral bottles of fine crusty Port. A veritable den it was, filled with what seemed to be the wrecks of philosophical apparatus dating back two or three generations—ill-fated ventures on the treacherous main of science. Here a fat-bellied alembic lolled lazily over in a gleamy sand-bath, like a beach-lost galleon at ebb-tide; and there a heap of broken porcelain-tubing and shreds of crucibles lay like bleaching ship-ribs on a sullen shore. Beyond, by the middle window, stood a furnace, fireless, and clogged with gray ashes. Two or three solid old-time tables, built when joiners were more lavish of oaken timber than nowadays, stood hopelessly littered with retorts, filtering funnels, lamps, ringstands, and squat-beakers of delicate glass, caked with long-dried sediment, all alike dust-smirched. Ronald involuntarily sought for some huge Chaldaic tome, conveniently open at a favorite spell, or a handy crocodile or two dangling from the square beams overhead, but saw nothing more formidable than a stray volume of Kant's *Critique of Pure Reason*. Taking this up and glancing at its fly-leaf, he saw a name written in spidery German script, almost illegible from its shakiness—"Max Lebensfunke."

"Your name?" he asked.

"Yes, mein Herr," answered the old man, taking the volume and caressing it like a live thing in his fumbling hands. "This book was given to me by the great Kant himself," he added.

Reverently replacing it, he advanced a few steps toward the middle of the room. Ronald followed, and, turning away from the windows, looked further around him. In striking contrast to the undisturbed disorder, so redolent of middle-age alchemy, was the big table that flanked the laboratory through its whole length. It began with a powerful galvanic battery, succeeded by a wiry labyrinth of coils and helices, with little keys in front of them like a telegraph-office retired from business; these gave place to many-necked jars wired together by twos and threes, like oath-bound patriots plotting treason; beyond them stood a great glass globe, connected with a sizable air-pump, and filled with a complexity of shiny wires and glassware; next loomed up a huge induction-magnet, carefully insulated on solid glass supports; and at the further extremity of the table lay—a corpse.

Ronald Wyde, in spite of his many-sided experience of dissection-rooms, and morgues, and other ghastlinesses to which he had long since accustomed himself from principle, drew back at the sight—perhaps because he had come to this strange place to clutch the world-old mystery of the life-essence, and found himself, instead, confronted on its threshold by the equal mystery of death.

Herr Lebensfunke smiled feebly at this movement.

"A subject received this morning from Berlin," he said, in answer to Wyde's look of inquiry. "A sad piece of extravagance, mein Herr—a luxury to which I can rarely afford to treat myself."

Ronald Wyde bent over the body and looked into its face. A rough, red face, that had seemingly seen forty years of low-lived dissipation. The blotched skin and bleary eyes told of debauchery and drunkenness, and a slight alcoholic fœtidness was unpleasantly perceptible, as from the breath of one who sleeps away the effects of a carouse.

"I hope you don't think of restoring this soaked specimen to life?" said Ronald.

"That is still beyond me," answered the old man, mournfully. "As yet I have not created life of a higher grade than that of the lowest zoöphytes."

"Do you claim to have done as much as that?"

"It is not an idle claim," said Herr Lebensfunke, solemnly. "Look at this, if you doubt."

"This" was the great crystal globe that rose from the middle of the long table, and dominated its lesser accessories, as some great dome swells above the clustered houses of a town. Tubes passing through its walls met in a smaller central globe half filled with a colorless liquid. Beneath this, and half encircling it, was an intricate maze of bright wire; and two other wires dipped into it, touching the surface of the liquid with their platinum tips. Within the liquid pulsed a shapeless mass of almost transparent spongy tissue.

"You see an aggregation of cells possessed of life—of a low order, it is true, but none the less life," said the philosopher, proudly. "These were created from water chemically pure, with the exception of a trace of ammonia, and impregnated with liquid carbon, by the combined action of heat and induced electricity, in vacuo. Look!"

He pressed one of the keys before him. Presently the wire began to glow with a faint light, which increased in intensity till the coil flamed into pure whiteness. Removing his finger, the current ceased to flow, and the wire grew rapidly cool.

"I passed the whole strength of sixty cups through it to show you its action. Ordinarily, with one or two carbon cells, and refining the current by triple induction, the temperature is barely blood-warm."

"Pardon an interruption," said Ronald. "You spoke of liquid carbon; does it exist?"

"Yes; here is some in this phial. See it—how pure, how transparent! how it loves and hoards the light!" The old man held the phial up as he spoke, and turned it round and round. "See how it flashes! No wonder, for it is the diamond, liquid and uncrystallized. Think how these fools of men have called diamonds precious above all gems through these many weary years, and showered them on their kings, or tossed them to their mistresses' feet, never dreaming that the silly stone they lauded was inert, crystallized life!"

"Can't you crystallize diamonds yourself?" asked Wyde, "and make Freiberg a Golconda and yourself a Crœsus?"

"It could be done, after the lapse of thousands of years," replied Herr Lebensfunke. "Place undiluted liquid carbon in that inner globe, keep the coil at a white heat, and if Adam had started the process, his heir-at-law would have a koh-i-noor today, and a nice lawsuit for its possession."

Ronald Wyde bent toward the globe once more and examined the throbbing mass closely, whistling softly meanwhile.

"If you can create this cellular life, why not develop it still higher into an organism?"

"Because I can only create life—not soul. Years ago I was a freethinker, now my discoveries have made me a deist; for

Ronald Wyde looked once more at the sodden features of the corpse, and smiled lugubriously.

"A mighty shabby old customer," he said, "and I doubt if I could feel at home in his skin; but I'm willing to risk it for the sake of the novelty of the thing."

The old philosopher's thin face lit up with pleasure.

"You consent, then?" he chuckled in his womanish treble.

"Of course I do. Begin at once, and have done with it."

"Not now, mein Herr; some modifications must be made in the connections—mere matters of detail. Come again tonight."

"At what hour?"

"At ten. Mein Vögelein, show the Herr the way out."

The girl, who had been moving restlessly about the room all this time, with her wild brown eyes fixed now on Ronald, now on the old man, and oftener in a shy, inquisitive stare on the corpse, lit a dusty chemical lamp and led the way down the awkward passages and stairs. Ronald tried to start a conversation with her as he followed.

"You are too young, my birdling, to be accustomed to such sights as this upstairs."

"Birdling is not too young, she's almost fourteen," said the girl, proudly. "And she likes it, too; it makes her think of mother. Mother went to sleep on that table, mein Herr."

"Poor thing! she's half-witted," thought Wyde as he passed into the street. "By-by, birdie."

Home he walked briskly, to be met under his flaming balcony by Lottchen's kindly afternoon greeting. How had mein Herr passed his Sabbath? she asked.

"Quietly enough, Lottchen. I met an old philosopher in the God's-Acre, and went home with him to his shop. Have you ever heard of Herr Doctor Lebensfunke?"

"Yes, mein Herr. Wrong here, they say;" and she tapped her wide, round German forehead, and lifted her eyes expressively heavenward.

"Sold himself to the devil, eh?" asked Wyde.

Lottchen was not quite sure on that point. Some said one thing, and some another. There was undoubtedly a devil, else how could good Doctor Luther have thrown his inkstand at him? But he had never been seen in Doctor Lebensfunke's neighborhood; and, on the whole, Lottchen was inclined to attribute the Herr Doctor's trouble to an indefinable something whose nature was broadly hinted at by more tapping of the forehead.

Ronald Wyde mounted the stairs, locked himself in his room, and wished himself out of the scrape he was getting into. But, being in for it now, he lit a cigar, and tried to fancy the processes he would have to go through, and how he, a natty and respectable young fellow, would look and feel in a drunkard's skin. His conjectures being too foggily outlined to please him, he put them aside, and waited impatiently enough for ten o'clock.

A moonlight walk through the low streets, transfigured by the silver gleam into fairy vistas—all but the odor—brought him to Herr Lebensfunke's house. Simple birdling, on the lookout for him, piloted him through the unsafe channel, and brought him to anchor in the dimly-lit room.

"All is ready," said the philosopher, as he trembled forward and shook Ronald's hand. "See here." Zig-zags of silk-bound wire squirmed hither and thither from the life-magnet. Two of them ended in carbon points. "And here, too, my young friend, is your new finger."

It lay, detached, in the central globe, and on its severed end atoms of protoplasm were already clustered. "Literally a second-hand article," thought Ronald; but, not venturing to translate the idiom, he only bowed and said, "Ach so!" which means any thing and every thing in German.

It was not without a very natural sinking of the heart that Ronald Wyde divested himself of his clothing, and took his gave him time to think connectedly over what had happened, and what he now was. His fellow-passengers cast him sidelong looks, and gave him a wide berth. Even the quaint, flat-arched windows of one pane each, that winked out of the red-tiled roofs like sleepy eyes, seemed to leer drunkenly at him as they scudded by.

Ronald Wyde's account of those days in Dresden was vague and misty. He crept along the bustling streets of that sombre, gray city, that seemed to look more natural by cloud-light than in the full sunshine, feeling continually within him a struggle between the two incompatible natures now so strangely blended. Each day he kept up the contest manfully, passing by the countless beer-cellars and drinking-booths with an assumption of firmness and resolution that oozed slowly away toward nightfall, when the animal body of the late Hans Kraut would contrive to get the better of the ani-mating principle of Ronald Wyde; the refined nature would yield to the toper's brute-craving, with an awful sense of its deep degradation in so succumbing, and, before midnight, Hans was gloriously drunk, to Ronald's intense grief.

Time passed somehow. He had memories of sunny loung-es on the Bruhl'sche Terrace, looking on the turbid flow of the eddied Elbe, and watching the little steamboats that buzzed up and down the city's flanks, settling now and then, like gad-flies, to drain it of a few drops of its human life. Well-known friends, whose hands he had grasped not a week before, passed him unheedingly; all save one, who eyed him for a moment, said "Poor devil!" in an undertone, and dropped a silber-gro' into his maimed hand. He felt glad of even this lame sympa-thy in his lowness; but most of all he prized the moistened glance of pity that flashed upon him from the great dark eyes of a lovely girl who passed him now and then as he slouched along. Once, a being as degraded and scurvy as his own out-ward self, turned to him, called him "Dutzbruder," asked him how he left them all in Berlin, stared at Ronald's blank look of non-recognition, and passed on with a muttered curse on his own stupidity in mistaking a stranger, in broad daylight, for his crony Kraut.

Another memory was of the strange lassitude that seemed to almost paralyze him after even moderate exertion, and caused him to drop exhausted on a bench on the terrace when he had shuffled over less than half its length. More than once the suspicion crept upon him that only a portion of his vitality now remained to him, and that its greater part lay mysteriously coiled in Herr Lebensfunke's life-magnet. And this, in turn, broadened into a doubting distrust of the Herr himself—a dread lest the old man might in some way appropriate this stock of life to his own use, and so renew his fast-expiring lease for a score or two of years to come. At last this dread grew so painfully definite, that he hurried back to Freiberg a day before his appointed time, and once more found his twofold self wandering through its devious streets.

It was long after dark, and a thin rain slanted on the slippery stones, as he again made his way through the deserted and sleepy paths of the town to the old philosopher's house. He was wet, chilled, weary, and sick enough at heart as he leaned against the cold stone doorway and waited for an answer to his knock. The plash of the heavier rain-drops from the tiled leaves was the only sound he heard for many minutes, until, at last, pattering feet neared him on the inside, and a child's voice asked who was there. To his friendly response the door was opened half-wide, and Vögelein's blank, pretty face peeped through.

Was Herr Lebensfunke at home? No; he had said that he wasn't at home; but then, she thought he was in the long room where mamma went to sleep. Could he be seen? No, she thought not; he was very tired, and, in her own—Vögelein's—opinion, he was going to sleep too, just as mamma did. And the wizened little face, with its eldritch eyes and tangled hair, was withdrawn, and the door began to close. Ronald forced himself inside, and grasped the child's arm.

"Vögelein, don't you know me?"

The girl, in nowise startled, gravely set her flickering candle on the door-step, looked up at him wonderingly, as if he were an exhibition, and said she thought not, unless he had been asleep on the table.

"Good heavens!" cried Ronald, "can this child talk of nothing but people asleep on a table?"

But, as he spoke, a thought whirred through his brain. He drew the poor half-witted thing close to him and asked:

"Can Vögelein tell me something about mamma, and how she went to sleep?"

The child rambled on, pleased to find a listener to her foolish prattle. All he could connect into a narrative was, that the girl's mother, some seven or eight years before, had been drained of her life by the awful magnet, and that, as the child said, "the Herr Doctor ever since had talked just like mamma."

His dread was well founded, then. The old man's one dream and aim was to prolong his wretched life; could he doubt that he would not now make use of the means he had so unwisely thrown in his way? He turned about, half maddened.

"Girl!" he cried, "I must see the old man! Where is he?"

He couldn't see him, she whined. He was asleep up there, on the table. At one o'clock he had said he would wake up.

He pushed past her, mounted to the long room, pressed open the unfastened door, and entered.

The old man and the corpse of his former self lay together under the light of a lamp that swung from the beam overhead. An insulated carbon point was directed to each white, still breast. From the old man's hand a cord ran to a key beyond, arranged to make or break connection at a touch. By it stood a clock, with a simple mechanism attached that bore upon a second key like the first, evidently planned to press upon it when the hands should mark a given hour. The child had said that he would wake at one, and it was now past midnight.

Ronald Wyde comprehended it all now. The wily old man's feeble life had been withdrawn into the great magnet, and mixed therein with what remained of his own. In less than an hour the key would fall, and the double stream would flow into and animate his young body, which would then wake to renewed life; while the cast-off shell beside it, worn to utter uselessness by a toilsome century, would be left to moulder as a mothed garment.

Surely no time was to be lost; his life depended upon instant action. And yet, comprehending this, he went to work slowly, and as a somnambulist might, acting almost by instinct, and well knowing that a blunder now meant irrevocable death.

Carefully disengaging the cord from the old man's yet warm grasp, and setting the carbon point aside, he lifted the shrivelled corpse and bore it away, to cast it on the white rubbish-heap in one corner. Returning to his work, he stripped himself, and laid down in the old man's place. As he did so, the distant Minster bells rang the three-quarters.

Was there yet time?

He braced his shoulders firmly against the brass plate under them, and moved the carbon point steadily back to its place, with its tip resting on his breast; the silk-wrapped wire that dangled between it and the magnet quivering, as he did so, as with conscious life. Drawing a long breath, he tightened the cord, and heard a faint click as the key snapped down.

The same sharp sting as before instantly pricked his breast, tingling thrills pulsed over him, beats of light and shadow swept before his eyes, and he lost all consciousness. For how long he knew not. At last he felt, rather than saw, the lamp-rays flickering above him, and opened his eyes as though waking from a tired sleep. Sitting up, he gave a fearful look around him, as if dreading what he might see. The drunkard's body lay stretched and motionless beside him, and the clock marked three. He was saved!

Slipping down from his perilous bed, he resumed the old familiar garments that belonged to him as Ronald Wyde, shuddering with emotion as he did so. Only pausing to give one look at the pale heap in the shadowy corner, and at the other sleeper under the now dying lamp, he quitted the room and locked its heavy door upon the two silent guardians of its life-secrets. When he reached the street, he found the rain had ceased to drop, and that the cold stars blinked over the slumbrous town.

Before noon he had taken leave of Frau Spritzkrapfen, turned buxom Lottchen scarlet all over by a hearty, sudden, farewell-kiss, and was far on his way from Freiberg, with its red-vined balcony and its dark laboratory, never again to visit it or them. And as the busy engine toiled and shrieked, and with each beat of its mighty steam-heart carried him further away, his thoughts flew back and clustered around witless, brown-eyed birdling. Poor child, he never learned her fate.

I heard this strange story from its hero, one sunny summer morning as we swept over the meadowy reaches of the Erie Railway, or hung along the cliffside by the wooded windings of the Susquehanna. When he had ended it, he smiled languidly, and, showing me his still-mutilated hand, said that the old doctor's job had been a sad bungle, after all. In fact, the only physical proof that remained to verify his story, was a curved blue spot where the ingoing current from the magnet had carried particles from the carbon point and lodged them beneath the skin. Psychologically, he was sadly mixed up, he said; for, since that time, he had felt that four lives were joined in him—his own, the remnant of Herr Lebensfunke's miserable hoard merged in that of poor birdling's mother, and, last of all, Hans Kraut's.

He left the cars soon afterward at Binghamton, watchfully followed by a stout, shabby man with a three days' beard stubbling his chin, who had occupied the seat in front of us, and had turned now and then to listen for a moment to Ronald's rapid narration.

A week later, and I heard that he was dead—having committed suicide in a fit of delirium soon after his admission to the Binghamton Inebriate Asylum. The attendant who made him ready for burial noticed a singular blue mark on his left breast, that looked, he said, a little like a horseshoe magnet.

AN INHABITANT OF CARCOSA

by Ambrose Bierce

*F*OR *there be divers sorts of death—some wherein the body remaineth; and in some it vanisheth quite away with the spirit. This commonly occurreth only in solitude (such is God's will) and, none seeing the end, we say the man is lost, or gone on a long journey—which indeed he hath; but sometimes it hath happened in sight of many, as abundant testimony showeth. In one kind of death the spirit also dieth, and this it hath been known to do while yet the body was in vigor for many years. Sometimes, as is veritably attested, it dieth with the body, but after a season is raised up again in that place where the body did decay.*

Pondering these words of Hali (whom God rest) and questioning their full meaning, as one who, having an intimation, yet doubts if there be not something behind, other than that which he has discerned, I noted not whither I had strayed until a sudden chill wind striking my face revived in me a sense of my surroundings. I observed with astonishment that everything seemed unfamiliar. On every side of me stretched a bleak and desolate expanse of plain, covered with a tall overgrowth of sere grass, which rustled and whistled in the autumn wind with heaven knows what mysterious and disquieting suggestion. Protruded at long intervals above it, stood strangely shaped and somber-colored rocks, which seemed to have an understanding with one another and to exchange looks of uncomfortable significance, as if they had reared their heads to watch the issue of some foreseen event. A few blasted trees here and there appeared as leaders in this malevolent conspiracy of silent expectation.

The day, I thought, must be far advanced, though the sun was invisible; and although sensible that the air was raw and chill my consciousness of that fact was rather mental than physical—I had no feeling of discomfort. Over all the dismal landscape a canopy of low, lead-colored clouds hung like a visible curse. In all this there were a menace and a portent—a hint of evil, an intimation of doom. Bird, beast, or insect there was none. The wind sighed in the bare branches of the dead trees and the gray grass bent to whisper its dread secret to the earth; but no other sound nor motion broke the awful repose of that dismal place.

I observed in the herbage a number of weather-worn stones, evidently shaped with tools. They were broken, covered with moss and half sunken in the earth. Some lay prostrate, some leaned at various angles, none was vertical. They were obviously headstones of graves, though the graves themselves no longer existed as either mounds or depressions; the years had leveled all. Scattered here and there, more massive blocks showed where some pompous tomb or ambitious monument had once flung its feeble defiance at oblivion. So old seemed these relics, these vestiges of vanity and memorials of affection and piety, so battered and worn and stained—so neglected, deserted, forgotten the place, that I could not help thinking myself the discoverer of the burial-ground of a prehistoric race of men whose very name was long extinct.

Filled with these reflections, I was for some time heedless of the sequence of my own experiences, but soon I thought,

"How came I hither?" A moment's reflection seemed to make this all clear and explain at the same time, though in a disquieting way, the singular character with which my fancy had invested all that I saw or heard. I was ill. I remembered now that I had been prostrated by a sudden fever, and that my family had told me that in my periods of delirium I had constantly cried out for liberty and air, and had been held in bed to prevent my escape out-of-doors. Now I had eluded the vigilance of my attendants and had wandered hither to—to where? I could not conjecture. Clearly I was at a considerable distance from the city where I dwelt—the ancient and famous city of Carcosa.

No signs of human life were anywhere visible nor audible; no rising smoke, no watchdog's bark, no lowing of cattle, no shouts of children at play—nothing but that dismal burial-place, with its air of mystery and dread, due to my own disordered brain. Was I not becoming again delirious, there beyond human aid? Was it not indeed all an illusion of my madness? I called aloud the names of my wives and sons, reached out my hands in search of theirs, even as I walked among the crumbling stones and in the withered grass.

A noise behind me caused me to turn about. A wild animal—a lynx—was approaching. The thought came to me: If I break down here in the desert—if the fever return and I fail, this beast will be at my throat. I sprang toward it, shouting. It trotted tranquilly by within a hand's breadth of me and disappeared behind a rock.

A moment later a man's head appeared to rise out of the ground a short distance away. He was ascending the farther slope of a low hill whose crest was hardly to be distinguished from the general level. His whole figure soon came into view against the background of gray cloud. He was half naked, half clad in skins. His hair was unkempt, his beard long and ragged. In one hand he carried a bow and arrow; the other held a blazing torch with a long trail of black smoke. He walked slowly and with caution, as if he feared falling into some open grave concealed by the tall grass. This strange apparition surprised but did not alarm, and taking such a course as to intercept him I met him almost face to face, accosting him with the familiar salutation, "God keep you."

He gave no heed, nor did he arrest his pace.

"Good stranger," I continued, "I am ill and lost. Direct me, I beseech you, to Carcosa."

The man broke into a barbarous chant in an unknown tongue, passing on and away.

An owl on the branch of a decayed tree hooted dismally and was answered by another in the distance. Looking upward, I saw through a sudden rift in the clouds Aldebaran and the Hyades! In all this there was a hint of night—the lynx, the man with the torch, the owl. Yet I saw—I saw even the stars in absence of the darkness. I saw, but was apparently not seen nor heard. Under what awful spell did I exist?

I seated myself at the root of a great tree, seriously to consider what it were best to do. That I was mad I could no longer doubt, yet recognized a ground of doubt in the conviction. Of fever I had no trace. I had, withal, a sense of exhilaration and vigor altogether unknown to me—a feeling of mental and physical exaltation. My senses seemed all alert; I could feel the air as a ponderous substance; I could hear the silence.

A great root of the giant tree against whose trunk I leaned as I sat held inclosed in its grasp a slab of stone, a part of which protruded into a recess formed by another root. The stone was thus partly protected from the weather, though greatly decomposed. Its edges were worn round, its corners eaten away, its surface deeply furrowed and scaled. Glittering particles of mica were visible in the earth about it—vestiges of its decomposition. This stone had apparently marked the grave out of which the tree had sprung ages ago. The tree's exacting roots had robbed the grave and made the stone a prisoner.

A sudden wind pushed some dry leaves and twigs from the uppermost face of the stone; I saw the low-relief letters of an inscription and bent to read it. God in Heaven! *my* name in full!—the date of *my* birth!—the date of *my* death!

A level shaft of light illuminated the whole side of the tree as I sprang to my feet in terror. The sun was rising in the rosy east. I stood between the tree and his broad red disk—no shadow darkened the trunk!

A chorus of howling wolves saluted the dawn. I saw them sitting on their haunches, singly and in groups, on the summits of irregular mounds and tumuli filling a half of my desert prospect and extending to the horizon. And then I knew that these were ruins of the ancient and famous city of Carcosa.

Such are the facts imparted to the medium Bayrolles by the spirit Hoseib Alar Robardin.

AMONG THE DEAD

by James H. Connelly

[I must write down here nothing of myself; but only that which is given me to write. Who thus commands me I see not, nor do I hear or know him. But these thoughts, and the words that clothe them, are his, not mine. They are formed in my brain, but not by me. I hold the pen—nothing more.]

WHEN they found me, in the morning, I was cold and still. "He is dead!," they said, as they put back the heavy silken curtains of my bed and let the chill gray light fall upon my face. "He is dead!," they said, "past pain, and care, and sorrow. He is at rest. But, for the sake of those he leaves behind, it is not well that men should know how he died." So the complaisant physician told the untruth, and the world believed it. But I, pulseless, breathless, lying there before them and hearing their speech, knew that the deed was my own. I had been weary of the strife of life; sad from that which had been; fearful of what was to come.

With ceremonious pomp, befitting one in my station among men, they buried me. Emblems of woe and symbols of mourning were all about me and piled upon my coffin. There was one who stood at my low-lying head and spake words of eulogy over me. They were mockeries. I, hearing them and conscious of the truth of what had been, knew my deep undeserving. Alas! for the frozen lips that could not gainsay his smooth flatteries.

Then deep-toned waves of solemn harmony awoke responsive trembling in the walls about and the high arch overhead, and even thrilled me where I lay in state that all might look their last upon me. Amid the many who thus gazed and cared naught were a few who loved me, whose tears dropped on my face as they bent to kiss my icy brow; and a passion of pity for their grief that I had brought upon them, and a vain longing to return to life that I might comfort them, came to me like a throb of pain.

Then they shut out the light from me and carried me away to my last resting place. And all the way, though I lay there in darkness, with unseeing eyes, deaf ears, and speechless lips, I saw the infinite loveliness of the dear living world I had abandoned, heard its myriad sounds of life blended into a choral of thanksgiving for the joy of mere existence, and, out of my remorseful yearning to again be part of it all, uttered a shriek of agony—heard and echoed only in my own soul.

Dully rumbled the earth falling upon my coffin; high in a mound above they piled it. Down where they had put me, all was still, and cool, and damp. When their work was done, they went away. Then, all was silence. The momentary pang of desire for life had passed, and I was resigned. Voluntarily I had died that I might sleep, at once and forever. But I could not sleep. Every sense was keenly awake. And now I knew that I would never sleep, that death is an eternal wakening. And that wakening, for me at least, was in the grave. A nameless horror, unspeakable and vast, overwhelmed me.

Lonesome and dark, at first, my surroundings seemed. But I grew accustomed to the obscurity, could in some measure penetrate it, and a consciousness grew upon me that I was not alone. Had I neighbors down there in the ground? Were others awake near me? If so, could I know of them, and in what forms might they appear to me? With appalling shapes my fancy filled the gloom that smothered me. Dimly I felt already that I was not as those by whom death had been unsought; that I un-bidden, had intruded upon them before my time had come to know them, and I feared them—as if I had still been alive.

But in much time they came no nearer to me, and were no more distinct than are vaguely-defined superior depths of shadow where all is shade. And I had nothing to do but lie still and think, always to think of myself, sometimes with pity, again with contempt, and often with rage, for I was very weary of being there and of thinking that I was so of my own will.

And all this while Nature was reclaiming from me that which belonged to her,—my form of clay. How hideous and loathsome it became to me! Yet I was bound in it, inseparable from it. With each fibre, in every tissue of the horrible mass that it became, my semi-material second self—my astral body—was inextricably interblended, and from it, as now I knew, could only be freed by its mouldering away and returning to the elements whence it had been drawn. Earth; air; water; each individually pure, yet how unspeakably revolting down there in the grave in their process of resolvement. And the demon Worm; resting not and sated never; who but the dead themselves can know what tortures he inflicts, to which all agony of living flesh is joy? Yet to all these dread abominations, their maddening defilement and their pain, the senses of my astral body, keener than those of men who live yet all ways like to theirs, thrilled with extremest consciousness. Oh! the unutterable misery, the loathing and the horror of that awful prison house.

With the slow progress of the changes thus upon me wrought, my concious second self by slow degrees gained freedom. Then I knew what was about me; penetrated with my sight the long, thick-peopled lines of houses of the dead, and knew my neighbors. And I saw that all graves were not fearsome prisons, hells, like mine. In some lay bodies turning back to earth, wherein no soul was pent. Souls whose brief earthly lives were all too short to know of evil purpose or of sin, and those who worthily had lived out their allotted days till, spent with kindly labor of good deeds, therein had left their earthly forms,—for them the eternal wakening was restful peace in realms of light. But those inhabiting there below, with me, were souls, like mine, impatient of their task of life. Not alone is he self-slayer who by violence upon himself abbreviates his earthly span. To the same fate attain the grasping souls who, by excess of toil for love of gain or satisfaction of ambition, and the sensual ones who, through abandonment to fleshly lusts and vices, will to the grave before their time. Such were my company.

Ah! what democracy there is in death! In that drear nether world, masks are unknown, efforts at pretence vain. Each naked stands, transparent to his fellow's gaze, each meriting the scorn of all and shunning each the other, self-reproach and vain regret in every one consuming thought of pity for his fellow's woe. Madness, that knows not, and despair, that is past caring, may not mercifully enter there. Man must be conscious, and not quite devoid of hope—even though that hope be but of some other kind of hell—, that he may suffer all the more. How long! Oh! Lord of Life, how long! until such hope springs up as can some comfort bring; until the end appears, remote but sure, when, through destruction total of the bonds of clay, deliverance shall be. To all, at length, that hope appears, and, as the years roll on, by progress slow is realized.

Up once again, when little more, if aught, than formless dust is left behind, the freed soul rises to the world of living men. So I passed, leaving one woe to learn another not less keen in anguish.

A weary time I yet remained within the narrow confines of the city of the dead, as if some potent spell still linked my soul unto the elements that had been mine; and all my days were filled with sights and sounds of human grief; and all my nights a myriad spectral forms, Remorse, and Sin, and Shame, and Fear—that had been human,—and the baleful bodiless things that hate men's souls, surrounded me. The dew upon the rank grass there seemed tears; the dreary moanings of the wind in the bare branches overhead were lamentations; and the moon's cold light, crossed by swift-moving clouds, did seem to shudder at our ghastly multitude.

Stronger and stronger on me grew desire to look again on those I loved in life, until at length my will sufficed to burst the bonds that held me near my grave, and I returned to them,—so plunging in another hell.

On them I saw descend, though far remote, the dire results of the rash deed that I had done, the curse that I had wrought; yet, in comparison, the atom to the Infinite is as my love and sympathy for them had been in life, to what it now was magnified. And herein lay my hell. Their perils and their griefs, cares and temptations, all to me were known, spread clear before me like an open scroll; and I could even read the fate awaiting them; behold the merciless hands—to them invisible—up-reaching from the abysms where souls are lost, to drag them down; mark their vain struggles to escape, and with unerring surety presage their defeat. And, all the while, my knowledge was no less of how they could be helped and saved,—yet I was powerless. Words framed by my immaterial lips made no vibration to their ears; the anguish in my eyes they saw not; thoughts that I strove to force upon their minds in passive sleep distorted were to idle dreams; and the malignant creatures of the air encircling 'round mocked at my impotence.

The end has come at last. Contrition, for rebellion past against the perfect wisdom of the Infinite Will, from Infinite Justice gains surcease of punishment, the severance of all earthly ties, and rest, and peace.

THE SERPENT'S BLOOD

by W. Q. Judge

IT was an old and magic island. Many centuries before, the great good Adepts had landed on its shores from the West and established for a while the Truth. But even they could not stay the relentless tread of fate, and knew that this was only a halting place, a spot where should be concentrated spiritual power sufficiently strong to remain as a leaven for several cycles, and that should be a base upon which in long ages after ages might be erected again the spiritual temple of truth. These blessed beings remained there for centuries uncounted, and saw arise out of the adjoining seas other lands, first of soft mud that afterwards hardened into rocks and earth. They taught the people and found them apt students, and from their number drew many disciples who were full of zeal as well as patience and faith. Among the least of those I was, and toiled long and earnestly through successive lives upon the Island. And the Island came to be known as the Isle of Destiny, from mysterious future events foretold for it by the greatest of the Adepts and their seers.

Yet I succeeded not in reaching the point when I could hope to pass on from the Island with the teachers, who said that at a certain day they must travel away to other lands, leaving behind them their blessing to those who willingly remained of the disciples; those who rebelled had still to remain, but without the aid and comfort of the benediction of the blessed ones.

At last the day of separation came and the kingly guides departed, leaving well established the true religion and practice. Yet we all knew that even that must have its decay, in which perhaps even some of us might have a hand, but the centre of power was not to depart from the Island until its destiny should be accomplished; the power might be hidden, but it would remain latent until the time arrived.

Many years came and went; still I found myself upon the Island again and again reincarnated. With sorrow I saw the ancient practices overlooked and different views prevailing. It was the power of the serpent.

On one well-known mountain the Masters had placed a gem, and at the mountain's base a tower. I knew that mountain well, and saw it every day from the tower at some distance away where my own duties lay. I was present when the wonderful gem was placed upon the mountain, and of all those who saw the grand event, I alone remembered. Since that day many centuries had rolled away, and the other disciples, reincarnated there also, had forgotten the event but knew of the gem. Some of them who in other lives had been my servants in the tower were now my earthly superiors because they had devoted their minds to formal outward power, which is only the weak symbol of the reality that should exist within. And so the tradition alone remained, but the diamond now blazed less brilliantly than in the days when I first knew it. By night its rays shot up into the heavens, and the priests month after month tried ceremonies and prayers in vain, in order to cause it to burst forth in all the glory of its pristine days. They knew that such a blaze was a possibility—indeed an old prophecy—but that was all they could tell, and were ignorant of the remainder of it, which, if they had known, perhaps none of their ceremonies would have been performed. It was that the great and glorious blaze of light from the mountain diamond would only take place after the last drop of the serpent's blood was spilled upon the Island, and that then the diamond itself would never again be found upon the rock where it had rested for so many ages. And I alone of them all knew this; but I knew not where the serpent was to be found. His influence was felt and seen, for in the early days he alone was the sole reptile that eluded pursuit, as his birth was due to the evil thoughts of a wandering black magician who had landed for a week upon the Island so long before that the priests had no record of it. This serpent had to be killed and his blood spilled upon the ground to remove forever the last trace of the evil done by the magician, and for that event only was the diamond kept upon the mountain through the power of the good Adepts who had put it there. It preserved the germ of truth from the serpent's breath, and would not be needed when he was destroyed. Had the priests known this, no cere-monies for increasing its brilliancy would have been tried, as they would rather suffer the serpent's influence than lose the gem. Indeed, they believed that their tenure of power was in some way connected with the diamond mountain. They were right. I knew the fatal result for them when I succeeded in discovering the place of the serpent.

Day after day and long into the darkness of the night, I meditated and peered into every corner of the Island. At the full moon when the diamond grew a little clearer, I saw the slimy traces of the serpent upon the Island but could never find his lair. At last one night a fellow-student who had passed on before me with those by whom the diamond had been set, and who now and again returned through the aid to help his old friend, came to see me and, as he was going away, said, "Look at the foot of the mountain."

So near the sacred diamond I had never thought it possible the foul reptile could be found; and yet it was there, through the evil nature of the high-priest, he had taken up his secure retreat. I looked and saw him at the foot, breathing venom and black clouds of the soul's despair.

The great day of ceremonies for the diamond was again at hand, and I determined that then should witness the death of the serpent and the last bright shining of the diamond.

The morning broke clear and warm. Great throngs of people crowded about the mountain-temple, expectant of some great result from the ceremonies. It seemed as if these natural psychics felt within them that the diamond would burst forth with its ancient light, and yet every now and then a fear was expressed that in its greatest beauty it would be lost to them forever.

It was my turn to officiate at the ceremony after the high priest, and I alone was aware that the serpent had crawled even into the temple and was coiled up behind the shrine. I determined to seize him and, calling upon our ancient master, strangle him there and spill his blood upon the ground.

Even as I thought this, I saw my friend from other land enter the temple disguised as a wandering monk, and knew that my half-uttered aspiration even then was answered. Yet death stared me in the face. There, near the altar, was the sacred axe always ready to fell the man who in any way erred at the ceremony. This was one of the vile degenerations of the ancient law, and while it had been used before upon those who had only erred in the forms, I knew that the Priest himself would kill me as soon as the diamond's great flame had died away. The evening darkness would be upon us by the time that the moment in the performance permitted me to destroy the enemy of our race. So I cared not for death, for had I not faced it a thousand times as a blessed release and another chance.

At last the instant came. I stooped down, broke through the rule, and placing my hand behind the shrine caught the reptile by the neck. The High Priest saw me stoop and rushed to the axe. Another moment's delay, and all hope was gone. With superhuman power I grasped and squeezed. Through my skull shot a line of fire, and I could see my wandering monk wave his hand, and instantly the Priest stumbled and fell on his way to the axe. Another pressure, and the serpent was dead. My knife! It was in my girdle, and with it I slit his neck. His red and lively blood poured out upon the ground and the axe fell upon my head, and the junior priest of the temple fell dead to the floor.

But only my body died. I rose upon the air and saw myself lying there. The people neither stirred nor spoke. The Priest bent over me. I saw my wandering monk smile. The serpent's blood spread slowly out beside my body, and then collected into little globes, each red and lively. The diamond on the mountain behind the temple slowly grew bright, then flashed and blazed. Its radiance penetrated the temple, while priests and people, except my wandering monk, prostrated themselves. Then sweet sounds and soft rustling filled the air, and voices in strange language spoke stranger words from the mountain. Yet still the people did not move. The light of the diamond seemed to gather around the serpent's blood. Slowly each globe of blood was eaten up by the light, except one more malevolent than the others, and then that fateful sphere of life rose up into the air, suddenly transformed itself into a small and spiteful snake that with undulating motion flew across the air and off into the night to the distant Isles. Priest and people arose in fear, the voices from the mountain ceased, the sounds died out, the light retreated, and darkness covered all. A wild cry of despair rose up into the night, and the priest rushed outside to look up at the mountain.

The serpent's blood still stained the ground, and the diamond had disappeared.

THE SENTIENT DAGGER

Julia Campbell Ver Planck

IN the boudoir of a charming woman of the world, this tale was told to me. If you do not believe it, I shan't blame you. Even now, I can hardly believe it myself.

The boudoir was a strange one for a woman. With Nina Grandville the unusual was always to be found. She was like, and unlike, other women. On the surface, *grande dame de par le monde*. Beneath that polished surface, which afforded no hold to the cynic claws of her own sex, who shall say what swift dilation of the nostril, what smouldering fire of the eye, what scorn in her walk amid the crass, material crowd might not confound the observer? Distinguished by a quiet elegance, the surface woman was accepted by all save the philosopher and the fool. I have always been a little of both. As I looked at the tiger skins, the panoplies or weapons, the savagely grotesque bronzes of her boudoir, refusing to blend with crown Derby and plush *poufs a la mode*, I wondered, for the thousandth time, more or less, over that hidden nature to which this admixture must be the key. The late Grandville, remarkable only for *fadeur* and a keen taste in sauces, was never responsible for it, I was sure.

Waiting there for the lady, my eye wandered down a sunbeam, its quivering point touching an object hitherto unnoticed by me. It was a small dagger, sheathed in bronze, with a figure of Mephistopheles holding up a wine cup while he mocked and sang, upon the handle. The impish deviltry of the little figure attracted me. It hung upon a velvet disk just above Madame's lounge, and when I unsheathed the blade it was a slim, oval-shaped bar of steel, sharp on both edges, with a wasp's sting point. A lovely bit of steel with only one defect where a dark stain marred the blue polish of that blade. Mrs. Grandville appearing at the moment, I held the dagger out to her, remarking, "What a pity to let such a weapon rust. Do let me have it cleaned."

She stood in the doorway, grasping the curtain, her lithe undulation arrested by my words. She turned from red to white—a fiery, luminous whiteness—and from that to ashy gray. Her throat quivered, but no words came. Her nostrils dilated, she went white again, her grand figure expanded, towered; by some subtle alchemy of nature the woman seemed to turn tigress before my eyes; in a bound she was at my side, clasping my wrist, and our eyes burned, each into the other's. As a spectator of some great natural upheaval, it did not occur to me to say anything. I held my breath and the dagger while we sounded one another a long moment. In her gaze I saw only a fierce question. What she saw in mine mast have satisfied her, for she relinquished my wrist and seated herself with a shrug and a laugh.

"Certainly, Lord Hatfield; take it to every gunsmith when you return to town and ask him to remove the stain. You will find that most of them know it. If they succeed I will pay them any price they may ask. And to you I will give one of the rarest things on earth, a woman's loyal and profound friendship."

While she spoke I had been looking at the stain on the blade. It somehow affected my brain with a kind of heat and tumult. I attributed this effect to the blade because of some emanation proceeding from it, like a hot and jarring mist, which blurred the mockery of Mephistopheles. Altogether, I was wrought up beyond my usual mood. So I looked full at her, saying:

"Suppose I wanted even more than that? Suppose I wanted what is less rare, but closer, more human,—a woman's love?"

I don't think I had known that I loved her until then, but I took a quick advantage and threw all my newly-found heart into my voice. Her eyes shone, then contracted; one saw she was happy, then sad.

"In that case I—I should tell you the tale of the dagger," she replied.

"Tell it to me, then."

"It is not easy, Hatfield."

"Say it is impossible, but tell it. Strong tasks are set to the strong. You are very strong."

A pink flush suffused her pallor at my praise. I have seen rosy sunrise clouds flit over the Jura snow peaks so. But in her eyes was a piteous dread.

"Tell me," I entreated again.

"That you may laugh?"

"That I may learn."

"Learn? What?"

"What a woman's soul is, when it is real."

She studied me briefly; then she plunged into this tale:

"I will tell you. When I have done, you shall pronounce the verdict, 'Guilty,' or 'Not guilty.' A horrid weight will be lifted from me. My mind will not revolve about it any more, like a trapped rat in a wheel. To know how a sane mind judges my moral status, this is the relief you offer me. It is a real and terrible thing I am about to tell you, but the majority of persons would call it a phantasm of the mind. Only the very sane can admit the reality of subjective phenomena. Few know that the unseen is more real than the seen. That stain is on the dagger, plain to every sight, but the ethical cause of it would be denied by most men and women.

159

"Before my marriage with Mr. Grandville, I lived with my mother in Italy. You know she was a Florentine. I had artistic talent and studied under Luigi Fiamamente, an artist of reputation. I became engaged to him. My cousin, Lavoisini, studied with me, and in view of these circumstances my mother's chaperonage often relaxed. What happy days those were! We were young, full of life and health, aspiring to high ideals, pure as daybreak. Ours was the blissful confidence of innocence, ignorance. It was disturbed. It was disturbed indeed.

"One day, as I painted, I heard a footstep coming up the long flight of stairs leading to the studio. Leisurely, emphatic, elastic, confident, it came on and on. Louder, more aggressive, self-assertive by the time it reached the studio door, I felt that an enemy stood there. The man who entered completed my instinctive dislike. In his auburn hair, his ruddy cheeks, his massive but supple form, scarlet lips and hawk-like, contemptuous eyes, the lust of life was exemplified. He came to buy a picture. He remained to insinuate the poison of materiality into our hearts. Into mine, hatred. Into Luigi's, fascination. He said that the artist refreshed him like spring water. At the bottom of the clearest human nature you may stir up mud if you will. The spring became polluted. Luigi became unnerved, listless, hollow of eye and cheek in a few days. He sought me less; when he did, he treated me with apologetic kindness. Marshall—so the stranger was called—appeared interested in me also. I repulsed him without disguise. He said that, since I would not receive him, he must content himself 'with our Luigi.' The words were a veiled threat. He soon held my poor boy as in a vise. Steeped in material pleasures, he winced under Marshall's contempt of all finer feeling; his ideals were rendered ridiculous, his virtues contemptible, but he submitted to the influence. I was not able to remonstrate. I was so young, you see; I could hardly define what had happened. But I hated Marshall. The hatred grew. It reached a climax one day when I found Luigi prostrate on the studio floor, his body convulsed with sobs. I begged him to tell me what had happened. He only muttered that it was too late. I told him it was never too late for truth and love. He replied that he had neither; he did not even desire them. His face, aged and lined, his wasted frame, his dimmed eyes, all confirmed his words. 'Hateful as is the gulf where I have fallen,' he said, 'I do not wish to leave it. Outside of the sensations it affords, I am a dead man. Even while I lament, an interior voice mocks me and assures me that my thirst for the lowest forms of pleasure is unslaked, that I shall soon enjoy them again, and with *him*, even as he enjoys partly through me. This promise delights me. Go; Nina; go.'

"Terrible words for a young girl to hear! I left him, loving him more than ever. I shut myself in my room, planning his release, nursing my detestation of Marshall. I did not perceive that he had thus infected my mind also. While I thought out various plans, all at once I seemed to see Marshall lying upon the studio lounge, where he took his noon siesta, after an opium cigarette. Above the lounge this dagger always hung. And then I seemed to see it planted in his heart. This picture delighted my fancy. A spark lit and flamed in my brain, while I mentally contemplated it. Then I laughed aloud. A new thought had struck me. There was a private passageway connecting our house and the studio. At noon, every one was asleep. And—why not? *Why not?* A Something seemed to harden, inside of me. I rose like one refreshed. I was young and strong. I loved Luigi. I would free him.

"Well; the day and the night passed somehow. Through the long hours I revelled in a mental picture of a dagger stained with blood. Life, for me, seemed to end with Mephistopheles sneering above a dead man's heart. Noontide found me in the studio; Marshall lay there, asleep. I felt as cool and as hard as a rock. I leaned over him, took the dagger from the wall, unsheathed it, planting myself firmly upon my feet. The sleeper turned towards me, smiling in his lethargy. I smiled back. I raised my arm, looked at the weapon to guide my aim. Heaven! What was that I saw upon the blade? What was the deadly stain? Whence came those drops of blood? The blade had a voice. It yelled MURDER at me. The air resounded with crisp tongues that took up the cry. I shrank. I cowered. I fled.

"Back in my room again, alone with the dagger, I tried frantically to remove the stain. I could not. The silent witness of my moral guilt remained. Marshall walked the streets, but I was a murderess. The thought was the deed; it lived, even though the final blow was wanting. I saw this, but I would not believe it. I stole to the studio and hung the unclean thing upon the wall again, quaking with fear lest someone should unsheath it and expose that eloquent stain."

She sobbed a moment, hysterically, from exhaustion.

"I will not keep you much longer. While I lingered, my cousin came in. I burst into tears at sight of him. He led me before Luigi's best work; it was cut to pieces with a palette knife. 'It is Marshall who obsesses him,' he said. 'Can nothing be done?' I shook my head and gazed at the dagger on the wall; hate was in my heart, together with the rage of impotence. His eyes followed mine; they dilated, then remained fixed. After awhile I left him, still staring at the dagger.

Next day the city rang with news of Marshall's murder. Later, my cousin was arrested with the dagger in his possession. He seemed benumbed, dazed, and did not defend himself. At the trial he admitted his guilt and said that the dagger had a blood stain upon it and a voice came from it, urging him to kill. Some thought him crazed. Others believed that he affected mental disorder to escape extreme punishment. He did escape that, having always been a gentle, peace-loving soul. They sent him to the galleys for life. Before going, he gave me the fatal dagger. 'You know its power,' he said; 'keep

162

it safe from human eyes.' In a short time, he too was dead. My heart seemed dead also. My love for Luigi was gone. The shocks had sobered him. Perhaps we might have raised one another, but we were both too tired to feel. Mamma brought me to England. The rest you know. And now, who murdered Marshall?" She rose to receive my sentence. "What do you say? Guilty or not guilty?"

I said nothing. With the force of that extraordinary tale upon me I stammered some consolatory commonplace and said I must have time to think. I got away to my rooms in town; the dagger was still in my hand and my brain felt light as a feather. I fell asleep from sheer exhaustion. Late next morning I awoke, right as a trivet, clear as a crystal, and all the cobwebs swept from my brain and my practical common-sense restored. My thoughts ran somewhat thus:

"Guilty? Poor girl! How should she be? The melodrama of her mother's blood is in her. Social strain has made her morbid. I'll tell her so. I'll tell her I love her, by Jove, and we'll go on a wedding tour to Norway. No air braces one up like that." With such thoughts I tubbed, dressed, took breakfast, and drove to my gunsmith's. I wanted to take her the dagger, clear and clean. The man said he could do it, then he was puzzled. Finally he said it couldn't be done, so I had to renounce that little plan. I was soon on my way out to Windsor, but concluded to walk through the park to calm myself, for I was as full of ardor as any lad, dreaming God knows what dreams of love fulfilled. Something rustled near me. There, beneath the branches of an oak, I saw a stately stag of ten, gazing at me. The next instant he turned to run. The hunter's thirst for prey must have taken me by the throat. I ran after him, feeling for some weapon: something flew from my hand; he fell; there was a dagger in his palpitant side, and Mephistopheles leered at me, while all the little voices or the wood cried "Guilty! Guilty! Guilty!"

I got home somehow. And I never again saw Nina Grandville. Between us there seemed to be the shadow of a crime. Absurd, if you will, but my soul gave the verdict "Morally Guilty." And I could not argue it down.

Somewhere about the world is a small bronze dagger, with Mephistopheles on the hilt and a stain on the blade. Let no man possess himself of it unless he desires to kill. It has been steeped in thoughts of crime until it has become an entity whose life is hatred, whose impulse is murder.

XARTELLA

by Florence Carpenter Dieudonné

I
THE DESERT

THE sapphire night slept on the desert's ghostly breast, our camp fires burned low upon the sands and wondrous hosts of stars marched across the skies. On one side rose a crumbling pyramid, on the other were the still tents, their striped folds tinged red from the dying embers. The camels, heaped in ungainly rest, had groaned themselves to sleep. The horses were motionless. Silence had fallen upon the explorers' camp.

I had cast myself down upon a pile of saddle-cloths and rugs to look awhile at the glory of the stars, to glance, with an eerie chill, at the darkening form of the old stone pile, to meditate upon the mystery which seemed to live with the sands.

Someone moved beside me. It was that old stranger who had joined us the day before we left Cairo. He might have been the spirit of the desert, he seemed in such accord with time and place. His tall form was wrapped with a cloak of white wool, a great white turban was on his head, his dark face was earnest and anxious, his eyes, fierce and black, glared 'neath heavy brows.

"You do not believe in Xartella?" he questioned.

I had been told that Xartella was a deathless creature, more than man, who had been seen, for centuries, in the vicinity of this pyramid. While I had not the slightest faith in these legends, noting the remonstrative expression in the aged face I hesitated to speak my skepticism.

"I confess—to me there seems insufficient evidence——"

"Come!" interrupted the stranger, "I will prove that Xartella has existed."

An adventure with a maniac, I thought, as I walked beside him.

"Twelve years have passed since the events transpired which I shall relate," continued my companion as noiselessly we crossed the sands. "I wish to find a certain broken spear handle."

Very mad but, likely, harmless, I thought. With him I climbed up the rocks until he paused and began to search among the rubbish.

"Look, friend," said he, "your young eyes may be able to find the point and part of the handle of a spear."

With assumed diligence I searched until I did find the spear. When it was withdrawn from the sands, in the starlight we could see that the two parts, one of which he carried, united perfectly.

"It is the very spear. My spear!" he said excitedly. "Now let me tell you of Xartella." We sat upon the crumbling stones, and as the stars paled for dawn, I heard this story.

"Xartella! Xartella!"

"When first I heard that cry rise from the foot of this pyramid it was white noon. The air shimmered like a veil above the hot surface of the stone. The waste of sand was blinding as it billowed into distance, broken only by those fragments of dead empires which marked their own graves.

"In unbelief I had come, with the others, to search for the lost daughter of one Vor, who was considered to be the wealthiest merchant in Cairo. The maiden had been for months infatuated, or hypnotized, by Xartella and had been watched, constantly, to prevent her flying across the desert to his home. At last she had escaped her guards. Immense rewards were offered and, I thought I might find the foolish lady. So, it chanced, there we all stood, in the blistering noon, when in an instant's time all doubt vanished. For there stood Xartella, at the foot of the pyramid.

"No wonder that they called him a god. A man so majestic that not even that mass of stone towering above him could dwarf him into human insignificance. Robed in fabric wrought over with gems, from head to foot he blazed like another sun. Beneath his antique crown was a face grand, dark, strong. It might have borrowed its repose from the Sphinx, its glory from an eternity, its cruelty from a demon.

"When the gaze of those wondrous deep eyes struck mine I could not move, I felt myself grow chill. I tried to call out, as did all the others, 'Xartella,' but my lips were cold and trembled.

"I could utter no word. Then the mystery looked away. I breathed again, moved and called 'Xartella' with the rest. With others hastened forward to capture him.

"Capture Xartella—Capture the stones of the pyramid. Capture the loneliness of the desert! The Arabs were right. He was more than human. He might be a thousand years old; ten thousand years old. When he looked with those terrible eyes across that plain, of which the very legends had been stolen by time, into what splendors of memory did the ruins lead him. What was that ancient glory of which he was left the only existing miracle? There was stern, supreme majesty on his face. There was mysterious menace in his taper bronze hand uplifted to the sun. There was a cloud of white—a dazzle in our eyes! Xartella stood not at the foot of the pyramid. No one was there. The brilliance had vanished. No more should I see that glorious face; it was gone!

"A yell of rage rose from the company, together men rushed to the spot where he had stood, searching in the sands for the print of his foot. They hammered the moveless blocks of stone and pried great slabs of rock from the dust, as if they thought the mighty man had digged himself a grave. Incantations and prayers mingled with beast-like howls of rage; we had all seen him and he had escaped us all.

"Through the weary day we searched until the parting kiss of the sun. The red light fell across the gray wide plain, and the wide plain was gray no more. In lines of scarlet and in lakes of golden mist the air slept, shining. Hill-tops burned crimson, for palms purpled slow in death of day.

"Then I saw moving, far off on the sands, a white-robed form. Hastily I raised my glass. Toiling among the purpling vistas was Vor's weary daughter. My horse——

"Xartella, Xartella!"

"He stood again like a fire-red star upon the summit of the pyramid. His dazzling majesty as he stood in the sun made me forget Vor's wandering daughter. Like a swarm the Arabs crawled up the steps of rock. Among them was I, who looked up at the radiant prize, then back at the demoniac faces as one python head after another peered above the terrace, each countenance stamped with the same ferocious determination. Was not Xartella afraid as he looked down from his surrounded standing place? How could he escape? They were not here to be foiled. They were closing the ring around him: more than two-thirds of the distance to the summit was passed. They were all well armed.

"Once more that fell gaze scathed me. I was dizzy; moved heavily, as one moves in a dream. I saw others clasp their eyes. Some leaned against the rock to rest. A stagnation seemed to fall upon them. They moved not forward. Then I heard a defiant shout; a derisive laugh came down to us. Some few lifted their heads to look. There was a blaze of red light, as if the gorgeous sun had shattered into fragments.

168

"No man stood upon the summit of the pyramid.

"Xartella was gone.

"At once rose the stricken ones; the blinded began to see: the trembling began to grow ferocious. I found myself still weak and clumsy. I leaned upon my spear—this very broken spear. The shaft was pressed into the crevice between the rocks. As I looked—bewildered—at the place where the flames had flashed, suddenly turned the stone upon which I stood and I fell into depth and darkness. As I scrambled to my feet the heavy stone swung into its place, shutting out the last ray of evening light. I knew that I was a prisoner within the mighty walls. Alone, forgotten, with only a broken spear in my hand. Already weary—already thirsty. Something told me I was Xartella's prisoner.

"At first I gave myself up to frantic desperation. After awhile I regained sufficient self-control to consider, remembering, resolutely remembering that delirium was destruction. Carefully I examined the walls until I found one narrow passage. A strong current of cool air made me hope that there was some outer door. For some time I proceeded so steadily and evenly that I felt encouraged. Then something crashed in the blackness, covering me with dust. Instinctively I turned back. A great stone had barred the passage. Whether it were a door or merely an accidental falling of rock I could not tell. I cried out in horror, then rushed on blindly—madly. No return now. The corridor was my fate.

"I seemed to see the sunny courts of Cairo. I was tortured with thirst; I could hear those fountains plashing under the trees. The corridor was growing lower, narrower. I could not go back. I crawled on my knees. How close it was. The current of air had ceased since the stone fell. If I lifted my head it struck the rock. I thought that soon I should be crushed by the weight above. I crawled like a snake. I lifted my head a little. The rocks were not there! I rose. There was plenty of room. I reached my arms about and touched no walls, and in the darkness danced and laughed because there was space in which to die.

"Then it seemed there was a tinge of light, but I scarce dared trust my eyes. It became brighter and I was obliged to believe. It was light. Soon I found a fountain of cold, clear water nestled in a vine-filled recess; farther on I could see the glow of lamps. One danger was passed. What now?"

II
VOR'S DAUGHTER

"Refreshed by the water I was resting, absorbed in speculation as to my best course, when close beside me passed the white-robed form of Vor's daughter. A slow moving vision of golden light seemed she in that black realm. Blonde and with wealth of yellow hair, she resembled not the women of Egypt. Her face and form were perfect, marvelous her beauty, but pale as one dead. She was staring, with no trace of expression in her fixed blue eyes. A hand, in hue and texture like the waxen leaf of a lily, clutched the remnant of a silver-cloth veil: the shoes were lost from her blistered feet, her robe was dust-covered and torn on the hem; it had trailed across wastes of sand.

"This patrician lady made no pause; did not even taste the water. I remembered the many times that we had halted at the wells. I wondered what had she endured to pass them all as she passed this fountain. How had she escaped discovery on the desert, in full sunlight, while hundreds searched for her? But as I thought she was fast leaving me, I rose to follow her.

"We soon came into a large hall of barbaric magnificence. Singular tiles and mosaics of shining and oriental brilliance lined all the upper walls. Open doors, portals and arches un-draped gave vistas of antique magnificence. Into this luxury intruded strange, crude relics of antiquity. Some of the apartments blazed with lights; one corner was shrouded in deep shade. Into its obscurity opened a hieroglyphic-marked gate which was hung between huge orange-colored posts covered with mystic characters in black.

"When Artossa, Vor's daughter, reached the central hall she dropped like an inanimate object upon the floor. I hastened to her side. She seemed in a stupor of unnatural slumber. I could not tell whether it were weariness or a mesmeric state. I brought water, and when I placed the cup at her parched lips she did not drink. Finding I could not rouse her, I sought refuge in the shadows beyond the orange gate. Such mystery and singularity were about me that I was scarcely sure I still retained my reason. I wondered if I really experienced what I thought I did, or if I had gone mad in that corridor. I almost was afraid to move lest I restore some horrible consciousness.

"It would have been better had I selected some other hiding place: no rest was here for a confused brain.

"A deep red hue steeped the gloom, through which slanted shafts of blue light looking like swords dipped in blood. Odd roundish bottles or huge jars were on all sides. A crimson liquid was in them. Peculiar spiced dust filled the air and clouded at every step. Cumbering the way were so many dark objects which yielded and crackled when I stepped upon them that I lighted a match and looked about. It was the only match which I possessed: it showed me—mummies. Hundreds of grinning mummies, piled and shelved and scattered about the floor. Their hideous faces were everywhere. Then the match expired.

"After some time I accustomed myself to the darkness and saw great cases of glass in which lay sleeping persons: some of these were young and beautiful, some were very like mummies. The feet of each one were bathed in the crimson liquid. The entire scheme was incomprehensible to me, who groped shiveringly among the horrors, hoping to find some unravelment of the mystery, and so doing found the most monstrous iniquity of all. It seemed a living mummy; it moved its eyes and head but did not speak. A tattered cloak covered with ancientest symbolic designs was heavily crumpled upon the withered body. I lifted a portion of the weight from the feeble frame. So doing, I struck down into dust a crown agleam with precious jewels.

"I heard the sound of Xartella's voice. Some powerful influence seemed to coerce me. I moved toward him. It needed all my strength of will, all realization of my danger to keep me in hiding while I beheld him once more.

"He paused beside Artossa and looked at her with deep solemnity upon his face. He seemed to note her torn veil, her tattered dress, her blistered feet. He lifted his hand and slowly moved it, beckoning. A bevy of beautiful slave girls came from an adjoining apartment. I noticed how singular was their step, their feet clicked like machines as they surrounded Artossa. Then Vor's daughter rose to her feet, opened her eyes. Amazement, horror, despair followed the first bewildered look of her face. She clasped her white hands to her brow and seemed confounded.

"Xartella watched, silently. After a time she turned as if to fly. Then, like a congealing, returned the somnambulistic state and with the same clicking step as the slave she departed into another chamber.

"Xartella, then, came into the Hall of Mummies where I was hidden among the jars. There was now no call upon me, and I could think and act independently. I watched as the mysterious man searched about among the cases, often speaking to the darkness. He removed the jar of crimson liquid from the feet of a beautiful youth, shook him, and lifted him up. The sleeper opened great vacant eyes and stared, sightlessly, at the dark burning eyes of Xartella. Then he followed him through clouds of dust. Click, click, sounded his step as he crossed the great rooms, drew aside a portière and dropped like a limp doll upon an inanimate collection of the same sort of humanity. Revealed to me by the lifting of the curtain were hundreds like him tossed into a pile of moveless loveliness, as were the mummies heaped in still hideousness.

"It occurred to my mind that these perfect men and women were resurrected mummies, restored only to physical life. Xartella was their soul. Not even by his art could a soul be hindered in its eternal progression.

"Astounded as I was, the more I considered on this idea the more certain I grew that it must be so. I determined to try an experiment. That elvish creature with the live head!

"I remembered that the jar which had held the withered feet was very small. In such a multitude of mummies discrimination was impossible. Xartella must have forgotten this one. I would restore it. I changed the small jar for one such as had restored the youth. I filled this jar to the brim with the crimson liquid. In these preparations I found again the crown, which I laid carefully upon the stone shelf. I was sure those dreadful eyes followed the crown with anxious watchfulness. After all this was done I returned, for secrecy, into a grove of large-leaved foliage trees which was outside the gate. Here I regaled myself with a delicious fruit, such as I had never tasted, composed myself to rest and fell into a deep slumber. I have always thought I must have slept for days."

III
APHLAH

"My first waking thought was of the dark room and my experiment. The Orange Gate was locked, but I climbed upon the stone partition wall and grew cold to behold some moving object. It was in shades and far but it was where I had left that mummy which lived. I crept, noiselessly, around to where the wall was above and beside it.

"A woman was there. She had risen and twined the dust-filled tatters of the hieroglyphed robe about her. Her words were maledictions, her breath seemed made of sobs. She held, clutched in her claw-like fingers, *that crown*. As she peered through a little wicket in the wall, I judged she could see Artossa, for thus she spake:

"'Thou infatuate dupe. Thou foil of fiend. Beware! For the glance of those eyes, thy life. For Xartella's smile, thy all Eternity. "Willingly a sacrifice," he said. And as he prophesied, the ages of this weary old earth have produced it.

"'She has come across hot sands at his call. Into this dark haven at his bidding. Crowned by his hand, throned by his side. Even while the glamour of her crown is new this maiden lays it down. All this! and, for him, consents to venture into an unknown futurity in hope to return again, to him, with souls for all these restored of earth.'

"'I am Xartella's Queen. Not thou, Artossa. Forsaken. Forgotten. I am Queen and once again I will put on this crown.'

"She rose to her feet; in the sword of blue light I saw her ghastly, impish face distort with rage. She lifted the crown with both hands.

"'It is a crown,' she cried; 'for this thing men have died. Have slain those ones best loved. Have whitened hills with rifts of human bones. Have colored rivers red with brothers' blood. It is an awful power, my own ancient crown forged in the fires built by primeval race. All newer crownlets shall fall down before it. I know the glorious life which the crimson fluid can bring back to me. Xartella!'

"Even in that mummy shape was some hint of grandeur, as in that blue she lifted both her leathern arms, raising aloft the crown to place it on her head.

"But it was too heavy. She clasped it to her breast and bowed her bald head upon its gems.

"'Xartella has forgotten Aphlah. He would send this puny, frightened woman of modern earth to bargain with Archangels. I should be sent. Not such as she. Cruel to steal my power, to let me almost perish, yet not quite. To forget me while the years roll into centuries. Was it that my beauty waned? No. Xartella's red jar would have given to me supernatural loveliness. Rather was it because he deemed my crown more blest than his.'

"I left this thing which I had evoked from mummy life. This creature of the shades. It was no forgotten fate. It was a woman who would restore herself to a majesty which would be most terrible to Artossa.

"But where had the living gone. The beautiful resurrected and the baleful restored became so unendurable to me, that, during the prolonged absence of Xartella and Artossa, I hid myself in the recess of the fountain. There I counted the slanting beams of fourteen sunsets before I heard weird music and the sound of Xartella's voice. Then I forgot my loneliness, forgot Aphlah and myself in the glory of the picture presented in the old stone halls.

"Artossa was enthroned beside Xartella. Rest had restored her resplendent beauty. Her hair was coiled and diademed. A gossamer robe of gold and rose was bound about with bands of gems. Her feet were cased in broidered shoes.

"Before the thrones whirled all the host of beautiful youths and maidens. Waving salutations with their white or tawny arms. Tossing their long, loose hair and moving, in a mechanical accord, with discordant music, twanged from stringed instruments struck by the hands of dark-skinned musicians. It was bewildering. Majesty, splendor, beauty centered upon the throne. Gorgeous hues burnished, motion glinted the foreground of the scene. Even the jarring music, here, was not unpleasant.

"A great sarcophagus, of transparent substance, stood, conspicuously, close by the thrones. The lid was raised. From time to time Artossa glanced toward it, almost with dread. But her white hand lay in the clasp of that one dark and strong. The touch seemed to control her.

"Then I heard Xartella explain, in a soft voice, with an oriental figurativeness of expression which transformed to a translation the real horror of the desired sacrifice.

"Artossa must consent to enclose herself in the mysterious casket. Death was sure in the thousandth of an instant. Resurrection, Xartella insisted, was, by his art, just as certain. She would be able to procure, through her intercession, souls for all his restored multitudes. When she returned more glorious than other earth creatures she should reign with him for centuries. Not in that dark, contracted realm, beneath a pyramid already crumbling, but in such visioned land as, I was certain, was not builded above the seas of earth and only had foundation in the imaginings of this half-god. And this must be a willing sacrifice.

"Listening for her answer Xartella paused, forgetting the lagging dancers. Like dolls they began to drop in their places.

"'You see,' he said, 'they have no soul but mine. For their new life, Artossa, will you go?'

"'I will go,' replied Artossa, very sad; 'but how can I go willingly and leave you?'

"'You will return.'

"'I may not find the weary way.'

"'Love will lead you back.'

"'In that other sphere there may be no love. Whence I am to procure all these souls love may be dead. Love may even forget.'

"'*Fond heart, there are not moments in eternity to make true love forget!*'

"It was Aphlah! and as she suddenly appeared before us and uttered these words I wondered had she not changed into

176

an angel. Her majesty and beauty paled those others as the sun pales the moon and all the stars. She might have been moulded from moonlight and robed in woven dew drops so marvelous was her humanity, so unreal her shimmering garments.

"Xartella sprang from the throne to approach her. A look of rapture transfigured his stern face.

"'Aphlah, my wife——'

"His words were interrupted, this woman of glory lifted to her bronze gold hair that same crown which I had lifted from the dust. And, as she raised it, in dust fell down the antique, brilliant crown which graced Xartella's haughty head.

"'Xartella, this is my crown. For this crown man has destroyed the one best loved. But, 'tis an ancient ring of power. Behold how newer diadems shall fall before it.'

"I had drawn close to the throne and as Artossa's crown crumbled into dust it fell upon my hand. The maiden, forgotten, at this supreme moment, by her captor, turned to me and with the cry of a young girl's terror, flew from the splendid throne to my arms.

"'I do not wish to die,' she sobbed; 'I do not dare to bring those souls. I wish to return to my father's palace. I do not wish to cross the chill river, death. O, to float once more in glory of sunlight on the Nile.' She fell at my feet, weeping, frightened, imploring my aid, and I comforted her with common words of earthly encouragement which seemed strangely out of place.

"Aphlah moved near the sarcophagus.

"'Xartella, upon what shore dwells man when he has died to higher life?'

"'Let others ask the question, Aphlah. Not such as thou.'

"'Not yet a soul for all these dear ones?'

"'There is but one dear, on earth. Let these dead rest. Go not across the boundary.'

"'I will be your ambassadress. I will seek some friendly

archangel and may return with the souls to light your empire of the dead.'

"Xartella moved to prevent her but he seemed chained. The thing which I had thought a fate forgotten now proved itself the more powerful of the two. Aphlah dropped, like a cloud of silver, into the fatal casket. With a heavy jar the lid flashed down.

"'Come back! I never meant to let you really perish. There is no light left in my earth. I do not know that I can bring you back. I only waited: O, Aphlah, I never meant that you should die or really be forgotten.'

"A fearful sight it was to see the powerful Xartella striving vainly to tear away the lid from the sarcophagus. To see the glinting of the crown through the transparent sides. To note the still face in the majesty of death. Xartella crashed article after article into shatters trying to break that seemingly fragile lid.

"'I have called too late. I have waited my repentant words until she hears me not.'

"Then he cast himself down beside the casket and hid his face. Around him lay the still dancers.

"I whispered to Artossa that we would seek an egress from the pyramid. Even then the great walls began to shudder as if shaken by an earthquake. Light, as if of sun, filled all the space. We two shrank away from something, vast and blinding, which neared Xartella. He rose and stood appalled. A voice like the serene music of a singing ocean uttered these words:

"'Call me not back.
   Hear ye that thunder gong
   Of the stampeding throng
In miracles of white
   In glory swept along?
It is vibrant chord
   Of that transcendent song
   Which earth can never sing.'

"'Only a man art thou, Xartella. Thou hast no power in heaven. Another cycle I have finished in the great wheel of the worlds. I shall no more return. Never may life go back. Come thou, come meet me here.'

"Then all was dark. Again the pyramid shuddered. Artossa clung to my arm. A great rock fell from the center of the pyramid and as it dropped it buried Xartella and the sarcophagus.

"The stars of heaven shone down on us. We saw two great white spirits sail grandly away into the distant blue."

The speaker ceased.

"Is that all?" I asked.

"My story is ended."

"But, Artossa?"

"She followed Aphlah's call and died three days after I had restored her to her father's house."

Then the old man pressed the spear into the seam of the stones. I was not surprised to see the rock turn and reveal a pit. But, in the gray dawn, I saw the flash of steel. Before my eyes the stranger fell, a corpse, into the black. I roused the camp. Now listen, this is the strangest of it all. We found that corridor. We found the great stone surrounded with bleached bones and mummied forms. We found dozens of great jars with a dry, red powder in them. One of the men stepped upon a white ball which burst and enveloped him in an impenetrable white light, in which he was invisible for half a minute. Another found a number of great fan-like structures of glass, in colors red, yellow and blue. These, when flashed open in the sun, gave the effect of a great dazzling star.

I found only this. I suppose it to be a piece of the broken sarcophagus. In all the earth I have found no other substance like it.

DEATH—LIFE

by *Will L. Garver*

THE carriage was driven rapidly for about five minutes when it came to a temporary stop, and I heard someone climbing up in front as though to the seat beside the driver. Then we continued on again for at least three hours without a single stop. During all this time my companion was as silent as the grave, and the only idea I could form of the route taken was from the turns which the swift motion of the carriage made plainly perceptible and the sound once made from crossing a bridge. At last we came to a stop and I heard a low whistle, shortly followed by another; then the carriage moved slowly forward and in a few moments came to a stand. As on the preceding drive my conductor handed me a hood, and without saying a word motioned me to put it on. Silently I obeyed, and together we got out. Pulling down my hood to see that it was actually on, my companion took my arm and we ascended a flight of steps. During a moment's stop at the top I heard a whispered conversation, but could not understand. We now crossed what I took to mark the door. Then my conductor's hand left me, and each arm was firmly grasped by a pair of strong hands, and I was hurried in a half run over a noiseless floor. In a few minutes we came to an abrupt stop and my hood was removed. Looking around

I found myself again in a large, cubical-shaped room with no apparent openings; but instead of being finished in black, as was the room of my former experience, everything was blood-red in color. Four lights, surrounded by red globes and burning with a red flame, filled the chamber with a dim and sickly light. Around a red center-table, as on the former occasion, were twelve figures, but his time all robed in crimson gowns corresponding with the color of the room. The first object to attract my attention was a gigantic black vulture standing by and eating from a large red bowl resting in the center of the table and filled with decaying flesh. As the bird ate his horrid mess a sickening stench arose. "My God!" I thought, "This is black magic sure." The noxious smell gagged me and I staggered back. As I did so a most diabolical laugh arose from the figures around.

"Ha! Ha! Ha! Ha!"

Then one of the figures lifted his hand—which was not a hand, but a gigantic, blood-besmeared paw—and pointing it at me said in a voice cold and heartless:

"Tomorrow your body will be his food." Then all around in chorus chanted as though in diabolical glee:

"Ha! Ha! Ha! Ha! Be his food, be his food, tomorrow!"

"Poor man," said the first speaker in the same icy tone, "you have yet one chance to return. Take it and go back."

Now came Garcia's warning; now did I think of Iole; the foul odors sickened me, but with a determination which bordered on desperation, I answered:

"No! Go on!"

Quick as thought the hood was again thrown over my head, and two strong hands seized me on each arm and forced me in a run for some forty steps, when I was again brought to a sudden stop and the hood removed. I was in a room like the one just left, but finished throughout in green; and, as though by instantaneous change, my conductors were dressed in like-colored garments, as also eleven figures who sat around a center-table as before. My conductors seated me at one end of this table and each took a seat beside me. The robed figure at the end opposite now drew forth some papers, and addressing me said:

"Are you ready for the oath?"

"I am," I answered firmly.

Passing me the papers in his hand to the figure at his right, the latter took them and in deep solemn tones commenced to read:

"THE OATH.

"I believe in the eternal, immutable, relentless and universal reign and rule of law.

"I positively do not believe in the forgiveness of sins, or the possibility of escaping or expiating them by or through any means of substitution or penitence. I believe that every evil thought, every evil wish, every evil word and deed brings to man a corresponding and not to be evaded pain.

"I do not believe that even God, angels, death, or all the powers that be, of heaven, earth or hell, can avert the sufferings that follow as the effects of evil thoughts, desires, or acts.

"I believe that from the humblest molecule of the most degraded and noxious matter to the highest and most exalted essence that pervades the minds of God-illuminated geniuses, all is life.

"I believe that every atom in my form is filled with life; I believe that every atom in my form is a life; but that all are bound by the power of my unconscious will to work together for the good of my organism as a whole.

"I believe that, even as my body is filled with a vast multitude of lives, even so is the circumambient air, the all-pervading ether and all-material and immaterial things, visible and invisible; through and in all are warming, innumerable hosts of beings, beneficent and maleficent.

"I have considered all this; I understand; I believe; yea, I affirm.

"And now, in the presence of all these and my superior, I do most solemnly swear and affirm; in the presence of my immortal soul, in the presence of God and angels, in the presence of all eternity, to reveal, without permit, the teachings, persons, symbols or proceedings of this lodge, either by word, act, sign or intimation.

"I further swear never to reveal the signs, pass-words, grips, symbols, times or places of this lodge and its members.

"And I further swear, that not even death, torture, cell, flaying, rack or flame can force me to violate this, my most sacred and solemn oath; neither will fame or ill-fame, power, misrepresentation or ignominy lead me to break this my most sacred pledge.

"Hear and register ye this my most sacred oath, pledge and affirmation, Gods, angels, demons, hear! Now have I sworn, and now do I, in calm, sound mind add this never-to-be-recalled invocation:

"O, swarming lives that fill my form, if I should ever, now or in eternity, violate this solemn oath, consume me! Gnaw in slow agony my vital parts! In awful cancer eat me!

"And thou, O, demons of destruction, who dwell in air around, when I seekrelief in death seize my surviving soul and force it back to earth again! There at thy pleasure give it pain, and thus may my eternal life be filled with awful misery! Thus do I swear, and thus do I evoke."

The reader ceased, and for a moment all was silent; then the leader spoke: "Man, you have heard the oath; do you understand, accept and sign?"

"I understand, accept and sign," I answered.

The leader handed the paper across the table, and, having again carefully re-read, I signed.

Having taken the signed oath, the leader handed another paper across the table and said:

"Write as I dictate."

I took the paper and pen and he commenced, as follows:

"Be it known to all whom it may concern, that I, Alphonso Colono, am tired of this life, and after due thought and consideration have concluded to drown myself in the Seine——"

"Hold on!" I interrupted, as I dropped my pen, "that is untrue, and will bring dishonor on my name."

"Ah!" said the leader, "you still care for the opinions of the world, do you? We thought you had killed out all thoughts of self; did you not burn the black square?"

I made no answer, but thought to myself this is risky business. Then, concluding to view it as a test, I took up my pen and wrote as dictated. "Now sign it," said the leader; and, with some hesitation, I signed.

"Now sign this," he commanded, as he handed another paper across the table.

Taking it up I found it to be a check upon the Bank of France, and reading as follows:

Pay to the order of Count Alexander Nicholsky Five Hundred Thousand Francs.
frs. 500,000—

Now the force of Garcia's warning came to me. "My God!" I said to myself; "what he said must be true—the White Masters never ask for money. They spurn all material recompenses or rewards. Are these the Black Brothers with stolen livery and symbols? Well, I have gone too far to turn back now, and, by the eternal I will proceed, let come what may. Yes, I will continue, even to the death. Count Nicholsky! Why, he is the famous Russian mystic who is supposed to be the richest man in Europe. Could it be possible that he had secured his wealth through this nefarious order? The leader noticed my hesitancy and said sternly:

"Well, will you sign?"

"Yes, I sign," I answered, as with a bold hand I signed away my entire fortune to an unknown man.

"'Tis well," said the leader. "If you pass you will need no wealth; if you fail, your last letter will identify your floating body in the Seine."

With this cold-blooded speech he put both papers carefully away in his rob eand drew forth a deck of peculiarly colored cards. These he shuffled and passed around the table, each figure shuffling in turn. Having passed entirely around, he cut the returned deck and laid it in the center of the table. Each man now drew a card in regular order around the table, the leader making the last draw. At a signal each one turned his card and an instantly checked murmur of surprise arose.

"Man," said the leader, with savage sternness, "do you belong to any other occult Brotherhood?"

"Not that I know of, " I answered.

"Well, Brotherhood or no brotherhood, you are surrounded by invisible powers, and this being the case, contrary to all precedent, we, even at this late hour, give you an opportunity to withdraw. We do not wish to assume the responsibility of what threatens. Woe to you if you fail; and woe to her! Man!" he exclaimed abruptly, and his tone was fierce, "we care naught for your poor, miserable life, but the fates here say that if you fail our virgin sister, Iole, is doomed."

"I will not fail; go on;" I cried, between my set teeth.

"Man! The elemental powers you evoke will shatter life and mind and make a raving maniac of your sister—forbear!"

"I will not fail; her blood be on my head. Go on!"

The words had scarcely left my lips when all was black as night, and the room was filled with strange and awful sounds. Strong hands seized me and a terrifying voice whispered in my ear—"Run!" Forced as I was, I obeyed. I soon found that we were in a narrow, vaulted passage. On, on, we ran, the stone floor echoing our footsteps. All was dark, but no longer having on my hood I could dimly discern the vault above, while my footsteps told me that we were going down an incline. On, on! My companions were panting for breath and I was almost exhausted. Still on and on; would we never stop? Suddenly I was tripped and fell to the floor, the hands of my conductors left me, and I heard the one word in a hollow, mocking voice—"Die!" Immediately I felt the floor sinking beneath me? down, down, down, into the very bowels of the earth; and all was inky blackness. At last it stopped with a jar, and looking around I beheld a phosphorescent skeleton standing at the opening of a dark passage. It had the power of motion, and in its left hand it carried a human skull which emitted a red light, while with its right it motioned me to follow.

At the same instant, and while I hesitated to follow this uncanny guide, a voice which seemed to speak from my stomach said clearly and distinctly:

"Follow, and never turn back; behind you lies destruction, your only hope is on. Follow!"

Having regained my breath during my ride downward, I arose and prepared to follow. As I did so the skeleton turned around, and as though floating proceeded along the passage, I following. The air commenced to become damp, cold and musty, but I continued in the wake of my grim guide. Suddenly, like vapor, it vanished, and I was again alone in an impenetrable gloom. Hardly knowing which way to turn or what to do I stood still, when the same interior voice again spoke and said:

"Advance; go on."

Reaching my hand out to the side I felt the wall; it was cold and slimy. Feeling my way I proceeded cautiously to ad-

186

vance, when the wall abruptly came to an end and I almost fell upon the floor which had suddenly become rough. Stooping down I felt a rock and concluded I would rest awhile; but as I sat down on its cold, slimy surface, a hissing sound arose, and my hand came in contact with the cold body of a snake. Hurriedly rising, a huge bat flew past my head and a swarm of others commenced to circle around me. Somewhat nervous, but still possessing a wonderfully cool head, I made another forward step. The air had now become full of flying bats and all around was the hissing and noise of serpents. "My God!" I exclaimed, "am I in truth deserted?" And again the mysterious voice within spoke and said:

"We never desert those who call with sincerity of heart and are worthy of our care."

This strengthened me, and I again thought of my divine self. But now a snake commenced to coil around my feet, and with a momentary terror I rushed forward, only to strike a rock and fall into a viscid pool. A suction drew me down; I could not rise, and commenced to sink. Vainly I battled; now to my breast, now to my neck it rises until it reaches my mouth.

"My God! My God! Have all indeed forsaken me?" I cried, as the viscid, tar-like mass reached my mouth. As though in answer to my last despairing cry I ceased to sink—my feet had reached the bottom. Now my mind again became quiet, and I felt for a place less deep. "Ah! Thank God, I have found it!" I cried, as I again rose in the glue-like mass until it only reached my breast. Laboriously I made my way along, each step making the pool less deep, when—oh horror! I am in another whirlpool and down I go! Vainly I strive, while the fluid is thick and viscous, the bottom seems to slide and I sink slowly to my mouth again. For the second time I stop sinking, and slowly and with toil reach a more shallow place, only to again be drawn into another pool. Now the truth dawns upon me. I am crossing a series of pools, and as fast as I get out of one I sink into another. Oh, merciful power! How wide is it? How long must I thus labor? Will I never reach the other side?

Again the inner voice speaks: "Have strength; persevere." How long I struggled thus I knew not. I could not go back, for all would then be lost; my only hope lay before me, so I continued to struggle. I had sunk into the fourth pool, which was denser than any before, and whose surface was covered with a putrid corruption which almost smothered me with its sickening odor, when, almost exhausted, and resting for a moment in the depths, a red light appeared in the darkness. Looking around I saw a boat approaching. It contained but a single occupant, and was drawn forward by a black rope which hung as if suspended in the air, and upon which were numerous bats. The red light shone from a skull fastened on the prow, and by its rays I saw that I was in a large cavern. As the boat drew near, I saw that the solitary occupant was a man dressed in red; his face was also red and had an evil look, while a red skull-cap with a bat's wing on each side gave him a still more sinister appearance.

"Lost man," he said, in a voice intended to be smooth, but which grated harshly on my ears, "pledge me your soul to do as I may bid and I will lift you from this mire and make you King of Earth!"

Raising my head sufficiently to speak, I asked:

"And who are you who would thus require a pledge before you give assistance?"

"I am King of Night, the ruler of the earth; matter is my element, all material things are mine."

"Then go," I answered, "I seek you not. Spirit is my element and I prefer to die, for death is but entrance into spirit life. Away!"

Without a word he tapped the rope, the boat was drawn rapidly away and I was left again in darkness. I had now concluded to die and end it all, for I was completely exhausted;

but no sooner had I surrendered when a new strength arose, and the inner voice, louder than ever before, spoke and said:

"I, thy God, the Christ within thy soul, am with thee. Fight on! Work! Work! Work!"

With renewed vigor I returned to my labor, determined at least to die fighting. Six pools had now been crossed and I was in the seventh. Whether it was from growing strength or less viscous pools, I knew not, but each pool since the fourth had been less difficult to cross. And now I had crossed the seventh pool and again reached land. A cry of thankfulness escaped my lips and I was about to pause for rest, when the inner voice again spoke and said:

"Go on! Go on! Never tarry; delays are dangerous."

Now relying solely on my inner guide, I started forward, and as I did so I saw a light reflected against the cavern walls from some place in front. The distance I had descended must have been deep down in the earth. Hurrying forward I turned around a projecting rock and came upon a smoldering campfire. Beside it sat a horrid looking hag affectionately caressing a huge serpent coiled around her body. The fire was evidently a center of attraction, for around it swarmed numerous other snakes and lizards, while the bats were constantly darting over it. When the woman caught sight of me she laid down her snake, and, advancing, greeted me with a blood-curdling laugh.

"Ha! Ha!" she screeched, as she extended her long bony fingers and curved them like claws, "Ha! Ha! Another victim." Then as she looked more closely at me, her manner changed and her frame commenced to shake, while she wrung her hands and broke into a mournful lamentation.

"Man! Man!" she cried, "go back! Go back! See this old hag! Ten years ago she was young and beautiful, a princess of a royal house! Now behold her, cursed victim of a gang of monstrous murderers!"

Then looking around as though she feared someone would hear her, she huskily continued:

"Like you, I gave up all for knowledge and sought admission into the Sacred Brotherhood, but was deceived and fell into the hands of this Black Order. Like you, I crossed the tarry pools; but I would not kill. No! No! I would not kill. Man, ten years ago my heart was turned to stone. Stone! Ay, more than stone; to adamantine flint. But thy face recalls what I once was. Ah! If they find out my life will be to pay; but I must warn you, for you have touched my long-lost heart. Heart! Ah! It is better to have a heart and die than to fester here among these vampires." Without giving me a chance to speak, she leaned forward, and peering at me with her sunken eyes said, hardly above a whisper:

"Man, down that passage they will meet you and command you to take a human life. No one can join their Brotherhood who has not killed a man; their compact is one of blood." As she spoke she pointed down a narrow passage to the right. "But," she continued, still speaking with suppressed voice, "one chance is left you. They demanded this of me; I refused, and they threw me back here in this dismal cavern to live a death amid the slime of earth. Ah! Who would think that I would thus speak—I, a monstrous hag! But you have touched my heart. Many souls have I sent along that dark passage, but you I cannot. Listen: For long years I was buried in this dismal gloom without one ray of sunlight; but one day I found a passage which leads out of this awful hole. It is not guarded, and it is your last chance. I risk my life in telling you. But, ah! How many lives have I, since my first refusal, helped to destroy? Some hellish power of theirs has made me a criminal with them. Blood! Blood! How many lives have I now taken? Then cannot I take my own? You have touched my long-dead heart. What! Has this hag a heart? Ha! Ha!" For the first time she paused and glared wildly around.

But I had determined to be guided solely by my inner voice, and this mysterious speaker within had, all through the woman's wild and desultory talk, kept saying: "Go to the right! Go to the right!" It spoke so loud that I thought the woman must have also heard it, but, as she continued to glare around in silence, I spoke:

"My poor sister, give me a firebrand to light my way; I will continue to the right, join the Brotherhood, and see that you are relieved from this dismal place."

"Lost! Lost! Lost!" she cried; then regaining her first appearance, clawed at the air and laughed that same witch laugh. "Ha! Ha! Ha! Ha! Yes, I will give you a torch; go on to your death—go on." She carefully brushed aside her slimy pets and got a flaming piece of wood. Handing it to me, she pointed her long bony finger down the passage, and with a leering laugh urged me on.

"Go on," said my inner voice; and with dripping clothes I hurried onward. The passage was rough and had many devious windings; swinging my torch, I must have proceeded along this way for about three-quarters of an hour, when I entered a narrow, vaulted passage leading upward. Along this I continued for about fifteen minutes, when it came to an abrupt end. A blank wall blocked the passage. Swinging my torch over my head I could see no opening. But stooping down I discovered a small hole near the floor on the right side. It was scarcely as large as a man's body, but, with torch in front, I crawled through, to find myself in a large, black room surrounded by a number of black-robed figures. A number of torches lit up the chamber, and looking around I saw a coffin beside a newly-dug grave in the center of the dirt floor of the chamber. In front of the open grave and coffin sat a man, bound in a chair like a captive. Now I recalled with a feeling of horror and doubt brings fear, and as these thoughts found place in my mind a tremor ran over me; but with an earnest invocation to my inner self for guidance and strength I gave no outward sign of weakness.

"Give him his robes," said a figure, who, from his dress, I took to be the leader; and as a masked figure with a suit of black clothes and a gown in his hands advanced, he addressed me and said: "Candidate, you have passed the first ordeal, but many more await you. Put on new garments."

Then turning to the man with the garments, he said: "To the bath."

Gladly I followed to a bath at the end of the chamber, thinking they at last were beginning to show some consideration for myself, but all the time wondering if they would try to make me take the life of another. Having changed my garments, all the time under the eyes of my silent conductor, I was led back to the chamber, and two figures advanced and took my arms and led me in front of the bound man, while the black-robed assembly gathered in a circle around. As I stood in front of the bound man, whose face was only partly masked, the leader advanced with a long, ugly-looking dagger, while another figure, robed in red, came forward with a bloodstained bowl.

"Candidate," said the leader, "it is your glorious privilege to secure initiation by meting justice to a traitor. This man, in violation of his most sacred oath, has revealed our secrets to the outside world. All to whom he gave these secrets must now die, but he must first expiate his crime; and it is your grand privilege to do the work and thus bind yourself to us by ties of blood. Carve out his traitorous heart and put it in this bowl." As he finished speaking he offered me the knife. I had now fully determined upon my course of action, and, raising myself to my full height, I answered with power and dignity:

"I will not take human life; by no man shall man's blood be shed; all life is sacred and vengeance belongs to God."

A hiss arose from the assembly and the leader, grasping the knife, advanced in front of me and said:

"Do you refuse? Do you defy our laws and orders?"

"Yes, when contrary to the laws of God and eternal law."

"Then you, yourself, shall die," he hissed, and raised his arm as though to strike, when a cry arose from those around:

"Stay! The coward, bury him alive; the worse than traitor—bury him!"

A dozen strong hands seized me. "Better truth than self," I cried, as they bound me hand and foot.

A storm of hisses greeted my remark, and, bound until I was rigid, I was thrown into the open coffin. All is over now, I thought; I have indeed fallen into the hands of those sworn to evil. Had my search for truth been but a chimera of my imagination? Had my deluding fancy led me to my ruin? Well, so be it; if the God-powers cannot protect me in my purity of heart and purpose, I at least can die in search of truth. As these thoughts passed through my mind, a calm and restful peace settled over me. How glad I was to die! How sweet is death! In their hurry they broke the glass of the coffin -lid as they fastened it over me.

Then I was lifted up and felt myself being lowered into the grave. "So end all cowards!" greeted my ears, and then the dirt commenced to fall upon the coffin. But how peaceful I was; a great joy filled my heart. "All for truth! All for truth!" I kept repeating. Suddenly the fall of dirt ceased, and I heard excited voices; then a loud report and an awful roar filled the room and I felt my coffin rising. It was lifted from the grave, the cover taken off, my bonds cut, and I was removed. As I stood erect once more, with mind calm and clear, I saw that not a black figure was in sight: all were dressed in indigo.

"We have bought you with a ransom," said the new leader; "one of our members has agreed to do your duty to the Blacks, and you are saved."

"I want no man to do my duty; every man should do his own," I answered.

"We will attend to that," replied the leader, then turning to one of his men, said:

"We have saved him from the Blacks; he seems a worthy candidate, and if he will pass our tests, we will accept him as a brother. Take him to our chambers, make his brand and get his number."

Instantly a hood was thrown over my head and I was led forward between two conductors. In a few minutes we came to a halt and, the hood being removed, I found we were in another large chamber with a glowing furnace at one end.

"Disrobe," said my conductor, as we came to a table near the wall. I had thus far obeyed and was yet alive; I therefore concluded to still obey and take all chances, and so without a word of dissent commenced to disrobe.

"Now let me take your measure," he said, as he motioned me to stand in front of a peculiar chart upon the wall. This chart was covered with small squares made by intersecting white and black lines upon a yellow background. In the squares were letters, symbols, signs and numbers, painted in various colors. Against this chart I took my stand with heels together and arms outstretched, while a man who had just approached, and who wore a white cube hat, marked my outline on the chart.

"What does he measure?" asked the leader, as I stepped aside.

"By the black lines, the four lengths which make his height are equal to the four which make his width, and he is therefore a perfect square. By the white lines, the seven which make his height are in exact proportion and equal to those which show his width, and he is therefore the square of seven or number of forty-nine."

"'Tis well; put on your garments," said the leader.

The white-capped calculator had now gone toward the furnace, and the leader continued:

"Bring on your iron," I answered, fully confident of my will power.

The brander now advanced with a glowing iron and I laid my bare arm upon the table.

"Brand the figure seven," ordered the leader, and in obedience to his command the red-hot iron was placed upon my arm. A darting pain shot through me, but with clenched fist I held my arm unmoved. Before he could complete the figure the word "Hold!" rang through the chamber. The brander drew back and the leader arose. "Who thus commands?" he asked. "A herald from the king," replied a white-robed figure who now advanced and handed a letter to the leader.

"Who informed him before the hour?" he asked, turning to the messenger.

"The secret wires which communicate all thoughts," replied the herald. "Candidate," said the leader, turning to me, "you are summoned to appear before the king. His herald will conduct you; follow where he leads."

At a motion from the herald I arose and followed. Straight toward a black wall we proceeded, but when we reached it a hidden door flew open and we passed through into a small vestibule-like room finished in pure white.

"Take off the black and don the white," said my conductor, as he opened a cabinet filled with white silk garments fragrant with perfume; "nothing that wears the black can cross the river and appear before the king."

Ah! I thought, the day begins to dawn. As I removed my black garments and put on the white, soft and pleasant to the touch, a feeling of indescribable happiness came over me. My heart seemed to be burning with a consuming love, and, although I had had no food for many hours, a new strength arose within me. An airy lightness filled my body, and looking at my form I saw it had become a pearly white. Having robed myself, my conductor led me from the vestibule into a large, white-walled cavern filled with a radiant light. It was of immense size, and the floor at our feet was of golden sand; thickly strewn with shells, while in front flowed a rippling river of crystal water. The distant shore was hidden from view by a white mist or vapor, and listening I heard the roar of a cataract below.

"Candidate," said the herald, "this is the last river; this stream you must cross in a boat without oars. If your faith is strong in truth and justice, if you doubt not that the pure and good are protected, you will cross in safety; for the Brothers of White never desert those who in purity of heart rely on the good for protection. But if you doubt, if your love for truth and purity is not strong enough to draw the powers of truth and purity, then must you drift over the falls and into the cataract whose roar you hear. Have you strong faith in justice, truth and right? Have you strong and pure love? Will you undertake the passage?"

As he finished speaking we reached a white boat drawn up on the sand by the river, and I answered:

"Yes, I will cross the river; I believe the purity of my motives will draw to me the protection of the masters." My faith, indeed, was strong, and a great love filled my entire being.

"Noble brother of tomorrow," said my companion, as he pushed the boat into the river and I got in, "may the power of your heart and mind reach the protectors of the good." With these words he gave a powerful push and sent the boat far out into the stream.

No sooner was the herald out of sight than the thought came to me, how am I to cross this swift stream without a single oar? But immediately the counter-thought came, the Gods and Masters will protect their children if found worthy. With this thought I became calmly indifferent, while the boat drifted down the stream. Quietly I lay in the boat, enjoying the rapture of the love that filled me. Louder and louder became the noise from the cataract; swifter and swifter grew the current, and the boat shot on; but, lost in the happiness of the interior light, I gave no heed. And now the boat darts forward like a thing of life, shaking in swift motion; but still I was lost in a subjective reverie and stirred not. Suddenly a strain of celestial music filled the air around and rose above the roar of water. My eyes had been closed, but I now looked up and— behold! The radiant light around me was full of angel-faces. I arose on my arm, and as I looked around I saw a white boat rapidly approaching. It was drawn by golden ropes, festooned with flowers, in the hands of angel cupids. Swiftly it drew near, and the floating throng struck up in chorus? "Love Brotherhood and Truth."

And lo! As I gaze a queenly form leans forward in the prow of the boat and—joy of heaven! It is my darling Iole. She reaches my boat, checks it with a golden anchor, and then extends her arms to greet me. Once more I was saved on the brink of the abyss. I was now no longer blind; the spirit had unfolded; and, conscious of my right to love her as brother of her sphere, I stepped in beside her and locked her in my arms. Tenderly our lips met to seal this purest union of two souls, purged, as it were, by fire. The cataract grew fainter; the boat, pulled by unseen hands, moved swiftly over the water.

"My noble brother, victorious over all things earthly," she said tenderly. "My darling sister, queen of love and goodness," I answered, with all the fervor of my heart.

"We love as God intended all should love," she whispered.

"Yes, my darling, that pure and holy love of soul for soul within the depths of spirit and where no thought of earth is present. All hail the divinity of love, pure love!"

A MONSTER'S BIRTH IN SPIRIT

by Freeman B. Dowd

DON locked his door and entered his cabinet. On the floor, enclosing the tripod, was a huge circle painted in the three primary colors, red, yellow, and blue, and in regular spaces were painted the twelve signs of the Zodiac, as in a horoscope The ruby light is exchanged for one of a dull yellow, and there are many magic mirrors now, instead of one. They are of all colors, black, white, yellow, red, blue, and compound tints, some made of baked clay, of glass, of paper, cloth, gold leaf, etc. This day, however, Don arranged before him a small box, closed on the four sides, with a light within shining through a small round hole one-sixteenth of an inch in diameter, shaded by a piece of orange paper. Ever since Ina's burial Don had been uneasy in his mind; the old sadness and unrest returned with redoubled force. His sleep is troubled and unrefreshing. His dreams are of monsters, who seem to clutch at him in a friendly way, apparently deriving strength and satisfaction from contact with him. Try as he will, he cannot banish the consciousness from his mind, that somehow, in some unaccountable manner, Ina's cause was his own.

Lying awake nights, he felt strange influences, like something cupping different parts of his person, a drawing, sucking sensation, which left him each day weaker and weaker, accompanied by a frantic desire to commit suicide. All the time he sensed weird, goblin-like influences—a rustling, a whispering, stealthy steps, pushings, and caresses that greatly disturbed him.

In vain he walked upon the bluffs, gazing at the scenes that Ina had loved, or sat musing upon the old log for hours, hoping to get a glimpse of her dear face. All in vain; no Ina came. Even the inner voice ceased its counsel, and the peaceful ecstatic feeling he loved so well, which came over him at Ina's presence, and presaged the presence of his second self, came no more. In vain he sat for hours, asking questions of his mirror. Failing to get answers, he busied himself making new ones, imagining that they lost their potency by use or that different colors were necessary to conform to his own changing conditions. It was all in vain. At last the thought struck him to make and use the "star mirror," considered the most potent of all. To this end he constructed the box referred to.

This morning he is feeling uncommonly bitter toward Dr. Parker. Mr. Albee's request that he should accompany him on his visit seemed to kindle hell fires within him. He could see nothing in Dr. Parker but an embodiment of all that is infernal. No excuses for his acts impressed his mind. "He is the cause of all my misery," sighed Don; "I'll destroy every vestige of him," said he, grinding his teeth. And suiting the action to the word, he looked around the studio for something to remind him of the doctor, but saw nothing save Ina's portrait turned face to the wall. Seizing upon it, with eyes like a basilisk, he thought to smash it over a chair; but his eyes caught hers, as he had painted them in her innocence and purity, with all the girlish mischief and trust looking at him, transformed now into something magical, heavenly. No wonder the hard look left his own face as he gazed at hers! No wonder he staggered as he set the frame against the wall, and gazed spellbound at the transformation! No wonder he was softened till the tears rolled down his cheeks!

The paroxysm of weeping soon passed away, and taking the picture reverently in his hands, he carefully hung it in his cabinet behind "the star mirror," so as to face himself when gazing. Then he wrote these words on his slate, which he hung underneath the picture: "Oh, thou infinite spirit! Thou who art all that is!—Thou who art the prayer, and the answer thereof!—show me, this hour, the workings of a curse! Let me see its potency, its effects, and the means of its operation! Oh, give me an object-lesson! Thou that art now and evermore!" and closing the door he sat on the tripod gazing into the fiery eye that looked out of the box at him. He essayed to get his mind into the meditative channel in which heretofore he had found calmness, tranquillity, "Samadhi," but his mind would not concentrate. There was no focus to his thoughts upon anything but Dr. Parker, and these were agitating rather than tranquilizing. His feelings grew more and more bitter. He essayed to call up thoughts of love, and tried to see Ina's face as he had seen it in the picture. Vain task! The face came, but it was distorted with a demoniac look of vengeance; thoughts of love mingled so with thoughts of wrong done to his love that there could be no calmness.

At sight of her face, gradually there stole into his consciousness sounds of whisperings, which, growing louder and louder, became an indistinct murmur of voices, incoherent, unintelligible. Then he became conscious of feeling cold, as if a cold wave of air was striking on his back. A feeling of horror crept into his mind as something cold and slimy crept up from his feet. On it came, without form, but tangible, creeping: now it is on his stomach, now on his chest. He tries to cry out, but his voice is unheard; he tries to leap from the tripod, but is powerless to move; while slowly—oh, *so slowly!—the thing* approaches his throat. He feels the blood pressing behind his eyes, his head is full, the *thing* has clasped his throat, and he loses consciousness with the thought in his mind, "This is death." But not for long was he dead.

Suddenly he awoke, sensing an awfully disagreeable stench, "Where am I?" he gasped as he opened his eyes in dense darkness; but no answer came. Gradually his eyes adjusted themselves to his surroundings, and he saw dimly, in a foggy atmosphere, a large room, the entire floor of an old building on the banks of the river, formerly used as a tobacco factory, but long since unoccupied, which he had visited many times. He saw, I say, dimly, an immense crowd of people. The stench was almost unbearable, but he became used to that, and began to take an interest in what was being done there. Gradually he became aware that the building was filled with a crowd, and the light grew stronger in the center of that motley crowd. Making his way, by much pushing, through the throng, whose touch as he passed left a cold, slimy sensation, nearer to the light, he found that it arose from a smouldering fire which naked men and women were fanning and feeding with some objects which he could not discern. Upon a raised platform, overlooking the strange performance, sat Don's old-time friend—"the stranger"—*he with the slouched hat and dark cloak*; while by his side, to Don's inexpressible grief and horror, stood the object of his love, the beautiful Ina, no longer sparkling with mirth and joyous good nature, but with set features, intense look, and glare as of some wild beast. Her hair, tangled in masses, fell on her shoulders, writhing and twisting together in huge clusters, only to unfold and curl again, ceaselessly, like a nest of serpents. All around was a sea of heads, of all tribes and nationalities on the face of the globe, and of tribes and nationalities long since extinct. The ancients were there in quaint costumes or none at all, and representatives of every sect and religion that have ever existed.

As Don gazed upon this strange gathering the old tobacco factory seemed to enlarge itself. It became immense, till at last it had no limits at all that he could perceive. The whole expanse was filled by this heterogeneous mass of gibbering, malicious, unforgiving, revengeful beings. They marched with banners; they shouted and they sang; they gathered in knots and crowds as if listening to someone speaking. Some were naked, while most of them were clad in various costumes. A continual roar of voices, like the wind among trees, confused and mingled voices and dialects, merged into unintelligibility, till Don despaired of learning anything touching the object of this meeting, and turned his eyes upon the center, where the fire burned more and more brightly, as it was fed by the naked men and women. Pushing his way nearer he became aware that there was a continual passing from the multitude, of objects which were cast into the fire. Looking closely, he saw that they cast in living reptiles, lizards, tarantulas, centipedes, toads, and all deadly things, each nation or tribe contributing those things which they considered most deadly, loathsome, and offensive. It was a spiritual concentration of evil.

As the strangeness of the scene familiarized itself to the mind of Don, his perceptions cleared, his intuitions began to teach him, and he awoke to the startling fact that he was a spirit among spirits, and was attending a conclave of the dead, representing all ages, climes, races, tribes, nationalities, and sects. He became correspondingly intent, trying to ascertain the object of this meeting. Suddenly he of the cloak raised a wand. The multitude became silent in a moment, and in a loud voice he said:

"The material of the altar is complete; now for the sacrifice! Let nothing be offered except such things as are an abomination to the Lord."

"Heretics are such," shouted a Catholic Bishop.

"The authors of the inquisition are an abomination to the Lord!" shouted the ghost of Martin Luther.

"Allah be praised!" cried a Mahomedan, "cast in all dogs of Christians!"

Shout upon shout arose until the whole heavens echoed and roared with mutual denunciations. Sect cursed sect, nation cursed nation, individuals cursed each other, till it was found there was no unison, and the meeting would break up in a row. Again the wand commanded silence. Already each creed or sect was massing its hosts and displaying its banners, getting ready to seize upon all others as an abomination, fit only for the sacrifice.

"Hush!" said the commander; "the universal sentiment of mankind is the voice of the Lord! There is one thing universally execrated among men. It is a liar!"

"Bring him forth! Who is he?" queried a little man with a lantern in his hand. "Catholics! Protestants! Heathen! All of you! I have been vainly searching, night and day, with this lantern, for an honest man these hundreds of years! Cast all in! they are only fit food for the gods, and I doubt very much if it prove a palatable dish. If liars are an abomination to the Lord, and He wants such for a sacrifice, ye need not search for one; take any, or all."

Then stepped forth a Buddhist Rahab and said: "If the universal sentiment of mankind is the voice of the Lord, there can be no Lord, because there is no universal sentiment. The sentiment of one age is not that of another, nor is the sentiment of one nation that of another. The same thing is true of sects, classes, and individuals. If there is any Lord, who shall speak for Him? who shall declare what sentiments are an abomination to Him?"

"I declare the counsel of God," cried a man, clad in long robes of black, holding a crucifix aloft, with a mitre on his head, "I declare!"

"Down with the priest, the abomination of the Lord! A hypocrite! a blasphemer! a pretender of holiness!" roared the crowd as with one voice.

A great tumult followed, of rushing, struggling, knocking down, tumbling in heaps, with shouts and yells, groans and curses, mingled with prayers; while Don, fearing for his own safety, began to look around for a place of exit.

In the midst of this pandemonium up went the wand again, and all was hushed in a moment.

Then spake he of the cloak:

"We have not met to philosophize nor to abuse each other, but to carry out the will of that universal Providence we all worship. And we all agree that He wishes vengeance taken upon the wicked. We know this, for every human heart feels glad when justice is done to the wrongdoer, and the heart echoes the voice of the Lord. Now we are called upon to be God's instrument of vengeance in this particular case. The universal sentiment, alike of savage and of civilized man (if, indeed, there are any truly civilized), is that rape is the most execrable crime which can be committed. And now we are to punish a crime that exceeds it as the expanse of heaven exceeds the small earth. Dr. Parker has committed a crime unknown in the annals of crime. His devilish ingenuity hath extracted the devil's power of control over mortals from the secret laboratories of hell, and, lacking even the pity of the damned, hath essayed to perpetuate this crime by calling from the darkest crypts of the abyss a spirit of whom the *devil himself is ashamed*, and infusing it into this pure virgin of heaven while in an hypnotic sleep, making it possible for this loathsome spirit to be born again among men, again to have a hold on heaven by reason of this virgin through the love of the expectant mother. But this has been partly thwarted by Ina's taking a bold leap from earth to your midst, asking for the help of God to punish this wretch, by taking from him all that hath been given to him—his spirit, his intelligence, his will, his very soul, if such be possible. The curse of Ina is even now destroying the life of his body, but it will take the united curses of the vast concourse of the spirit world to totally eradicate his spirit from the universe, and thus put an end to the growth of this prostitution of the powers of heaven, *this hypnotic crime*. The monster that Ina's curse has invoked is ephemeral, i.e., it depends wholly for its power upon her will; but the female heart is full of pity, and in the lapse of the ages, at sight of his sufferings, she is liable to forgive him the wrong he has done. Then this monster of her volition will die; Dr. Parker will be born again among men, with his soul still reeking with the filth of unexpiated crime, again to multiply himself and perpetuate crime, till there shall be no good left! The altar of sacrifice is complete! Bring forth thy unwelcome, undesired, unloved, unborn baby, thou daughter of heaven! sweet sinless Ina! It is a fit sacrifice, not to appease the wrath of God, but to inflame it—an abomination, a stench in the nostril of the Lord! Poor little lifeless lump of clay," he exclaimed, stretching out his open hands over it and looking up to heaven, "we realize that thou art only a nucleus of attraction around which that monstrous spirit hovers! We send thee back to him who called thee from the abyss! We send thee back through this vortex of fire, tinctured with the anathema of all lovers of order, love, and decency, praying, dear Father, that this curse may live till thy vengeance be satisfied!"

He bowed his head, and taking the little bundle from Ina's arms, stepped from the platform and cast it into the flames. A spluttering, a hissing, and the flames lowered themselves till darkness obscured the scene, when a voice again rang out like a trumpet: "Let the priesthood of the fire organize." In the course of a few minutes the flames again burst forth, disclosing a strange, weird spectacle. A circle of twenty-one, men and women, totally naked, of many nations, climes, and times, had formed around the fire, and holding each other by the hands, were marching slowly around to the left, chanting, in doleful, long-drawn strains, some not unmusical, the wild barbaric words. The flames shot higher, the circle quickened its movements, the drums beat, and another circle formed outside the first one, which revolved to the right. Faster and faster they whirled, till, letting go of hands, each one of the inner circle struck into a dance, whirling, leaping, and bounding like a top, to the left; while the outer circle did the same to *the right*—a wheel within a wheel, revolving in different directions. Drums beat outside, and the multitude sang, shouted, roared, and danced, all in perfect time, though in such apparent disorder and confusion. A perfect pandemonium; and yet a certain harmony breathed through all, intoxicating, alluring, till Don, catching the general feeling, felt like joining in the mad revelry. Faster and faster revolved the circles. Wilder became the shouts and cries, while the gestures, contortions of bodies, the violent swaying of heads from shoulder to shoulder, the frantic leaping increased as the flames rose higher and higher. Froth oozed from gasping mouths; tongues lolled out blood-red. A translucent yellowish mist seemed gradually to envelop the dancers and move in circles with them. Don noticed that this yellow mist issued from the bodies of the dancers, and was attracted to the fire. This mist increased in density, till the dancers were half obscured. They seemed then, to Don, like demons dancing in a flame.

At last, one by one, those of the inner circle in motion passed over them as if there were no obstacles in the way. At last the inner circle all lay prone upon the ground. In some unaccountable manner they had, unperceived by Don, arranged themselves with their heads pointing towards the fire; but the outer circle increased the rapidity of its motions. Then there began an agitation in the fire. It swelled up as a bubble, and bursting at the top, black smoke issued therefrom like a volcano. But it was heavy, and rolling down over the flames, was reabsorbed at the base, accompanied by a hoarse roar like the waves of the ocean as they break upon the shore. Gradually the fire decreased in size and brilliancy, till it was like twilight, in which semi-obscurity the burning pile seemed to open in the midst, as if cleft from the top, showing some dark object struggling amidst the flickering flames. It grows stronger; it assumes shape; it lashes the fire as a sea-monster does the ocean; fire-sparks fly from it in streams. It crawls out and goes, like a serpent, thrice around the fire, slowly turning an indescribable face towards the people as it goes. Crawling, serpent-like, it had no legs, a body like an alligator, with scales of a dark color on one side and orange on the other; its body ended abruptly, the caudal extremity terminating like that of a craw-fish, while a head, somewhat human-like, projected, without the appearance of a neck, from the other end. The eyes, small and fierce, stood wide apart, projecting as if choked out. A huge snout took the place of a nose, with wide, distended nostrils; and the mouth opened, blood-red, lipless, from ear to ear, without chin or lower jaw. Raising itself on its tail, it shook itself out straight like a column full ten feet high, without a sign of a limb. Then the skin opened, like flaps covering pockets, and limbs projected therefrom, not unlike a man's in shape, but terminating in huge claws or talons. Stretching out its arms, it disclosed wings like those of a bat, extending from its hips to its hands. Snorting like a porpoise, it strolled around the fire a few times, then walked deliberately through it, lashing it with its tail, and stamping it till the fire died out and left a soft phosphorescent glow illuminating the room like pale moonlight. Every vestige of the fire had disappeared, but the inner circle lay there still, while the outer circle, having long since ceased moving, stood clasping each other's hands, like an impassable barrier.

The monster, as if in great wrath, with its tail lashed the earth, which it dug up with its claws, vomiting fire and smoke at the little circle. It bellowed in an awful voice, but all in vain. Its rage came back upon it: the fire from its mouth, the smoke from its nostrils, recoiled from contact with the circle. Even the lightning-like sweep of its claws and tail could not touch one of the sleepers who surrounded it. They were like a wall of adamant.

All at once a trumpet sounded, and a voice proclaimed:

"Dr. Parker is dead! he comes! prepare for the judgment!"

A dead silence prevailed. Even the monster stood in rapt attention. A dark speck appeared in the circle, surrounded by a small halo of silvery white.

"It is his soul!" announced the trumpet. "Now behold how it clothes itself with a form!"

Gradually the white vapor increased in size and arranged itself in form, darkening and becoming more dense as the outline became visible. Shortly a human form was seen stretched upon a couch, in a strait-jacket, with feet lashed to the bedposts. It was Dr. Parker just as he was at his death.

Then arose the master of ceremonies—*he of the cloak*—and said, stretching forth the wand:

"There, lying all unconscious before you, Apollyon, is your charge. You will take from him all that the great God hath given him, for he hath only abused the gifts, turning them into false channels. For the sake of knowledge he hath destroyed the happiness of others. To build up a fortune for himself he hath robbed the poor. Believing not in God, nor in the indestructibility of human life, he hath taken upon himself to stand in the place of God Almighty in controlling that freedom of the will and of choice and action vouchsafed to every mortal on earth, by means of which only is heaven attainable. Thus hath he set himself at variance with the purposes of God in order to aggrandize himself or to experience a momentary pleasure. Of all the gifts Providence hath bestowed upon him there is none left worth saving. He hath not improved upon his intelligence by using it for the benefit of others, for self hath been the underlying motive of every act. Had he improved upon his ten talents he would have discovered a soul in himself and others, and thus have found out God. Love is immortal, if he had any of it; but there is nothing left of him but brute instinct. In annihilation he believed; let the individuality known as Dr. Parker cease to be! It will take long ages of slow disintegration before he will get down to the base from whence he came! Dog he was, let him be dog again! As for you, Apollyon, you are as eternal as *human hatred of evil*. So long as one human heart harbors hate for the wrongdoer shalt thou exist, for thou art the concentrated wrath of all time, a product of man's anger; void of pity, conscience, and soul. Hate, animated by a modicum of moral sentiment, monster of the infernal regions of man's incomprehensible soul, away!"

While this address had been going on Dr. Parker had regained consciousness. He did not know he was dead. He seemed surprised at the strange faces crowded around, and raising himself, asked for the doctor, whereupon Apollyon stepped from the crowd with his hideous mouth wide open, looking as if his head were half cut in two. At the same time that his eye fell upon Apollyon, Ina came from the crowd, the crowd, whereupon he yelled,

"Take her away! she is dead! Why does she torment me so? take her away! Oh, doctor, loose these bonds! I am as well as anyone! give me my freedom!"

Ina immediately set him free. Leaping like a tiger from the couch, he struck like a madman to the right and left, getting away from Ina as fast as he could. But Apollyon with a fearful roar seized him by the neck, and holding him up, shook him till he was as limp as a rag, then dropped him on the ground, saying in an unearthly voice,

"Now, dog, salute your mistress!"

The doctor raised himself upon all fours and went whining to Ina, fawning around her like a dog licking her feet. She, stooping, clasped a chain about his neck and placed the end there—of in the hand of Apollyon.

"Now God have mercy, when we have none: Go!" cried a loud voice.

A roar! a crash! as if all the thunderbolts of heaven had been let loose. The old tobacco factory groaned, shook, trembled, reeled like a drunken man. A flash of lurid lightning illumined the place for a moment, during which Don saw the building falling upon him and the flying crowd. Then he knew no more.

MY ANCIENT CAT THEOSOPHUZ

by W. P. Phelon

EOW! Meow! M-e——o————w!

These sounds broke upon the still air of a summer afternoon. The first two were rapidly uttered, as if in great mental excitement, and bodily action; the last projected in a shrill crescendo of defiance.

Then another voice took up the conversation:

"You ole, black debbil, I cotch you yet! Jest you wait; then I'll tan yer ole hide!"

As the echo of these objurgations, flung like a handful of sharp gravel, rattled against the side of the house and the windows, and penetrated the halls, an enormous black cat bounded from the broad piazza overlooking Lake Michigan, into my study. Here, leaping into a cushioned arm-chair, devoted solely to his use, he winked at me solemnly, with his big, opaline eyes, and began deliberately to arrange his toilet, which was in a slightly rumpled condition.

"Been enjoying another fracas with the cook, Theosophuz?" I questioned, in response to his greeting.

The cat said nothing, but made a little grimace, and a motion as like a nod of the head, as a cat could make.

At this time, Theosophuz was a stately animal, black as coal tar. There was not a single white hair upon his whole body.

The manner of his coming to me was most peculiar. I am a widower, attached to a business house in Chicago, and like thousands of our people, live in one of the suburbs, on the lake shore, and go back and forth daily on the railway trains.

One bleak, stormy night, bending to the blasts of a fierce north-east wind, I was trying to reach my home from the railway station. Above the shrieking of the storm, I heard, in a sheltered bend of the road, a feeble wailing, like the cry of an infant. Guiding myself by the repeated sound, I discovered crouched behind a big stone by the wayside, not an infant, but a very juvenile cat. Bundling it in my arms, under my umbrella, for I had not the heart to leave anything that I could aid, unprotected, from the pitiless storm, on such a wild night, I hurried on to the house. There I turned the bedraggled, shivering thing over to Dinah, the black cook, whose sympathy was at once aroused for the poor bit of misery. Some warm milk was tendered and eagerly accepted. An old basket, and the ruins of an antiquated quilt made its temporary bed, by the kitchen range, for that night. When the rays of the morning sun strayed into the kitchen, the kitten had once more attained selfhood which he has never for a moment since, laid aside. As he grew in size and strength, he showed no signs of leaving us. As a cat had never been one of our blessings, the adoption of the stranger was mutually agreeable to both the contracting parties.

For a long time he was nameless. One day, as he sat in front of me in a chair, to which he was partial, and which, when he sat up,, brought his eyes within easy reach of mine, he was busily occupied with the functions of his solemn toilet. Every few minutes, he would stop and blink owlishly at me with his mystical eyes, which, on this occasion, were particularly weird and hypnotic in their expression. If I ever allowed my own eyes to rest upon them for a fractional moment, they seemed to possess the fascinating charm always attributed to the eyes of a snake. This was followed by a changing expression of the whole face, which becoming grave and mysterious beyond conception, filled me with an unusual sense of awe. As my look lingered, I heard a voice as from a great distance, saying: "I am Theosophuz, the favorite cat and messenger of Queen Chalmi, of the land of Khem. My mummy rests yet undisturbed, in the land of the fathers."

"But," I gasped, in a terrified sort of bewilderment, "do cats come back? I mean in that way. Are you the same cat that you were then? That is, are you really the Queen's cat?"

"Oh, yes, as soon as vital existence acquires any soul-force, it begins to reincarnate. All domestic animals are impressed with soul-force, from the people with whom they associate. I have always been able to carry away out of the lives more than I brought into them. But the mummy idea was no good. The real cat can never get on with his mummy, any more than a ten-year-old child could wear its ten-year-old shoes. But that's all, now. Call me 'Theosophuz' and I'll come 'most always."

The voice died away, and I came out from under the awful shadow of the ever-changing eyes. Pulling myself together, I remarked: "Well, Theosphuz, I am glad to make your acquaintance, and I hope we shall be of mutual benefit to each other."

Staring somberly at me for a moment or two, as if mentally translating my words, he jumped down from his seat, and thenceforth, his name was Theosophuz.

With all his good points; with all the advantages of his high ancestry, association and culture of the past; in his present incarnation, he was an incorrigible thief, and was constantly raiding the cook's exposed stores. This always brought the clash of arms. When driven from his usual haunts, if hard pressed, with all convenient speed, he made his way to me, having very quickly learned to recognize in me a friend that was at once provider and protector, while his antagonist contented herself with a storm of objurgations and epithets, never to be carried out, but simply repeated on the occasion of the next raid.

While thus temporarily in disgrace, he would sit before me, in his favorite seat, staring at me with those wonderful eyes, into which, if I ever dared to look for a moment, something therein enclosed, began to cloud, and take tangible form.

On this particular occasion, as, like a young tiger, he came bounding in through the open window, the pleasant fragrance of an early summer morning was about me. I had just finished, quite satisfactorily to myself, a Mss. for the printer. There were a few spare moments. After signing my name, I stopped work and lifted my eyes to those dangerous scintillating orbs of his. It was an hour before I got back, an hour that condensed centuries in its grasp, and this was the manner of the vision:

In the depths of those cavernous eyes that seemed to widen and widen without limit, mists and wreaths and masses began to float, rolling out from center to circumference. Then all limitations disappeared from a constantly enlarging center of clear light. I was borne up, as if I had become a bird. Resting thus, immovable, in the realm of mid-air; beneath me lolled, in the heat of a blazing, tropical day, a stretch of land too large to be called an island, and yet too small to be numbered with the vast continents of our day.

A voice, answering my unvoiced questioning, said plainly: "This Continent lies where the West Indian Archipelago is now situated. Its diversity of hills and mountains, is represented by the contour of the islands in that land-strewn sea, so well known to your geographers and historians. Look and Learn!"

At these words, as when one turns the screw of a spy-glass, the view of the realm beneath became plainer and plainer. Out of the gray shadows lying close to the earth, as if springing toward the upper air, came into sight a vast city of temples and palaces, whose white, marble walls, and gold-decorated roofs, towering aloft in turret and pinnacle told a story of profuseness in plan and magnificence in building, both as to material and construction, that has no parallel in present existence, anywhere upon the Earth. Tropical vegetation is on every hand, and the flash of cooking fountains inviting to rest and refreshment. Save only, on the Great Wharves, was there toil and unrest, about the haven built in from the sea, and solidly walled. There, were crowded the operators and operations of a world-wide commerce.

On the Southwest, great chimneys carried the smoke from the blaze of fierce fires, where the Cyclops of that time, forged weapons, instruments of various uses, and vessels of honor and dishonor, out of that peculiar bronze, whose secret of composition remains with them to the present time as one of the "lost arts." Sometime it may become once more known. They only could make the Damascene blades of that early day. They only supplied the men of the Stone Age, with means for slaughtering their enemies and the wild beasts, and we know they did not exempt their friends from sacrifice, if there was a scarcity of other suitable material.

But, in the Northeastern corner of this wonderful island continent, stood a building, unique in its situation, design and construction. It was built partly on an artificial plaza, and partly dovetailed into the mountain of rock, turned like a book leaf, over into sight. But upon the fair page of this planetary book, are indellibly impressed lasting records of word and deed, that have influenced all the planet, down to the present day. Right here, bearing itself aloft, into the clear blue, a great white tower arrests all attention, not so much for what it appears to be, but because of some peculiar emanation from it, that sways all currents of thought now upon the earth, or that shall be. I am fascinated with this marvelous condition, and continued looking at it. From its base a light begins to coruscate, and the wall of the tower, to my gaze grows thinner, until it is transparent. I see all as if I stood within the room, as it hollows itself out before my vision. It is not large, and is evidently a secret retreat. It is furnished luxuriantly. One would imagine it was of the present day, so closely do its furnishings and textiles correspond with the products of our own hands and machines. It is almost solidly lined with gold. The decorations show both taste and lavishness. Two figures present themselves, a man and a woman. The woman half reclines upon a sort of couch, and the man sits leaning against her. They are both fair specimens of the Aryan race. She is of royal family, and her dark bronze hair, wonderfully luxuriant, falls in uncurbed masses over the shoulder of her companion, who looks into her eyes with love and the deepest devotion. His dress is that of one of the High Priests. She is a daughter of the reigning House. She has been Temple taught, and having met the priest, they have yielded to the obligation of the former lives, have become lovers, and are at one of their trysts. I hear them speak.

"But have you considered well the results possible from the assumption of power over all planetary conditions? Are you sure that you have sustaining force to carry it through?" she asks, and her soft tones thrill like the notes of a silver bell.

"I have considered well. Everything that can be done under the law, will be done. We must succeed. Then no human power can stay our hands. Obedient to our wills, all things become. Existence, and undying youth with all its heritage, will be ours, dear. Then for us will all creation wait."

"Yes, I know how brilliant seems the prospect, and how sweet will be the living of unnumbered ages, together, when no physical weakness shall limit the highest enjoyment. But I fear me, that The Most Mighty One will not brook the seizure of His knowledge, and that some awful disaster waits for you, my beloved."

216

"Nay, nay, we can but fail, and we may succeed, and then you shall be Empress of the Earth," and the triumphant tone of arrogant will, seemed to assure success of the design, whatever it may be. He holds out his arms, and as she, with her face lighting up with the love of the ages turns to him, the picture fades. As I strainingly look, the voice out of the Silence that is acting as my Mentor, says; "Thou dost perceive the 'Lost Atlantis' before it was lost. Now see how it was lost."

A moment or two of expectation. It might be Eons upon Eons of time, for there is no standard of measurement by which to realize condition of space.

Again I see plainly the man and the woman in the secret room, on the island Continent, so prosperous and so happy. But now the man wears the badge of the Supreme Leader of this powerful nation. The emblem, flashing upon his breast, proclaims him the Senior of the "Mighty Three." He reclines upon a divan, and she nestles in his arms. She has grown more queenly, more self-reliant and assertive. In this attitude of mutual devotion, they are evidently discussing some subject of intense, common interest. I hear words of a strange language. I know it to be Aramaic, the mystery language of the ancient temples, while at the same time I am sure that my knowledge is not out of the present consciousness. I know certainly that this is the fact. But the purport of it all is this. She is talking:

"My best beloved! why will you persist in seeking the accomplishment of this awful thing? You know more now than any one man of the past, or of the future. Why must you seek the danger, you say you are certain awaits you?"

"Wise counsellor and dearest of all earth's gifts! I cannot put aside the clinging desire to know about something of which God alone now knows. I also would, of my own power, remove from you the overhanging anxieties of physical death, so that while yet living, you might become immortally young. It would only anticipate the final outcome."

"But, beloved, will not that destroy the fullness of the unfolding sequence, thus preventing the perfection we seek?"

"Nay, all things exist in the Great Forever, and sequence is only in our perception."

I can plainly see that the woman's trust in the power of the man is leading her to consider favorably the project, whatever it may be, upon which his will is set. It seems also necessary for its success, that she must consent, or her trained, potent will, may become terribly obstructive, at the point of final outcome.

They fade. I am conscious of a massing about the great, white tower; about the Temple; and about all that beautiful land, of almost irresistible invisible forces, marshalling under the call of an imperious human will incapable of taking denial from those who serve it. Like an army of occupation they close around the great city. Clouds snatch away the day. The crash of sheeted lightning; cyclonic bursts of wind; and an awfully continuous downpour of water, indicate the revolt, for a little while, of the elements against the Four Great Angels, their rightful rulers. It is the result of the temporary destruction of the Earth's equilibrium. The balancing of positive and negative, so simple in itself, which holds, with such mighty energy, all things steadfast, ceases for the moment to be. The movable Elements, unrestrained, hurl themselves incessantly against the immovable, upon this hither-to favored land. The foundations of the earth give way under the pressure of these new conditions. It disappears from mortal sight, carrying down with it all records of the most glorious nation that ever existed. For centuries these records are to be guarded by the Angel of the Water. The ambition of Lucifer, the Light-Bearer of the Ages, has brought this swift destruction. From the time when its appalling incidents were first mentioned with bated breath, even down to the present day, it has ever been called the Great Flood.

Then the cloudy mists roll in, as the beauty and glory of the first great city of the Aryan race disappears beneath the treacherous waters, so soon to show, in their sun-kissed depths, no sign to the mortal eye, of the treasures concealed below. I continue to look upon the tossing unrest, until a clearing light once more shines over a tropical country. A great river flowing from mountains at the South, and making its way directly North, rescues the land and its people from the heat and arid deserts of a Continent having very nearly the latitude of the first scene. A long, narrow strip of country thus fertilized, supports a teeming population, by its ever-flowing waters. Nowhere, in all that long journey from the equatorial zone, to the temperate waters of the inland sea, is there any intermission in the strip of green of varying width. No rains fall there, the only fertility develops from the slowly flowing river. Upon its bosom forever floats an empire's revenue. Like a huge python, it receives from everywhere, and through its sinuous coils, transmits for the benefit of its own people, the products of other people's brains and hands. As I look closely, I see that his people have exalted death over life. Their tombs are palaces. Their temples are statements in stone of the great glory of the Spirit, which they term the Real and Unseen. Their pyramids are the records of their men of letters, who thus made note of the knowledge they had acquired by the centering of determined and transmitted research.

Armies, led by generals and kings who never knew defeat, march forth from conquering to conquer. They return, bearing the spoils of many lands, and hundreds of captives, who henceforth will, as adopted citizens, instill new blood into the original stock, and thus prevent the nation's dissolution.

It is a land of wealth and power, and strong impulses on the thought planes. The leaders force their way in the silence, by thought projection, and hypnotic suggestion. I can see a strong resemblance between these men and the men of the former nation. Indeed, it seems as if the former men possessed the bodies and conditions of these, as much as if they were actually returned Atlantians. The genius of their past civilization has been transmitted to themselves of the now. There is a strange similarity in the architecture; in the inscriptions; in the characters; and in the truths they teach; for I can understand perfectly what was intended to be set forth by the curious hieroglyphics, to this day found both in Central America, the last remnant of Atlantian civilization, and in Egypt's storied temples. Looking and longing to know all, the scene begins to waver, as if a hot mist was going up from the whole land. Directly, I lose sight of everything in the revealing of the darkness; while a voice, low and insistent says: "Wait."

As one passes through the striking of a clock; so with scarcely perceptible change from the centering of the dimness, again appears clearly the land of the Nile. As if it were only yesterday, instead of thousands of years ago, I recognize my two former acquaintances of Atlantis. But now, she is radiantly beautiful, and like one of the immortals. Surely to her, all things might now belong. But to him, has come a chastened beauty of face, an evident result of that victory of the ages, the conquest of Self. Still he wears the priestly garb, but the fashion thereof has changed. It is evident that he is speaking to his queen, for she wears the double Uraeus crown, of Upper and Lower Egypt, and still looks upon him with kindly eyes, the outcome of the long ago. These effects assimilated into the Ego, must forever influence all its actions. They are talking of the revival of the mysteries of the Mighty Brotherhood of Wisdom which controlled Atlantis; and has ever since, to a greater or less degree, exercised its potent force on man's development. He says:

"My Queen, there is no place in all this broad, flat, desert land where a chamber of initiation could be placed, without making it a center of curious, discordant thoughts vibrations, which so centered would destroy the object of retirement."

"Priest of the Royal line, let us build the Chamber of Retirement in an excavation and place over it a mountain of stone. Then will concealment be ample."

"Thou hast a mighty wit, worthy the spouse of the Great Cheops. But will he do this thing for the priesthood?"

"Aye, my friend and counsellor, he will do anything for *me*. He will not hesitate to make war, if it is necessary, to obtain the slaves that will be required to do the building."

Then I see an immense excavation dug in the desert sands. This is lined on the sides with a vast facing of stone. In the center, stands a set of three chambers. Entrances and hidden ways are provided. When all is ready, walls are slowly reared by the combined labor of thousands of men. When the last stone is laid at the top, King Cheops' Great Pyramid stands out in the clear sky, as it stands today, the wonder and mystery of the world, for it holds within its impenetrable and silent bosom, the secret of both the Sphinx and the Brotherhood of Wisdom.

For a third time, the cloud lifts, and now the scene of the vision has moved still farther East, and an island partially land-locked, in the blue-green of the tropical seas, spreads before my gaze. In its mountains are cut temples and monuments. On the walls of these are inscriptions providing the fact that the same hands and thoughts planned and wrought them as inscribed the strange characters on the tablets of Atlantis and Egypt. More than that, the story they tell is of the fall from their hands, as their grasp weakened, of an almost omnipotent power. This was held as a common heritage, by the first great races of men upon the Earth. By an overweening desire for that which they could not lawfully possess, they brought disaster and destruction upon themselves, and all with whom they were associated. Not only was this fully impressed upon my mind, but I could see in the inner recesses of the great rock temple, here carved out of the mountain, a secret closet, holding upon its walls an index of the depositories of the Alexandrian library, which thus preserved its contents from the fury, alike of the Christians and the Caliph Omar. In these depositories, from which some few Mss. have been once more put into literary circulation, will finally be found all that the world has hitherto supposed to have been lost, when the Great Library was destroyed.

Then the knowledge of all this fades away from the memory of the nations of the Earth, in the same manner as the picture disappears from the range of my vision. In its place, reappears the black outline of Theosophuz with his lips slightly parted; his eyes emitting the same quizzical, cynical, faraway expression.

Looking at him, it seems very natural that a Black Cat should be able not only to do such wonderful things, but most fitting that he should make a success of all his aims and objects. I noticed, however, when he jumped down, it was not with his usual vivacity, but with the languid movements of a hypnotizer who had been strenuously exercising projected power.

It was some months before I was at leisure to again give much notice to Theosophuz, who went and came, quarreled with the cook, and altogether seemed in his action more like a dog than a cat.

But just before Christmas, my attention was called to his facial expression and actions. He seemed to have become another kind of a cat. His dignity and airy moods were almost supercat in their humanness. The evening before Christmas, he had come to my room in the twilight, and as usual was sitting in the chair close by mine. We were both basking ourselves in the flame and heat of a cannel coal fire. The gas was turned low. I was having a fit of meditation, through which ever and anon streamed strange scintillations of forceful energy, as if from some competing source.

Suddenly, I was aroused by a half-human, quite audible sound from Theosophuz. He was sitting bolt upright, staring at me, his great eyes distended to their fullest capacity, and well, the events of that night are beyond my comprehension, and almost beyond my description. I have simply tired to write down the words of the Black Cat, capable of telling such marvelous stories and illustrating them too! I only transcribe from notes made after I came back from somewhere. Who can tell?

No sooner had I glanced at Theosophuz' big eyes, than my own seemed held immovably and irresistibly in the grip of a darkness so impenetrable, it could be likened to nothing else than the insects hermetically sealed in amber. All consciousness of the present environment had passed out of my memory, and although thus firmly held, there was a sensation like a faint recollection, that I was only waiting. All present feeling was absorbed in a restful dallying with Silence and Darkness, unmeasured by any of the paltry standards of the human mind. I might have been in this condition an hour, or 10,000,000 years, there was absolutely no recognition of any difference between either time or eternity. Suddenly, a thrill shot through the entity I called "me." I felt and recognized the vibration, which translated into words, meant: "Let there be light." As the intensity of feeling faded, I perceived a loosening in the grasp of the relentless hand, hitherto detaining me. I was coming back, thanks to the Existent, into a re-created day of energy and life. Again and again, the flushing thrill of presage passed through me, and enlarging, boundless space was filled with whirling worlds. Each, adapted to its balancing in the whole, was fitted with its great army of inhabitants, accurately numbered and recorded in the great books of the Universe. All was adapted to the glories of the natural scenes, so incessantly shifting as to be named illusion, under the constant impulse of the mighty creative Word, which once spoken becomes Eternal Law. To the inner of the innermost, sounding from afar; to the ever-existent I, came the words: "Thou hast beheld the beginning of the great day of Brahma."

And, now, I am floating upward into light abundant, into freedom inexpressible. I come once more into largess. From the infolding of darkening vapors, constantly opening and closing, as when a pot boils, growing more and more distinct, amidst the constantly moving nebulous masses, I see a mountainous country, small in extent, but filled with a restless and ambitious nation. For the time being, they are the guardians of the sacred knowledge, transmitted from mouth to ear, through the ages, to oathbound keepers. It is the time of one of their sacred feasts. A Just Man, whose teachings have since echoed and re-echoed through the whole world, is suffering execution, under the Roman method, to a slow and most horrible death. The ancient Egyptian symbology of the triads, three crosses, three bodies, three spirits, is perceivable, in which the lower triad, the shadow of the shadow is transmuted into the substance of the higher. But that which is not perceived is the wonderful gathering of the disembodied angels and ministering spirits; who are watching this man, tested, as but few men are tested, in their lives; as to whether he shall regard the doing of the will of the Father, as of supreme consequence; and as a man, shall die a hero; as an ego out of many lives, shall lay aside his body like a god. The heavens darken, the earth quivers, the Veil of ISIS, before the Holy place of the Temple, is rent in twain. Men's hearts grow faint with fear within them. Their souls become lead; while with the supernal exclamation: "My God, my God, why hast thou forsaken me?" he passes from contest and struggle, to victory and the acclamations of the invisible hosts.

It does not require outer suggestion, to tell me that I have witnessed out of the Astral Light, the incidents known to this generation of men, as the "Crucifixion."

A short pause, a feeling of relief from strained attention; and then I am compelled to look into Space, at the revolution of the Earth upon its axis. I must, also, compelled by a power I cannot resist, notice the revolution of the Moon about the Earth; then of the two about the Sun; then of the whole system of the planets about the Sun. Then I notice that the Sun and its satellites are moving about some far off center. Our own astronomical wrappings are but a reduced condition of the Greater. What we are to the sun, each other, and the Zodiac, is repeated, only magnified many-fold. In all Astrological conditions, we are controlled by a Greater as well as a lesser Zodiac. The power of the former is even more far reaching and eternal than our own. It is an involving of revolution after revolution, until, through billions of millions of years, the last great cycle has returned upon itself. As the first great series of rounds closed its circuit, I heard a bell, thrilling and overpowering in its silvery cadence, strike one. I knew then, that all this interrelation of measured space has completed but one hour of its existence, one twelfth of the awful, irresistible motion, following the impulse of the Creative Energy, which thought and it was done.

Now, Nature seems to rebel. I feel as if I would like to struggle back to mortal consciousness, but the influence abiding in, and shining out of those eyes of fiery depths, held me fiercely and firmly, as the voice said: "Be patient a little longer. Look and attain Wisdom."

As I looked, the whole earth became peopled with all those who were counted to it. There was no more death, and Time had ceased to be.

"The Resurrection," the antithesis of the "Crucifixion," had come upon the Earth. It was not a renovation of dissolved and mummified bodies, but a reconstruction with spiritualized atoms of the already existent forms of men. The previous physical atom had become a living entity of itself.

Man's ego, full of the immortal attributes of the Ever Existent, had reached the point of being able to clothe itself with a body worthy of its high aims and powers. In wondering maze, I perceived a curious thing. In the same fashion as the setting sun appears to withdraw to itself all the light of day, so the light shed throughout the Universal spaces, was apparently reversing its motion. The twilight of the night of Brahm, little by little, was falling upon all manifestation. Creation stirred and animated by the Great Breath, vibrating as light, heat and color, was returning upon its cycle of completion, into its source, the Great Forever. I could now see how the rest and solitude, where one day is as a thousand years, and a thousand years as one day, would hold all in its inexorable embrace; as soon as time should cease to be. The darkness grows. I pass from contemplation to a recognition of the present, and consciousness of my surroundings dawns upon me once more. Instead of knowing myself to be 100,000 years old, I find myself in a sixty-year-old body, with a little cloudiness of mental power, as if hypnotically impressed.

I rub my eyes, there sits Theosophuz, his iridian-hued eyes slowly coming back to their normal condition. I look at him with mixed feelings of admiration and wonder. I am puzzled, more than ever, to know whether he was he, or some other, who, sent to teach, had chosen this method of presentation. Which was it?

I have never looked into the eyes of the Black Cat since.

WITHIN THE TEMPLE OF ISIS

by Belle M. Wagner

I

THE REVELATION OF THE ASTROLOGER

ALTHOUGH the hour was very late, near midnight, the Priestess had just retired to her apartments for repose.

The Rites of the day had been extremely long and fatiguing, as they always were for a Priestess of Isis attendant upon the burial service of one in high rank; and a great nobleman of the land, as well as a near relative of the Priestess herself, had been buried that day.

Thus personal sorrow had mingled with and added weight to the impressive and solemn grandeur of the occasion, yet, strangely enough her mind was neither with the events of the day nor the dead, but her thoughts were resting now where they had wandered many times throughout the day, namely, to her little handmaid and special attendant, as well as Vestal in the Temple, Sarthia.

Sarthia, who at the very beginning of the Chants and Litany, had failed in her part and had, with such a pitiable moan and beseeching glance at her, been hastily withdrawn from the assembly and assisted to the private courts.

Poor child, she thought, the strain upon her emotions, the solemn occasion, was too great for her in view of the crisis, which all unknown to her, must be now impending. However, upon learning from an attendant that the young girl was resting quietly and apparently not ill, she had not herself personally visited her, but concluded to wait until morning.

Once, twice, thrice, just as the Priestess had, as it were, passed the border-land of sleep the pale face, with its pleading eyes and plaintive cry, had started her back to vivid consciousness.

"Ah! this will never do," she said, springing to her feet. "Something is indeed wrong," and taking up her mantle she glided swiftly through the corridors, and a few moments later was bending over the silent and motionless form of Sarthia.

Noiseless as had been the approach of the Priestess some interior vibration had informed Sarthia of her coming and, with a quivering and swift movement, she sprang from her couch and threw herself impulsively into the arms of the Priestess.

"Ah! sweet Mother, well beloved of our blessed and divine Isis, hear me and help me," said the girl, in a whisper, tense and low, so low as only to reach the listening ear of the Priestess.

"Speak child," answered the Priestess, caressingly clasping Sarthia to her bosom with one strong arm, and with the other making soft, mesmeric passes over her trembling body.

"Ah! thank you, sweet Mother; this is so good and kind of you to come to me tonight. I have suffered so all day from your thought; you have been disappointed in your Sarthia and with reason, too. A Vestal, who all but faints at the sight of death, is not made of the stuff required in the Temple Service. But, believe me, dear Priestess, the trouble is far deeper than appears upon the surface. The Ritual this morning but furnished the occasion or, rather, hastened some crisis that

228

was already near at hand. For some time now I am haunted by most potent premonitions of a violent death. Night after night, dark apparitions hang around my bed, and only last night I awoke to find the Bird of Nu, the Owl, from out the inner Sanctuary of the Temple, perched upon my pillow and shaking his head and croaking at me most mournfully."

"What!" exclaimed the Priestess. "The Bird of Nu. Ah! this is indeed very serious. The matter must be investigated at once. But, my child, if all these portents prove true, do you fear death? Have all our teachings been in vain? Have you made so little progress in knowledge and the philosophy of existence as to be overcome by dark shadows and grow faint in the presence of the sentiment and show of an external ceremony? The pageantry, which appeals so overwhelmingly to the emotions of the outside world, is the necessary means of teaching the people these awful and stupendous mysteries of life and death. But the Initiate should be sustained by actual experiences within these hidden realms and possess a knowledge of their inner nature which places him on a plane far above the reach of Fear; besides being endowed with that burning love for wisdom which calmly discerns good in evil, and immortal life in the shadow, called death. Do not think I am chiding you, my child. I am only seeking to recall my real Sarthia, who is incapable of Fear, back to this physical expression called body.

"There, already the bright soul shines again with its usual clear light. Hold it firmly and do not let it flicker so again, and now I must leave you to seek an interview with the chief of the Astrologers. The record and Horoscope of your birth must be carefully looked up, and the meaning of these portents determined. Good-night, my child."

With a kiss, fond and maternal, the Priestess withdrew. She proceeded leisurely and thoughtfully toward a distant part of the Temple, having first dispatched a messenger before her to announce her coming, seeking an audience, well knowing that at this now early hour of morning the Astrologer Priests would all be in the midst of their busiest studies, calculations and most profound observations.

But Sarthia, when left alone, although marvelously calmed and comforted by the tender presence and lofty words of her idolized Priestess could not compose herself to sleep. Instead, she soon floated into a state of restful contemplation, drifting from one topic to another, until suddenly she found herself confronted by a most intensely vivid and startling vision. "Can it be?" Yes, true enough, there sat the venerable Astrologer holding in his hand before him, her chart of birth. Beside him, engaged in completing the necessary calculations, sat the scribe and youthful Astrologer Priest, Hermo. There was a strange pallor over his face and a compression of the lips which betrayed unusual emotion. The Priestess was partially facing them, composed, yet with a serious thoughtfulness of mien.

At last, Hermo, looking up, said, "The directions for the present year of life are made out, and the fatal arc carefully computed, Venerated Master," and handed his work to the Astrologer who took it, studied a moment briefly, and turned to the Priestess.

"What is the result, Venerated Father?" she asked gently.

The Astrologer slowly shook his head and replied impressively, "According to all the laws of our Science, and you know how true they are, the physical organism of Sarthia can not survive this present cycle of yonder fair Goddess of the night." And, with a majestic move, he pushed aside a curtain, revealing the Moon now low in the west.

"So short a time," said the Priestess. "Tomorrow night will be the full, and must we indeed lose our Sarthia before another new Moon? What is the nature of these evil influences?"

"The planets, in their configurations, indicate sudden and violent dissolution," was the reply.

"Ah, now," said Sarthia to herself resolutely, at this point turning away from the vision, "now I understand it all," and with a feeling of amaze at her newly-attained clairvoyance she fell into a deep and refreshing sleep.

II
IN THE PRESENCE OF THE HIEROPHANT

With the first waking moments a sharp pang recalled to Sarthia the vision and its revealments of the previous night. But her mind had fully recovered its philosophic tone and she proceeded about her customary routine of duties, calm and firm, and, as is often the case, in view of some inevitable and stupendous catastrophy close at hand, life only seemed larger, more intensely real. So, when later in the day she received summons to meet the great Hierophant and High Priest, what, at any other time, would have seemed a most momentous event, appeared now only in the light of the expected and necessary.

As she was ushered into the presence of the Holy Father the whole apartment seemed pervaded by an atmosphere of genial warmth and electrical-giving life which somehow emanated from the inner nature of the Priest himself, radiating also spiritual and mental, as well as physical force.

For some moments the Hierophant regarded the young Vestal in silence, but Sarthia was conscious that he was reading her inmost thought and motive like an open book, even down to her vision of the Astrologer and his fatal announcement regarding her life.

"My child," he said at length, "are you ready for the great change now already at hand?"

"No, Father, not ready but resigned to what seems to be the inevitable decrees of the planets that rule my physical destiny."

"Thou hast well said thou art not ready. Your life has yet but only begun for you. Its experiences, its many lessons and duties, are all unlearnt and you would pass to the spirit world immatured. Your young soul, like fruit plucked from the tree too soon, would ripen slowly, losing many of its flavors and never attaining certain of its best and highest qualities, for as you well know, progress in the next stage of existence depends upon the attainments in this.

"Thou art not ready, yet say you are willing to bow to the inevitable. This is wise, still have you not heard it said many times that man is the arbiter of his own destiny and that the soul was the inheritor of God-like powers by which it could rise to the plane whereby it ruled, instead of obeying the blind or planetary forces of Nature?"

"True, O Venerated Father, I have indeed heard all this, but I am very ignorant. Are there such possibilities for my soul?" and somehow imperceptibly hope began to dawn within her heart and quicken the life forces.

"Ruling the blind forces of Nature is very like ruling the wild beast, although the beast is much stronger than man and capable of tearing him to pieces, yet man, by forethought, can evade or trap and chain or otherwise overcome him. So my child, there are ways wherein man, assisted by his own knowledge, and by the instruction of departed spirits; aye, by the immortal Gods themselves, can evade even the malefic planets in their devastating course.

"To my clairvoyant vision, as I now at this moment look at you, every minute atom of your physical organism is in the subtle process of depolarization from unity toward chaos and disintegration. You are not yourself conscious of this condition only as it has been revealed to you, for your soul is so alive that it has become almost unconscious of its physical expression and for this very reason the shock of dissolution would be all the greater when it did come; for example, witness your unexpected collapse yesterday morning. Ah! sudden death is a most deplorable calamity, and your pitiable state of mind was but a foretaste of what would be the state of your soul for many long years, if you had died then, and will yet be, to a less extent now, unless this swift-coming blow can be evaded.

"However, in case the worst comes to worst, you have about ten days more of this external life and under our special care and preparation you can live years of experience in hours of physical time, and your soul thus equipped may courageously enter upon its journey to the spirit world. Rest assured, my child, everything possible shall be done for you."

"Ah, thank you; thank you, kind and good Father," exclaimed Sarthia, casting herself at the feet of the Hierophant and, with tears streaming from her eyes, kissing the hem of his robe.

"But, truly life is sweet, especially to the young, is it not, my child?" said the Priest, gently raising Sarthia to his side and holding her trembling form in a firm clasp. "Happily, there is an alternative which we have to offer for your most careful consideration and decision.

"Listen now, and give me your closest attention. Know you the young Princess Nu-nah?"

Sarthia bowed assent.

"For now these many weeks she lies in a semi-conscious condition, the soul hovering about its earthly temple uncertain whether to go or stay. In some respects her condition corresponds with your own, only that with you, as dissolution approaches, your soul grows brighter and more active, while hers becomes more and more latent; this result being largely the difference of environment—a contrast of the soul unfoldment possible in Temple life and that amid the distractions of the outside world.

"Tonight, the night of the full Moon, the Princess Nu-nah will be brought to the Temple and the Rites performed initiatory to the soul's great change. You, also, my child, must bear her company. The same journey lies before you both and you can go hand in hand through the dark valley of the shadow of death.

"And now, right here is a point where all will depend upon *your* decision. It is possible for us, by aid of the arts of Magic known to us, to bring your two souls in such magnetic rapport that at a certain point the vibrations of the two will, for a single instant of time, be in unison. At that momentous instant the polarity of the two souls can be interchanged so that the subsequent vibrations of your soul will draw you toward Nu-nah's body, while Nu-nah's soul will be drawn toward your organism, and thus will be accomplished the first great step in the drama.

"This great change will hasten the physical crisis in each organism. But your soul, while connected with Nu-nah's body, can easily overcome the malefic planetary influences which would destroy it if she were there; while her soul in your body renders *nil*, by its very non-resistance, the influences which would be absolutely fatal were you still there when the evil descends. And thus do you evade the blind forces of Nature. Two lives are spared for the duties and experiences of this world. This will be the second part of the drama, and now comes the third and last point to consider, the Result.

"In just the proportion as this is a most stupendous change in your soul life, so indeed, perhaps, even appalling to your present comprehension, will be the effect.

"After your soul has once entered its new temple it will be obliged to remain there polarized by the new forces set in operation while passing the crisis. Then, Sarthia, our bright and well-beloved Vestal, will henceforth be known as Princess Nu-nah, and will be obliged for a time to live the life and perform the duties of the Princess.

"On the other hand, the Princess Nu-nah will put on the external body of our Vestal Sarthia and enter upon the life of

234

the Temple Service, but with this difference; that while this change is consciously made by you, Nu-nah will probably never know it until she passes finally to the spirit world. Her past life has already faded from memory while consciousness of the new life will dawn gradually as upon an infant, and therefore, since she can not be consulted in the matter, the decision rests solely with you.

"Tonight, at midnight, your answer will be required. Until then, fare thee well, and God be with you."

III
THE MIDNIGHT OF THE FULL MOON

It yet lacked several hours of the fateful midnight, as Sarthia, her body perfumed and annointed, according to the prescribed rites, was borne by faithful attendants from the bath into the courts of the Sanctuary and placed upon a couch beside another, upon which already rested the unconscious form of the lovely Princess Nu-nah.

But Sarthia, although to an external observer as unconscious as the fair Nu-nah, was never more intensely awake, every atom of her being and soul alert to all transpiring about her and conveyed to her through her marvelous new gifts of clairvoyance and clairaudience.

Never, with the external eye, had she seen more vividly the vista upon vista of columns and corridors winding in and about the Sanctuary, now illuminated by the full-orbed Queen of the Night, which she could see shining through a certain archway, and her heart thrilled as she counted the number of archways fair Luna must pass until, at midnight, she would shine down through the one just above her.

Already had begun the weird chants, interspersed with solos of exquisite harmonies of stringed and wind instruments—responses and echoes.

Incense burned and perfumes arose and blended in an indescribable union with melody and motion, while as the fragrant vapors from the burning censers wafted and wreathed about the colonnades and porticoes, Spirit forms added their presence to the sublime scene, bringing with them flowers, aromas and harmonies from the divine abodes of the very Gods themselves.

Oblivious of the passage of time, while intently absorbed in every minutest detail of the wonders passing about her, Sarthia was almost becoming drowsy, when suddenly, the Moon looked in upon her, fast nearing the final archway, and yet she was undecided. She turned and gazed upon her companion, mentally asking, "Can I become Nu-nah?"

Nu-nah was very beautiful and a Princess. But Sarthia was also beautiful and the blood in her veins was royal, though of a different branch from the present ruling House.

Nu-nah was cold and haughty, accustomed to rule and be obeyed.

Sarthia was humble externally, a Vestal of the Temple, but in her mind and soul as imperious as a Queen of the realm of Heaven. Passionately devoted to the pursuit of Wisdom and the possibilities of obtaining knowledge, even Magic was open to her, in the Temple Service. Could she leave her Temple home, her opportunities for growth, her idolized Priestess, to go into the environments of Nu-nah?

The thought seemed to her worse than death itself. "Every one has to die," she mused, "and I may as well die one time as another."

Then another thought came into her mind—Hermo. He had begun to teach her the mysteries of his science of Astrology. Hermo, for whom she had a pure sisterly regard and who was so proud of her swift proficiency in his favorite study. And then she recalled the vision of the previous night when Hermo had shown to her clairvoyant eye his agitation at her impending doom.

"But if I become Nu-nah and Nu-nah becomes Sarthia, Hermo will never know the difference and thus be spared the pain of loving his young sister. And furthermore, Nu-nah has a lover to whom she is betrothed and would have married, ere this, but for her lingering malady, the superb young Prince Rathunor, whom I have never seen."

Ah! here was indeed a most dire complication. Love was a most mysterious and unknown emotion to her. She might hate Prince Rathunor and "then we would both wish I had died," and she half laughed to herself at the domestic comedy thus presented to her mind.

At this period, either as a reaction from the light thrown, or lighter thought upon her overwrought nature, or possibly from some subtle, potent influence emanating from the censer burning near her, Sarthia lapsed into sudden and most profound unconsciousness.

A few moments later—it seemed to Sarthia as if ages had intervened—she began a fierce struggle to awake. "Why, how is this?" she thought. She seemed enveloped in a dead wall of some kind. The brain, the heart, the infinite ramification of nerves in no way responded to her will and her utmost effort. Almost worn out with the unequal battle, it began to dawn upon her that she was really endeavoring to animate the other body. "Am I becoming Nu-nah?" Yes, in the excitement of the moment she raised herself upon her couch and, resting upon her elbow, gazed upon the rigid form of what a moment before had been herself.

But her movement had startled a form beside the couch, someone who had approached, unobserved by Sarthia, during the interval of unconsciousness.

A young man who seemed to her the most God-like being she had ever beheld and perceiving her glance, with a low exclamation of joy, sprang toward her, clasped her hand in his, and turning her face upward, gazed with most passionate tenderness into her eyes.

"My Nu-nah, you will live," he murmured. "Do you know your Rathunor?"

Thrilled to suffocation by the love in his eyes, every atom of her soul vibrating to a new-born and overwhelming emotion, she felt herself slowly but surely losing control of her new body. With, however, one supreme effort she pressed the hand holding hers and returning the look in his eyes she gave one deep, quivering sigh and was gone.

When again she regained consciousness she was within her own body. Rathunor had vanished and the first slanting rays of the Moon were descending the last aperture.

It was midnight, and she found herself in communication with the Hierophant, who, from a different portion of the Sanctuary, was seriously regarding her and again reading her inmost thoughts.

A few moments before she had all but decided that she could not be Nu-nah, that death now, here in this Holy Sanctuary were better far than hundreds of years as a Princess of the realm of materiality. But, a new factor had now entered her being. A force, more subtle than all Wisdom,—more potent than life or eternity itself,—had transfused her soul— Love! Love, the first, the highest, the all-embracing force of the mighty Universe, and with this new love had been ushered also into being, Jealousy.

"Rathunor loved Nu-nah! Am I not a strange interloper? Was it not worse by my decision to rob Nu-nah of her lover than to deprive her of continued physical life?"

For, it seemed to her now, that life without love would be more than the agonies of the lowest hells. Then again, to live with Rathunor as his wife, while he all the time thought her to be Nu-nah, would be an incessant torture, keener and more intense than if she were chained by, as a third person, to behold him loving the actual Nu-nah in her own body.

"Holy Father and revered Hierophant," she moaned, "help me, I can not decide."

"My child," came the mental response to her call, "if you could be assured that Rathunor would love *you* in Nu-nah's body, would the decision be easy?"

"Aye, indeed, dear Father."

"Then rest assured it will be as you desire. We give you our sacred word that Rathunor will love *you*."

Then, raising his arm, as in benediction, he slowly repeated thrice, like an incantation, the words, "Rest in Peace," and, ere the echoes of his voice had died away, the soul of Sarthia had left forever its earthly abode and Temple.

IV

WITHIN THE ADYTUM

For several days, after floating from her body into the Astral world, Sarthia remained in a state of profound, dreamless slumber and then gradually passed into a condition of semi-consciousness with occasional fitful gleams of memory until one day she realized herself in close proximity to two persons engaged in earnest conversation and became fully aware of the momentous events that had just transpired and her present disembodied situation. And with a thrill indescribable she recognized the voice of Rathunor addressing the Hierophant.

"And so, most revered Father, all things are progressing favorably and toward a satisfactory culmination?" he said.

"Even so, my son," was the reply.

"And yet," continued the Prince, "save the one momentary gleam of recognition, upon the first night of the ceremonies, the soul of the Princess Nu-nah, to all outward appearance, has left entirely. The body is sustained, apparently, by some magical process, the nature of which I do not understand."

"True, my son, but that need not disquiet you. The resources of Nature are many and far from being exhausted. But then, youth is naturally impatient. Did you so deeply love the Princess?"

At this point Sarthia would have withdrawn but she found that her desire to stay chained her to the spot, and glancing at the Hierophant she realized that her presence was known to him and that he wished her to remain.

The Prince mused thoughtfully for a few moments before replying and then said with a half sigh, "You know, O Father, that I myself did not particularly desire that marriage. From my earliest childhood I have been fond of my cousin and playfellow. As she matured I have admired, with family pride, her perfect beauty of form, her haughty spirit and her ability to rule. And yet, as you, who can so easily read the innermost secrets of the heart, must know, I have not been able to discern the happiness for myself in this union that my soul would crave, or that you led me to expect in wedded love. If my ambition irresistibly impelled me to fill the external destinies of mankind, to become a monarch of unsurpassed power and magnificence, then would Nu-nah be the royal consort absolutely adapted for such pride and pomp. But, you know, O Father, all these things are as empty bubbles and child toys to one aspiring to become a Priest King, to him who hungers and thirsts, day and night for wisdom, for knowledge of the more inner secrets of Nature, guarded so jealously by the Priesthood but revealed by the very Gods themselves to those worthy to know and fit to use and assist in carrying out the plans and orderly workings of the very Universe itself.

"In form and feature Nu-nah's image meets my highest ideal, but when I would speak of the thoughts and ambitions upon which my soul dwells, then her cold look of incomprehension appalls me with the vast difference in our natures. Her thoughts can never penetrate the realm wherein my life-forces are all centered. Never have I experienced from her the response my love would crave."

"Have you then never at any time felt that Nu-nah's love for you could be trained and in time evolved to the plane whereby she would respond to you?"

"Nu-nah does not seem capable of the love of soul. She accepts me as a lover due her, and whose attention and presence gratify her pride and vanity. Never once, or perhaps only once, have I ever seen or imagined I saw a recognition of love, and that was the night of the full Moon, during the recent ceremonies. As, with your permission, I for a moment drew near the couch on which she reposed, she suddenly raised to a half-sitting position and seemed strangely startled by my presence. With a thrill of hope, that finally love was awakening, I sprang forward and spake anxiously and fondly to her. For the first time in all my life her glance vibrated to my heart's very core. My brain reeled with intoxication as she pressed my hand, and the love from her eyes burns now into my soul as I recall that one second of bliss. But, alas! she fell back into her former lifeless state and lingers so until I am in doubt if after all it were not some illusion connected with the wonderful Magic of that night."

"Nay," said the Hierophant, "I can assure you that what you experienced was *real* and that if this matter reaches a successful issue you will henceforward find in Nu-nah all that your soul desires, that ever will her eager spirit lead yours in the pursuit of knowledge and the highest wisdom."

Then the Hierophant turning, mentally addressed Sarthia, the unseen witness of the interview, "Am I not right in making this pledge for you to Rathunor? Think you we have also fulfilled our promise that Rathunor shall love you?"

But her heart was too full to reply. He then directed her attention to her location and surroundings and for the first time she became aware with amazement, almost terror, that she was within "THE SACRED ADYTUM—THE HOLY OF HOLIES," while the Hierophant and Rathunor were within an adjoining court and private apartment of the High Priest.

"My child," said the Hierophant in reply to her speechless inquiry as to the meaning of this wonder, "there are no barriers to the disembodied soul. This place, so religiously guarded, so inaccessible to the ordinary mortal, is open to any soul having passed a certain grade of initiation into the divine mysteries of Nature and attained unto that purity of heart whereby man may see his God.

"Tomorrow night, on the occasion of the new Moon, will be consecrated within this Holy Chamber, the union of your soul with that of Rathunor's and here also will be consummated that mystic transfer between your soul and that of Nu-nah's.

"And now, I leave you here while I accompany Rathunor. As you gradually lapse into the sweet silence of this Holy place, observe the meaning of some of the stupendous mysteries of Nature revealed here openly to the one having eyes to see and possessing the gift of understanding."

Her first sensation on being left alone was, that she was floating like the vapor of a breath upon the swaying wreaths of burning incense, and as she reclines thus in blissful repose there dawned upon her vision a view of the vast Temple in its absolute entirety. It assumed the strange outline of a gigantic human body, all its intricacies becoming orderly correspondencies of the human organism in its multitudinous ramifications. Then all the vast ceremonial of this body passed in review before her mind, each rite symbolic of some function, physical, mental and spiritual, and she marveled at the adaptability of the parts to each other and then to the grand whole.

But, above all, was she impressed by the depth in depths of meaning of this Sacred Adytum in its symbolic relation to the whole structure. However, ere she could tarry to reflect, the nature of the vision changed as if her eye had been turned suddenly from the lense of a Microscope to that of an immense Telescope. Before her view stretched the starry Zodiac, in outline, the same as its prototype, the human body—the Grand Temple. The Sun and its solar system corresponding to various vital functions in the human organism, but the crowning wonder of all came as she comprehended the relation which our planet, mother Earth, bore to the Grand Man of the skies, and her soul was overwhelmed as all the implications of this relation rushed in upon her being.

V

THE TRANSFER

According to the calculations made by the chief Astrologer Priest it was just at midnight that the conjunction of the luminaries took place in the Zodiacal sign belonging to the Moon. This union of the luminous orbs of the day and night is powerfully magical in its results.

The vibrations, set in motion by this mighty union of the positive and negative forces of Nature, react, not only upon the waters and the Earth, but the human family. Not only does the mighty ocean obey this wonderful influence in the ebb and flow of its tides, but the Earth, as she rotates upon her axis, obeys this mighty power and manifests in her depths and heights in her serpentine movement about the Sun.

Nature's laws are very exact and man, to become the Arbiter of his own destiny, must blend his energies in harmony with those of Nature.

Agreeable to appointment and the arrangements to be made it was necessary for the Hierophant and the Holy men of the Temple to assemble at an early hour, although the Transfer was not to take place until midnight.

Much preparation was necessary as a most momentous ceremony was to be performed this night; one that rarely ever was performed, owing to the fact that few of the Temple

Priests were initiated into these sacred Magical Rites. They were too Sacred and Holy to be imparted to many, too dangerous for possible failures, too infinite in responsibilities accompanying such undertakings. Only those where the mind, soul and spirit, blended as one in their organism, were ever entrusted with the interior knowledge of the Sacred Adytum—The Holy of Holies.

Only the invocations were to be made, the chants and ceremonies belonging to the Holy Sanctuary were to be observed. The air was ladened with the sweet fragrance of incense and those subtle perfumes that are so delightful and enticing to the soul. Hours before the solemn Rites were to be performed, every part of the Holy Temple must be permeated with their magical and mystical influence.

The bodies of both Sarthia and Nu-nah lay in state before the Altar in the Holy Sanctuary, both robed and perfumed as if for burial.

The Hierophant of the Temple, the Priests and the Lay Priests, and the Priestesses with their Vestal Virgins, were now assembled in their respective places.

The hour of midnight had arrived. The chants now begun, set in vibration the spiritual forces that appeal only to the soul and spirit.

The subtle, silent will of the High Priest mentally commanded the presence of the departed spirit of Sarthia. At his bidding, she came floating toward him, and when within a certain distance from her inanimate body, she remained hovering over it. Most willingly and joyfully she came, knowing the promise of the High Priest would be realized when she became able to animate and control the body and mind of what was still Nu-nah's.

Rathunor was present at the urgent request of the Priest. He little dreamed why his presence was so much desired, and how he, who was so ignorant of the Temple rules and service, could be of any assistance.

A spark had been kindled within his very soul, the night that Sarthia found herself in Nu-nah's temple and for a moment consciously remembered and spoke, that had been burning deeper and deeper until now, it was ready to burst forth as an ever-living flame at the first breath of hope that this new emotion was of the soul—real and immortal.

Did he dare for a moment listen to the whispering of the interior self? Fear alone made him drive back and quell the monitions that sprang from within, for O, if they were only vain hopes could he survive the disappointment? The thought was crushing, and better, he thought, not to hope than believe an illusion.

The magnetic chord that yet held Nu-nah to her frail, prostrated body had not yet been severed. The unconscious soul hung or rather floated about its temple, apparently waiting for a stronger force from the interior realm to call it away.

The Hierophant stepped to the front of the Altar and, raising his hands, invoked the presence of the Gods and their assistance in this Sacred ceremony of making that Transfer of the spiritual life-line that binds the spirit to soul, and soul to body.

As the two souls hung suspended by these magnetic life-chords above their own bodies, through the magical influences of the Priests, the chants and music came closer and closer, as if drawn together by some strong magnetic attraction.

Sarthia, now, as well as Nu-nah, was unconscious of what was taking place. Nu-nah's was the natural unconscious state of an undeveloped soul in passing from the physical temple to the realms beyond, while Sarthia's was purposely induced by the magical will of the Operator.

The middle of the mystical hour had just been reached when the two life-lines met and blended for one single instant, then separated and, obeying the powerful wills of the Priests, became polarized in each other's body.

The magical invisible agency that had been animating the body of Sarthia was now withdrawn, and the soul of Nu-nah's gradually but faintly began to supply the animating force to revive and control the apparently lifeless form.

Sarthia's spiritual consciousness was not immediately allowed to return. The awakening must be gradual to her, for knowing what was being done, the joy and ecstacy of a prolonged life in the holy bonds of pure love with Rathunor would be disastrous if suddenly conveyed to her consciousness.

The High Priest, turning to Rathunor, said, "Our beloved pupil, return now to your usual duties, but fail not to return to the Temple a little before twelve o'clock tomorrow night."

Now the bodies of Sarthia and Nu-nah were removed to another part of the Temple. The Priestesses and Vestals, with the choir and musicians, were dismissed as the first part of the solemn and sacred Rites was over, but the Priests remained, never stopping in their magical work, for yet the vibrations of the new-born souls were not of sufficient strength and power to remain unassisted, especially that of Nu-nah's.

VI
THE AWAKENING

The constant presence of some of the Priests of the Temple had been near the bodies of Nu-nah and Sarthia continuously for the last twenty-four hours, and by their magic assistance the vibrations of the souls to their new tenements grew stronger and quite harmonious.

The hour of midnight was again near at hand. The reviving forms of the two young girls were again brought into the Holy Sanctuary of the Temple and placed in front of the Altar and the Hierophant who had already taken his position.

The Priestesses of the Temple with their Vestals were quietly and solemnly wending their way to their usual places. The choir had begun to chant the opening service when Rathunor with one of the Priests approached with slow and measured strides as if a false movement would disturb the solemnity of this midnight's mystic silence.

As they approached the spot where the two bodies lay, there was a perceptible movement, as of consciousness in the silent form of Nu-nah.

Just as the distant chimes pealed forth their announcement of the midnight hour the Hierophant arose and stepped forth to the front of the Altar and, at a silent signal, there broke forth, as of one voice, the low-distant strains of the most enchanting music. The voices and the tones from the musical instruments were so harmoniously and wonderfully blended that the result was magically effective. The strains increased in volume—they seemed to approach nearer and nearer— until the whole edifice resounded and re-echoed as though filled with one vast orchestra sounding forth the Anthem of Creative Life, "We Praise Thee, O God."

This enchanting music continued for some time, then gently died away until only the breathings of music could be heard, when the Hierophant raised his hands as if in supplication. The solemn, awful stillness of the hour was awe-inspiring.

Once, twice, thrice, the voice of the Hierophant resounded throughout the Sanctuary as he thus spoke to their souls:

"Arise, O ye daughter of Isis, come forth and again enter the daily lives of a Vestal and a Princess. Many years now are granted to your service, and now that you have both been beyond the dividing line of this and the other plane, your lives henceforth should be guided and influenced by that experience."

At this he descended from the Altar and took the helpless hand of Sarthia to magically convey to the silent, lifeless body the electric forces of life.

Turning to Rathunor, who stood near, beckoning him to his side, he took his hand and led him to that which *was* Nu-nah's body, and gently raising the apparently lifeless hand of the silent form placed it within that of Rathunor's. The effect was indeed magical.

Rathunor was held spell-bound, the thrilling sensations, the emotions that sprang forth from the heart were electrifying. He could feel the tense vibrations passing from his hand to that of her body, the source of which he could not fathom nor understand, and little did he care at that moment when he perceived the slight tremor that was creeping over the heretofore lifeless form of his Princess Nu-nah.

Here, Rathunor would have been overcome by his emotions of joyful bliss and thrown himself prostrate at the feet of the Priest in thankful gratitude for the restoration to life of his lovely Nu-nah, had not the Hierophant just at this moment laid his hand upon Rathunor's shoulder saying, "My child, have you become unconscious of the place and the occasion, and the solemn promise you gave me to bravely follow my instructions without a show of weakness. Let not an outward manifestation of your feelings escape you again. Are you yourself again?"

With a mighty effort of his will Rathunor commanded an outward calm at least, but he could not speak, he could only bow his head in assurance and being told to retain the hand of Nu-nah, the Priest continued audibly, "In the name of the Almighty and ever-living God I now join these two souls as one. May their consciousness of this, their soul-union, dawn upon their outward memory as time proceeds, and then journey together in conscious union on the eternal path of progress to the Divine Throne of God. Amen! Amen!"

Rathunor heard but did not understand and being overcome by the silent over-powering influence surrounding him, fell insensible to the floor beside the reviving form of Nu-nah.

248

As soon as he had been conveyed to an outer court, the Hierophant again continued. Turning his attention to Sarthia, mentally he called three times, "Nu-nah, Nu-nah, Nu-nah, henceforth you shall be known as Sarthia the Vestal. May the guardian angels that have been placed over your reviving body, keep and hold the soul with it until health of body and strength of mind returns. God bless our new-found Vestal. Amen."

As the last echo of the Priest's voice died away the music burst in a joyful song of praise, and continued until the bodies of each of the young girls were removed. Sarthia's to that formerly occupied by the Vestal, and Nu-nah's to that of the home of the Princess.

Rathunor soon revived in the fresh air of the outer court and now being summoned by a messenger from the Hierophant presented himself again before him.

"My son," said the High Priest, "go to the home of the Princess and remain, either with, or near her until three cycles of seven shall pass by. At the end of twenty-one days you may return to your own home and enter the accustomed life of a Prince, until that time shall come when the Prince of the world shall enter the path that leads to a King of Wisdom," and with a fervent press of the hand and a benediction for his soul's welfare he bid him good-night and retired from the Holy Sanctuary.

VII
A VISIT TO THE CHIEF ASTROLOGER

A few weeks after the preceding ceremonies, a messenger announced to the Astrologer Priest that the Priestess sought an interview.

Hermo was at his post making the usual, daily calculations for the Priest. As the Priestess entered, Hermo arose, and was about to withdraw, when the Priestess, by a wave of her hand, gave him to understand his presence was required.

The Priestess began, "O, most Venerated Father, I come again to ask assistance, with your astrological knowledge, in behalf of Sarthia. The memory of the past seems to be entirely blotted out. Is there any aspect showing that memory will return, and if not, at what time do the planets indicate a commencement of the training of the mind that will bring a successful issue in spiritual things? We will have to commence with her as a child and train the body, mind and soul to Vestal Service."

The Astrologer turned to Hermo and said, "Hear you the request of our Priestess here? Make note, and see at what time the planets point favorably to the initiation of our new Sarthia into the Temple Service of Isis."

"How is our new Sarthia?" inquired the Priest.

"Nothing, as yet," answered the Priestess, "but that does not disturb my hope and faith that she will become all that we wish and desire of her, and instead of having but one Vestal we shall have two, for ere long Nu-nah will also be numbered among our Vestals, and Rathunor as one of our Priests."

Thanking the Priest for his promised service the Priestess withdrew.

The Astrologer returned to his studies and was soon absorbed with them, when, suddenly he turned to Hermo and said, "Hermo, I shall place Sarthia under your special tutelage as soon as she is ready to commence her studies in Astrology."

The suddenness of the Priest's remarks quite confused the young scribe and set him to seriously thinking. Strange thoughts came into his mind, "why should Sarthia *not* continue her studies with me, why would she become a special and *not* a fellow student?"

He could not account for these strange thoughts that had been excited within his mind, and the rest of the hours of work did not show the usual amount accomplished.

250

At an early hour the next night, before Hermo had arrived for his night's work, the Astrologer Priest sent for the Priestess. She hastily responded to the summons feeling there was some very important news to be received. As soon as she entered, the Priest said, "Most noble Priestess, I find by the calculations made, that not before another month may our infant child, Sarthia, be initiated, as a pupil, into the Temple of Isis. Two days before the full Moon the spiritual rays will be most active and potent, and being of so harmonious a nature we may hope for the most satisfactory results. The task will be slow and require much patience, my Priestess, for the hereditary tendencies of the brain, that have so far influenced that soul's life and experiences, will have to be polarized in other channels and gradually awakened to consciousness. The life of the body it has been animating in past years was not of such a nature as to mature a healthy soul.

"The work now, with our new Sarthia, is with the Soul, to make it equal to the brain that has been cultivated and enlarged in spiritual ways; while with Nu-nah, the work will be in arousing and developing that brain to the conscious response of the matured soul. Do I make myself plain to you? In my young pupil, Hermo, we will have a most valuable assistant in our work with Sarthia, for I have discovered that the divine relation of brother and sister exists between them. They are blest with being the emanations from the same divine state and children of the same spiritual parents. I spoke to Hermo of Sarthia last night, at the same time *willing* that my new discovery might be imparted to his soul, which I could see had been partially accomplished.

"We will allow them often in each other's society, and that holy love of brother of sister, and sister of brother, which can only be kindled in the outer heart when this spiritual relation exists.

"This will soon be recognized by each of them, and this alone will be a most potent influence in nourishing and teaching the soul of Sarthia. Nothing lies in Sarthia's path that portends serious evil for many years to come. Therefore, my good Priestess, take new hope and courage, and not many Moons will grow and wane before an inward pride will be born for your new Vestal."

The Priestess retired after thanking him most cordially, and could hardly conceal her emotions of joy and rapture until she was safe in her own apartments, where she could give full vent, in tears and cries of joy and gratitude.

As soon as all traces of the effects, which this knowledge had produced, were erased, and she became perfectly calm and composed, she sought Sarthia's chamber. The young girl was reclining upon a couch that had been drawn near the window, apparently much absorbed in studying the heavens. Scarcely did she notice the presence of the Priestess until she knelt beside her and said, "What thoughts are being born in my Sarthia's mind as she views the mighty heavens above with its millions of silent monitors, awaiting our pleasure to read and understand? Are they speaking to my darling child? Do you hear their silent voices and feel their subtle and powerful influences upon you?"

The young girl did not reply immediately. The body was still very weak and feeble, the mind was as one just awakening from a prolonged slumber.

"My beloved Priestess, did you speak to me of the stars, those loving lights in the heavens? They do seem to speak, but I can not understand and know what they say. Do you, dear Mother, and can you tell me?"

This first ray of awakening memory was more radiant to the Priestess than a thousand stars could have produced if all their rays could have blended into one. But calmness was her external bearing. Seldom any manifestation of an unusual emotion, was permitted to find an outward expression either in manner or speech. She had attained that perfect command of herself that neither joy nor sorrow, good nor evil, praise nor blame, could unbalance the perfect poise and tranquillity of her developed Soul.

"My Sarthia," replied the Priestess, "I can not know what they are saying to *you*, but they do speak to me. They tell me that life is immortal, that the growth and the progress of the soul are eternal, that we may know and read their language while in these bodies if we try; then as we draw nearer and nearer to them, as our souls grow and become familiar with their teachings, we can know them as well, if not better, than our Astrologer Priests do, also as well as your brother Hermo is learning to do."

"My—brother—Hermo," and there was a perceptible light of intelligence in the eyes for a moment.

The Priestess was not speaking to the mind, but to the soul, at the same time willing to find a response there. The mere words availed nothing to her, only in so much as they expressed the longings and desires of the interior self.

As Sarthia said no more, the Priestess arose and, moving quietly about the room, gave a few directions and cautions to those in attendance, then presently withdrew.

That night was passed by the Priestess in her own private chamber, not in sleep and rest, but actively and earnestly engaged in silent prayer for her new-born children, Nu-nah, Sarthia and Rathunor.

VIII
PRINCESS NU-NAH

The morning following the Priestess' visit to Sarthia's apartments, she sent a messenger to inquire for the welfare of Princess Nu-nah.

She was reported to have slept well, seemed much stronger, but a peculiar change had taken place during her almost fatal illness. She spoke strangely, almost weirdly at times, which excited much comment and anxiety amongst her immediate friends and relatives.

The Princess had been a general favorite and much admired by those occupying the same station in life with herself; but by those who were subject to her commands and rule, she was looked upon as cold, stern, and heartless, kind in her way when obeyed, but the slightest disobedience brought scornful reproaches and often punishment.

The Priestess, knowing the source of the peculiar change spoken of, felt that all was well. No other attention than the presence of Rathunor was needed. The developed soul of the Vestal Sarthia would soon come into control of the brain she was now trying to find expression through.

Then, too, the organs of the brain that Sarthia's soul would naturally vibrate, had never become active, nor developed; they, as it were, were dormant, fast asleep, awaiting the pulsating vibrations of the spiritual influx to give them life and usefulness. While those that had been so fully developed in the brain, by the life of the Princess, found no corresponding vibrations from the soul.

Truly, a strange commingling of the two opposing forces, and one in which time was required to bring about perfect adjustment.

The High Priest had commanded all visitors to be excluded, except Rathunor, who was to have access at all times, and as the Hierophant's word was that of God to them, so, purely from a religious standpoint, they were strictly obeyed. While the Priestess and others of the Temple knew the secret of the Priest's strict injunctions, they likewise knew that none of Sarthia's associates dared approach, lest their presence would too suddenly awake to consciousness the slumbering soul, before the brain had yet fully responded and vibrated to the new animating spark of life.

Rathunor, most of all, observed the change in the Princess; at the slightest touch there was a response within—his very presence struck the chords of sympathy that existed between them. This was, to him, a very unaccountable change. In all his life association with Nu-nah these emotions, that now seemed to spring from the soul, had never before been experienced. He was very much inclined to attribute it to an abnormal sympathy aroused by her sickness and terrible suffering. Still, the words of the High Priest haunted him and the feelings born from within, on the night of the solemn Rites at the Temple, could not be vanished by any amount of reasoning; still he would not allow such thoughts to be nourished by the slightest hope—much less be watered by the spirit of faith and allowed to grow. Although Rathunor was brave in external pain, and daringly courageous in acts of chivalry, he was an infant when subject to disappointment. Here was the battle of self going on.

"Have I the strength and manly courage to bear the disappointment born from a delusive hope? Not yet." So he suffered and heeded not the whisperings from within, until he could not endure it any longer, when he sought the presence of the Hierophant for advice and enlightenment. Scarcely able to hold in check his impatience he burst forth without the recognition due the superior presence of a High Priest.

"O, most Holy and Revered Father, tell me, am I wrong in not listening to the monitions that are racking my inmost being? May I hope the love that is growing within my soul will be surely recognized and reciprocated by Nu-nah on her return to physical health? Is this love a vain delusion on my part, an imagination born from sympathies that will vanish as soon as health is restored and we enter the whirl of the social world again? If it is in thy power, O Father, tell me the truth. Repeat thy assuring words once more, and I will be guided by them in the future, and never again allow the shadow of doubt to cross the threshold of my mind."

"My child," said the High Priest, "once more I assure you of the loving response of Nu-nah's soul and mind, as soon as she is herself again. But, mark you well, at the return of consciousness, be not rash in any of your words or acts; remember, her return to life is as a new-born babe—weak, tender and easily impressed by stronger minds and wills than its own. You are the stronger at present, and all patience and indulgence are exacted from you. Let her imaginations and fancies play as they will for awhile; yours must be calm, loving, sympathetic and unwavering in hope and faith that all will eventually be well; and again, I assure you that not many years shall pass before you will enter the path and the life your soul is now longing for. Princess Nu-nah will more than compensate you for all the kind attentions you now bestow upon her in the guiding, teaching and leading your soul in the paths to spiritual knowledge and the spiritual life, while still inhabiting the physical form.

"The hungerings of your soul shall be more than satisfied by her ministering spirit. The interior consciousness will gradually dawn upon you both, but to Nu-nah first." Then, taking Rathunor by the hand, he continued, "Doubt no more, my child, have faith in the Infinite Wisdom that guides and directs the struggling soul through the intricate ways of evolution up to the final consciousness of Immortal Life. God be with and bless you."

Rathunor had no words to express his gratitude. But they would have been useless to the Hierophant, for the new-born light that shone forth, though dimly, was more to the Priest than a world of words.

He merely looked, bowed, and with a fervent pressure of the hand, was gone from the presence of the Holy Priest. As he retraced his steps toward the home of Princess Nu-nah, a holy calm pervaded his whole being; his doubts fled as an enemy; his excitement was transformed into tranquil earnestness;

a sublime sense of the realities of life filled his brain, and a willingness to await the progress and development, that time would bring forth and mature, possessed him, until he was so changed that he scarcely recognized himself.

Was this change volitional?

IX

THE INITIATION

Days of weary watching, and toilsome care that the newborn Vestal would not be misled in her awakening thoughts, were necessary. The body needed but little care other than the proper nourishment and attention of any one in usual health. Sarthia's physical organism had not become depleted by disease and suffering, and the disorganization that had commenced was checked by the magical agent that had been placed over it, even before Sarthia had entirely left it.

The lethargy was more mental than physical. It was that semi-consciousness that precedes sleep, or that one sometimes experiences when awakened suddenly out of a deep, profound slumber.

The Priestess visited her many times throughout the day when she could spare the time from her duties in the Temple. In the course of a few days Sarthia was able to be assisted in short walks about the halls and corridors, but took little heed of things about her. Day by day, the body grew stronger and a new light began to dawn in the eyes and shone upon the countenance of the fair young girl.

In the meantime, Hermo had been apprised by the Astrologer Priest of the true relation existing between himself and Sarthia. His joy knew no bounds, for neither his heart nor soul had ever thrilled with the love of mother, sister, or kindred. It had been his misfortune to be deprived of his parents before his young mind and heart could be moved by the tender emotions of love, but now it needed no more than the Priest's revelations to kindle into flaming fires that something, he knew not what, that had been smoldering in his bosom all his life.

Now, the Astrologer's words were clear and the cause of the strange thoughts that were excited in his mind was revealed. Over and over he asked himself, "Can I wait to see my beloved sister?"

His impatience became equal with his joy, and days that had before passed as moments now seemed as ages. One morning, much to the Priestess' surprise, a messenger announced that Hermo desired an interview with her in the waiting-room below. The Priestess descended to where Hermo was waiting and, with a questioning look in her face, clasped his hand in a firm but anxious manner, inquired, "Is all well with our young Astrologer, Hermo, this morning? Does he bring tidings from our revered Father? Has any new testimony been given by the stars that portends evil to our Sarthia?"

Hermo stood in mute astonishment. "How could the Priestess receive such forebodings from his presence when his whole being was throbbing with pulsations of unbounded happiness," he thought.

"Nay, my dear Priestess, quite the reverse. Has not our worthy Father acquainted you with my new-found joy, my Love—my Sister? Know you not the divine relation that exists between Sarthia and myself? The hours have seemed days since this knowledge was revealed to me and I now beg to see my new sister and walk with her and yourself upon the lawn in the private grounds of the Temple. Can my request be granted, O Priestess?"

She still retained his hand and, again pressing it warmly between her own, said, "Our brave and noble Hermo deserves this blessing as a reward for his honest toil alone in his struggle for Truth and Knowledge. Yes, my dear Hermo, I was made aware of the relation between you and our new Sarthia and have been anxious for this moment to arrive when you would be sent to escort Sarthia in her daily walks about the grounds, but I caution you to be guarded in your words. Remember she is yet but an infant and must be taught as a child. Remain here and I will go and bring Sarthia thither and we will walk together."

It was not long before the Priestess, Sarthia and her attendant appeared. The Priestess was leading Sarthia and as they approached Hermo placed her hand in that of his saying, "Sarthia, I place you in the care and protection of your brother Hermo."

"Hermo! Hermo!! My brother Hermo?" said Sarthia.

To the penetrating eyes of the Priestess and Hermo the light of consciousness was momentarily seen and to the clairvoyant vision of the Priestess a startling scene was beheld. The vibrations of soul to soul, the love that had been kindled in Hermo's heart and soul went out with such intensity that it aroused into a vivid activity the slumbering soul of Sarthia, and the brain, being already so finely tuned to the higher vibrations of the Spirit, responded at once.

The fresh air, the green grass, the beautiful flowers and shrubbery, with the inspiring presence of Hermo, were like magic to quicken the pulsations of body and mind and bring to her cheek and eyes the flush of health and life. Not much of the conversation was directed to Sarthia, but when reference to the stars was made, she instantly inquired, "Brother Hermo, do the stars speak to you, and do you know what they say? Our lovely Priestess here can read them, and how much I would love to speak with them, too."

"I will teach you how some day, my sister, as soon as you are able to commence your studies."

"Will that be soon?"

"Yes, in a short time; so soon as you become an attendant in The Temple of Isis."

Sarthia was silent, and the Priestess reminded them it was time to return,—Sarthia to her room and Hermo to his studies, while the Priestess' presence was required in the Temple.

※

These walks continued daily with most satisfactory results to the Priestess and the Hierophant. All fears of the perfect harmonizing of the new soul to the body of Sarthia were allayed. The animating spark of life was growing stronger and the vibrations from soul to body were complete; not with consciousness, but that involuntary vibratory exchange that exists with the majority of the people that make up the earth's human family. As only the higher portion of the brain of Sarthia had been active the soul must necessarily manifest itself through those organs. Often were the much beloved Priestess, Hermo and Sarthia's attendants, surprised at her expressions and profound questions on spiritual subjects.

It was nearing the time when Sarthia was to take her initiatory step as a Vestal in the Temple of Isis. In fact, only one more day intervened before the ceremony was to take place. As the incidents relative to the transfer were known to all the Temple attendants, it was looked forward to with much silent rejoicing and gratitude that they had not been robbed of their lovely Vestal who always was held in sacred esteem by them all.

All had been notified to prepare for the Initiatory service— the music, chants, and ceremonies sacred to this occasion, must be in readiness. The night had arrived; the fair Goddess of the night shone forth in all her radiant splendor, seemingly conscious, that she was shedding forth the magnetic influence necessary for the sacred Rites now about to be performed. It had almost reached the Zenith when the solemn march of the

Priestesses, Vestals and attendants that were to conduct Sarthia to the Holy Sanctuary of the Temple started. The Priestess walked beside Sarthia. Sarthia was clothed in pure spotless linen, her head was bare with the exception of a wreath of laurel leaves that rested lightly upon her flowing hair. In her hands she carried a white-bound volume which contained the songs, chants, litany and regime for the Vestals of the Temple.

Just as they reached the door, the High Priest arose, and simultaneously the music burst forth in joyful strains that spoke welcome, courage and love to the heart of Sarthia. When they reached the foot of the altar, where stood the Hierophant, Sarthia knelt upon a velvet cushion at his feet. The music ceased while the High Priest stood with uplifted hands in silent prayer. At a signal, the choir began chanting the Litany. Sarthia was bidden to rise, when the Priest, in measured and solemn tones, addressed her:

"Do you come to pledge yourself to Temple Service? Is it your desire to become a Vestal of Isis? Do you take the pledge of celibacy to the virgin Rites of the Temple; your time, energy and purpose to be devoted to the duties that devolve upon a Vestal?"

The low, clear voice of Sarthia was heard throughout the Sanctuary as she bowed and answered in assent.

"So be it, my holy virgin. I now commit your soul to the Guardian Angels of this Sacred Sanctuary to guide, guard and protect your budding soul to perfect at-one-ment with its divine center, that you may inherit immortal life while yet with us. Amen!"

Sarthia opened the book within her hands and, kissing its pages which she had already subscribed to, handed it to the High Priest. He took it, and held it in his left, while he placed his right hand upon her head, and said:

"I bid thee welcome, my Vestal Sarthia, and commend thy soul to the Gods above, that ever keep watch o'er the children of earth. God bless thee. Amen! Amen!"

Then, as if they were voicing the words of the Hierophant, the chants grew louder, the music poured forth in grander tones as though to join the invisible hosts above in praise to God most high.

The ceremony was over and Sarthia was conducted back to her chamber, a Vestal of the Temple of Isis. The occult powers that had been evoked in behalf of Sarthia soon became manifest in her daily life. The zeal and zest with which she pursued her studies and the understanding of their interior meanings were sufficient evidence of her teacher's inspiring influence. She was soon placed under her brother Hermo's instruction in astronomical and astrological lore, and here also displayed a proficiency in learning that surprised Hermo and delighted the Astrologer Priests. At Temple Service she was all devotion and, as an Attendant, ever true and faithful. The brother and sister became devotedly attached to each other and the Priestess often observed this attachment, which sent a pang through her heart, lest such joy and happiness might not be granted Hermo for the remainder of his life. Then instantly would she offer a silent prayer that such supreme happiness would be theirs throughout eternity.

X
THE PRINCESS' WEDDING

The Princess' recovery was very slow, owing to the great depletion of the physical body during her recent illness. Much care and attention were bestowed upon her by her royal friends. All the luxury which wealth alone could procure, and the kindly influences of loving associates were brought to bear to speedily hasten the restoration of their Princess to her former health and spirits. Health was slowly but surely gaining the ascendency, but the spirits of heart and mind were not of that buoyant, external nature that she formerly displayed.

With her return to health, demands of a social nature were made upon her. She enjoyed pleasures but a seriousness attended her every movement that much annoyed her friends. The attendants and servants were excited to wonder at her kind and thoughtful interests of them—while many thought it was due to her weak physical condition, others remarked, how much the Princess' sickness had improved her. Those that before feared her, now began to love and seek to please and serve her.

Rathunor was a daily visitor, and remembering the advice and instructions of the Hierophant he was calm, silent, and patient in his attentions to her and apparently took no heed of her fancies and strange conversation. She would constantly plan amusements and social entertainments on a grand scale, but with such a seriousness of purpose that it quite annoyed Rathunor at times and caused him to wonder if this was really his former Nu-nah.

While the annoyance came purely from the external, there was an interior attraction that was, irresistibly, holding him spell-bound to her side. His happiness now was greatest when they sat, rode or walked in silence. Little did he dream, while in that silence which so enraptured him, the soul of Nu-nah was blending and drawing the electric life-essence from his own to hers. That interchange was going on wherein there is no robbery, but an inter-blending of the magnetic and electric life-forces that cause to spring into activity the harmonious vibrations of a complete whole, and the reaction upon both brain and the physical organism was health, contentment and happiness that rises above all external cares, sorrows and discords.

Although the soul of the, now known, Princess was highly developed it could find but few responsive echoes from the dormant spiritual organs of the brain. These she must arouse to sensitiveness and action. It was this that gave rise to the peculiar ideas, expressed in her conversation, that so mystified her friends. Visitors soon began to pour in upon her congratulations, presents and invitations to once again enter the gilded salons of fashion and the round of amusements that are the daily life of a favorite Princess. To all she gave a modest, quiet reply, neither accepting nor rejecting their attentions, which left them in wondering doubt at times of her sanity.

In the midst of some grand occasion she would be suddenly missed and on being sought out would be found concealed in some pleasant nook, or even out in the open air, or beside an open window, absorbed in meditation or gazing into the heavens. When her attention was attracted she would start and, with a strange, far-away look in her eyes that would indicate to a superficial observer she had been asleep, would allow herself to be led back and enter the festivities of the hour.

With all their efforts they could not enthuse her with the excitement and merriment surrounding her. But, if any one should become serious and express thoughts that appealed to the interior, she was all attention and the questions that were so ready when such an opportunity afforded showed plainly that, although present in body, the soul and interests were in other realms and spheres than this.

No one but Rathunor could hold her attention for any length of time. With him she was animated, and charmingly beautiful and joyous and would, with some enthusiasm, enter into the pleasantries of the hour which brought to her face the charming attraction of natural beauty. Behind those orbs of vision there seemed to shine forth a light that was more radiant than the gorgeously brilliant illuminations of the salons. Her beautiful face, her perfect form and bearing, made her the center of attraction and she was much sought after. But, as soon as she was induced to leave Rathunor's side, that which made her presence so irresistibly attractive and radiant before, faded out.

Thus time passed on, and as health returned, Prince Rathunor pressed his suit. There was now no apparent reason why he could not claim his promised bride and make the Princess Nu-nah his own. His more earnest friends cautioned him to await further developments and, in an undertone, reminded him of the peculiar and unnatural bearing of the Princess at times. They were sure, in time, their once lovely Princess would be herself again. Rathunor listened, knowing their kindly interest sprang from good motives, but he was silent—he could not speak for none would understand. The yearnings of his heart and soul would not be quelled by any outward show.

While to the world Nu-nah was a source of mystical wonder, to Rathunor she was his stay and comfort. He needed no further evidence and assurance of Nu-nah's love for him. Too often had he experienced the response from within to her silent pleadings for light, truth and wisdom. The attraction of the outer world was losing its fascination for him, the longings from within grew stronger and more clamorous for outward expression until, one day, he advanced the subject of astrology to the Princess Nu-nah. For an instant, her whole being was illuminated by that mysterious light—for a single moment the soul arose to the supremacy of the brain and found a faint glimmering expression that was visible to Rathunor's ever-watchful eye.

"Astrology, my Rathunor, fascinates me with its name and the wonders and mysteries it is said to reveal. Do you think those Astrologer Priests of the Temple know whereof they speak, and do they read the stars and gain from them the wisdom they are said to possess?"

Here was the first opportunity to present these sacred subjects to Nu-nah's mind. He tried to think and, feeling that the present excitement of the brain's higher organs was of a temporary nature, he was really at a loss what to say that would be most effective and impress itself indelibly upon her awakening brain.

"Yes, my dear Nu-nah, I believe they do possess the knowledge they claim and I also am convinced that much of that wisdom and knowledge is gained through their understanding the laws of astrology. Those celestial bodies in our heavens were not placed there by our Divine Creator without a purpose. I believe they have an influence upon us that can be learned, defined and utilized by those who study and know this influence through astronomy and astrology. Nu-nah what is that which produces the interior longings to know? Is it not that there is something to know—something that our common brains can not grasp and analyze? Do you not think that silent, yet persistent, monitor which lies concealed somewhere within our being is excited to action from some source other than our outward selves, and that longing to go out must be accounted for by a something without that calls and attracts us to it? May this not be the stars that we see twinkling and motioning to us as we gaze into the midnight heavens?"

He stopped, wondering what the effect of his words would be, when, to his amazement, there appeared a more vivid consciousness in her eyes and features than he had ever seen since her return to physical health and, taking new hope from this manifestation, he continued, "Do you love the social world longer? Is there not that longing, too, within your bosom for something more real, more ennobling than the pastimes of worldly pleasures?"

At the mention of the worldly things, the light from her eyes died out and was gone. Rathunor said no more but silently thanked God that he had for those few moments assisted the soul of Nu-nah to vibrate, too; and had set in motion the vitalizing currents to the spiritual portion of the brain and earnestly prayed that this might be the beginning of many opportunities that were to follow.

Realizing that only he could arouse the dormant organs of her spiritual brain, he became more anxious than ever to have her constantly in his company. He again pressed his suit and the day for the wedding-nuptials was to be at once submitted to the Astrologer.

Rathunor again sought the Astrologer Priest for advice. He wished to know when the stars would point most favorably toward such a momentous event. This the Astrologer was not long in finding out and soon conveyed the news to Rathunor that at an early date such might be consummated. As the Prince arose to go the Priest took his hand and said, "My child, in taking the Princess Nu-nah as your wife, you obey the holy intuitions of the soul and not only will you be united in soul but in body and mind. I wish you the eternal bliss that attends all who are truly mated. Farewell, my child; my blessings go with you."

Rathunor was too much absorbed in other things to understand the mysterious words of the Priest, but notwithstanding this the seed had been again sown that would sometime spring up unannounced and unexpected.

The announcement of the wedding was soon made and invitations sent out, far and near. Congratulations poured in from every source, although some would have refused, had they been true to their own sentiments, for the remarkable and unaccountable change which had taken place during her terrible malady was too evident to be altogether right and should be righted before the Prince should make the Princess his wife.

Rathunor was satisfied, never forgetting the Hierophant's sacred words, and none other need be consulted. In their silent hearts they wished the wedding might be private and the holy ceremony of the Temple be performed by the High Priest. This, of course, could not be owing to the station and position they occupied in life, for the lives of a Princess and

Prince are not wholly their own, so to the public they must bow and pay obeisance.

Preparations for the wedding commenced at once, for it was to be a grand affair. Nothing was to be spared that would add beauty and grandeur to the occasion. Extravagant expenditures were indulged in, until money seemed at a loss to supply more. The trousseau was exquisitely magnificent and, on the wedding night, the beaming radiance of the countenance of the Princess was neither dimmed by the rich silks, nor the rare, priceless laces and lovely jewels that glittered and sparkled with the living spark of life within them, that adorned her form.

Never a bride so fair; never a couple so happy. It was that quiet, subtle happiness, which permeates the very atmosphere about them and leaves its traces in every susceptible heart that breathes it.

XI
THE RETIREMENT

After the wedding the Prince and Princess were, from necessity, drawn within the whirl of social pleasures with attentions in the way of entertainments, court suppers, balls, drawing-room receptions, etc. The interior longings were compelled to creep into the background until the external was gratified to exhaustion. The Princess' seriousness departed for a time and they were very happy in the round of pleasures that were planned for them. But as time sped on they began to grow weary of the show, pomp and shallowness of external life. The seeds that had been sown in Rathunor's heart and brain, and that which he had aroused in Nu-nah's slumbering, spiritual organs of her brain, had taken root and now began to spring forth into activity, first as weariness of the superficial pleasures of society, then a desire to gradually withdraw from this life into a more quiet and secluded one, where they might listen to the inner voices and gain pleasure, as well as knowledge, from this source.

The Prince anxiously awaited another opportunity for speaking to Princess Nu-nah on spiritual subjects. The Hierophant had given him to understand that at no distant day Nu-nah would become interested in spiritual things and be his teacher. He had not been made aware of the transfer—that was to be revealed to him by Nu-nah herself. He had begun to wonder how and where Nu-nah's spiritual awakening would take place when an opportunity presented itself in a most unexpected manner.

One lovely evening they were taking a stroll about the grounds of their castle, when the full Moon arose in a flood of light, it rose higher, fuller, until the whole world seemed bathed in her magical beauty and in order to longer enjoy her light and magnetic influence the Prince suggested a longer walk. Unconsciously they chose the path that led them towards the Temple, which was only a short distance from their home. As they neared the Temple distant strains of music attracted their attention. They listened, and it seemed to speak in the plaintive tones of a hungering soul; they hastened their steps until they had quite reached the private grounds of the Temple of Isis, Nu-nah was in advance of Rathunor, being irresistibly drawn by some invisible power, when she suddenly stopped and clasping his arm, as within a vice, cried out, "My Rathunor, do you hear that music; what is it? I have heard it before, but where, O, where? How came I to know the chants and music of the Temple Service?"

They were held spell-bound to the spot, when the Prince was warned, by the trembling and the gradual loosening of Nu-nah's hand upon his arm, to quit the spot at once. The Prince placed his arm about her waist to support her as he urged their return home, but she stood immovable apparently chained by the magical power of some invisible force.

Stronger grew the mystical power of the spell until the Princess seemed compelled to rush madly on and into the Temple, if the Prince had not held her back in a firm grasp, and at the same time trying to attract her attention by his words. "Come, my darling, let us retrace our steps and as we walk I will tell you all I know about what you have heard."

"O, my Rathunor, speak to me quickly before I have time to forget. I can not remember this long, yet it as a recurrence of a vivid dream. Tell me while I am awake, where I have been. I saw, and felt, and know I was there—there in the Sacred Sanctuary of that Temple. O, that I might go again and remain there forever to listen to that enchanting music and the solemn heavenly voices of that choir."

A quiver ran through her whole frame and with a mournful cry she fell fainting in the arms of Rathunor. Here his innate born courage and bravery sustained him, and instantly there flashed into his mind the words he had once heard the High Priest use while passing his hands over an insensible form. So, gently laying her inanimate body upon the grass, he repeated in slow, but firm and commanding tones these words:

"Return, O soul, to thy physical body. Return, I command thee, and reanimate this lifeless tenement of your soul. Come, come, I command thee, come."

Scarcely had the last words been uttered when a movement of the hands and limbs announced to Rathunor the return of life. She was soon able to rise and, being supported by the Prince, they slowly wended their way back to the castle. She walked as in a dream, but as her step was stately and firm, the Prince did not become alarmed until he had her safe in her room, when the extent of the occurrence dawned upon him and then he hurriedly called her maid and sent at once to dispatch a servant for their physician. Nu-nah had become quite herself before the Doctor came and after he had administered a little palliative, withdrew saying, "The Princess will soon be well. It was only the result of fatigue induced by the constant excitement of social pleasures."

The Prince was silent and, seeing the Princess was so comfortable, he retired to his own apartments with strict injunctions, he should be notified at once if any symptoms of the prostration should appear. When once within his private chamber he threw himself down in a chair and fell into a profound study. Over and over he reviewed the incidents of the evening. "What was there in that music that so enchanted Nu-nah? What did she see and hear that revived a faint memory of something in the past? What magical force was it that drew her so irresistibly toward the Temple? What produced that quiver which preceded her falling insensible into his arms?"

He was half inclined to blame the Priests for it all, for he knew something of the power of magic and its psychologic effect. The more he reasoned the farther he wandered from a solution. Now he mused, "If that had been the beautiful Vestal, Sarthia, I could understand why she would be so powerfully attracted to the Temple, but Nu-nah, who had never entered the Holy Sanctuary except for those sacred Rites that are administered to all who are supposed to be bordering on the land of the spiritual world; only those two nights, to his knowledge, had she ever been in the Sacred Sanctuary; there was something in those ceremonies that he had not as yet understood; there must have been some mystical, magical power employed to restore the frail, feeble, unconscious Nu-nah to life and health and, to him."

He thought and reasoned until his brain was on fire, and still no solution of the mystery was presented to his understanding.

"Well," he at last exclaimed, so loud that he startled himself, "I will have to accept it as a mystery and patiently wait time's own pleasure for the explanation."

He began to prepare for retiring, but he could not calm himself—a restlessness took possession of him that he could not quell; he walked the floor, tried to read, and resorted to many ways to restore his tranquillity, but all in vain.

"I must see my Nu-nah once more before I can sleep," and, hurriedly readjusting the clothing he had removed, he repaired to the Princess' private room. A gentle knock brought the attendant to the door.

"Is the Princess quiet and sleeping," he inquired in a whisper.

"No," answered the servant. "She is awake and feeling well, and just now remarked that if she thought you were not sleeping she would have you called for she had something she wished to tell you."

His presence was at once made known to the Princess, and, with a low cry of delight, she called him to her side. A signal sent the attendant from the room, when the Princess began, "My Rathunor, my beloved husband, I am so glad you came. I have something to tell you that I might forget before morning. Tonight, when we came within the sound of the music in the Temple, I felt as if I left my body and you, and by some unknown power was drawn into the Sacred Sanctuary. I saw the High Priest, the lovely Mother Priestess, the Vestals, the choir and musicians, all earnestly engaged in some holy ceremony. The music, the heavenly spiritual influence of the atmosphere, the exquisite fragrance of incense and perfumes, with the purity reflected by the Vestal attendants, so enraptured and enthralled me that the thought that I would ever have to leave its sacred boundaries caused me to lose consciousness and, when I awoke, you were bending over me."

272

Seeing a strange look in Rathunor's eyes and interpreting it to mean jealousy, she continued, "but that was not all, my Rathunor; you were there, too, for awhile. I tried to keep you, but could not—something drew you away from *me* and I, for an instant, suffered the same pangs that are torturing your heart now. I thought you would rather go than stay, and a feeling of jealousy entered my heart, but the strange fascination of the place was more to me at that instant than you, my Rathunor, so I longed to stay but could not. I have been trying to think what it all means. You must help me for already I feel the memory of the event passing away."

She ceased speaking, and in a few moments was fast asleep. The Prince kissed the hand he held, then gently laid it by her side and quietly left the room fully conscious that the mystery had been partially revealed, and that now the Princess would sleep for the rest of the night. After returning to his rooms he again flung himself into an easy chair determined to seriously think and arrive, that night, at some immediate steps to take his Nu-nah from the excitement she had been subjected to for so long, so that a recurrence of the sad event might not be repeated. Before another Sun arose the Prince had decided upon his future course. "I will take Nu-nah away, ostensibly on a long tour of the country for pleasure. Aye, for pleasure, but not the kind we have submitted to since our marriage."

The next morning, as soon as the Princess could see him, he requested her presence at once. He met her at the door and with a loving inquiry as to her health, led her to an easy chair beside the open window where the rays of the morning Sun could fall upon her as they penetrated the delicate lace which hung at the window. Drawing a chair to her side he began to unfold his plans, at the same time watching every motion and expression of the face to see what effect they would have upon her. She did not betray her thoughts until he said his object was not so much for travel as to retire to some quiet, pleasant nook, where they could be excluded from the world, and those they knew, for awhile, and instead of spending their time in the superficial pleasures of the world they could enjoy each other's society and learn something about the invisible mysteries that surrounded them.

When the motives of his plans were mentioned a perceptible change flashed across her countenance and a light appeared in her eyes that he had not seen for some time and, by the time he had finished, her whole face was beaming with an inward delight, that urged the Prince to further reveal the plans that he had laid during his midnight reasonings. The Princess raised not a single exception to his schemes but, on the contrary, entered into them with a zest that surprised even the Prince.

"O, to be alone, Rathunor, where we could think and study that which we choose has been the longing of my very soul these many weeks; can not we go at once, today if possible?" She felt she could not wait the necessary time for the preparations to be made.

There was a duty toward their friends that must be fulfilled. The devoted attentions that had been showered upon them for so long must not be ignored. So, it was decided to give a farewell reception, before taking their departure for an indefinite stay in strange lands.

Accordingly invitations were issued to a grand state occasion, when the Prince and Princess would bid their friends and associates Farewell. Ah! farewell. Little did those who were of that brilliant assembly dream, as they clasped the hands of the Princess and Prince in cordial and sincere goodbye, that it was indeed a Farewell to all. Neither did they conceive for a moment what those Farewells meant to the Princess and Prince. It was hard for them to conceal their happiness as every minute of time brought their departure nearer, and what their guests took for the happiness of their presence, was really induced by the thoughts of the future.

They were soon off and we can only follow them in thought for a time. Let those thoughts be kind, for, knowing thoughts are potent, send them out lovingly toward the awakening mind of Princess Nu-nah.

XII
THE RETURN TO A NEW LIFE

Several years have elapsed since we bade our Prince and Princess farewell. Only at long intervals had they communicated with their friends. The outer world had almost forgotten them, but not so with the Hierophant and the Priestess of the Temple. Daily, had their prayers gone in behalf of their souls' welfare. Although not in communication with them in body, they were in spirit, and from this source they knew all was well. The High Priest, in his astral visits, could see the growing power of the soul over the slowly-evolving brain of the Princess, and with the electric soul-force, the great nourisher and renewer of life, though unconscious to him, the rounding out was fast nearing completion of the soul's mastery over the brain and body of Nu-nah.

They had settled in distant lands, near a little country village that lay just at the foot of the mountains. It was made up of the simple peasantry, where life was free from cant, suspicions, criticism and morbid curiosity. Here they could live and follow the bent of their minds, undisturbed and unobserved if they so wished. They kept their identity unknown yet the villagers knew from the Princess' delicate beauty of form and features she belonged to some noble family and station in life, but her kind, thoughtful bearing towards them won their love and esteem at once, and equally did they esteem the Prince for he was ever lavish with his money and attention to those who appealed to him for assistance. The mountains soon became their favorite resort. Long walks were taken daily, and rests made in the quiet nooks on the mountain side. One place particularly became a very dear retreat to them, for never did they stop there but that some inspirations were born. It was here that Nu-nah took her first lesson from Rathunor; it was in this sacred spot that Rathunor gently but cautiously revealed to her the Initiatory Rites of the Temple that had been performed over her unconscious body. This excited an intense curiosity, if not deep interest, in Nu-nah's mind. She began to question and think and, as she thought, there came a vague, glimmering memory of the past, and when Rathunor would inquire the cause of her almost unconscious moods, she would raise her hand to silence his voice, and whisper, "I am dreaming—O, something so grand, so solemn, so sacred haunts my mind; just wait and it will all come by and by," then her dark eyes seemed to grow larger and larger and to burn with a concentrated fire.

The Prince's delight knew no bounds as these expressions led him to believe they sprang from deep desires and interests, so the time seemed to shorten for the day to come when their whole time and attention would be turned to the study of Nature's mysteries and the secrets of life be revealed to them, thus satisfying that inward longing for the realities of life. Also, he knew, the new love that had been born in Nu-nah's heart for him was more than that love that the external only can know. Its depths he could not fathom nor its source pursue, so he was content to wait that promised time, predicted by the Astrologer, that Nu-nah would lead, guide and teach him these spiritual truths and reveal to his already awakening soul the laws of the spirit.

Now, a new joy was revealed to the Prince when the Princess made him aware that a new soul had been entrusted to their tender care and keeping. The thoughts of maternity filled her heart with bliss. Blessed privilege, to bring to this plane of existence a soul awaiting incarnation in human form, to live, grow and experience on this planet the last grand objective existence that the soul can know. What care, what pleasure would she take in training that little soul to know its God and the mysteries of life and in maturity stand forth to teach mankind Wisdom and Truth.

The pleasure in preparing for its advent made days pass as minutes. Time, borne on the wings of love, passed quickly. Her soul had gained that control over the mind that it was full with pure, holy and spiritual thoughts. Her mind could not get beyond her husband and the young soul that had been transmitted to her keeping. The divine joy of love was singing in her soul. Rathunor left her alone in her happiness, knowing that in her condition any great effort on his part to draw her mind-thoughts into new channels might lead to dire results.

At last the Natalday arrived. The magnetic, as well as the physical, period of gestation being completed, to them a son was born. Never was there a human soul greeted with greater love and welcome than this one. Not only was it the offspring of the physical union, but that of the souls. Welcome, thrice welcome, to the children born of such love. The physical condition of the Princess was very critical for several days. The Prince's grief and anxiety was almost unbearable; neither sleep nor food took a moment of his time during her severe illness, and often did he think that again Nu-nah's soul would take its flight and wend its way to the realms above.

The eighth day after confinement was one of stupor and unconsciousness. Not a moment passed unheeded. It was near midnight when, the attendants having retired for a short rest, and Rathunor sitting alone by her bedside, her eyes suddenly opened and bent their gaze upon him. Beautiful, calm, divine Nu-nah, her wonderful eyes shone with a surprising brilliancy and they were so riveted upon him that he dared not move, much less speak. The minutes that intervened between her waking and speaking seemed as an eternity to Rathunor.

"My darling husband, are you beside me—are you where I can speak to you, and are we alone?"

Only by a gentle pressure of the hand could he respond, and, gently laying his right hand upon her brow, he assured her by this act of his presence. She began speaking—her voice was low, yet clear and distinct, "My Rathunor, my true-soul companion, I have returned with the knowledge I now impart to you. While you so patiently and tenderly watched beside my frail and almost lifeless body, my soul was away gaining knowledge and experience in the soul-world. There I learned who I am and my relation to you. Do you know, O my Rathunor, that our souls sustain that divine relation to each other that makes us immortal, because of being complete? The whole, the two rays of the Divine Ego, are joined and blended as one in our union. Can you hear me further?"

The agitation of his grief began to assuage and he could now listen calmly and without emotion to her words.

"Yes, go on. What you have already said has been indelibly burned upon my mind and soul. Let me hear all you have to impart."

"Know you that this body was Nu-nah's and this soul that of Sarthia's?"

It was here that only by a mighty effort of his will was he able to keep in abeyance the emotions of his heart, but the superior and God-like power of an invisible Presence sustained him. The Princess took no heed of his silence and continued her revelations.

"Do you know that on the night of the full Moon, the solemn and sacred Rites performed over the unconscious bodies of Sarthia and Nu-nah in the Sacred Sanctuary of the Temple of Isis, our souls were transferred by the magical power of the High Priest and the invisible assistants? Nu-nah's soul was polarized in Sarthia's physical temple and that of Sarthia's in this of mine. Both were prostrated, even to dissolution by the malefic influence of planetary arcs, and this method was resorted to, that both our lives might be spared to round out our necessary physical existence while yet in these bodies, and also for your sake was this undertaken by our Holy Father that you might have that love which you so much craved and the longings of your soul might be satisfied with the knowledge it thirsted for. This will explain to you the great change observed at times in your Nu-nah, and the unnatural, dreamy moods that possessed me sometimes. The brain was slow to respond to the wonderfully developed soul of Sarthia and it was at those times that the soul gained the supremacy, that the greatest change would manifest. You now have the true devoted love of your soul companion and the lovely form of Nu-nah for your wife. My Rathunor, are you satisfied? If a pang of disappointment cross your heart, our darling child here may blot that out as he grows and learns our mystic lore and become also a soul companion of his fathers in climbing the ladder to higher wisdom and spheres than ours."

The Prince could not speak. He sank on his knees beside the bed and buried his face in her bosom. Here silence was more profound and spoke deeper wisdom and contentment than ever words could do; how long he remained in this humble attitude and poured forth his gratefulness in prayer he knew not; but when he arose the Princess was sleeping quietly, the breathing, though feeble, was deeper and more even. He gently crossed her hands upon her bosom, adjusted the clothing carefully and left her side, full of a new hope he had had for many days. Life again appeared in all its glory, not a shadow appeared upon its horizon; weariness and anxiety forsook him and he went about as if walking on air, but not a word escaped his lips—nor an act betrayed his new-born joy.

When the nurses returned they at once remarked the change in the Princess. They, too, became hopeful and assured the husband that his wife would soon be well. The Princess recovered rapidly, and it was not long before her gentle presence and noble influence shed its effulgence in the home as she moved about it.

As soon as Rathunor could spare the time from Nu-nah's side he sent the Natal hour of his first-born to the Astrologer Priest. Anxiously did he await the reading of the stars and what they indicated for his child. The calculations were made, the judgment submitted in writing, but "Shall I transmit them to the Prince and Princess, can they yet receive and philosophically accept the revelations therein made?"

He left the study-room and repaired to the apartments of the High Priest to seek advice and instructions. Then, by the exercise of his potent will, he made the necessary observations to see if it were wise to convey the knowledge of the predictions to his children, Nu-nah and Rathunor.

"Not yet will we send the reading. Our Nu-nah has not sufficiently recovered to bear any unpleasant news."

Rathunor became impatient and thought, at times, he would write again—the letter must have been lost—but something withheld him. At last strange forebodings haunted him. He knew too well the promptness of the Astrologer Priest; there must be something that could not be revealed to Nu-nah. He thought he was strong enough to bear resignedly all that might come, but when it did come all his forebodings had not prepared him to receive it. It was only a letter—no calculations—no reading, as indicated by the stars, was in it. The letter had been dictated by the Priest and transcribed by the scribe Hermo, and read thus:

"Our darling children, Rathunor and Nu-nah, bear bravely the news I now impart to you. Your first born, the offspring of true inspiration and soul-love, can not remain with you long in the physical form. The stars deny a prolonged life, and my interior knowledge of the planetary influence, also tells me his life upon our Earth's plane will be of short duration. His already matured soul does not need much of Earth's experience to round out its objective existence, before entering the true life in the spiritual realm; there it will remain, my dear children, ever beckoning you on, and contributing to you that energy that will ever spur you to greater effort to realize while yet in the physical form Immortal Life. Tend it carefully, but when the Great Powers that Be summon its soul to go, do not try to hold it here, but add the strength of your united prayers to its flight and bid it depart to its home in the spiritual realms above. God bless and give you the strength, my children, is the prayer of your devoted Father. Amen! Amen!"

The strength of spiritual force that seemed to accompany the letter and his loving advice imparted courage to their hearts, and instead of giving way to grief, began to philosophically reason and console themselves that God's ways were wiser than man's.

Not many months did their lovely spiritual child remain with them until its soul took its flight to realms beyond, where truly it became as a beacon-light to the souls of its parents. Its departure left the Prince and Princess sad and lonely for a time and their struggle to reconciliation was great—but this was of the heart and not of the soul. Time healed the external wound and the interior vacancy was filled by study, investigation and the development to external consciousness of the knowledge within.

Again, they became restless and plans were laid to leave their happy home near the mountains, and the devoted friends they had made among the villagers who were sorry to part with them and, as memento to their honest, noble friendship, they distributed their household and personal effects among them. They revealed to no one where they were going. They disappeared as mysteriously as they came, but where? Only one place on Earth could tempt them to leave that sacred home, where such extreme joy and sorrow were known, and that was the former home of the soul of Nu-nah, The Temple of Isis. Nu-nah was to enter as an aspirant to a Priestess, and Rathunor as a Priest King.

The Return to a New Life, was hailed with joyful welcomes from all of the Attendants of the Temple. Rathunor and Nu-nah soon passed the ceremonial Rites of the Temple and none were more faithful in their efforts and studies than these new-born children—the especial care of the High Priest and the Priestess.

We leave them here, wishing them the progress, the happiness and that Divine Peace and Understanding that comes to all Perfected Souls. God be with them.

AS A MAN THINKETH

by Marie Saltus

"YOUR deductions are correct and logical, Professor, but your premises are absolutely false. In consequence, your arguments, though clever, are useless."

Professor Hinton-Garow faced the speaker with a frown. His paper on "Contagious and Infectious Diseases" had been anticipated by the medical convention as its basis of action; and the fact that he had traveled from Glasgow to Calcutta expressly for that purpose gave additional weight to his words. The committee, though comprised of only a handful of men, was an important one—having the financial support of the home government and the moral support of the world. The monster terrors of Asiatic cholera and the "black death" gave unmistakable signs of a gigantic onslaught, and at the note of warning a dozen physicians and scientists of eminence and ability had been gathered from the four quarters of the globe to probe the secrets of contagion and infection, and, understanding, find ways and means to combat, and if possible to destroy. Such was the motive of the gathering, and Professor Hinton-Garow, upon whom all eyes were turned, had just given a most comprehensive address on the nature of contagion, and the possible uses of electricity and concentrated heat and light in killing the bacteria in the early stages of development. As the words of protest were uttered, the attention of the listening group was directed to a slight, small man of extreme old age whose erect form, clear blue eyes, and serene composure were in contrast to the thick white hair that waved about his head and the white beard that hung like a breastplate to his waist. With unclouded brow he gazed earnestly at the faces before him.

"Gentlemen," he said, "we are here for the good of mankind. Let us be practical. This is no time for speculation or controversy. Let us found our arguments upon facts, not theories; let us get at the bottom of the trouble, not sidetracked into experimenting with its growth."

The chairman called the assembly to order. "Professor Adam Adair," he said, "the greatest scientist, chemist, and psychologist of our times, is with us. At his extreme age we hoped for but scarcely expected his presence. That he is here, and that he is also to address us, is an honor to everyone present."

The men moved their chairs to get a better view of one whose fame had preceded him. A curious smile played upon the old man's features as he continued:

"Gentlemen, we are here for a practical purpose, and it is idle for us to speculate upon the best method of attacking disease while in complete ignorance of what *dis-ease* really is. Let us start at the foundation and work upward; let us begin with the fact, absolute and incontrovertible, that *there is no dis-ease of the body*. That which is so called is, when rightly understood, but the outward manifestation of a disordered *mind*. Our human bodies are but the visible productions of the mind within. Harmony, or, as we call it, *health*, is our natural or positive condition: dis-ease the negative or outward sign of inner discord. The mind makes us what we are. Consciously or unconsciously, daily and hourly, we are making and manifesting bodily conditions and environments, which are called into existence by mental pictures vividly conceived and continually looked at—to say nothing of the currents of thought-atmosphere in which we are magnets or centers. Thoughts are things, and the power of constructive imagination rightly used is stronger than electricity and greater than the combined energy of the world. We make ourselves what we are. We are constantly constructing new bodies. Why can we not make them according to our fancy?

"Those who do not *fear* cholera rarely if ever take it. Since the mind alone can kill, why cannot the mind cure? I am, as you know, an Englishman, and at an early age I accompanied my parents to India. It was there I was educated, and there I first studied the metaphysical lore of the East. When I left Oxford, many years later, I married; and my wife and I, accompanied by our only child, a girl of three, went to India to live. For years I devoted my time to research and study. An Indian by associations and affections, I was encouraged and welcomed by the greatest teachers; and Yogis of profound learning opened many of their sacred books to my inquiring eyes. It was there I learned the fallacy of 'disease,' and there—but of that later.

"I will tell you how I put my convictions to the test. When my girl was six years old my wife died, and in order to divert my sad thoughts I took the child and traveled round the world. We visited many lands and saw many interesting sights, but our arrival at Honolulu was followed by an event that was destined to change not only my life but my ideas and theories as well. So appallingly strange and unusual were the consequences of this occurrence that it has almost revolutionized the realm of my individual thought.

"We had been in Honolulu a week, my child and I, when I became acquainted with a certain Father Sebastian, a Jesuit, whose duty it was to send reading matter and other supplies from the little mission of which he was in charge to others of the order on the island of Molokai. No one could live on that isle of the living death and return to his fellowmen, but the priests of the mission would row out to a fixed place with books and provisions while those from the island would come up in their canoes to effect a transfer of the articles. Thus personal contact was avoided and the safety of the transfer insured.

"For years Father Sebastian had done this, and it was with the greatest interest that I listened to his story of the living horror not many miles away. I asked permission to visit these stricken creatures and acquaint them with their rightful inheritance of health—to urge them one and all to coöperate with the gigantic forces of Nature working in their behalf, and hold to the desire that their *children* at least might be born free from the taint. Disease is *not* hereditary—it cannot be; but the mind of the parent acting upon the unborn germ of life may plant the *suggestion*, which is developed after birth by the thought atmosphere impregnated with the false idea of disease transmission. Thus the appearance of disease is inevitable

"In vain I urged my request. The good priest shook his head. My ideas were not in accord with his own, and he thought it would be a mistaken kindness to help me to gain access to that place of horror whence the law would not permit me to return. That I was above the law of 'disease' while I held faithfully to the mental picture before me, I well knew; but my arguments were useless, and after repeated requests I abandoned the idea. It was the night before we left Honolulu that I went to bid my friend goodbye. He knew we were to sail for Japan in the morning, and this hour had been appointed for our meeting. It was late in the evening before I arrived at the mission. Father Sebastian was alone, save for the presence of a little girl—a sweet-faced, bright-eyed creature of unusual beauty. After the first word of greeting the priest's face grew grave. 'Professor,' he said, slowly, 'I was unable to help you in your honest efforts to aid your fellow-men in the way you wished, but God in his inexplicable wisdom has granted your prayer in a most remarkable way. It sometimes happens that a child of leprous parents is born apparently free from the curse. happens rarely, but when such an instance occurs the child is if possible isolated and cared for at some mission. Almost invariably the disease shows itself later in life—you would ascribe it to the thought-atmosphere by which the child is surrounded. I am not prepared to accept this explanation, but I am going to help you to put your belief to the test. This child at our feet is the offspring of leprous parents. She was born six years ago apparently free from the stain, and during her short life has been cared for by the sisters of our mission who live on the island. So far she has evinced no signs of the malady—her health is evident; but, as even in our mission there are some who are becoming its victims, I communicated your theories to the sister in charge and it became her desire to give this child the benefit of the possible chance. What I have done is against all rules and regulations, but we effected a transfer to our boat and hence to the mission here. The child knows nothing of her people, nor has she ever heard of disease. She is so young that the memory of the mission will become but a dream to her. It is one chance in a million; and now I ask you, as a man and a Christian, will you take her with you tomorrow and do for her as we would if we could?'

"To say that I was surprised is inadequate. It was minutes before I could realize the truth of his words, but when I did a light seemed to break in upon me. 'Father,' I cried, 'give me the child! She is the age of my own little one. Henceforth they shall be sisters, and I will have two daughters to care for me in my old age. You have given me a chance not only to perform an act of mercy but to demonstrate beyond doubt the greatest psychological fact of the century. Races unborn will benefit by your thoughtfulness. I accept your gift as a sacred trust. Come here, little one.'

"The child understood no English, but she did understand the mute appeal of my outstretched arms. She hesitated a moment, but the tone of my voice reassured her, and running to me she climbed up in my lap and put her dark curly head against my shoulder. Simultaneously I bent over and kissed her, and so sealed our eternal compact. Mr. Chairman," continued the speaker, after a pause, "it is a long story and a painful one—shall I continue? Let me know the sentiment of the meeting."

A hush had fallen upon the audience, but now they found voice. "Please proceed, Professor!" "We must hear the sequel!" "You must not stop!" exclaimed the members present.

The old man paused a moment or two as if to recall more vividly some picture latent in his mind. Then, opening the leaves of an old journal, the Professor read the following account:

May 27, 187—.—Yesterday dear sister was married. How radiantly beautiful and happy she was! Dear Thora—I am so glad! Never have I seen Father so proud and happy! Lord Blakesley is a fortunate man, and I believe he knows it. Now that she has really gone I begin to realize what I have lost. We have been so much to each other—Thora and I. Perhaps it's because we never knew a mother's love. I know I shall be very lonely, but when I feel sad I will think of Thora's happy face and Captain Mattison's sympathy and sweet attentions. He is a great friend of Lord Blakesley's (I cannot think of him yet as Albert). I wonder if he will call?

Blakesley Castle, July 2.—How quickly time has passed! I have been here two weeks already with dear Thora, but it seems like two days. Captain Mattison is here also for a visit, and we have been so happy together. Albert calls him "Arthur." Somehow I like the name. Last evening we went for a walk in the sunset, and he told me that the glory of the heavens was like the glory that had come into his life, but that he hoped, unlike the sunset, had come to stay. I felt so stupid—I could say nothing. Everything seems changed. I wish I could see Father.

July 10.—The world is too small to hold all my happiness. I cannot express how happy I am! Arthur has told me that he loves me, and we are going to be married in September. Thora and Albert are so pleased, and dear Father is coming out to see us next week. He must live with us when we have a home—he is too much absorbed by his studies. I want to make him as happy as I am today!

September 8 (Paris).—Arthur and I were married yesterday, and we are the happiest people in the world! Arthur has no fortune, but I do not care for that. Thora has given me jewels fit for a princess, and Albert has given us a lovely little home near the castle—and Father will divide his time between Thora and me. Father seemed strangely affected the day of the wedding. I wonder why? I hold always to a picture of health and harmony: no harm can come to me. Perhaps dear Father was thinking of his own wedding. I write my new name, and it looks so strange—Myra Mattison.

April 3 (Home).—We have been here in our little home over six months. Not a shadow has crossed our path. Dear Thora has a son and heir—a fine, beautiful child. There is great rejoicing at the Castle, but I am worried about our own dear Father. He has aged lately, and sometimes when Thora and I are together he looks at us in a queer way as if he wanted to know something he dared not ask. He has sent up to London for his books and papers, and tomorrow he will come to me to stay.

April 18 (Home—Hell).—Which way I turn is hell! Am I mad, or only going mad? Objects dance before my eyes and my head swims. I am ill, horribly ill—I, who have never known pain or illness in my life! Can this ghastly thing be true? It happened last week, though it seems years—years. Father's things came from London and I thought to put them in readiness for him. I was arranging some books on a shelf when one arrested my attention. It was strangely printed and

I was curious to see more. The language was unknown to me, and I was about to put it away when a sheet of closely written paper fell to the floor. My father's writing! What demon drew me to my destruction? I know not. It was there—the hideous truth! Each word is written on my heart in letters of fire:

"*Honolulu.*—On this Bible, I, Adam Adair, write this solemn oath. Never by thought, word, or deed will I betray the origin of the little girl who has this night come so strangely under my protection. She is mine. Henceforth I shall have two daughters. Mine is a noble mission. The child of leprous parents—born on an island of lepers—has been born free from the taint, and she shall prove to the world the supremacy of mind over matter. With a vivid mental picture of health ever before her, her physical body shall remain above the law of disease and discord. A hundred years hence, when we all shall have entered the great beyond, shall my experiment be made known. From time to time I will take notes on her condition, and the matter thus collected I will put in safe hands until the time is ripe for its revelation. As I deal with this child, accursed of humanity, so may Infinite Justice deal with me!"

Such is the awful document. I see it here, there, everywhere, in letters of blood. Memories like forgotten dreams have come to my aid, and in those dreams I can recall the tall grass and palm-trees of a tropical clime. In the great Bible that no hand has touched for years I read the record of one birth—no more. It is all true—true! The accursed thing is in my blood—and in that of my unborn child. I have no name, no people—I am accursed!

April 15.—How have I lived these days? They tell me I am *not* ill, but when I see my haggard face in the glass I know it is true—true! I can speak of this to no one, least of all to Father (but who *was* my father?). I am afraid to hear the truth—the awful details. One fact alone is sufficient: I am the child of lepers! God help me! So far I have had no signs of the curse. How long can I put off the evil day?

May 17.—Father is watching me closely. I can see it—feel it. It is I, not Thora. His manner alone is conviction. There is something he has on his lips to tell me, but he restrains himself. What if he guesses that I know? It is not possible. Thora and her child are with me almost constantly, and my husband is devotion itself. They cannot know of the demon in my heart. How will it all end? The picture of health has left me, nor can I recall it. My mouth and tongue are parched and dry, and my hair seems to be falling out!

May 30.—It has come. I know it. There are spots on my face and hands—scaly spots like the skin of a fish. I can no longer disguise the truth. I am a *leper*—accursed of God and man! Do my family suspect the truth? They already look at me with frightened eyes. Must I bring into existence a child to be accursed also?

June 12.—I have told them—they know it now. I have told them all but the finding of the paper and the discovery of my parentage. It would kill Thora—at least *that* she shall be spared. She and Father are with me constantly. They are telling me that my *mind* is diseased—not my body. They are trying to reason with me. What they say is true, but I cannot realize it. I feel the loathsome thing in my blood, and I see *red!* This morning Arthur left me to go up to London. He will bring down two specialists with him. I fear I am going mad.

Here the diary ended, but, opening a copy of the *Times*, the old man continued to read:

"*July 2.*—A most extraordinary and phenomenal case has just occurred among us. Young, beautiful, and apparently in the best of health, Myra Mattison, wife of Captain Arthur Mattison of Her Majesty's Fusileers, has been stricken with leprosy. So rapid has been the progress of the disease that scarcely three months from the time she first noted its appearance it was beyond the power of medical science to retard it. She has been removed temporarily to a private hospital at K——. The origin of the disease is a mystery. Mrs. Mattison is the daughter of Professor Adam Adair, whose fame is such that he needs no introduction to the English public. Her mother was before her marriage Miss Adelaide Gordon Hastings. Never in any way has she been exposed to the awful malady, and the physicians in charge are almost hopelessly looking for a solution of this most unusual and mystifying case."

The following he read from an issue of the *London Daily Telegraph*:

"*July 30.*—Lady Blakesley, the well-known and beautiful sister of the unfortunate victim at K——, is prostrate with grief. The sisters have been inseparable always, and the greatest devotion has existed between them. Lady Blakesley is utterly unable to account for the unprecedented circumstances other than her belief that her sister's mind had become affected by some story of disease, and by constant brooding thought had produced externally conditions latent in her mind. Lady Blakesley is absolutely unafraid of disease, either for herself or her child. She was with her sister constantly until the time of her removal, and is even now most anxious to share her isolation, and would do so if not prevented by the medical authorities."

The old Professor then read the following from the *Times* of August 3d:

"The unfortunate victim of leprosy, Mrs. Arthur Mattison, is now at rest. At half after three this morning she died in child-birth. The child died also. Death was indeed an angel of mercy in disguise. Lady Blakesley was present at her sister's death. By some telepathic or psychic power she felt the truth, and in spite of the nurse and physicians present she found her way to her sister's apartment and held the suffering woman in her arms until the last. Great fear is entertained for her safety, and as yet she has not been allowed to return to her home."

The concluding paragraph was from an issue of the Times of a year later. It read:

"Captain Arthur Mattison of Her Majesty's Fusileers has been stricken with the awful disease that took his young and beautiful wife nearly a year ago. The servants who were employed at Ivy Cottage are stricken as well. All have been secretly removed. Strange as it seems, Lady Blakesley, who attended her sister when she died, has escaped the curse. Though regularly examined by experts, she remains strong and healthy. Last week she gave birth to a daughter, and both are remarkably well. Medical science is baffled. Let some science mightier than *materia medica* give us a solution of this most perplexing and phenomenal mystery."

When Professon Adair finished reading there was an oppressive silence. Tears were in the eyes of many of his listeners.

Professor Hinton-Garow was the first to find his voice. "You are right," he said, slowly. "There is some force about us some terrific power—of which we are in ignorance. Your story is pitiful to a degree, but was it not the young woman's knowledge of her parentage that quickened the latent malady already in her blood? The mind, as you assert, acted upon the body in a powerful way, but the germ was there potentially, though for the time quiescent."

The old man brushed his hand across his eyes. "Gentlemen," he said, with an effort, "you have heard my story; but the sequel answers the point in question. *Lady Blakesley, happy and well, with a group of healthy children about her, was the little girl I took from the mission.* Myra, who went through that death of horror, was the child of my own flesh and blood."

THE ALCHEMIST'S WINE

by Samuel S. Neu

A SPANISH gentleman, recently looking over the library of a friend in London, and noting several books on metaphysical and Theosophical subjects, remarked that he had at one time been connected with an occult society. Upon his friend inquiring why he had discontinued his membership, he related a strange story, which is here given.

When I look backward I cannot convince myself that we were altogether foolish, and yet no sane men would ever have wasted their time and energies in the mad way that we did. Personally, I have had enough since the terrifying episode I am about to relate. You may tell me it was all imagination, yet it was real enough to me, and the streaks of gray in my hair since that terrible night bear silent but forcible witness to the frightfulness of the thing.

There were eight of us who conceived the mad idea of forming "The Secret Circle of Occult Searchers." As if by some unseen though powerful force we had been drawn together, having nothing in common but an intense desire to arrive at the truth in Spiritualism. It was in the days when Spiritualism was new and rampant, when men's minds were more readily interested and attracted by the mysterious than today. I mention this only as partial extenuation of our otherwise foolish act in forming our Secret Circle.

We held our sessions Friday evenings. Seeing clearly that nothing could be accomplished by the investigation of phenomena alone, we decided that we must become familiar with all the available literature of the occult sciences. On this we were most fortunate, in having among us one who bad devoted all the leisure of an already long life to kindred studies, possessing a well-equipped library of occult works. Naturally we made him our leader, gave him the title of Grand Yogee, had him appear at each meeting arrayed in————. But I cannot make public our rites: the oath of secrecy that bound us must not be violated even though we have long since disbanded.

After six months of systematic earnest study, we thought we had delved deep enough into the mysteries of Nature and Man. It was then that we came across an old manuscript in which was given the recipe for a concoction, one taste of which would, it was affirmed, open to the taster the world of the *so-called* spirits, a world which our studies told as lay midway between our old world and the true Spiritland. In an instant we were on fire with eagerness to test this wonderful drink and solve the ultimate mystery. In vain did the Grand Yogee strive to dissuade us. In vain did he warn us against dangerous experiments without sufficient knowledge. Were we not there to make experiments? And as for that had we not learned enough in six months' conscientious study to avert any dangers? Yes, we would try the experiment, and in spite of the deep sigh and the sad grave look of the Grand Yogee, we proceeded to prepare the devilish mixture. It was tedious work, requiring both care and patience, but at the end of the month we were rewarded by having one glass of the liquor before us.

Then came that eventful meeting on the fourteenth of March, at which the experiment was performed. That date I can never forget. The fourteenth of March. It is burned indelibly into my memory. For it was to me it was allotted to drink myself into the other world, literally drink myself into death. Eager as we had been to test the drink at the beginning, now that the time had come we were assailed with fears. Finally I, who had ever been the most courageous—or rather, most daring and foolhardy—volunteered to risk my life in this cause.

Holding the glass aloft I looked for a last time around that Secret Circle, at each of the Brothers, at the Grand Yogee with the sad, apprehensive look. Then, smiling at his fears I lifted the glass to my lips and tasted.

Then I stopped, for the face of the Grand Yogee suddenly turned pale. He seemed to gasp for breath and writhe. A veil suddenly lifted from my eyes and I saw upon his shoulders a horrible thing. Its eyes were greenish yellow, an ape it seemed, yet not an ape for it had horns—and wings. Its tail was about the Yogee's neck, strangling him, and with its clawed hands it was beating upon his bald head. I sprang at once to assistance intending to grasp the monster, but my hands went through it as if it were air.

Then I suddenly remembered having read that only two metals could affect spectres of the middle world. My oath forbids me to say what these metals are, but let us call them copper and lead. I called to the Brothers to get me some lead. any leaden object. One ran to an adjoining room and brought an old leaden candlestick, with which I proceeded to beat the spectre over the head. Uttering an unearthly shriek it fled, but not before it had seized my arm and closed its sharp teeth through the forefinger of my right hand.

Then I had to describe to the other Brothers what I had seen, what to them had been but pantomime, and long into the night we discussed the apparition. Not until we were about to adjourn did I notice that my forefinger, where the shape had bitten me, was swollen to twice its normal size and very painful. Next day my physician applied a poultice, but all he did only aggravated the wound and made the pain unbearable. Five specialists I consulted during the next two weeks, but each had to admit that he was powerless, that never before had he seen a similar wound.

For a month we discussed the wound in the Circle, and finally it was decided that it would never heal until the Spectre had been laid low and that no one could lay it but myself.

So arming myself with a "leaden" knife and a "copper" chain to hold the monster, I once more lifted the fatal glass to my lips. Again the lifting of the veil, and again the monster perched upon the shoulders of the Grand Yogee. No time was to be lost.

In an instant I was upon it, the copper chain about its waist. I tried to run my knife through its heart, but the thing squirmed and the knife entered its neck. Very well, thought I, I will behead it. So I pressed the knife down, down, the creature—screaming with agony and terror. I was relentless, and grasping the spectre by the jaw, I gave the knife a last vicious thrust and the head was severed. I held it aloft, exultant, victorious. But as I did so a veil again lifted from my eyes; the form of the headless spectre seemed to take on human shape—no, worse,—seemed to become the Grand Yogee himself. And the object in my hand? There, by the beard, I held the Yogee's head, the red blood streaming out on the table.

Imagine, if you can, my horror. Small wonder my hair has streaks of gray. A miracle that reason remained. I took one glance from the hideous thing in my hand to the headless man,—and then I could stand it no more. I staggered backward, and as I sank into my chair the head slipped from my hand to the table. The last I remember was a crash of glass. At last I awoke and looked dazedly about. "Where am I?" I asked. "What has happened?" No answer. Then I half remembered. "Tell me," I said appealingly, "what has happened." Then somebody spoke. "Don't you remember? You raised the glass to drink. It just touched your lips and you sank into the chair."

Could it be possible! The voice of the Grand Yogee! I looked and imagined I saw him alive and sound. How I wished it could be true! No, I must be dreaming. Or had I gone insane?

"And you dropped the glass, spilling all that precious fluid," someone remarked ruefully.

Then a great light began to break on me. "What day is this?" I eagerly inquired. "Why, the fourteenth of March."

Then it was clear, thank God! That horrible occurrence had been a dream, a dream of one short instant. There had been no spectre, no blood, no murder. I looked at my finger. No sign of a scar.

They noted my bewildered looks and asked the cause. And when I had finished telling them there ensued a long, loud laugh—in which I did not join. Perhaps to them my experience appeared as a monstrous joke. Perhaps it so appears to you. To me it must ever remain the most terrible two months of my life—two months though occupying but an instant.

Then and there, without a word, I left the "Secret Circle of Occult Searchers" never to return. I learned from the Grand Yogee, whom I met five years afterward, that the Circle had disbanded shortly after, but he did not give the reason.

I have no doubt that there are many things concerning Life, and Mind, and Death, that those who search can find. And may those who search have luck in finding. But for my part, I shall live out the remainder of my natural life, and after that, if it pleases God, I shall know the mysteries of that other world. Until then, may the book be sealed to me.

SHERAU, THE PARASCHITES

by Justin Sterns

Lo! Desire is potent. But linger; the Path that you choose
Leads, perchance, where the Sun hides his face,
and the Hell-waters ooze.

SHERAU, the paraschites, having made the eight incisions required by law in the body of the most noble Rameses I. fled for his life from the shower of well-directed stones that were his immediate portion.

For his life in very truth, since this was one of those happily rare occasions when the body desecrated by the abhorred knife of the embalmer's most vile but necessary assistant, the paraschites, was that of a Pharaoh. The stones hurled at him were twice the size used by the onlookers to express their rage at the mutilation of the dead body of a slave, or even a citizen. Moreover, the throng in the City of the Dead, that lay across the sacred Nile on the hither bank from Thebes, was many times greater today than on days of less notable embalmings. In fact, if no chance directed stone of the many that rained about him found its mark and made him even as the great Rameses now was, then indeed had the sheltering arm of the god of the outcast paraschites been over him during his mad race.

Sherau stumbled on into the shelter of the nearest thicket, cursing the fate that had caused him to be born a paraschites, bruised and stinging from the stones that had found him but freer than on some former occasions from downright hurt. He threw himself face downward among the papyrus reeds and laid his forehead on his crossed arms, breathed and shaken by his wild run and trembling with relief. For Fear of Death and Lust of Life had stalked at the right shoulder and at the left of Sherau the paraschites since the hour he knew that the king was dead, and that the doubtful honor of assisting to prepare the royal mummy was to be his.

"Now by the great God Seth," gasped Sherau, under his breath lest any pious Egyptian should hear him call on the name of the god of all evil, "if I had but the power of Rameses, son of Rameses, over the thrower of every stone flung at me this day for just one little hour; one little, little hour! Ah-e! but I would wring their necks! With my two hands I would wring them." And his two hands could have made short work of the necks of most men.

"If I were but Rameses the Living! Ah-e! Ah-e! Ah-e! They should make me sport for a thousand years, those throwers of stones and shouters of evil names. Ah-e!" Sherau was reviving.

He drew himself up furtively, into the most reverential attitude of the praying Egyptian, and sucked in a long breath.

"O Mighty Seth! Give me the power of Rameses—the power of Rameses—the power of Rameses!"

The veins stood out swollen and blue on his neck and forehead, and on his clenched hands, and he prayed without ceasing till he fell over on his side, exhausted.

He roused up when the tumult of the people who followed the chariot of Rameses II as he returned across the river to Thebes, reached him.

Sherau crept to the edge of the thicket, and lay concealed where the whole sweep of the road for half a mile spread out below him. His eyes were set wide open, and blazed like the unwinking, jewel eyes of an idol. As he sprawled full length among the reeds he dug his naked toes into the soft, black earth and his hands reached out and clutched all they could hold of the slender papyri and crushed them together savagely. While he watched the passing pageant his lips writhed over his strong, white teeth, making of his face a most wonderful series of gargoyle masks. At any moment, as he beheld the approach and departure of the Pharaoh and his attendants, his head was a fitting model for a heathen idol of the sort they appease with the sacrifice of little children.

Presently Sherau betook himself to his hovel, in the mean quarter where the Thebans allowed such outcasts as paraschites to live, and there ate, drank and made merry with others of his calling because, having mutilated the body of a Pharaoh that day, he was neither a corpse nor a cripple at nightfall, an escape unparalleled since men first became mummies. But in the middle of the hot and windless night that followed, sleepless in spite of the wine, Sherau left his hut and sought a place he knew on the Nile bank a little beyond the City of the Dead.

Directly he reached the spot he set about what he had come to do, for it was not the aimless restlessness of insomnia that had sent him night-wandering, and it was not the first time, nor the second, nor the tenth, that he had spent the hours before dawn in his present occupation.

He stalked the bushes skillfully until he succeeded in laying hands of violence on a small she-bird with her three young ones. Long practice had made him deft at this. Tonight, the male bird escaped. Had the best of luck been his he would have had that also.

Sherau drew from the bushes a small wicker cage in which he put his captives. The young birds presently gave over squawking and the mother bird, worried and wakeful over her changed surroundings, settled again on her nest to make the best of it.

Sherau's eyes sought the moon. It was still an hour too high for safety in his main enterprise. But fair sport could be had in the interval. He threw himself down and tore up the thick vegetation leaving a level, cleared space under his eyes, as he supported himself on his elbow. A luckless dragon fly lit in the little arena. Immediately, Sherau's great hand covered it. Through his fingers he watched its agitated fluttering.

"I am mightier than Rameses," he muttered. "I am Sherau the Great, king of land and sea. King of the whole world. Every nation is mine or pays me tribute. A thousand slaves in my palace sweat daily in my service. An hundred thousand are building my tomb, that shall be the wonder of the ages. My name shall never be forgotten. I am Sherau the King.

"This slave here," he mumbled on, "hath crossed my path in somewhat. I have cast him in chains. How shall I serve him, that he may feel the displeasure of the King of the World and all my subjects tremble at his fate? Hold! 'Tis a woman slave. See! she flaunts in gauze. I have but wearied of her. Therefore I will graciously spare her life. I will merely strip her of these costly garments of gold embroidered gauze and cast her out—to be the dancing girl of the paraschites. Ah-e! from the palace of Sherau the Great to the dens of the paraschites! That were worse than death!"

He caught the dragon fly carefully and held it down firmly by its outspread wings, reveling in its struggles.

"So! my fair one! Thou dost not wish to be shorn of thy finery and leave the palace of Sherau the Emperor? 'Tis thine own fault. With thy great beauty thou shouldst so have charmed me that I would never have parted with thee. Nay, thou mightest have sat on an Empress's throne. 'Tis without use that thou strugglest. By thy mighty master's commands thou art stripped of thy gauds—one by one!"

302

With the deliberation of an executioner Sherau robbed the creature of its delicate wings and let it go.

"There! Get thee hence and queen it over the paraschites. Ah-e! 'Tis almost too much favor to those dogs that they should have thee! Mayhap some day when other pleasures pall, I will seek thee out in thy den and thou shalt thank thy king that he spared thy life tonight."

He lolled back on his elbow and waited, for Sherau played the game scrupulously by the rules he had made for it. Only those creatures that ventured into the little arena represented the unfortunate objects of the mighty Sherau's displeasure.

Suddenly he leaned forward with stopped breath. A sacred beetle! lo! a sacred beetle! Never before had the power that ruled provided a scarab to become the object of the royal anger.

Sherau the paraschites threw himself flat on his chest in an ecstasy, and reaching forward with both hands caged the new prisoner where it stood. There was not a spark of awe for the holy things of Egypt in him. Instead a tremulous delight and a huge sense of power at being able to torture and finally to slay that which it meant death to an Egyptian to kill, even by accident, if the fact became known.

"An high priest!" whispered Sherau, with sparkling eyes. "An high priest! Now, indeed, hath Sherau the King fit sport!"

Carefully prisoning the beetle with one hand, with the other he stripped from a reed a fibre of the strength and flexibility of thread. He looped it about his quarry, between the first and second segments, and holding an end in either hand he settled down to gloat over its struggles and to weave great dreams of absolute power out of them, that should trick him into forgetting that he was a dog of a paraschites.

"'Tis Ami," he muttered, "who bade me prepare the body of that dead dog of a Rameses today. Now shall he get his deserts!" With dilating nostrils he tormented the insect a while, letting it seem to escape and dragging it rudely back.

"So! Didst thou think to flee the vengeance of thy king, unhappy priest? Nay, now, the hour of thy death is set and written. I do but play with thee a little space, ere I deliver thee over to the executioner. Fit sport for kings! Fit sport for kings!" he muttered.

"Now, now, thou wretched one," impatiently, "if thou wilt not be quiet—we must see what can be done to quiet thee. My hands weary of keeping such constant hold on thy rope."

One by one, he removed the legs of the insect, thrilling at each desecration of the sacred creature as though it were in fact the living body of his enemy, the high priest, that he mutilated.

"Now, at last, thou art content to be quiet, art thou? But thy submission cometh too late to avail thee aught. Thou shouldst have bent the knee to Sherau, and ceased to cross his mighty will, ere, by his orders, thou wert shorn of thy sacred office. His word is given. Thou must die."

He put the beetle through the bars of the wicker cage, and roughly prodded the bird awake. But she refused to touch it. Perhaps the impulse to eat lay dormant in her during the hours belonging to sleep.

"Then will I be thy executioner," snarled Sherau. With a quick jerk he tightened the loop of reed fibre, and directly the body of the sacred scarabæus of the Nile lay dismembered before him.

"Carrion," he muttered, poking it out of sight among the reeds.

He looked at the moon.

"One more! There is time for one more!" he whispered, gluttonously, and settled himself to watch.

"The next shall be Setos, the wine-seller," he mused. "He hath done me an ill turn this day concerning the price of that fourth bottle of wine. 'Twas half water—ah-e! Setos! welcome!" Sherau's long arm shot out in greeting. He grasped by

304

the gorgeous wings the moth that had come unwittingly to play the sorry rôle of Setos.

"Thou goest finely clad, O Setos, charger of three prices for thy diluted wine! 'Tis simple justice that I should take from thee this gaudy cloak thou gottest by such thievery. There! Henceforth go afoot, and clad in rags. 'Tis properer so. And harken, Setos! Hadst thou not spat upon me for an 'outcast dog of a paraschites' when I told thee of the water in thy wine, then would I have spared thee this further punishment. Seest thou this house of twigs I build thee with mine own hands? Therein shalt thou stay till thou diest of hunger and thirst. For thy sins, O Setos. Ah-e! Setos! Sherau the Mighty is long of arm and strong of hand. Thou wilt never sell poor wine again."

He looked for the third time at the moon, and getting up stretched lustily. His night of pleasure was not half over. If that which was to follow did but equal what was just completed, then would the days of terror he had endured since the death of Rameses be altogether wiped out. He took up the cage of nesting birds and plunged deeper into the thicket.

Presently he reached a small pit covered with a lattice of twigs, and cunningly contrived to escape notice. Many an anxious hour had Sherau spent on the construction of this dungeon, knowing perfectly that discovery would cost him his life. Now, after a thorough reconnoitre, he put in his hand and drew forth his royal prisoner—a starveling kitten some six months old. Of a truth, this Egyptian holdeth nought holy! In his mad lust for power he layeth violent hands on all that is most sacred to his race. Nothing could save an Egyptian who was known to have killed a cat. It is a tremulous joy to Sherau, when life is hardest and he is made most keenly to feel a miserable outcast, to remember that thrice already he has done what not one of his persecuters would dare do—and yet he lives!

There was water at all times in the den of the half-starved kitten, which Sherau had risked his life five months before to steal. Food he brought as he had brought it now, not too often, lest his coming be observed. Moreover, there was vivider delight to be had from the antics of his prisoner when its hunger was keen. Sherau laughed aloud now, as the kitten glared at the birds and began to lash its tail.

He threw himself down again on his belly, with his puppets within sweep of his long arms. And first, disregarding the agony of the awakened mother bird, he took the cat in his brutal hands and looked it over sharply. The creature bore the scars on its thin body of previous torture. Not hunger only did Sherau the Great mete out to his royal prisoner.

"Ah-e! Rameses the Little! Thy namesake is dead. This day have I thrust my knife into him. Shall I therefore do likewise unto thee? or save thee a while that thou mayest make sport for me? Art hungered, little king? emperor that was? dethroned one? So! then thou shalt kill but not eat! kill but not eat! kill but not eat! Thou that wert king, thou shalt be executioner, despised of the people and profiting not by the deaths of thy victims."

He put the cat back in its hole and turned his attention to the birds.

"Thou first!" to the mother bird, "that thy squawking may cease."

He looped a cord about her neck and under her wings and then, with evil ingenuity, wound another one around her bill so that her fear was no longer audible. Returning her to the cage he bound her offspring in the same way.

"The anger of the mighty Sherau is great," he muttered to them. "Ye slept, and danger threatened the life of the king your master, whom ye were appointed to guard. Treason! Quick death were a thousand times too merciful. Sherau will show the world a king's displeasure. Ye shall die a death not known to man until this day. Ye shall be thrown to the lions.

Ah-e! Never again will a soldier of Sherau the King fall asleep at his post."

He took out the starveling cat, and slipping the loop at the loose end of the rope tied round its neck over his wrist, he watched his frantic assaults on the cage, chuckling at the madnesses of terror and hunger being enacted for his pleasure. At length he drew back the cat, and taking out one of the birds held it by its tether, cleverly playing one against the other until, satiated, he permitted the kill.

He threw the bird into the hole and beat the cat off cruelly when he tried to follow, at length taking another bird from the cage and thrusting it almost against his muzzle to distract his attention. So the game went on. But at the third kill, as Sherau beat him off when he tried to follow and eat, the half-crazed kitten turned on him and did quick havoc with his claws. Sherau caught him round the neck, cursing savagely, and almost strangled him. Presently he muttered, loosening his clutch: "Thou shalt die tonight for this that thou hast done." The blood was streaming from his right hand. "But first complete thy work. There is yet one other needs thy claws. Then will I strangle thee, O Rameses, with this same hand that thou hast torn—as I would I could strangle thy namesake, who sleeps tonight in the bed of his father."

The moon was close on an hour lower when they broke in upon him, the lifeless kitten still hanging limp in his blood-stained hand.

Sherau sprang to his feet at their storm of hostile cries, swinging the kitten defiantly about his head with a loud scream of laughter. Death had come to him, death so certain that the idea of seeking to escape it did not enter his mind. Instead, Fear of Death and Lust of Life stood again at his right shoulder and at his left, and they rent his brain between them so that he went altogether mad.

"I go to the Halls of Osiris," he shouted. "Yea, I go! but come thou with me! I go not alone! not alone! I am Sherau the Mighty, king of the earth and of men. If I go this night to the Halls of the Dead, I go fitly attended. Come with me, thou! and thou! and thou!" He felled them like oxen.

The moon dropped lower and hid behind the thicket, leaving the Nile in starry darkness and Sherau, with four others, lying stark beside the stark kitten.

A DREAM OF ROSES

by Blanche Cromartie

THAT Dreamer who has Mercury (☿) and Venus (♀) in Aquarius (♒) dreamed, and in her dream she saw, reaching on all sides to the horizon, a vast desert, entirely covered with stones; stones neither rare nor precious nor even picturesque, but misshapen, ugly, incrusted with soil and dust—a weary sight.

And the voice that speaks without words said to her:

"These stones are the souls in the world." Thereupon the Dreamer turned her eyes heavenward and there beheld more beauty than the world of men's souls dreamed, for in the blue vault there arose a vast cross, white and luminous, and its extremities seemed about burgeoning into flowers. From its center beamed star-wise five streams of golden rays and hanging upon the Cross there seemed to be a wreath. But the Dreamer hardly heeded this, being engrossed by the wonder of the five-pointed star, for its rays were more golden than the finest gold and each one, though myriad their number, was clear and individual, like a gleaming hair.

From the two lower star-streams the rays fell upon the stones and she saw that one ray went to every separate stone, to every stone one. And lo, they were stones no longer: everyone of them had become a rose.

And the voice that speaks without words said to her:

"See how these roses smell."

And the Dreamer laughed at the thought that perfume could be seen.

The surface or the world was now completely covered with roses and she saw how, in response to the rays from the star, each rose (which had been a stone) sent an answering ray, not pure golden-bright, like those shed by the star, but rays of colors, hues, beautiful exceedingly and endlessly varied. For every rose sent its own responsive ray and no two were alike, for all the colors of Dreamland were there, matchless in beauty and variety, far beyond any which are seen by those who think they are awake!

The rays from the roses reflected to their source and fell upon the wreath of roses which hung upon the Cross. And just as the rays from the Cross had changed the stones to roses, so now the rays from the roses worked a wondrous transformation, for, as they touched them, the Dreamer saw no rose-wreath but a halo formed of celestial beings like glowing fire, which whirled and turned like wheels, so exquisitely bright that for very joy the Dreamer awoke.

SHADOWS

by Alma Newton

IT was dawn. The hour when beauty alone should reign, but in man's world it is the time for death as well as for birth—the end as well as the beginning. At that hour I slept. My soul travelled far into strange and terrible regions, weird neighbourhoods of men. It was like a bird with a broken wing. It merely drifted with the strongest current of air. Now the strongest current at that hour on this morning was moving toward a prison. Before I realised it, I was there in that place called prison but commonly known as Hell, for it possessed not only evil spirits, gnashing teeth and broken hearts, but foul odours, sinister warnings, weird messages of death.

Suddenly I was in a room with strangers. It was dark and heavily shadowed. These shadows seemed to move on the wall grotesquely.

A tall young man with clear blue eyes said to me, "I think I will go tomorrow, I will wait until tomorrow." I said, "Yes," as I looked into his deep blue eyes, not knowing why I did so. "Yes, you will go tomorrow!" A little woman in a brown dress said, "I wonder if it's over yet." Another said, "I'll see," while the shadows again regained their motion and seemed to glide around the wall.

An officer appeared in the door and said, "You can come in now." Mechanically I followed him down a long aisle to a room which I entered with the others. In this room of death there was a figure of a man clad in gray, lying on a cot close to the floor. His neck was twisted horribly to one side and there was the pallor of death upon his face. The breathing had ceased and yet he smiled!

At first I thought it was the smile that sometimes comes into a face after death, the smile of peace; but I looked again and to my horror I saw that he was speaking to *me!* Out of the smile, the lips moved and he spoke to me! The others knelt down beside the cot and sobbed, while the young man with the deep blue eyes cried aloud and said, "O John! John!" and the others then cried aloud, and I turned and walked away. . . .

I awakened. The vision was so keen and hideously real that I could not forget it.

All that day it followed me. I knew then the reality, the torture of being haunted; of not being able to escape a soul in the other world when it desires to be near one. All that day I walked, walked, trying to send it away, but as the evening came on it seemed to cling more closely to me! In the night it crouched by my bed as though afraid.

At dawn I awakened. He was standing at the foot of my bed, his neck still twisted, his poor face smiling and his lips still moving.

"Oh," I cried, "it's real, it's real! But what can I do for you?" And again I said, "What can I do for you, dear?" as I would to a wounded child. "Can't the others, your friends, help you? Those that love you and cried at your feet? The young man and the little woman in brown?"

"No," he said wearily. "That is why they cannot help me. They love me and they cry at my feet; you can help because you do not cry and because you know the Way."

"What way?" I asked. "What way?"

"The Way," he answered, "through, on, on to the Brightness! I don't know what you call it, but you are not afraid of the road and you know how to go."

"I see, I see," I answered. "You want me to take you through the astral world, up to the White Kingdom of God."

"I don't know what *you* call it," he answered. "I know I am in darkness and so near the earth I can still see the chair, I can feel the current and hear those voices and the crying . . . I see the shadows there—here—everywhere!"

"And yet you smile," I said; "how strange it is!"

"I smile because you came, because you can take me away, because you saw, you heard and did not cry," he answered eagerly.

Lovingly, tenderly, I went toward him. My fear had vanished.

"Give me your hands, your poor dear hands—hold fast to my hands and never let go for a minute. Never fear, never look back—just trust to me as you would to your mother, for you say that I know the way! Let us drift on, on, far away, but to do this we must first sleep and then in a moment we will be there! There where every shadow is turned into a golden dream; where torture is changed into ecstasy, where your hands will grasp stronger, kinder hands than mine—where there is only the noon of things; no dawn, no twilight, no cares, no sighs—— Now we are *going*, don't think, just trust to me. . . ."

And then I found myself singing to him as I would to a child, a sort of little prayer on the way. Soon the darkness goes, the music comes, music you never heard before, each plane is a melody, each melody an echo and the echo is for *you*. Each echo has a color and each color has a flower, each flower is a promise and the promise is for *you*. Each promise is a symbol, each symbol is a prayer and the prayer is for *you*. Each prayer is a poem, each poem is a blessing and the blessing is for *you*. . . ."

On—on—I sang until he slept.

And after my sleep I awakened to feel a sense of perfect peace in my room and more that of a radiant happiness! For a stranger had come to me, someone had asked me to be a pilot on a strange astral sea, to push aside elementals, to pass the Dweller on the Threshold, to rise from one plane to another, to take a frightened, desolate soul on toward the Brightness! *To serve while the body rested!*

The next day I took up a newspaper. Casually I turned the pages. On the top of the fourth page my eyes fell upon these words:

> Two men went to the chair yesterday morning at dawn, —— Prison. One of them a middle-aged man, unusual refinement, beloved by his fellow prisoners, John ——.

The newspaper fell to the floor. *I could read no more!*

THE LAST HOURS OF A SPY

by Max Heindel

HE was sitting in the ruined garden of an ancient monastery looking at the confusion of flowers and weeds, children of care and carelessness; the latter seemed to be gaining the upper hand since war had driven the original owners away, for the soldiers who now camped there had no time for flowers.

He was not one of them; he was a captive, a spy. Caught with important papers, he had been sentenced to be shot, and was now waiting for the firing squad which would end it all.

But would that *end* it? What a foolish question. He had been brought up to believe in a hereafter, but soon after entering the University he fell in with the common attitude of mind, the scientific mind, in that institution. The higher criticism had proved the fallacy of the Bible. In the dissecting room the mechanical machinery of the body was made plain, chemistry could account for the action and reaction of the organism. Psychology offered an amply sufficient solution of the marvels of mind; in short, man was proved to be a moving, thinking machine, capable even of perpetuating itself by means of offspring, which carried on the work when the parent machine was worn out and consigned to the scrap heap in the cemetery. Sovereign or subject, master or man, saint or sinner, all were but shadows upon the screen of Time.

But somehow or other he was not quite so certain since the war had brought him face to face with murder *en masse*. He had watched hundreds dying on the field, in the trenches and hospitals, and their absolute conviction of life after death was catching, at least it was disturbing. Could there be any truth in their assertions that they had seen "Angels" both on the battlefield and at their deathbeds? Pshaw, it was an hallucination due to the strain of the situation. Yet, so many had seen these things, fellows like Lieutenant K and Captain Y, level-headed and cool, and the captain never swore after that day at the Marne; more than that, he carried a prayer book, and had preached quite a sermon to a sergeant noted for his vitriolic tongue. And there were others.

Well, he would soon know; at five he was destined to face the firing squad.

He went into the room where he had slept last night. The guard who had been standing at the doorway while he was outside followed, rifle in hand, and watched him while he threw himself upon the rude cot. He looked up and saw a copy of Leonardo da Vinci's famous painting, *The Last Supper*. He had never been particularly fond of art, but something seemed to draw him to the Christ at that hour. He had undoubtedly been a noble character. He was martyred for a cause, and this portrayal of His last supper brought home the analogy to the man on the cot, for he had also partaken of earth's bounty for the last time.

Then there came into his mind the story of how Leonardo da Vinci had asked a friend to criticize the picture when it was finished, and the friend remarked upon the incongruity of the expensive goblets from which the apostles drank. Da Vinci rubbed his brush over them and sighed; he had put his whole heart and soul into the face of the Savior, and had hoped that glorious face would attract the attention of the beholder and efface everything else; instead, one of the most unimportant and insignificant details had caught the eye of his friend, even to the complete exclusion of the Lord of Glory.

"Is that also my case?" thought he that lay upon the cot. "Have I also fastened my eyes upon the unimportant things of life? I have looked upon death too often to fear now that my turn has come, still, there is so much to do in this world that one dislikes to think of oblivion.

"Christ said, 'But one thing is needed,' and if He was right, then I have been like da Vinci's friend, my attention has been riveted on nonessentials. Instead of seeking things eternal, I have bestowed all my time on temporal tasks.

"Heigh-ho! What is the use of moaning? If I keep on, my knees might begin to shake at the appearance of the firing squad."

He rose and, followed by the watchful guard, returned to the garden where he was attracted by an old sundial. He read the inscription: "*Oros non numero nisi serenas*" (I count only the sunny hours).

"What a fine motto, to forget all the sordid and 'small' things in life, and to recognize only the good, the true, the beautiful!" Looking over his life, now about to end, how near had he lived to that motto? Conscience compelled him to confess that he had fallen short.

And now it was too late. Lost in contemplation, his eyes clung to the shadow on the dial. There was something uncanny about its silent creeping progress towards the fateful five when the firing squad was due to appear.

He was not bothered about death, but he had begun to grapple with the problem of Life, and there came over him an overwhelming desire for a solution. But there was that shadow on the dial, "that intangible nothing" creeping on and on with slow but fateful force. Oh, that he might have the chance to seek light upon the problem of Life!

It was customary to execute those condemned under martial law at sunrise, but he had been politely informed that a suddenly ordered movement of the division which held him prisoner made delay inexpedient, and he would be required to face the firing squad at sunset instead. At the time he had answered with a bow and a shrug of the shoulder. What did it matter whether sooner or later, he would be ready. Now he was beginning to covet those hours that he might reason it out.

As he turned from the shadow of death on the dial, its silent progress seemed more eloquent than any sermon on the fleetness of life and the inexorable certainty of death.

Again he stretched himself upon the cot to think upon his problem of existence. In less than half an hour he would know all or nothing; either he would be annihilated as soon as the light of life was extinguished by the bullet that would inevitably strike his heart, or else he would be a free Spirit. It all depended upon which of the two theories were true, and the feeling of suspense was growing more intense with every moment, the longing for life becoming so great that it was positively painful. Of all the people who had professed their faith in the immortality of the soul no one had ever seemed to know; they all believed—that is, all but one.

And there flashed across his memory the recollection of meeting a man of strange and fascinating personality at a popular seaside resort where he had gone for rest and quiet on a certain occasion when his nerves had been overtaxed by the strenuous study of a scientific subject. This man, quiet, refined, and unassuming, had attracted him from the first, and on one occasion when their conversation drifted to the theories of life he had taken the materialistic view, and the stranger had confronted him with a number of seemingly unanswerable arguments. Yet it was not the force of the argument that struck him now but his remembrance of the voice of authority, the manner and demeanor of one who knew what he was speaking about, that made the impression and filled him now with a burning intensity of inquiry.

"Did the stranger really and truly know?"

He had spoken of men who "leave their bodies at will just as we leave a garment behind us when we enter the water for a swim. So," he had said, "do also those who enter certain invisible worlds."

He had called it "The Land of the Living Dead," and he had claimed that the so-called dead function there in a finer body in possession of all their faculties and with a full knowledge and memory of the conditions which existed around them while they lived in this life. Oh, that this stranger were here now, that he might talk with him and find out more about this matter which had now assumed so much importance in his mind.

But what was that which appeared in the corner? Was that the stranger, that cloudy, misty form in the dark corner yonder? And now he seemed to hear a voice, *"I will meet you when you step out of your body."* Then the figure vanished.

Oh, pshaw! that must have been a figment of his fancy, an hallucination of his disordered brain, he thought. The wish had made him see things that were not there; he would speculate no more. And again he went out into the garden to watch the sundial as its shadow crept on toward the fatal five.

There they found him, with a bright smile on his lips, as he greeted the officer of the firing squad and begged to be spared the ignominious process of blindfolding. Together they walked toward the wall at the further end of the garden, where he turned and faced the firing squad, while the officer stepped to one side and quickly gave the command which sped the bullet that found his heart.

He heard the detonation of the guns and felt a prick of pain as if a white-hot iron had seared his soul. Then a mighty wrench, and involuntarily his hand sought his heart—but how strange! Before it had reached his breast the pain was gone, and quickly he returned his hand to the hanging position at his side—he must not let the enemies of his country think him a coward.

Again he turned his attention to the firing squad, expecting momentarily to feel the impact of the bullets which he had already felt by anticipation, for in no other way could he account for the shock and the pain in his heart.

But what did it mean? The firing squad was standing at attention, and the officer was walking away from him to lead them out.

"Had they fired a blank charge?" No, that was unthinkable. He examined his clothing and found three holes in the coat right over the heart. He stuck his finger into one of them as far as it would reach and pulled it out again, bewildered at the absence of pain and blood. Evidently he had been struck by three bullets, and according to all the canons of experience he ought to have fallen in a heap, dead on the instant, yet here he was more alive than he had ever felt himself. How could it be?

Impulsively he ran after the departing officer, caught him by the arm, and asked for an explanation, but the officer seemed to disregard both the restraining hand and the excited query, continuing to walk towards his men as if he had neither felt nor heard.

"Am I dreaming, am I mad, or what?"

"Neither, my friend," answered a voice beside him and as he turned there stood the strange man—"Rosicrucian" he had called himself. With an intense feeling of relief, the spy turned towards him. Perhaps he could shed light on this perplexing experience.

"But how did you get here? I did not see you enter with the firing squad."

"Your eyes were not then yet attuned to the Spirit vibration; you were still blinded by the veil of flesh," came the answer, but it carried no intelligence to the spy, and he began to doubt the sanity of his companion.

"I see you do not understand and that my answer is only adding to your perplexities," the stranger continued; "you do not realize that you are dead."

"Dead! You surely must be mad. How can I be dead when I am standing here talking to you?" answered the spy in greater perplexity than ever.

"I did not express myself properly; I should have said, 'Your body is dead,'" replied the Rosicrucian.

But the spy gazed at him in utter helplessness and hopelessness; this was getting more and more bewildering; either he or this man was insane, or both.

"'My body is dead!' But how can you say such a thing? Am I not standing here, moving my lips and talking to you? I can move my limbs and walk just as well as you, though I confess I am at a loss to know how I am alive with three bullets in my heart."

"I see your perplexity, my friend, and I will explain presently, but first come with me to the place where you stood facing the firing squad; there is something there which will interest you."

Together they walked to the place.

"Look there among the flowers, my friend," said the Rosicrucian.

And as he followed the direction of the other's eyes the spy saw partly hidden by the tall weeds and flowers which grew so rankly over the garden, what appeared to be himself lying face downward. He bent down and sought to turn the fallen form to settle this impossible dilemma, but perplexity seemed to heap itself on perplexity without end, for as he grasped the inert form by the shoulder to lift it, his hand went through it as if it had been made of thin air and not flesh and blood.

Again he straightened himself up and turned to his companion.

"For God's sake, straighten this tangle out for me, for if I am not insane already I shall go mad in another minute!"

"Patience, my friend," answered the Rosicrucian, "it is all right, and I shall set you at ease in a few minutes; what has happened is this:

"When the firing squad fired the fatal shots three of the bullets entered your heart with such fatal effect that you only felt the pain for a fraction of a second before the ethereal body that you now use was wrenched free from the physical body, which then fell forward on its face. Henceforth this ethereal body will serve you as well as and better than the dense body you have discarded by death."

"Ethereal body," stammered the spy, still unable to follow him.

"Yes, my friend. Does it seem so strange that man has an ethereal body? Science puts forward the hypothesis that all things from the densest mineral to the rarest gas are permeated with ether, and it is right in its guess. The human body is no exception to the rule, it also being interpenetrated by ether. When that escapes, death occurs as demonstrated by Dr. McDougall in the Boston General Hospital a decade ago when he put on scales a number of people about to die, where they invariably showed a loss of weight at the moment of expiration.

"What doctors and scientists do not know is that this ether continues to retain the form and similitude of the dead dense body and remains *the house of the everlasting spirit* though invisible to those who are still in the physical body."

A great light and a look of intense relief spread over the face of the spy. "But how did the ether come out of my clothes, for I am wearing the same clothing as the dead body, and how did the bullet holes reproduce themselves in my present clothing?"

"That is a trick of the subconscious mind, my friend," answered the Rosicrucian. "Though you were not aware of the harm done to your body, the exact circumstance was registered upon a little atom located in your heart when you drew your last dying breath, for each breath drawn into the lungs contains ether which carries a picture of all the things in your environment, on the same principle that it carries the picture to a sensitized plate in the camera. The ether enters the blood stream, which carries it to the heart. There the seed atom corresponds to the photographic film, each successive breath producing a new picture, and so there is imprinted upon this little seed atom a series of pictures of the life from the cradle to the grave. This molds our destiny after death, and is the occult basis of the saying, 'As a man thinketh in his heart, so is he.' When the so-called 'dead' step out of their bodies the ether forms their clothing; it reproduces the physical peculiarities with absolute faithfulness according to the pattern of the last picture on the seed atom, the soul of which the man takes along as the arbiter of his life in the future."

The spy remained silent and lost in thought for some time, examining the explanation of the Rosicrucian from every angle. It seemed perfectly sound, logical, and in harmony with the known discoveries of science. Nor was it an insurmountable difficulty that the seed atom spoken of by the Rosicrucian must be extremely minute. Had not the eye of a fly numerous facets each of which made a picture of its surroundings, and had not the microscope opened the world of wee things? Who would dare draw the limit?

"But must I go on forever then with holes in my clothing and wounds in my breast, or will they heal, and can I procure other clothing?"

"Nothing easier, my friend; as I told you, here in the land of the living dead it is a law that as a man thinketh in his heart so is he. The poor fellows who fell by the thousands upon the battlefields, horribly maimed in the beginning of the war, were terribly distressed at their condition until we taught them to think of themselves as they were before going to war, hale and hearty. It was quite a task to get them to believe that that was all that was necessary to restore them to health, and it was slow work for there were many to be helped and we were few. But by degrees they were convinced and fitted to help later victims of the war so that now there are thousands of helpers ready to care for and help the thousands who are slain.

"Ah! you are an apt pupil; I see you have already mended your clothing and healed your wounds."

"Yes," answered the spy, "and thank you. I can never repay you for the relief you have given me. But I have one more difficulty. How was it that my body seemed thin air and my hands went through it? I know that it is solid."

"Oh, yes! That is amusing; the people in the physical world think of the so-called ghosts as being composed of intangible, filmy stuff like a wreath of smoke, that is, if they take stock in their existence at all. Their own bodies they regard as solid as a stone. But once they have passed beyond the veil to the Land of the Living Dead they are shocked to find out that people still in the flesh are as immaterial to us as we are to them, and that it is just as easy for us to poke an arm through them as it is for them to walk through us. In fact, they are as ghostlike to us as we to them.

"You are now a citizen of the Land of the Living Dead. Come, let us go hence and see the sights. But first, is there anyone you would like to speak to, for during the next few hours your spiritual body will be more dense than at any other time during your post-mortem career, and it will therefore be more easy for you to manifest to your friends at this time than at any time afterwards."

"I have a sister, but she lives in the town of X——, which is five or six thousand miles away. There is no one around here who would know or care."

"Distance is no barrier to the Spirit," said the Rosicrucian. "Think yourself there, and we shall be at the house of your sister within two minutes," and together they floated away, yet the speed did not seem extraordinary to the spy as he passed over one town and village after another. He seemed to have ample time to note the various details of the country, the architecture of the houses, the clothing of the people, etc. While passing over a great stretch of water he noticed a number of ships with the crews and passengers upon them engaged in their various tasks or pursuing their pleasures. In fact, the time did not seem either long or short; time seemed to be nonexistent in his consciousness, and he marveled in his own mind that he took it all in such a matter-of-fact way as if he had all his life been floating around through the air and seeing things he was now observing.

One thing though was strange and did bother him somewhat at first: the air seemed to be peopled with Spirit forms floating through it, just like himself and the Rosicrucian. At first he tried to avoid them but found it impossible; he braced himself for a collision when to his surprise he found that these people floated right through him and his companion just as if they had no existence whatever. This filled him for the moment with consternation and bewilderment until the Rosicrucian, observing his dilemma, laughed reassuringly and bade him not to mind, saying that that was the custom in the Land of the Living dead, for there all forms are so plastic that they easily interpenetrate one another at all times, and there is no danger whatever of losing one's identity.

Arrived at the home of his sister, they found her seated in a comfortable living room. The spy impulsively rushed over to her and embraced her only to find to his dismay that she was absolutely unaware of his presence, and that his hands, instead of clasping her form, went right through it.

Again he turned to the Rosicrucian, and asked the question as to what he should do to make himself felt. "Stand over in this corner here where the light is dim, for the etheric vibrations of light are stronger than the vibrations you are able to set up. Then make clear in your mind the message you want to send her and think it with all the intensity of which you are capable. It was the intensity of your thought before you faced the firing squad which came to me in my home and caused me to leave my physical body for a while in order to come to you and give you a helping hand in your hour of transition. If you can think with a similar intensity of the message you want your sister to have, she will receive it and her eyes will be drawn towards you."

Thus instructed the spy formulated the message: "I am in the Land of the Living Dead; I have passed beyond the veil." Fixing his gaze upon his sister, he stood there immovable, reiterating that message for several minutes. Suddenly the eyes of his sister sought the corner where he was standing, and perceiving her brother standing there, she commenced to tremble, and fell fainting upon the floor. Immediately the spy rushed forward to lift her up, when with a glad cry she threw herself into his arms.

"Oh, how did you come, Bob? It is only a few days since I had a letter saying that you were leaving on a dangerous mission, and here you are. How did it happen?"

Again blank amazement spread itself over the face of the spy; he had seen his sister fall, and here she stood! Was she also dead?

"No," explained the Rosicrucian, as he stepped forward and was introduced as a friend of Bob's. "No, she is not dead; she merely fainted, and she will have to go back into her body. There it is, lying upon the floor just as your own body did after they had fired the fatal shot. She probably will not have any remembrance of speaking with you now, nor will she know that you are in the Land of the Living Dead, but will have only the impression that she has seen your ghost and that something has happened to you; that is, unless you have been successful in impressing her sufficiently with your message stating that you have passed beyond the veil and are now in the Land of the Living Dead. Every night, however, when she goes to sleep, you will have the same chance as you now have to speak to her, for when we are asleep we are really in the same place as those whom the world calls 'dead.'"

At this moment the spy's sister seemed to fall asleep and was irresistibly drawn towards the body lying upon the floor. Gradually the spy saw her melt away and disappear into that form, which then began to moan and move.

"Come, let us go," said the Rosicrucian. "While you were speaking with her I worked over her body and have done all that can be done to ease her return to consciousness. You can do nothing more for her, so come, let us go hence."

ABOUT THE AUTHORS

ALVEY A. ADEE (1842-1924), born in Queens, New York, and educated at Yale University, Connecticut, was a diplomat who worked for the State Department for twenty-six years and whose chief claim to fame was due to his position of acting United States Secretary of State for a brief period in 1898 during the Spanish-American War. Having to write countless memos during his tenure, he was known for his punctiliousness with language, and Rex Stout, who was a friend of his, said that he used him as a model for his detective Nero Wolfe. In the early part of his life he published poetry in various newspapers, but he only wrote a single work of fiction, "The Life Magnet," which first appeared in the August 1970 issue of *Putnam's Magazine*.

AMBROSE BIERCE (1842-c.1914) was a prominent American writer, remembered especially for his short stories, many of which had supernatural themes. At the age of fifteen he became a printer's devil for the *Northern Indianan* newspaper and then joined the Union Army during the Civil War, and later found himself in San Francisco, California, where he lived for a large part of his life. In December 1913, while accompanying Pancho Villa's army as an observer, he disappeared. "An Inhabitant of Carcosa" was first published in the December 25, 1868 issue of the *San Francisco Newsletter*.

FITZ JAMES O'BRIEN (1826-1862) was born in Cork, Ireland, and was educated at Trinity College, Dublin. He moved to London upon receiving an inheritance of £8,000, ran through the money in four years, and then immigrated to the United States, where he dedicated himself to writing, quickly placing his short stories, many of them of supernatural and occult significance, in some of the foremost periodicals of the day, such as the *New York Times*, *Harper's Magazine*, *Vanity Fair*, and *Putnam's Magazine*. When the American Civil War broke out, he enlisted in the New York National Guard and subsequently died of a wound received. "The Lost Room" first appeared anonymously in the September 1858 issue of *Harper's Magazine*.

BLANCHE CROMARTIE (18??-19??) was a member of the Rosicrucian Fellowship and contributed a number of pieces to that organization's magazine, *Rays from the Rose Cross*, the November 1915 issue of which contained "A Dream of Roses."

FLORENCE CARPENTER DIEUDONNÉ (1850-1927) was born in Munnsville, New York. Her poetry and articles were published in various magazines and newspapers, and then, in 1882, she self-published her long occult poem, *A Pre-Historic Romanza*. This was followed by the novels *Zardec* (1885) and *Rondah, or Thirty-Three Years in a Star* (1887). "Xartella" first appeared as a self-published booklet in 1891.

JAMES H. CONNELLY (1840-1903) was a journalist, a member of the Aryan Theosophical Society, and an associate of W. Q. Judge, whom he helped produce interpretive translations of *The Yoga Aphorisms of Patañjali* (1889) and the *Bhagavad-Gītā* (1890). From Russian he translated Nicolas Notovitch's *The Unknown Life of Jesus Christ* (1890) and, in

330

the same year, published *Neila Sen and My Casual Death*. His articles and stories appeared in numerous places including the *San Francisco Chronicle*, the *Chicago Tribune, Lucifer*, and *The Path*, the December 1888 issue of which contained "Among the Dead."

FREEMAN B. DOWD (18??-1910), was a lecturer and phrenologist, who was possibly born in Davenport, Iowa, most likely in either 1825 or 1828. Sometime in the 1860s, he became a follower of Paschal Beverly Randolph, who, in 1970, selected him as the Grand Master of the Imperial Order of Rosicrucia, a position he held until 1907. In 1885 he joined the Hermetic Brotherhood of Luxor. His publications include *The Temple of the Rosy Cross* (1882), *Evolution and Immortality* (1900), and the novel *The Double Man* (1895), from which "A Monster's Birth in Spirit" is taken.

F. C. EWER (1826-1883) was a priest, freemason, and leading nineteenth-century Anglo-catholic. He was born on Nantucket Island, Massachusetts, raised in New York City, and attended Harvard College, where he embraced atheism. Upon his graduation in 1849, he went to join the gold rush in California, where he found work in the newspaper business, first as editor for *The Pacific News*, then as editor for and part owner of *The Sacramento Transcript*, then as reporter for *The Alta Californian*. In 1854 he became editor of a new monthly magazine called *The Pioneer*, the September 1854 and October 1854 issues of which serialized "The Eventful Nights of August 20th And 21st." While taking part in a conversation in a bar room in a mining town, he decided to abandon atheism and became Reverend of the Episcopal Church in San Francisco and then later returned to New York, where he eventually founded the New York Church of St. Ignatius. His publications include *On the Relationship Between Masonry & Christianity* (1862) and *The Stability of Freemasonry* (1866).

WILL L. GARVER (1967-1953) was an American architect, author and Socialist. He was born in West Virginia and raised in Kansas and Missouri. While still in his teens he began working for his uncle, the architect and engineer Morris Frederick Bell, through whom became a Freemason. In 1890 he went to Topolobampo, Mexico, where he spent a year at a utopian socialist cooperative and then, in 1891, in Halcyon, California, joined the Temple of the People, a Theosophical intentional community. In 1892 he was appointed superintendent of construction of the David R. Francis Quadrangle at the University of Missouri, and in 1908 he was the Socialist Party of America's candidate for Missouri governor. Though he wrote numerous articles and pamphlets on Socialist subjects, he is most remembered today for his occult novel *Brother of the Third Degree* (1894), from which "Death—Life" is taken.

"MAX HEINDEL" was the pen name employed by Carl Louis von Grasshoff (1865-1919), a Danish-born occultist and mystic. At the age of sixteen he left home to learn engineering in the shipyards of Glasgow, Scotland, and subsequently became, first, chief engineer of a commercial steamer, and then that of a passenger steamer which operated between Europe and America. In 1895 he moved to New York City, and then in 1903, to Los Angeles, California, where he joined the Theosophical Society and began to study astrology. In 1907, after attending a series of lectures by Rudolph Steiner in Germany, he received a visit from the etheric body of an Elder Brother of the Rosicrucian Order. Returning to the United States, he published *The Rosicrucian Cosmo-Conception* (1909) and founded the Rosicrucian Fellowship, the organ of which was a magazine called *Rays from the Rose Cross*, the November 1917 issue of which contained "The Last Hours of a Spy" under the title "Facing a Firing Squad; Before and After: The Last Hours of a Spy."

WASHINGTON IRVING (1783-1859) was one of America's great men of letters. Born in New York City, he began publishing in 1802 under the pseudonym "Jonathan Oldstyle." He wrote some of the world's most famous supernatural short stories, including "Rip Van Winkle" (1819) and "The Legend of Sleepy Hollow" (1920), and was an influence on Edgar Allen Poe, who sought his advice for his own story "The Fall of the House of Usher" (1839). "The Adventure of a German Student" is taken from *Tales of a Traveller* (1824).

W. Q. JUDGE (1851-1896) was born in Dublin, Ireland, and with his family moved to the United States at the age of thirteen. He studied law in New York, becoming a specialist in commercial law, and this activity brought him into contact with another lawyer, Henry Steel Olcott, President-Founder of the Theosophical Society, and subsequently Madame Blavatsky, whom he represented in her divorce from Michael C. Betenelly. He became Council for the Theosophical Society in 1875, and then, under guidance of the Masters, worked for the Society in Europe and India. In 1886 he became General Secretary of the American Section of the Society, and began publishing *The Path*, the January 1889 issue of which contained "The Serpent's Blood," under the pseudonym "Bryan Kinnavan."

GEORGE LIPPARD (1822-1854) was born on a farm in Chester County, Pennsylvania, and grew up in Philadelphia. In 1841 he began writing for the daily paper the *Spirit of the Times*; the following year, in 1842, his first short story, "Philippe de Agramont," was published in the *Saturday Evening Post*; and in 1843 he took an editorial position at *The Citizen Soldier*, the newspaper in which "The Dream of the Damned" was first published as part of the serialization of *The Ladye Annabel, or The Doom of the Poisoner*, which appeared in book form in 1844 and was later republished under the title *The Mysteries of Florence*. During the second half of the 1840s Lippard was the most widely read novelist in the United States; though he published a great many books, he is most remembered for *The Quaker City: Or, The Monks of Monk Hall* (1844). In 1850 he founded a secret society called the Brotherhood of the Union. According to the famous occult author R. Swinburne Clymer, Lippard was a Rosicrucian, and also a friend of the occultist P. B. Randolph.

SAMUEL S. NEU (18??-19??) was a New York based inventor and a regular contributor to the monthly magazine *The Word*, the October 1906 issue of which contained "The Alchemist's Wine."

ALMA NEWTON (1886-1955) was born in Mississippi, educated in New Orleans, and spent most of her adult life in New York City and Chicago, where she wrote mystical books and articles, including, in the last category, one on Algernon Blackwood. Her bibliography includes *Love Letters of a Mystic* (1916), *A Jewel in the Sand* (1919), and the collection of short stories *Shadows* (1921), from which "Shadows" is taken.

W. P. PHELON (1834-1904) was born in England and later immigrated to the United States, though when and how is uncertain, as his own accounts differ greatly from publicly available information. In any case, in 1865 he graduated as a physician from the State University of Iowa and by the early 1870s was a school teacher in Indiana. In 1874 he and his wife Mira moved to Chicago, Illinois, and in 1875 founded the Hermetic Brotherhood of Atlantis, Luxor and Elephanta. In November of 1884 he became a member of the Theosophical Society and was the Corresponding Secretary of the Chicago

Branch. In 1887 he joined the Hermetic Brotherhood of Luxor and also founded the Ramayana Theosophical Society, into which he inducted L. Frank Baum, the future author of *The Wonderful Wizard of Oz*. Furthermore, during this period he started the Hermetic Publishing Company which published, among other things, a novel he wrote with his wife, *Three Sevens, a Story of Ancient Initiations* (1889), and a journal called *The Hermetist*, the July 1897 and August 1897 issues of which serialized "My Ancient Cat Theosophuz."

JULIA CAMPBELL VER PLANCK (1851-1915) was an American Theosophist, lecturer, and writer. In the early part of her life she wrote, both under her maiden name Julia Campbell and the *nom-de-plume* "Espérance," poetry and short stories which were published in various periodicals, including *Harper's Magazine*, and the *Galaxy*. In 1886 she joined the Aryan Lodge and, mostly under the pseudonyms of "Jasper Niemand," "August Waldensee," and "Julius," published numerous articles and stories in periodicals such as *Lucifer*, *Theosophia*, and *The Path*, the September 1890 issue of which carried "The Sentient Dagger" signed with her real name.

EDGAR ALLAN POE (1809-1849) was one of the foremost American writers of the nineteenth century, known especially for his poems and short stories, many of which dealt with occult subjects. In 1827 he published *Tamerlane and Other Poems*, and later, from 1835-1837, worked as assistant editor of the *Southern Literary Messenger*. In 1838 his novel *The Narrative of Arthur Gordon Pym of Nantucket* appeared, and the following year he became assistant editor of *Burton's Gentleman's Magazine*. In 1840 his highly influential collection *Tales of the Grotesque and Arabesque* was published, which included "Ligeia," though the story had first appeared in the September 18, 1838, edition of the *American Museum*.

PASCHAL BEVERLY RANDOLPH (1825-1875) was one of the most influential occultists in America. Born in New York City, to a white father and a black mother, he went on to become a doctor, teacher, and medium, playing an important role in Spiritualism before recanting it in favor of his own brand of Rosicrucianism. His numerous writings include: *Dealings with the Dead* (1862), *The Wonderful Story of Ravalette* (1863), *Casca LLanna* (1872), and *Eulis!: The History of Love* (1874). "Lara" was originally published in the November 1861 issue of *The Hesperian*.

MARIE SALTUS, *née* Marie Florence Giles, (1880-1960) was born in Morristown, New Jersey and began writing at an early age, her first novel, *The End of the Journey*, being published in 1897 when she was only seventeen. The novel sold out and was republished the next year as *Her Game of Consequences*. Her second novel, *Though Your Sins Be as Scarlet*, also appeared in 1898. She was a Theosophist, an occultist, and was influenced by the New Thought movement, and, when she met and then later married the famous writer Edgar Saltus, it was under her influence that he joined the Theosophical Society. "As a Man Thinketh" was first published in the July 1902 issue of *The Arena*.

"JUSTIN STERNS" was the pen-name employed by Justin Sterns Lewis (18??-19??), who was the author of the occult poem "The Song of the Boy" (1906) and the plays *Undine* (1910) and *Flower of the Peach* (1914). "Sherau, the Paraschites" was originally published in the November 1908 issue of *The Word* as part of the serialized novel *Osru: A Tale of Many Incarnations*, which first appeared in book form in 1910.

BELLE M. WAGNER (18??-19??) was a follower of Thomas H. Burgoyne, one of the founders of the Hermetic Brotherhood of Luxor, who, subsequent to his demise, chose her as his spiritual successor and as his representative in that organization and, furthermore, dictated to her from "the subjective plane of life" the second volume of his *The Light of Egypt, or the Science of the Soul and the Stars* (1900) which was published by the Astro-Philosophical Publishing Company, which had been founded by her and her husband in Denver, Colorado, in 1892, as the publishing arm of the H. B. of L. "Within the Temple of Isis" was first published in 1899, as a stand-alone book, by the Astro-Philosophical Publishing Company.

OTHER BOOKS IN THE SERIES

The Zinzolin Book of Occult fiction (edited by Brendan Connell)
The Vermilion Book of Occult fiction (edited by Brian Stableford)
The Zaffre Book of Occult fiction (edited by Brendan Connell)
The Alabaster Book of Occult fiction (edited by Brian Stableford)

A PARTIAL LIST OF SNUGGLY BOOKS

G. ALBERT AURIER *Elsewhere and Other Stories*
CHARLES BARBARA *My Lunatic Asylum*
S. HEZOLNRY BERTHOUD *Misanthropic Tales*
LÉON BLOY *The Tarantulas' Parlor and Other Unkind Tales*
ÉLÉMIR BOURGES *The Twilight of the Gods*
CYRIEL BUYSSE *The Aunts*
JAMES CHAMPAGNE *Harlem Smoke*
FÉLICIEN CHAMPSAUR *The Latin Orgy*
BRENDAN CONNELL *Metrophilias*
BRENDAN CONNELL *Spells*
BRENDAN CONNELL (editor)
    The World in Violet: An Anthology of EnglishDecadent Poetry
RAFAELA CONTRERAS *The Turquoise Ring and Other Stories*
DANIEL CORRICK (editor)
    Ghosts and Robbers: An Anthology of German Gothic Fiction
ADOLFO COUVE *When I Think of My Missing Head*
QUENTIN S. CRISP *Aiaigasa*
LUCIE DELARUE-MARDRUS *The Last Siren and Other Stories*
LADY DILKE *The Outcast Spirit and Other Stories*
CATHERINE DOUSTEYSSIER-KHOZE *The Beauty of the Death Cap*
ÉDOUARD DUJARDIN *Hauntings*
BERIT ELLINGSEN *Now We Can See the Moon*
ERCKMANN-CHATRIAN *A Malediction*
ALPHONSE ESQUIROS *The Enchanted Castle*
ENRIQUE GÓMEZ CARRILLO *Sentimental Stories*
DELPHI FABRICE *Flowers of Ether*
DELPHI FABRICE *The Red Sorcerer*
DELPHI FABRICE *The Red Spider*
BENJAMIN GASTINEAU *The Reign of Satan*
EDMOND AND JULES DE GONCOURT *Manette Salomon*
REMY DE GOURMONT *From a Faraway Land*
REMY DE GOURMONT *Morose Vignettes*
GUIDO GOZZANO *Alcina and Other Stories*
GUSTAVE GUICHES *The Modesty of Sodom*
EDWARD HERON-ALLEN *The Complete Shorter Fiction*
EDWARD HERON-ALLEN *Three Ghost-Written Novels*